D1401238

WHITE
SANDS

Also by Simon Gandolfi

Golden Girl
Golden Web
Golden Vengeance

WHITE SANDS

SIMON GANDOLFI

HarperCollinsPublishers

ISBN 0-06-018720-4

97 98 99 00 01 RRD 10 9 8 7 6 5 4 3 2 1

For Antony, Mark, Joshua, and Jedediah.

IN GRATITUDE

The action of this book takes place during the Pindling administration rather than in the time of the present Bahamian Government.

Firstly my gratitude to Clarissa who acted as my sounding board for the characters of Charity and Jacket. My thanks also to Patricia Glinton-Meicholas for her wonderfully humorous and accurate *Talkin' Bahamian* and to Mark Firth of Roxton Bailey Robinson for his knowledge of the water surrounding Andros Island and for his hospitality at Small Hope Bay Lodge.

I also thank Seth Marshall of Sunseeker International, Poole, England, for advice on marine matters, and Sunseeker's Miami agents who very kindly took me out in a Sunseeker Apaché – one of the most thrilling experiences of my life.

My gratitude to the staff of American Airlines and American Eagle, particularly the personnel at Miami airport, for having directed and conducted me with safety and great courtesy throughout the region.

Most of all I wish to thank the people of the Caribbean, especially those in the village of Guayacannes, for their hospitality, their kindness, their patience and their great sense of fun.

PROLOGUE

The dead boy lay on the aluminium table in the morgue at Princess Margaret Hospital, Nassau. Gulls had alerted a fisherman. The boy wasn't a pretty sight. The elderly pathologist hadn't touched him yet. He said, 'At a guess, he was in the water at least twenty-four hours.'

'What about the Colombian?' The Chief Superintendent of the Royal Bahamian Constabulary asked.

'The funeral's in the morning. Maria Duncan at Good Shepherd over on Montrose is doing it,' Dr Jack said, naming the most prestigious of Nassau's funeral parlours. 'Old Trail Cemetery. The American from the DEA picked up the tab.'

'O'Brien?'

'The fat one – Anderson. Seems a nice man.'

The Chief Superintendent didn't respond. Six foot seven inches and thin as a stick, he was known throughout the Bahamas by his nickname, Skelley. The fluorescent lighting glistened on his shaved scalp so that the taut black skin seemed to be polished bone. His eyes were deep-set pits of shadow – a skull on a pole. He had been standing over the body for twenty minutes, most of the time not so much seeing it as using the boy's death to goad his mind as he tried to fit together the pieces of the puzzle. He was angry, very angry. And determined. He would have to come to an arrangement with O'Brien, resident head of the US Drug Enforcement Administration, the DEA. O'Brien first, then Trent.

Drug money had corrupted the Bahamas. However, Skelley trusted the short tubby pathologist as much as he trusted anyone. 'I'd prefer people to believe it was a normal drowning,' he said, his accent British softened by Bahamian undertones. 'Keep him on ice. Once it's dark, I'll bring a friend up to look.'

*

Skelley was too tall for any normal car. On formal occasions he rode in a fifteen-year-old London cab he had imported from England after a course at the police college at Hendon. Off duty he drove a World War II American jeep with the top down. A Stars and Stripes bandana protected his shaven skull from the sun. He had changed into ragged cotton pants that gave up halfway down his calves and an outsize T-shirt that was the right length but ten sizes too wide. He had cut the toes out of his rope-soled espadrilles.

He turned the jeep off the main road down a sand track that led to a short crescent of white beach with enough sharp rock in it to keep the tourists at bay. A double line of coconut palms shaded a half dozen fishermen's huts. A bunch of six- to ten-year-olds of both sexes were playing cricket between the palms with a homemade bat and a ball that was older than any of them. Two old men playing dominoes hadn't bothered shaving in a few days nor did they bother looking up at the police officer.

An open-fronted thatch shack faced out on to the beach. The owner of the shack operated without a licence selling cold beer from a lead-lined ice chest and fresh snapper grilled outside over the coals in one half of an oil drum. Recognising the jeep as it came through the trees, he dipped hurriedly into his ice chest for a Kalik.

Skelley told him to save his energy.

The sloop-rigged catamaran, *Golden Girl*, lay at anchor two hundred yards offshore near the line of breakers which marked the reef. Built by SailCraft in England of cold-moulded marine ply to MacAlpine-Downey design, she was an ocean-racing machine. The reverse sheer of her white hulls gave her the look of a pair of leaping jaguar.

The owner had been christened Patrick Mahoney. He had worked for eighteen years in that department of British Military Intelligence which concerns itself with combating terrorism. His expertise had been in infiltration and in the removal of those enemies of his government who posed too great a threat to be left at large. And he had been leased to the men at Langley by his Control for tasks prohibited by Congress – wet jobs in Americanise, wet for blood. Now he was known as Trent, a name supported by all the requisite documentation. He was the resident head of a Japanese agency specialising in insurance fraud.

Trent's employer, Tanaka Kazuko, had been a detective chief inspector in Kyoto. Pressure from politicians to leave their criminal friends in peace had lead to Tanaka's resignation. He had studied

2

English from a private tutor for seven years only to discover, on visiting England, that he spoke with a broad Liverpool accent. To save face, he posed as a Beatles fanatic. He had learned the Beatles songbook by heart. His Kyoto apartment and his office were filled with memorabilia. He had named his agency the Abbey Road Investigative Unit. In private he listened to Bach, classical Indian raggas and the most esoteric end of modern jazz.

He gave as his reasons for employing Trent that Brits came cheap and that he'd never find anyone else dumb enough to stand in the way of the bullets. Trent was something of a hermit and seldom went to the office on Shirley Street. Skelley's elder sister, Lois, worked officially as Trent's secretary but to all intents and purposes was the manager.

Trent was visible in the *Golden Girl*'s cockpit. Skelley knew the Anglo-Irishman too well to bother hailing. Striding fully dressed into the sea, he swam the last hundred yards out to the catamaran in a steady crawl.

He approached the yacht from the stern. Steps with anodised aluminium handrails were built into the reverse transoms. Grabbing one of the rails, he wiped the water out of his eyes.

A patio the size of the *Golden Girl*'s cockpit would have doubled the rent on a New York apartment. Trent sat at the table with books and papers spread. Already fluent in seven languages, he was studying Japanese.

A full beard disguised his features and made his age difficult to gauge. He wore a Walkman under a battered planter's Panama, a loose off-white cotton smock with short sleeves and mid-calf cotton pants tied at the waist with a drawstring. A strand of coral beads held a small throwing knife hidden beneath the dark thick curls in the nape of his neck. He could hit a playing card with the knife dead centre at thirty feet. Skelley had watched his practice routine; Trent had never missed.

Skelley climbed the steps and perched on the cockpit coaming with his legs drawn up so that his knees were alongside his ears. 'Lois said you were here. She said to tell you all's quiet at the office.'

'Go away,' Trent said.

Shrugging his bony shoulders increased Skelley's resemblance to a black heron in a children's cartoon book. 'I need you to look at a dead boy I've got in the morgue.'

A slight tightening in Trent's hands was the only sign he gave of

3

having heard and nothing showed in his eyes as he looked up from the Japanese grammar. Absolutely nothing. It was as if he had retreated inside himself, Skelley thought. Skelley hadn't wanted to come here. He had known it would be like this.

He said, 'There's no one in the Bahamas with your expertise.'

Trent gazed out to sea but there wasn't anything out there that would help. Without looking at Skelley, he said, 'I'm an insurance adjustor.'

'I'm sorry,' Skelley said.

Trent looked at him then and Skelley said, 'I'm not trying to manipulate you into anything.' It was a lie and he shifted as if cramped and uncoiled his legs into the cockpit. 'I'm asking you to look, Trent.'

Trent pushed his headset back and closed his book. 'Look?'

'Look,' Skelley said.

'That's all?'

Skelley didn't answer.

Trent watched a frigate bird drift along the reef. 'Bad?' he asked after a while.

'If I'm right, very bad,' Skelley said.

Skelley parked the jeep in the top car park at Princess Margaret Hospital and led Trent down the ramp and across the yard piled with black plastic sacks leaking refuse each side of the morgue's rear doors. Dr Jack let them in. He had given the duty guard ten dollars, telling him to pick up a pizza at Nancy's and deliver it to his home. Recognising Trent, he sighed and said, 'So it's one of those.'

'Let's not jump the gun,' Skelley said and followed the pathologist through to the cold room with Trent trailing behind.

Trent didn't want to be there. He had seen too much death. The cold and the stench of formaldehyde were too familiar.

'They found him out on the reef,' Skelley said in warning and Trent braced himself as the pathologist peeled back the rubber sheet. It was worse than he had expected.

Skelley said, 'I wanted you to see him before Dr Jack goes to work, but his guess is about twenty-four hours.'

To be able to think, Trent had to shut away the horror but he was out of practice. He turned away to the rear exit. The stink from the refuse sacks made him retch as he hurried across the yard and up the ramp.

'The door will be open, take your time,' Skelley called.

4

Trent turned right on Shirley Street, then right up Collins Avenue. He counted to himself as he climbed the tree-lined street over the ridge that divides downtown Nassau from the rest of the Bahamian capital. He had walked two blocks before he realised that he was keeping to the shadows: once this had been second nature. He wanted to curse Skelley for trying to involve him but he liked the man too much and Skelley never played games.

If the boy had drowned out at sea the big fish and the sharks would have had him so he must have drowned inshore or on the reef itself. Judging by the flayed flesh, he must have been tossed by the surf back and forth across the coral. Strange that none of his major bones had been broken – Trent would have noticed.

He was surprised to find himself almost back at the morgue. He was ready now and in control as he walked down the ramp and pushed the door open. He wanted to get it over with. He gave the two Bahamians a quick nod and crossed directly to the table.

In life the boy had been well muscled. The remnants of a scar on what was left of the skin on his right fist and another above his right eye-socket suggested that he had been a bit of a tiger. In death he looked small and very frail.

Dr Jack said, 'I'll turn him over when you're ready.'

The boy's back was equally flayed but there were minute differences. Trent had seen enough. He knew the type of man responsible.

1

JACKET

Thirteen-year-old Jacket Bride listened to his mother mutter as she stirred in her sleep. Her bed was made of uneven wooden slats and she tossed and turned through the night. Jacket could tell when she was sleeping deeply because she gave a little snort each time she rolled over.

Jacket shivered as an owl hooted up on the ridge behind the Bride hut. The hut occupied a square plot a hundred yards inland from the rest of Green Creek settlement on South Andros island in the Bahamas. It was a single room, twelve feet square, raised on stilts, and built of the same leftover planks as the bed. Jacket slept behind a curtain of rice sacks on a two-foot-wide shelf. A kerosene lamp hung above a rough table, three upright chairs and a cupboard with a stained and peeling mirror on the door. Jacket's mother cooked on an open fire under a palm tree and there was a sweet-water well over in the far corner of the plot.

Jacket and his mother lived alone in the hut. The boy had been five years old when his father deserted them. The boy had worn his father's old cotton jacket for the next two years, rain or shine. Finally the jacket had fallen to pieces but Jacket had earned his name.

Rumour reported that Jacket's father had joined the US army and Jacket watched every war movie shown on TV down at Mr Jack's bar. He wove their plots into his own fantasies in which his father was sometimes present, though more often in the background, a colonel in the Special Forces or a pilot flying a secret mission behind enemy lines. This night Jacket was a courier for the French Resistance in World War II.

It was past midnight before Jacket was satisfied that his mother was

7

properly asleep. The owl hooted again, a warning from the Resistance look-out. Jacket listened to the German patrol, their boots striking the cobbles of the narrow street in time to the thump of his heart. In minutes now they would fan out to search the village for the radio transmitter. His duty was to escape with it to Bleak Cay.

He was scared as he climbed out of the one window and sneaked down the sand track through the village. The night was peopled with enemies who hid in the deep shadows between the palm trees. Double lightning marked the SS officers' black uniforms; steel helmets and rifles dripped the night dew.

A dozen skiffs lay at moorings off the beach. Jacket's friend, Dummy, always moored the *Jezebel* furthest out so that Jacket could row clear without being heard.

The *Jezebel* was a typical Bahamian skiff, sixteen feet long and painted with tar. She was built of pine plank an inch thick on the sides and an inch and half thick on the bottom. The bottom planks were nailed in a herringbone pattern. The solid pine mast and boom lay fore and aft along the seats with the sail rolled and lashed round them with the rigging. An iron bracket supported the big lantern that stuck out over the transom and the butane tank for the lamp was lashed to a U cut in the stern seat. There were two pairs of oars and a heavy gaff. All in all the skiff weighed the best part of a quarter of a ton.

Jacket was small for his thirteen years and he rowed standing up facing the bows so that he could throw his full weight behind each stroke. Even in a light breeze the four miles out to Bleak Cay would have been an easy sail – however, he needed the sea smooth to be able to see the crawfish.

Charity Johnston surfaced a half mile up the coast and tipped her dive gear on to the battered windsurfer she had converted into a dive tender. A marine zoologist by training, she was recording the population of an isolated coral head and had dived on the head two days and two nights a week for the past six months. Diving solo was against PADI rules but Charity had little respect for regulations other than those she set herself in the classroom at the Green Creek school. Her contempt was particularly strong when the rules were set by Americans, and PADI was an American organisation.

Turning the sailboard south, she spotted the shadow of a skiff outlined

8

against the horizon. The skiff was out of sight by the time she reached the shore and dragged the board into the shelter of the trees.

She wondered if Jacket was the oarsman. She had repeatedly warned the child against going out at night by himself but, like Charity, he was a loner. She was tempted to walk along the beach to check whether the *Jezebel* was at its moorings but to do so would have been to spy, and she had her log to write up and there was school in the morning.

Schoolmistress at Green Creek for the past year, Charity was familiar with the talents and shortcomings of the children in the settlement and she had a shrewd perception of what would happen to each one of them in adult life. In class she tried not to show favouritism; however, Jacket was the only pupil who read and studied for pleasure. He was intelligent and imaginative – perhaps too imaginative for his own good. He also possessed a stubborn courage – necessary in defending himself against the village bullies. It was this courage which drove the young boy out fishing for crawfish at night.

2

STEVE

'They'll kill us,' Steve said. He had never been this scared. Not even as a child. The fear thrust up between his legs like a knife blade, his belly had collapsed and the sour taste of bile made him want to throw up. He longed to shoot Bob in the gut and watch him bleed to death at the bottom of the boat.

The boat was thirty foot in length with a dipping foredeck over a day cabin furnished with two settee berths, a head with freshwater shower, and a galley counter that was too small for serious cooking. Three sprung racing seats furnished the padded cockpit amidships. The after sundeck covered an 8oohp V8 Mercruiser engine. At five thousand revs the big out-drive slammed the boat over the water at sixty miles an hour – fifteen faster than the top speed of the Bahamian coastguard cutters.

Steve and Bob had spent the afternoon in the boathouse camouflaging the white hull with black tape so that it wouldn't show in the dark and they had dismantled the radar arch from behind the helmsman's seats as well as the chrome rails and bow pulpit in case they registered on the coastguard radar.

At least they'd been lucky with the weather. The evening breeze had died to leave the sea spread like black oil under the half moon. The humidity was high, the air thick with the stink of warm salt and iodine. Lights flicked at them across the shallow water: two beacons to the east marked the edge of the Great Bahama Bank: Lobos Cay Light stood midway down the channel separating the Bahamas from Cuba; Big Cay and Ram Cay to the west; South Andros to the north. Bleak Cay lay hidden in the darkness a mere three miles off their bow – three miles that made the difference between getting rich and getting killed. The beacon on its north tip flashed every four seconds, taunting Steve's helplessness. Steve was from New York City. He disliked the sea unless it was breaking gently on the beach at the Hamptons and the only boat he trusted was the ferry across to Staten Island.

Bob was the sailor. Bob, reputed to be a great mechanic, had been working on the big Mercruiser engine for the past hour and all Steve could do was curse him and curse the engine and all the sons of bitches who had got him into this mess.

Top of the list came the Colombian de Fonterra brothers, Xavier and Jose. He had come across them first at prep school in Connecticut. Steve had won a scholarship to the school and had gone on to earn a Master's in economics at NYU. He was a high flier in a bank on Wall Street when he met them next. They had lunched a few times at the Hudson River Club and spent evenings together but Steve had never rated a weekend. He had done a little money laundering for them, twenty grand, sometimes fifty, casual stuff that hadn't seemed important, and he hadn't covered his tracks.

'Hey, come on,' he'd blustered when summoned to the senior vice president's office to be interviewed by the Treasury agent. 'These guys were at school with me. Xavier was at Oxford. Their dad's a goddamn judge. He breeds horses, for Chrissake. The ones that go sideways up hills.'

The grey man in the off-the-peg grey suit said, 'Pasofinos.' He didn't even have a file, it was all in his head.

The bounce went out of Steve. 'Yeah, that's right.'

The bank hadn't fired him. Not then. Instead he got shifted to the bond department in what appeared to be a natural move. Six months later they let him go along with three others in a slimming operation planned months ahead.

Steve wasted six months looking for a job. The people who interviewed him were polite and he hadn't wanted to believe that he was on a blacklist. Finally he tried a cousin who ran the trust department at a small bank in Philadelphia. Steve and the cousin weren't close friends. His cousin was bad at hiding his thoughts. Embarrassed, he rolled a blue Waterman pen back and forth across the Morocco desk blotter while humming and hawing how the economic climate wasn't strong. In the end he came out with it: 'Look, Steve, maybe you should try something else. You know? Do something on your own. If there's some way I can help . . .'

Complacent son of a bitch – University Club, blonde wife with deep social connections, two kids, a four-bed colonial with pillars, BMW 320i with twenty thousand careful miles on the clock, a two-year-old Volvo stationwagon and a Kabota lawn tractor. Steve had wanted to murder him.

What was he meant to do? He needed to live somewhere cheap while he worked things out. The apartment had to go. If he sold it fast he'd lose money. He listed it with a woman realtor he'd dated for a few months a couple of years back and flew down to the Dominican Republic. He rented a studio apartment a couple of blocks back from the beach fifteen miles out from the capital at Boca Chica. Mornings he worked on his Spanish, afternoons on his tan. Nights it was like a bat cave. Every woman in town came out on the street. He'd cruise round with a German he'd met, beckon the women over, inspect them as if they were sheep at market, tell them they were too old or too ugly or order them into the car. The whole damn country was a whorehouse. Sure there were families in the capital who were different but meeting them was akin to breaking into Fort Knox. The rest were prostitutes. Ten dollars for light relief in the back of the car. Fifteen for a couple of hours in a motel with a sex film playing on video while a girl did what he ordered. Two months and his confidence was rebuilt and the apartment sold.

He met a bunch of Colombians on holiday who were impressed by his claims of friendship with the de Fonterra family. The Colombians told him stories of the big houses the de Fonterras owned, the horses, haciendas the size of a goddamn country. But what were they? A couple of Hispanic jerks, and they'd wrecked his life. Screw them. They owed him.

Steve didn't trust American Airlines. They were too hot on security and he suspected that he was on some kind of list that might alert a DEA agent with access to AA's reservations computer. So he flew charter to Bogotá, four hundred and fifty dollars for a week, hotel included. He called the brothers from the hotel and they sent a chauffeur: a nice old man with a fringe of grey hair showing under a peaked cap, suit well pressed, very respectful but no small talk.

Steve had expected to be driven to a house or an apartment, dinner with silver on the table and a half dozen servants. Instead the car slowed at a corner in an upmarket suburb and the elder brother, Xavier, slid in. He raised the glass partition and adjusted the volume on the radio before settling back.

Five foot ten in height, the Colombian was slim, country club fit, and freshly barbered. He wore charcoal-grey flannel trousers with inch-and-a-half turn-ups, a tweed jacket with a single slit and the corner of a Paisley handkerchief showing in the breast pocket. Plain but heavy gold links buttoned the double cuffs of a pale blue cotton Oxford shirt, Paisley tie, brown brogues mirror polished. It was the upper-crust English look that few upper-crust English could afford after the thieves and incompetents on the Lloyd's insurance market had cleaned them out. The look was hard to imitate. Xavier had it exactly right, even down to slight embarrassment at his social superiority.

Carefully adjusting his trousers so they wouldn't crease, he said, 'I won't pretend that I'm pleased to see you, Steve. You've caused considerable unpleasantness.'

Steve kept his rage hidden. 'You were the one with the coke money.'

'Coke?' Xavier gave a little sigh. 'You North Americans have a conception of the world based on your own greeds. Latin America, Middle East, Far East. Drugs, oil and painless routes to spiritual enlightenment . . .'

Steve made to interrupt but Xavier silenced him. 'You need something from me, so you can listen for once. Few of you have a sense of history. The de Fonterras have owned the same land here for three hundred years. We think in terms of generations. Some of us have tried to be socially responsible but we are neither stupid nor selfless. Given the problems of our country and the uncertain political climate, we wisely hide a little of our income each year. We employed you to do the hiding because we were at school together. You were careless, Steve, and you got fired. We had people from your Embassy sniffing around and both Jose and I have been stripsearched flying into Kennedy. A distasteful process . . .'

He picked a thread from his flannel trousers and placed it carefully in the clean ashtray. Then he faced Steve again. 'I'm going to give you a telephone number of a man who used to manage one of our coffee plantations near Medelin in the days before your drug money corrupted our economy. He has a reputation for absolute honesty and is in need of

13

capital. You thought you were laundering drug money for us, Steve, so he may be where you belong. Whether you call him is your decision.'

He leant forward and tapped on the dividing glass. The chauffeur eased the big car into the curb. Xavier said, 'Don't call me again. Ever . . .'

Steve walked a mile before finding a taxi. All the way he thought of how one day he'd get even. He'd kill the son of a bitch. He'd kill him slowly and laugh in his goddamn face.

But he made the call.

The meet took place at a café alongside a Texaco gas station twenty miles from the capital. Steve hired a Budget Ford. The road wound through the mountains. For the first miles shacks spread like refuse landfill each side of the road. Finally Third World misery gave way to trees. Trucks were a menace, no brakes and the drivers oblivious of which side of the road they drove.

Steven had been instructed to wait at a table beneath the flamboyant tree that shaded the dirt terrace outside the café. Four Colombians drove up in a mud-spattered Mitsubishi four-wheel-drive double-cab pick-up. They were dressed in well-washed khaki chinos, cotton shirts with button-down pockets, boots with dirt packing the welts. Three of them carried pump-action twelve-gauge shotguns – mestizo farmers back from a hunting trip.

It was all very casual on the surface but the driver left the motor running and stayed by the truck, his eyes flicking back and forth along the road, cab doors open to let in the breeze. A second man strolled over to check the gas station office, then propped himself against the wall so that he could keep an eye on whoever drove up. The third man ordered coffee on his way through to check the bathroom in the rear of the café. Last came the boss.

In his mid-forties, he was a square man with a broad paunch beginning to spread over his belt and a face like a cracked concrete block. He toed a chair back from the table and beckoned the waitress to fetch him coffee.

'I understand that you have some money which you wish to increase, señor.'

'That would be nice,' Steve said.

'And that you are without experience . . .'

'Yeah, well . . .'

14

'And that you have been careless once in the past.' The Colombian shrugged. 'A lesson, señor. In the future you will be more serious.'

He shifted a half inch in his seat as a black Lincoln town car pulled in for gas. The driver was a woman in her fifties. Seeing the gunman leaning against the office wall, she changed her mind halfway to the pumps and drove very slowly back on to the road towards Bogotá. A short stocky Indian waitress with a sagging bust brought the boss's coffee in a small cup with a blue line a third of the way down from the rim. The mestizo poked the cup round with a blunt forefinger till the position of the handle suited him. He sniffed at the coffee before taking a little into his mouth. Failing his standards, he spat it neatly into the dirt between his boots, then replaced the cup in the exact centre of the saucer. Every movement was the same, painfully slow and methodical – a real hick. Steve imagined him trying to cross the road in New York.

Watching the highway, the Colombian said, 'You will need a house in the Bahamas, señor, a quiet house on one of the less popular islands – and a fast boat with a white hull so that you can disguise it. You are young so you should work. Otherwise people will suspect . . .' They required Steve as a cut-out. He would receive the cargo. They would watch him for forty-eight hours before taking delivery. In payment they would invest fifty thousand of his dollars in the cargo at a ten-to-one return.

The midday heat and the humidity were soporific. The Colombian's voice droned on, unemotional, the instructions precise and detailed. Steve closed his eyes for a moment.

The Colombian struck like a snake, trapping his hand on the table. 'This is serious business, señor. I should like for you to look at me.' His eyes were placid, fatherly, his smile gentle. 'No mistakes, señor,' he said and tapped Steve lightly on the temple. 'You have much education. Remember, you must think all the time. All the time,' he repeated and nodded to himself. 'That is what I ask of you – to think and to be honest with me, señor. You should look into yourself and see if this is possible.' He dug a nail suddenly hard and deep into the back of Steve's hand. 'You understand?'

'Yeah, sure,' Steve said – another man to hate.

But he had agreed and now the whole damn thing had gone wrong. The fear came at him again so hard that he retched over the side, then swore and hammered a fist on the fibreglass coaming.

15

'Hey, take it easy,' Bob drawled without looking up. 'Sound travels miles over the water.'

Who gave a shit? 'We don't get to Bleak Cay on time to meet the plane, they're going to slit our goddamn throats.'

3

VINCENTE

Vincente was scared of what he had agreed to do – not of the proficiency required, but that, in flying the mission, he would lose his soul. Twenty-eight years old, he was slim and fine featured, his hair a mop of untidy curls, dark, as were his eyes. He came of what are called in Colombia the Engreidos, families who have never mixed their blood with the Indians. The great landed families who settled in the country back in the seventeenth century such as the de Fonterras, the Casasnuevas and the Valleras are Chinis. So are the bankers – the Cabreras and Tur del Montes. There are other families such as Vincente's who emigrated to Colombia in the latter part of the 1800s. Proud of their integrity, they produce much of the professional classes – doctors, teachers, book-keepers. Vincente was a float-plane pilot. A highly skilled one.

He had been in the indirect employ of the United States for the past three years, spraying cocaine plantations with defoliant from his own plane. His airfields were mountain lakes six thousand feet and more above sea level. These lakes were subject to sudden squalls that spun without warning off the mountains so that each take-off and landing was potentially lethal.

The spraying was as dangerous, the plantations hidden in small clearings in the jungle. Vincente had to fly within feet of the treetops to control the spread of the spray, the plane continually subject to air-pockets and up-drafts. The DEA had begun by using their own pilots and big helicopters but the expense and danger had been too great. No one in the States cared a damn if Colombians died, while losing American citizens could put the whole programme at risk.

Vincente's fiancée refused to support the continual anxiety and eschewed agreeing a date for their wedding. Nor did she want him working for the DEA or any other branch of US government.

An history graduate of Cartagena University, she had a youthfully enthusiastic social conscience. She could list with relish every crime the United States had ever committed in Latin America, from the plunder and annexation of New Mexico and southern Texas on through to support for the British in the Malvinas war. Impossible that she should marry a servant of such people: 'They pay you half the wage of their own pilots because they consider you inferior, Vincente. You shame yourself by accepting . . .'

The heavily built mestizo who approached Vincente was well aware of her views. The mestizo made his approach at the roadside café of the pension where Vincente stayed while spraying. Dawn glinted gold off the whitewashed walls and off the tin roofs of the small town and tinted the mountainside. The mestizo sat at the neighbouring table on the pavement with his back to the wall, a middle-aged farmer with thick hands that had worked the earth for years, earth the same brown as his ill-fitting suit. He was gifted with the outward placidity of the Indian and spoke in a quiet monotone so that at first Vincente thought that he was speaking to himself.

'The pilot who flies from the lakes. For the North Americans. A young man, but of great competence. So people say. Even the North Americans speak with admiration of his skill – yet there are those of his own people who speak of him as a traitor. Can this be true?' The gentle sadness in his voice was that of a teacher, disappointed yet philosophical.

The mestizo's voice droned on: 'The campesinos complain that the pilot destroys their income and poisons their soil. They say their older children grow sick with the chemicals that he spreads and that their babies are ill-formed. That there is danger in drinking the milk of their animals. That the leaves fall from the trees and that the trees die. This is what people say.' He nodded to himself, lower lip minutely pursed for a moment in wonder at this litany. 'Even some of those closest to him say this . . .

'They say that he is the owner of the plane – true, that the bank also possesses a part of it, but not so big a part that he need continue as a servant of the North Americans. It is true that they also say he has given his word to the bank that he will continue with the North Americans until his debt is paid. They say that he is nervous that the bank will take the house of his parents. There are those who have some sympathy for him because he is thoughtful of his parents. They say that a man of influence should speak with the bank so that the pilot can be free of such worries.' Again he nodded to himself.

'There are others who say that the young man should pay the bank what he owes – that only then will he be free of his worries. They say that there are other uses for his plane. Uses that would benefit his people rather than their oppressors. They even say that he could pay all his debts with one flight, a flight without danger to one so skilled . . . not even a flight to the United States, which is always dangerous, but to the islands out beyond Cuba . . .'

As Vincente watched for the spread of the trees or ripple across the water that warned of a squall, so now he saw the mestizo raise a finger a half inch and spotted the campesino leaning against the lamp-post at the nearby intersection. A second man dozed against the cab of a four-by-four Mitsubishi pick-up across the street.

Nerves tense, he listened as the mestizo continued: 'It is said that his plane is insured through the bank. Were the plane to be damaged, the bank would take their money, but would they advance the pilot sufficient for a new aeroplane? Would the insurance cover him for a second time?'

A red Camaro convertible eased round the corner, salsa on the radio. The young man at the wheel was a graduate of the same flight school as Vincente. He lived in Bogotá and had no reason for being in this small town at dawn. Spotting Vincente, he waved, then accelerated on down the street past an ancient Mack truck piled high with burlap sacks of coffee beans.

'Toys,' the mestizo chided as the convertible rounded the next intersection. 'A man should have better interests. Land, a respectable house, good education for his children . . .'

Vincente had little faith in coincidence. There had been many suggestions in the past, but from people more within his own circle and made laughingly so that he could choose whether to take the offer seriously or as a joke. This was very different, this slow, quiet, methodical build-up of threat and promise.

Vincente watched an Indian in a dun-coloured capa and sweat-stained straw hat lead a train of laden donkeys down the street. The donkeys teetered on high heels, picking their way over the cobbles. A dog, half Alsatian and half nondescript, slunk behind the Indian.

A fly settled on the lip of the mestizo's cup. He sighed and slid a five-peso note under the saucer. Pushing himself up from the straight-backed chair, he stretched the stiffness from his shoulders before stumping heavily across the street to the Mitsubishi. A second man came out of the café and followed him, four men in all, all of the same square build.

Vincente paid his bill and fetched his old jeep from the shed at the rear of the pension. The lake lay twelve miles away from the small town and the dirt track that ran up the narrow valley was like a ploughed field. One of the Americans from the base intercepted him.

'Jeez! I'm sorry, Vin. Some son of a bitch torched your goddamn plane.'

Vincente followed the American back to the lake. He had himself under control by the time he reached the DEA base. It was a small camp – six prefabricated sheds erected on three sides of a lake-side clearing in the forest. A light rain had begun to fall. The rain drew the scent of rotting leaves out of the soil, tainting the cool mountain air. The trees dripped and the rain streaked the sides of the two Airstream trailers used by the DEA agents and collected in pools on the tarpaulins covering the gas drums fenced in on one side of the camp and on the drums of defoliant lined up behind a stockade of pointed iron posts painted with red lead.

A hundred yards out from the shore twin float tips protruded from the rain-speckled water – the floats and the red holding-buoy, nothing else.

The dozen Colombians and the two Americans stood around in the wet like mourners at a funeral. Vincente sat on the small beach and watched the squalls chase each other across the lake. The wind wrinkled the dark waters and swirled up through the treetops that cloaked the steep flank of the mountain opposite and boiled the edge of the grey heavy blanket of cloud that hung down from the peak.

The others left Vincente alone after a while. The float tips reminded him of dolphins. It was easier not to blame his own countrymen for the loss of his plane – the mestizo and his threats. Instead he thought of the rain washing the defoliant from the trees, rivulets joining together and flowing into the streams and rivers. The US armed forces had done the same in Vietnam. A nation of gypsies, they left their filth where it fell and moved on.

Boots squelched down the path from the shed that served as their admin building. It was the senior of the two Americans, a burly man with a red face who was running to fat and sweated a lot. He had a couple of initials but everyone called him Anderson. He had spent too many years in the bush and had lost whatever roots he had. Love was something he searched for in cheap brothels. A simple man, he wasn't one for long speeches – Vincente had never seen him read a book – and he hated paperwork, but he had tapped out with two fingers a report for the insurance company. He sat beside Vincente on the wet sand with his feet drawn up and his beer-belly resting against his thighs, sweat mixing with the raindrops.

A grey-winged woodpecker sped low across the water and behind them a dog barked.

'I'm real sorry, Vin,' Anderson said. He passed Vincente the envelope.

Vincente shrugged. 'They don't like the spray.'

'Yeah . . .' Anderson shied a pebble at the float tips. It fell short by eighty yards. The two men watched the rings spread over the lesser circles made by the rain. The first ring reached the shore and the American grunted, perhaps in satisfaction. It was difficult to tell. 'Bitch,' he said and, after a while, added, 'It's a job, Vin.'

Though they had little in common, Vincente liked him. Anderson was loyal to his men – too loyal for the good of his career, which was often the way with expatriate North Americans.

Vincente drove back to the pension and packed his gear. Then he walked over to the telephone office and called the insurance company and the bank. He hadn't the energy for the drive into Bogotá and he wasn't ready to face his parents nor his fiancée. Instead he sat out on the curbside terrace. He knew why he was waiting. One of the mestizo's men drove up in the Mitsubishi pick-up at five o'clock and parked on the other side of the street.

A half hour later Anderson came tearing into town in the DEA cherokee. He swung out of the jeep and grabbed Vincente by the hand. 'Jeez, Vin,' he said, 'I was scared you'd gone. An Agency man in Miami called over the radio. Wanted to know whether I had anybody on the team who'd bid on a Beaver float plane that's coming up at customs auction in the morning. Says it's in real good condition.'

Anderson was as delighted as a child at his own birthday party. The chair creaked as he slumped down beside the pilot. 'Jeez, do I need a beer. That goddamn track kills me.' He shouted in through the door for two bottles of Castellos: '*Bien fria, señorita.*'

He turned back to Vincente, suddenly embarrassed. 'Vin, I said he should go to twenty grand. It's savings I had sitting in the bank. Pay me back when you get the insurance and stuff straightened out.' He had the details on a sheet of paper. Gratitude scared him and he swallowed his beer in a couple of gulps. 'I have to get back. Take good care of yourself.'

Vincente knew that Anderson wasn't part of it and he felt bad. He didn't blame anyone. The money was just too big. He watched the Cherokee out of sight, then he crossed the street and clambered into the Mitsubishi truck.

Now, a month later, he was paying his dues.

The de Havilland Beaver was a great plane and it was a perfect night for flying with almost no wind and excellent visibility out over the Caribbean. Leaving Colombia, he had headed for Port au Prince at twenty thousand feet, then turned west along Cuba's south coast past the US navy base at Guantanamo Bay. Hugging the Sierra Maestra, he had swung north and dipped low, crossing the Old Bahama Channel at fifty feet. The small beacon on Bleak Cay lay dead ahead. Any moment now the reception committee would light the lamp to mark the start of the landing zone.

4

JACKET

Jacket had rowed out to Bleak Cay nineteen times in the past three months. One more good night and he would have enough money saved to buy his mother's birthday present. She had never had a present since Jacket's father ran off to the United States – or none that Jacket knew of.

The dunes hid the beacon on the south tip of Bleak Cay but he could see the loom. The beacon marked the end of a jagged reef that surfaced at low tide. Surf broke on the reef in any sort of a wind and the crawfish kept to their holes. On a calm night they came out of the coral and hunted the sand of the lagoon for small shell. Only twelve feet of water covered the sand at low tide and the crawfish were plainly visible in the light of the butane lamp. There were nights when they formed chains, all crawling in the same direction. One such night Jacket had caught thirty in an hour, none of them less than a pound and a half in weight. Dummy ran them up to the Emerald Palm resort at Congo Town.

Jacket rowed short strokes in the steady rhythm taught him by Dummy. It took him an hour and a half to reach the reef. The only channel in through the coral to the lagoon was a nightmare of twists and turns and was too shallow for a skiff carrying the weight of two grown men. Jacket knew it by heart. Once into the lagoon he turned south and rowed along the reef until he came to an outcrop of coral heads that projected in towards the shore like giant stepping stones.

Jacket let the skiff drift a few yards back from the outcrop before heaving the rock that served as the skiff's anchor over the side. The water looked dark and forbidding. However, the monsters that lurked below were his own creation, invented to people the stories he acted for

Dummy with his hands when they were out fishing and which made the old man smile and nod and make those high-pitched squeaks behind his throat that served him instead of language.

The previous Christmas Dummy had melted ten pounds of lead scrap to make Jacket a weight with a handgrip. Jacket balanced the weight on the corner of the transom and coiled twenty feet of light line on top of it. Spitting into his mask, he rinsed the glass into the sea so it wouldn't fog and pulled the strap back over his head. It was an old mask and the perished rubber leaked but his mother would have been suspicious had he bought a new one.

Drying his hands on his pants, he opened the tap on top of the butane tank and flicked the lighter to the lamp mantle. He could see plainly in the lamplight the edge of the coral and the sand stretching back under the skiff. A crawfish froze dead in its tracks immediately below the lamp.

Jacket dragged an old sock on to his right hand and doubled it back to form a pad. Slipping over the side, he pulled his mask down and reached up for the weight. Then he piked, shot his feet up and let the lead take him down. Grabbing the crawfish behind the head, he abandoned the weight and surfaced. The crawfish went into the fish box under the centre seat. Then Jacket hauled up the weight and heaved it back on to the transom.

There were no other crawfish in the circle of light so he raised the anchor-stone just clear of the bottom and let the skiff drift. He had travelled about fifty yards back from the coral heads before he spotted the procession. There were forty or fifty of them crawling head to tail. Jacket had never seen that many. He swallowed water in his excitement. From way in the distance came the drone of a small plane.

Steve heard the plane way to the south. 'For Chrissake do something,' he cursed.

Bob looked up. 'I am doing something,' he said. 'I'm rebuilding the motor. If you'd waited like I said so I could check the boat out, I'd have told you the valves were shot and we could have bought something else.'

He was a big man, Steve's age. They had met in the Hamptons the Sunday of a weekend when Steve's Jaguar convertible blew a head gasket and his current woman walked out. None of the other men in the beach house Steve shared that summer was much interested in the girlfriend, but one of them said that Bob down at the marina was a great mechanic and a nice man always ready to help.

Everyone said Bob was nice. However, he was a slow though painstaking worker and finally got fired because his hours cost more than the marina management could charge for the work he did.

From then on he worked freelance but his niceness was always getting him into trouble. One time a man whose chauffeur was sick paid him to drive a big Mercedes into Kennedy and collect a German business associate flying in from Europe.

'It's important, Bob,' the owner of the Mercedes said. 'Get there an hour and a half early and wear a suit.'

Bob started out on time but he got flagged by an elderly woman with a broken Ford. She didn't have the money for a garage so Bob spent three hours under the hood fixing the motor and arrived at Kennedy an hour late. Both he and the driver's seat of the Merc were covered with grease. That was Bob. And he smoked a lot of grass.

The grass was why Steve had approached him. Familiar with boats and engines, he'd seemed a natural. Now Steve had to hold on to the coaming with both hands to stop himself from battering Bob in the face.

'The goddamn plane's coming. What the shit are we going to do?'

'Maybe you should flash a light or something,' Bob said. 'You know? So he knows we're coming? I've got to get the head back on. That's all. And connect things up. Thirty minutes.'

Bob's thirty minutes were infamous.

'What the shit's the pilot meant to do? Fly circles?' Steve demanded as he eased forward into the cockpit and swung the big spot round to face south. He would be able to tell if it was the right plane because it wouldn't have lights showing.

'The lagoon is smooth as a pail of milk,' the mestizo had told Vincente. 'There's a row of coral heads four hundred yards north of the beacon. Our man will light a lamp dead centre on the coral heads. The night breeze blows from the south so the lamp marks the start of the landing zone. Come in low and put down as close as you can to the lamp. The closer you put down, the more room you'll have.'

They had blackmailed him for his skills. Vincente was about to show them just how skilful he was. His grip was light on the controls as he banked the de Havilland Beaver into a slow turn. A powerful spotlight flashed at him from the north – perhaps the coastguards. They had told him that the entrance to the lagoon was too shallow for the coastguard cutters so he wasn't worried. What happened after he dropped the cargo was their affair.

Steve flashed the light and heard the plane turn away. The engine note changed and Bob said, 'He's going to put down.'

Bob had been cursed out by more people in one year than most people get cursed in their entire lives but he remained an optimist. It was one of his traits that made people say he was nice. 'They'll have given him the bearings and there's the moon,' he said. The beacon on the south tip of Bleak Cay reef flashed at them but the cay lay between them and the lagoon and they couldn't see Jacket's lamp.

This was the best night that Jacket had ever had. As he dropped each crawfish into the skiff, he converted it into Bahamian dollars, setting the value off against the cost of his mother's present. The present had been central to his fantasy world for more than a year. Now, with success certain, he felt oddly empty and somehow disappointed.

Bleak Cay was a dark blob in the moonlight. The reception committee's lamp blazed bright white on the coral heads. Vincente lined up the lamp with the beacon and came in at twenty feet. He wore coated Raybans and slitted his eyes to protect his night vision from the lamp. He knew within inches the height between the bottom of his floats and the lamp. He smiled as he thought of the men in the boat. He imagined the beat of the big propeller blasting them as they dropped flat on their bellies. He was going to scare the shit out of them . . .

5

Jacket surfaced into the roar of a huge monster that dived at him out of the moon. His bladder voided and prayers tumbled from his lips. Then there was a great rending crash as the monster tore into the coral heads.

The monster tipped and Jacket saw the tail-plane outlined against Bleak Cay beacon. He clung to the skiff while the tail sank, his entire body trembling with shock. It couldn't have taken long but it felt long. Shame overwhelmed him. There was at least one man in the aeroplane. Jacket stuck a foot into a loop of anchor rope and tumbled in over the skiff's bows. Speed was paramount but he was a careful child and he coiled the rope neatly as he raised the anchor-stone.

He threw every ounce of his weight into the first strokes. Once the boat was moving it was easier. He counted the strokes to calm himself. It was a habit he had developed over the years of loneliness that had followed his father's disappearance. He had capsized the skiff twice under sail and knew that there would be air trapped in the plane – perhaps enough for the pilot and passengers – however much the silver bubbles bursting on the surface frightened him. In his hurry he scraped the skiff along the side of a coral head.

He had to get beyond the plane to bring the lamp over it. That was the worst bit, crossing over the bubbles and feeling the plane grate along the skiff's keel. Then he was clear and tipped the anchor-stone overboard.

He took the crowbar Dummy kept in the skiff and dived over the side. In the heat of his desperation, he fogged the glass and had to wash the mask out. The plane was upside down. The floats had been sliced open, the entire undercarriage torn off. One of the wings had been ripped away, the other folded up towards the surface like a fin. The engine had broken loose, the propeller shattered. The cabin was intact.

Jacket dived and grabbed the wing tip, pulling himself down hand over hand. Imprisoned air filled what was now the upper half of the cabin. The pilot was alone. He hung upside down in his seat harness, head and shoulders in the water. Jacket tugged at the door handle but there was too much water pressure on the outside. He had to fight to steady himself. He jammed the crowbar into the side of the window and heaved back. Water spurted in but Jacket couldn't wait for the pressure to ease. His lungs were already burning.

He gulped air and dived again. With the cabin half filled, he was able to raise the window flap. He wriggled his head and shoulders through and grabbed at the pilot's seat harness. At first he didn't understand how the fastenings worked. Then they clicked open and the pilot slid down. Jacket's lungs were close to explosion and tears blinded him as he grabbed the pilot by the shoulders. He dragged him round, trying to force his head into the air bubble. He couldn't do it.

Reaching the surface, he dog paddled for a moment, gasping. He needed to stay there but he had to get back down. Then shame shook him as he realised that he could have breathed in the plane. He raised his mask to let the water out, straightened it, and dived to the wing. Snatching the crowbar free, he dragged himself over the plane and pried open the other window. He was frightened of getting trapped and had to force himself inside. He got his arms round the pilot's shoulders and held him into the air bubble. A gash across the pilot's forehead wasn't bleeding and his head lolled on his chest. Jacket pushed it up and it fell over to the side. The pilot's eyes were open but empty.

Jacket wanted to slap the pilot, curse him till he agreed to live. It wasn't fair, and he sobbed, holding the pilot in his arms, the man's head drooping every which way like the head of a chicken that has had its neck snapped.

In Jacket's thoughts the pilot became confused with the father of his daydreams. He wept with guilt for the thousands of times that he had fantasised his father's death: death because it could be made valiant, while desertion implied that his father hadn't loved him – or hadn't loved him enough.

Jacket couldn't abandon the pilot.

He laid him over on his side and manoeuvered his head and shoulders out through the door. The yellow horseshoe around his neck was a life vest. Jacket pulled at the strings. The vest suddenly hissed and expanded. In his fright, Jacket let him escape and shoot to the surface.

Jacket chased him up and wasted time trying to lever him over the gunwale into the skiff. Finally he gave up and swam with him to the shore where he rolled him up the beach clear of the tide mark. Jacket knelt beside him, not knowing what to do. He had to do something.

He swam back out and dived to the cabin. One of those small black cases the young Mormon missionaries carried on their bicycles floated against what was now the roof. Two rows of metal boxes were lashed upright in the compartment behind the pilot's seat. Jacket took the case to the surface first and dropped it into the skiff.

He hung there in the light, the hiss of the lamp fiercer than the roll of surf tumbling on the reef. He judged from the moon that half an hour had passed since the crash. He had to be home before his mother woke.

The metal boxes were probably valuable. They belonged to the pilot – to his wife and son. Jacket's thoughts went to his own mother – ashamed of her poverty, she wouldn't allow visitors in their hut.

He dived and cut the boxes loose. They were identical, twelve inches by twelve inches and eighteen inches high. The lids were sealed with heavy tape. He manoeuvred one to the door and tried to swim with it to the skiff but it was too heavy. Surfacing, he untied the line from his dive weight, dived, and looped the line twice round the box in a knot learned from Dummy – an Englishman on a yacht had told Jacket it was a clove-hitch.

There were twenty boxes in all and it took Jacket a further half hour to load them into the skiff. Once they were loaded, he shut off the butane from the lamp. The extra weight of the boxes made the passage out through the reef impossible so he rowed to the shore and set them on the beach. A dull silver, the sun would reflect off them in the morning – someone would see them.

Jacket was close to exhaustion, ahead of him lay the long row home and he was short of time. He tried to avoid looking at the pilot but it was no good and he walked up the beach in search of a hiding place.

Bleak Cay was a low waterless ridge three quarters of a mile long and a hundred yards wide. A few clumps of coarse grass and thorn sprouted from the sandy earth that filled the cracks in the dead coral. Hiding the boxes in the sea would be easy and he almost turned back – but anyone circling the lagoon would see them against the sandy bottom. Finally he stumbled into a dip at the foot of a dune where picnickers had built a fire. He brushed the ashes to one side and scooped out the sand. Then he fetched the first box . . .

Steve had been standing in the cockpit ever since the plane had landed, leaning over the side as if he could control the pilot by being that bit closer to Bleak Cay. Over the past hour a breeze had grown to the south and now a gentle swell rolled in across the shallow waters of the Great Bahama Bank. A keelboat or a catamaran would have hardly moved but the fast day boat had neither beam nor weight below the water to hold her steady and she rolled with the swell through twenty degrees. It was a slow sluggish movement culminating in a slight pitch of the transom as each swell slid away to the north.

Steve's stomach had cramped with the tension of the past three hours. They had eaten fried grouper with French fries before setting out; the oil and taste of the fish lifted now into his throat with each lift of the boat. He stood with his hands clamped on the cockpit coaming and he gritted his teeth every few seconds while silently cursing Bob or the pilot – mostly the pilot: I'll kill you, you Spik son of a bitch. Take off and I'll goddamn kill you.

The slightest sound that drifted to them across the sea was a threat. His eyes watered with the strain of staring into the dark. A blade twisted in his right temple.

Bob got to his feet and said, 'It's done.'

Bob had been wearing a plain black T-shirt when they left the boathouse. He had taken it off before starting work on the engine and had used it as a rag. He wiped his hands carefully before closing the engine covers. Most people would have tried the engine first but Bob claimed that a man was in the wrong line of work if he didn't know when he'd done it right. There was enough light from the moon for Steve to see him smile. That was Bob. The Colombians were going to murder them but Bob was happy within the cocoon of his expertise.

Steve fought his hate down. The boat fell to starboard into the trough, the bows lifted, the boat righted herself, then rolled slowly to port. The transom rose and, with it, the grouper steak and the French fries and the oil. The boat gave an almost imperceptible shudder as the swell passed. The transom dropped and he threw up.

*

Each box weighed fifteen pounds. The metal was slippery and there were no handgrips. Jacket carried them one at a time clasped against his chest in both arms. The distance to the dip was a hundred and twenty-two paces. He stumbled over the rough ground in the dark, driving himself with promises that he could do it and that it would be all right. He didn't know what would be all right but it was important. More important even than his mother's present. It was to do with the pilot.

Jacket could feel him lying there on the beach as if waiting for the work to be finished so he could leave. He was tall and black and he was very brave to have landed the plane in the dark with the enemy so close. The boxes had to be hidden before he could take off. He couldn't help carry them because of his broken leg. He didn't say anything to Jacket, neither about the boxes nor the pain. He was always like that, quiet and never asking for anything.

'I's all right, Dad. I's manage,' Jacket told him. Jacket didn't look at him because he didn't want him to see his tears.

Out beyond the far side of the cay an engine coughed and fired, then settled into a heavy thrum. Thousands of yachts cruised the Bahamas, many of them power cruisers or sports fishermen and Jacket was familiar with the sound of engines. He was almost certain this was a V8.

Steve rinsed his mouth out with bottled water, spat over the side, and wiped his lips. The controls for the electric winch were to port of the wheel. Having winched in the anchor rope, Bob had gone forward and stood with his feet well apart to steady himself as he lifted the three metres of chain and the anchor carefully over the bow.

With the rails dismantled there were no handgrips on the deck and Bob made his way cautiously back to the cockpit. Making him hurry would have been as difficult as getting a heavyweight boxer pregnant and Steve didn't try. They had been due at the rendezvous at 01.00 hours. They were two hours late.

There was a slight thump in the gearbox as Bob eased the throttle open. The propeller spun foam and phosphorescence, then bit properly and drove the bows up so that the boat squatted back on its tail like a spaniel puppy about to pounce.

Bob listened to the engine, then nodded in satisfaction and gave the boat more power. The propeller rammed the transom up. The bows dropped as the boat lifted on to the plane. Only the aft third of her hull touched the water as she sped across the sea in a wide arc towards the north tip of Bleak Cay.

Ducking into the cabin, Steve returned to the cockpit with a Ruger .45 magnum. A single bullet from the big handgun would drop a rhino. Steve didn't know what to expect but he wasn't going to take any shit.

Jacket could see, through his tears, the white V of the bow wave as the patrol boat rounded the cay. The crew were small men, slit eyed, dressed in drab khaki tropic fatigues and those funny caps. A corporal crouched behind the cannon mounted on the foredeck. Two ratings port and starboard of the open bridge manned heavy machine-guns. Depth charges were aft and a second cannon. The sergeant stood at the wheel while the captain scanned the beach through binoculars.

Jacket froze with the last box in his arms but his dad chuckled softly. 'No panic, kid. We've got natural camouflage. You'd best hide the skiff. Hide it the other side of me from where you're stashing the explosives . . .'

'I can't see shit,' Steve snarled.

Bob had dropped the engine revs as they rounded the point. A broken white line of surf showed the reef. Bleak Cay lay in the black smoothness of the lagoon like a huge jellyfish. The plane had to be there. Maybe the Spiks had camouflaged it black in the same way that he and Bob had camouflaged the boat. Steve wanted to use the spot but his orders were no lights once the plane was down.

'The dumb son of a bitch probably landed the far side of the goddamn beacon,' he said.

Bob didn't answer.

Bob had been reared on a farm by a father who was a great one for giving orders one on top of the other. Bob had tried to do everything at once only to be cursed for whatever was only half done. Now he did one job at a time at his own speed. He still got cursed but he could live with himself.

At present he was steering the boat. On the plane, she responded to the lightest touch; however, she was tough now to keep on course as they crept south towards the beacon.

Bob didn't fly but he knew boats and navigation and could visualise how it must have been for the pilot flying all that distance only to find one end of the landing area unmarked. If Bob had been the pilot he would have swung round again and come in over the beacon. That way he would be going slow as he began to run out of room.

'He had to know north from south to get this far,' Bob reasoned. 'Maybe he's parked up on the beach taking a nap.'

He had spotted the faint shadows painted by the flat angle of the moon across the swirls surrounding the coral heads in the lagoon. Dropping the anchor, he set it firmly into the bottom with a burst of the engine, then switched off and lowered the inflatable dinghy.

The patrol boat was little more than a hundred and fifty yards away when Jacket heard the clatter of chain and the anchor splash, followed by the purr of rope whipping out through the hawsepipe. He had to carry the last box, then he was done. The weight dragged a pain round from his shoulders and all the way down his arms.

Behind him he heard his father say, 'They'll put a landing party ashore.'

They were hunting his father. And the boxes. The Green Berets had to have the boxes so they could blow up the dam. They had chosen Jacket's father for the mission because he was the best. Now it was up to Jacket. He had it all clear in his head as he staggered to the dip.

He laid the box down and began shovelling sand back between his legs like a dog. The splash of paddles warned him of the landing party. They had come in over the reef and were paddling up the lagoon towards the beacon. They were speaking English, so the traitor was with them.

Steve had been almost calm as they rounded Bleak Cay. Now the panic was back in him. He knelt in the bows of the inflatable while Bob paddled. The light from the beacon snapped at them. They reached the south end of the cay without sign of the float plane.

'Where in shit is he? I'll kill the son of a bitch,' Steve said.

Bob spun the dinghy round on the paddle and backtracked. He knew what had happened. Steve had said the pilot was a real pro. The mystery for Bob was why he had landed from the north. The float plane must have been flying at around eighty miles an hour. He wondered if the pilot saw the coral before he hit.

Steve was cursing up in the bows. Bob didn't like guns and wished that Steve would put the Ruger away. Unclipping the waterproof flashlight from his belt, Steve poked him in the back. 'You'd better look. Keep the lens underwater so people can't see the light.'

Jacket knelt looking out to sea at the pale yellow halo glowing in the water. It was very close to the plane. They would hunt him once they discovered the boxes were missing. He had covered the boxes with six inches of sand.

'You'd better make certain it's enough,' his father said.

Jacket dug his feet in hard as he crossed the dip. There were a couple of places where he could feel the boxes.

'You're a lot less weight than a man,' his father said.

Jacket blinked back his tears and knelt again, scraping more sand off the windward bank.

Steve's instinctive reaction to finding the plane was relief that the pilot was dead and unable to tell the Colombians that he and Bob had messed up. The Spik must have got cut up in the crash – blood in the sea.

Turning to Bob, he said, 'You'd better get down and have a look.'

Bob was already fitting his mask. He was like a fish in the water and too dumb to be scared. He dived and was down what seemed a long time to Steve. Finally he broke surface and hung on the side of the inflatable, shaking his head.

'What the shit's that meant to mean?' Steve demanded.

'The plane's empty.'

Steve didn't believe him. Lowering himself into the water, he snatched the flashlight.

Bob handed him the mask. 'You can pull yourself down on the wing.'

It was a lot more difficult than Bob made out and there were sharks and every other kind of carnivore down there. Steve grabbed at the open door. He poked his head in. The flashlight slid over the seats and severed lashings.

Steve kicked for the surface. Grabbing the inflatable, he rolled in and lay there panting with rage. 'The son of a bitch ripped us off.'

Bob wasn't so certain but with Steve in this mood he kept his mouth shut.

Steve was marshalling the facts. The pilot must have crashed to have smashed the plane that badly. He wouldn't have crashed deliberately so the rip-off wasn't planned. He crashed with a million dollars of coke on

34

board. He escaped from the wreck and swam around awhile, waiting for the shore party. Then he thought: Hey, I'm rich.

He must have had an inflatable or a life raft on the plane to unload the cargo. He couldn't get far without a motor and he wouldn't want to get caught out in daylight with half a ton of coke on board.

'He's hiding on the cay. He'll have left tracks,' Steve said. He hefted the Ruger. 'He so much as moves, I'm going to kill the son of a bitch.'

6

Small, and with no father to protect him, Jacket was easy meat for school bullies. He had learnt how to hide from them in the pine dunes. He replaced the ashes and charcoal in the centre of the dip, scattered a few handfuls of dry grass, then used his shorts to brush away his tracks all the way back to the beach. The enemy were coming now. He set off at a jog for the far side of the island.

The pilot lay on his back with his eyes closed and his head at the wrong angle. The deep gash across his forehead was white at the edges.

'Someone must have got him out,' Bob said.

'The rip-off artist . . .' Steve kicked the body, then scouted the sand and found Jacket's tracks in the soft powdery sand inland from the pilot.

'Come on,' he said to Bob, and followed the trail over the dunes to the far side of the cay and along the water's edge. The prints were clear in the damp sand. Steve couldn't believe his eyes. He had the Ruger out, finger on the trigger. 'Shit,' he said. 'It's a goddamn kid. You go the other way,' he told Bob and began running along the beach in search of the kid's boat. If it wasn't there, the kid had to be out in the lagoon or on the way back to where he'd come from. Green Creek was the closest settlement. Ten miles further came Congo Town.

Jacket knew exactly what he had to do. It was as if he was watching a movie and acting in it at the same time. He had his knife ready as he raced across the beach to the landing party's inflatable. He sliced both sides, then sprinted for the skiff. There was no time to hide his footprints. He eased the boat clear of the shadows of the rock and looped the painter around his waist. Out by the reef the surf would camouflage the dip of his

36

oars. First he had to get there. He swam a careful breast stroke so as not to splash. He was only halfway to the reef when he heard the shout.

The bows of the skiff had left a deep V in the sand and the kid's bare feet had dug deep as he pushed off. The tracks looked fresh. Hands round his eyes, Steve searched the lagoon. A sliver of moon sat on the horizon. He could see the pale line of surf out on the reef – that was all.

Back when he was a banker Steve had jogged a couple of miles in Central Park every workday evening and had ridden a bike at weekends. He remained in good physical condition and his breathing was steady as he ran to meet Bob. He could see the kid's footprints in the sand, two to each of his own, and a lot shallower. Police would have an equation to calculate the height and weight of the boy but Steve didn't know it. The kid was small, maybe in his early teens – or a runt.

Bob was on his knees. He had a dumb grin as he showed Steve the sliced inflatable, almost proud. 'This is some kid,' he said.

Steve's belly lurched as he looked out towards the surf. He needed to think. He said, 'His boat was hidden in the shadow of a chunk of rock. Looked like it had a flat bottom. Heavy . . .'

'Skiff,' Bob said. 'That's what most of them have.'

Steve was building a picture. The boy must be very familiar with the cay to have brought his boat in through the reef. He must come from close by. Almost certainly Green Creek. Small. A loner. With balls to come out this far at night. There had to be something of value to make the trip worth while. The fishing was better out beyond the reef. Lobster – that must be it. And now he'd found a fortune in coke.

He said, 'We checked the reef. There's no way he could get a heavy boat out with a load on board so the coke's here.'

'Buried,' Bob said.

'Maybe . . .' The kid had time. Steve squinted at the reef. He imagined the settlement at Green Creek: thirty clapboard houses each side of a dirt street, a couple of shacks further back. Midway down the street the constable's two-room cinder-block with a flagstaff in the front garden. A tin chapel – Seventh Day Adventists. School with the teacher's rooms at the back. A store that stocked the bottom end of everything at a price that must make the owner rich – including gas from a hand-pump screwed in the top of a drum. That was Green Creek. A small kid who fished lobsters at night. He'd be easy to trace.

Steve wondered if the kid would tell anyone. He would return to Bleak Cay, that much was certain – alone or in company. Steve would be waiting.

He said, 'Bob, you need to get the boat back before first light. Take a couple of turns round the cay. If you don't find him, head on home. Get the tape off the boat and the rails and stuff back on. Then come out again tomorrow night.'

'What if the Colombians call?'

Steve didn't want to think about the Colombians. He wanted to find the coke first. 'They've got too much sense.'

'I hope you're right,' Bob said. Slow but always practical, he had brought bottled water and a pack of sandwiches for the pilot. Get what's left of the inflatable buried. Going to be hot out here,' he warned. 'Best find some shade. Don't drink too fast.'

Steve watched the big man walk firmly out into the sea. Even the thought of swimming out across the reef made him shiver.

Tying a fresh foothold into the painter, Jacket tried to heave himself into the skiff. There wasn't any strength left in his arms and he fell back. The splash scared him. He could feel them out there listening on the patrol boat. He choked back a sob, got his foot into the loop, and grabbed at the gunwale. His finger held for a moment then slipped on the smooth wet wood. He hung on the painter, panting, salt stinging his eyes as he blinked. The surf was pushing the skiff back towards the shore. 'Oh God, please . . .' he whispered out loud so that God could hear.

'You can do it,' his father said.

Jacket wiped his face on the back of his arm, put his foot back into the loop, held the painter with one hand and straightened his leg. He got his free hand over the gunwale and immediately grabbed with the other. He hung there, fighting to get his breath.

'Take your time,' his father said. 'Wait for the wave.'

He nearly lost his grip as the bow lifted. The wave rolled on under the skiff. The stern rose and the bow dipped.

'Now,' his father said.

Jacket focused the last of his energy in his arms and in the leg that was in the loop. He got his head over the gunwale, then his chest was on it. The wood bit into him as he fought to get his free foot round and up over the side. His heel caught on the inside and held. One last effort and he

38

rolled over and lay gasping in the bottom of the skiff. The next wave came.

'On your feet, son,' his father said.

Struggling to his knees, he swung out the oars. He made a short stroke first to straighten the skiff, more weight on the starboard oar, then a couple more strokes to get her moving. Each stroke winded him for a second as he threw his weight against the oars. His hands circled slowly – lift, lean back, drop and push.

Entering the lagoon had been comparatively easy with the surf behind him. Now he had to fight the sea all the way out through the twists and turns. He had to spin the skiff to face the breakers, hold her within the channel while the surf creamed down the sides, then swing her back on course. It wasn't far, fifty yards at most, but if he misjudged the sea, a breaker would catch him broadside on, slamming the skiff down on the razor-sharp coral. He hadn't strength left to get her off. The next wave would capsize the skiff, shattering one side and tipping him out. He might survive if he could see and he wore his mask round his neck; without it, he would be cut to bits.

Bob swam steadily out towards the surf. The coral didn't scare him. It had to be dealt with in the same way that he might have to deal with the Colombians. It happened, you did your best.

That the crossing would have been easier in daylight didn't cross his mind. Nor did he consider that he was playing the more dangerous role. Steve's money and connections had set up the deal. Steve had hired him because of his experience with boats and engines and the sea. The money was more than Bob had ever earned in a full year – enough to buy a boat, which was what he wanted more than anything else. But the amount didn't change his role or his attitude – he was working for wages.

He tried to read the wave patterns for signs of a way through the reef but it wasn't easy at night. Danger lay in being trapped in the shallows where a wave could dump on him, its weight grinding him into the coral. Gripping the coral edging his route, he held himself steady and hunched his back against the weight of the waves, then brushed the coral ahead gently with his gloved hands, feeling for the spines of sea urchins or other dangers before drawing himself forward another few feet. Twice he found himself in blind alleys and had to retreat. Finally he was through, and swimming hard for the boat.

He began his first circle of the cay a hundred yards out from the reef. The day boat made five knots at 700 revs. The only sound from the big Mercruiser came from the exhaust and he ran without lights. He had calculated that he could make three full circles before heading back to base. The kid couldn't have got far. Using the spotlight, Bob could have picked him up in minutes. In the dark and with the moon down, it was more difficult but not impossible and he remained hopeful as he stared over the windshield, eyes quartering the sea ahead.

Jacket heard the soft bubble of the exhaust. He had expended the last of his energy in gaining the open sea. He lay on the floorboards. He had nowhere to hide.

'Remember, we've got natural camouflage,' his dad had said.

Jacket unlashed the sail from the mast and gathered it foot by foot into the bottom of the boat. His trousers were filthy from sweeping the sand but paler than his skin and he took them off. He lay on the sail. He could hear the scratching of the crawfish in the fish-box and in the net; the plop of a wave against the skiff; the exhaust. It was close now. The boat was travelling slowly. There was a hiss and sigh as its bows caught a wave. Not more than fifty paces.

The black knight sat motionless on his black steed in the shade on the edge of the small forest. A small river ran down the valley below. The white baron approached the ford at the head of a hundred of his most vicious soldiers. The black knight wasn't afraid. Some day soon he would attack, now the odds were too great. The horses below snorted and he heard the scrape of steel bits and the soft splatter of the river where it dipped over rocks below the shallows.

'Stand, boy,' he whispered as his steed shifted weight. 'Stand, stand . . .'

An hour remained before first light. The boat had circled three times. Now Jacket heard it slip away towards the north. Getting to his knees, he stepped the mast and lashed the sail back. It was then he saw the small suitcase lying under the transom seat. He thought of dropping it overboard but it belonged to the pilot. The breeze was coming now.

Already he could smell the deep water of the Tongue of the Ocean, fresher and cooler than the Great Bahama Bank, less rich.

His mother always woke with the breeze, dressed, and began her walk across the south tip of the island to the American's house which she cleaned every day. She had tried for a job at a hotel in Congo Town but there had been trouble with the assistant manager and she had come home with her eyes swollen, a sign that she had been crying. She didn't cry often, not even in the first weeks and months after his dad ran off.

'You have to get the papers through,' his dad said.

The black shape of the case was barely visible. The plans were in it. As Jacket slipped an oar into the sculling U in the transom, his thoughts were with the General. The General had been waiting all night for the plane to return from behind enemy lines. Jacket's dad had given his life. Jacket wouldn't let him down.

The breeze came slipping across the sea, quiet as a lizard, and touched the edge of the sail. A second tremor stirred the light cotton. A third. The sail filled for a moment, only to collapse, then filled again. Jacket caught the breeze with the sheet, trapping it within the light rice-sacking so that the sail lifted first then swelled gently, no strength in it yet as the edge fluttered. There was a slight change in the plop of water against the hull as the skiff stirred. Jacket drew the oar in a fraction to bring the bows up closer to the wind, then quickly eased it before the sail had time to collapse. A pattering came now from the bows and a sudden slap as the skiff leant awkwardly into a swell. Jacket could feel the breeze on the back of his ears as he shifted his weight to windward. The skiff steadied and rose smoothly to the seas.

7

Jacket was missing. His mother closed the curtain on the shelf where he slept. She knew he was fishing and she crossed the hut quickly to the door – only a light breeze stirred the upper fronds of the pines.

There were times when she worried all night as she thought of him alone out at sea. Deserted by his father, the sooner he learned to stand on his own feet the better and she had never told him that she knew he went out. She wondered what he was doing with his money. He lived too much of his time in his imagination . . . and in watching war films on the TV down at the bar because of the rumour that his father was in the US army. Another rumour said he was in jail, which was more likely. Feckless man, always building a legend.

She sighed as she slipped her feet into sandals and straightened up. It was the walk that did for her. Six miles each day. She did it every day, Sundays and Christmas. Mr Winterton didn't need her to come every day or expect it of her but it was the one job she had been able to find. She didn't intend allowing Mr Winterton any reason or excuse for dismissing her. In seven years she had never even asked for a raise in pay and she never gossiped.

Mr Winterton boasted that he could let friends have the house any time that he wasn't there, confident that they would find it spotless. The present two guests were unusual in that they slept in separate rooms. The smaller one, Mr Steve, had been staying at the house for two months. He had explained to her that he was writing a technical book on currency investment policy. His friend, Mr Bob, had arrived with a fast motorboat more recently. They intended staying a further six weeks.

Searching her bag, she found a pencil stub and an old shopping list. She wrote on the back in careful capitals: DON BE LAIT FO SCHOOL.

Fishermen were slipping out on the dawn breeze as Jacket tacked round the point into Green Creek. Most days Dummy was one of the early birds. Jacket saw the square figure in the big hat waving from the water's edge. Rather than pick up his moorings, Jacket ran the skiff into the beach. Dummy waded out to meet him and grinned excitedly on seeing the night's catch and made odd squeaking noises in the back of his throat.

He was over sixty years in age and a rim of grizzled curls showed as he tipped back the faded red felt hat with the big rim that a young American woman had given him years before. The hat had faded but remained serviceable. The same could be said for Dummy. He was a deep chocolate in colour, his face lined and marked with an almost permanent smile that showed three yellow teeth; barrel chest, bow legs, toes splayed by years holding the mesh of his fishing net taut as he repaired the holes.

Jacket almost fell into the old man's arms. He stood in the water, hugging him round the waist, his head against Dummy's chest. He wished right then more than ever before that the old man could hear. With daylight, his fantasy worlds had retreated. He wanted to tell Dummy everything. To get rid of it all – the responsibility for having done the right thing or the wrong thing. He had to report the pilot's death to the constable and what he had done with the metal boxes.

But Monday was his mother's birthday. Jacket was determined to cross to Nassau and buy her present. The constable would stop him. He was a slow dull-witted man. Grown-ups mocked him for clinging to the big book of regulations on his desk more than he did to his wife.

There was Jacket's teacher, Miss Charity. If Jacket waited until she had gone into school, he could slip the case on to her porch with a note. She would inform the constable, but Jacket would be already out of reach. First he had to leave a note for his mother, telling her that he was going to Nassau.

Releasing Dummy, he pointed to his hut and acted changing his clothes, then pointed down the coast towards Congo Town and drew a big square to represent the resort hotel.

Dummy nodded happily then frowned as Jacket took the case from the skiff. The old man signed, wanting to know what it was and where Jacket had found it. Jacket didn't want to offend him, nor did he want him involved. Turning quickly, he trotted up the beach.

He was almost through the trees to the main street when Vic seized him and swung him round. Vic was king. Two years older than Jacket, tall and broad in the chest, he had won the inter-island boys' boxing cup for his age and weight three years in a row.

Jacket tried to tear himself loose but Vic had him by the ear and screwed his face into the sand so that he couldn't yell. Vic sat on him and grabbed the case.

'What is dis?' Vic demanded. He lifted Jacket's face an inch clear of the sand and shook him.

Jacket hadn't thought to try the locks. They were brass and solid-looking. He tried to shake his head as Vic ground his mouth back into the dirt.

'Where's you get dis?'

'I's found it,' Jacket said. He was determined not to betray the pilot. The pain was fierce as Vic gave his ear a further twist. He was tired. So tired. He fought back his tears. 'Bleak Cay,' he heard himself say. Shame shook him as he stuttered into the sand that a plane had crashed on the coral. Then he heard angry squeaks and Dummy charged out of the trees wielding a stick.

Vic fled with the case.

Still squealing his rage, Dummy lifted Jacket to his feet and held him. Jacket knew that Vic would take his revenge on the old man. They were always doing it, Vic and his gang, throwing rocks at Dummy, creeping up from behind and tripping him. The guilt was more than Jacket could bear. Everything had gone wrong, Jacket had never been to Nassau. He didn't know what days or hours the shops were open. He didn't know how to find the right shop. He didn't even know if the hotel at Congo Town would pay them straight off – all Jacket's earnings were banked with the manager. He had been stupid to even think that he could do it.

Dummy stroked his head and shook him gently. Squeaking encouragement, the old man pointed first to Jacket's home and then back to the skiff and to Congo Town. He gave Jacket a push and squeaked again as he grinned and nodded his head so that the brim of his red hat shook.

Bleak Cay was an oven. There was no shape to the sun. It spread overhead, a vast white fire in the bleached sky. Bob had told Steve to keep in the shade but there wasn't a tree on the island. Steve tried to cool himself in the sea but the sun drove him back, burning his face and his arms. First he had buried the inflatable. Then he had hidden the pilot in the dunes. Now he sat beside him and dragged the shirt off the body, wrapping it round his head. Still the heat bore down. Steve's fear grew with the heat, grew until he was on the edge of panic. He had always been afraid of pain. Now he imagined himself in the hands of the Colombians. His only hope lay in finding the cocaine before they arrived.

He had begun his hunt at the rock where Jacket had hidden the skiff. He had searched thirty paces each side of a centre line across the cay, poking the sand with a stick. Having crossed the cay, he had drawn a deep mark in the sand above the tide mark, taken fifty strides south, marked his new centre line and begun a fresh traverse. He had covered less than a quarter of the cay before the heat defeated him.

He was certain the cocaine was on the island. It had to be. He peeked out from under the pilot's shirt. The sand reflected the heat up into his face and he whimpered and quickly drew the shirt closed. A gull screeched. He heard it's wings beat against the coarse grass as it hopped towards the pilot. Wings beat the air as a second and a third bird landed. Claws scratched in the thin crust formed on the sand by the dew. Frightened the gulls would attract attention, he cursed them and threw sand, though without looking out. One of the gulls squawked an angry ke-ruh, ke-ruh.

Steve's face and his forearms were on fire. He thought of Bob asleep back at the house. The whole goddamn situation was Bob's fault. Bob and the three hours he had taken fixing the motor. And the kid.

The kid might have told someone at Green Creek about the plane crash. Maybe everyone knew. Steve opened the shirt a slit to check the sea. The only boat in sight was a mile away. A two-masted yacht with a white hull, its sails hung slack as laundry in a back yard. The crew had rigged an awning over the cockpit. Steve imagined them sipping Cuba *libres*. Screw them. He hoped their brains fried.

The sand burnt his knees and knuckles as he crawled up the dune to look out over the sea to the other side of the cay. The heat twisted the water into undulating mirrors that separated the white wake from a speedboat racing towards the tip of Andros. A lone skiff seemed to float on air way out beyond the reef. Damn kid. Jesus, what he'd do to him.

A gull laughed at him and he rounded to see half a dozen of them circling the pilot. They had blackish heads and a white border on the rear edge of their wings. He might as well wave a goddamn flag. The shirt fell back as he hurled a rock and the sun struck him full in the face. His skin was crisp as bacon. He cursed the sun, the goddamn gulls, Bob, the kid.

There were tears of rage on his cheeks as he scuffled like a crab back down the dune to the pilot. The body had begun to swell and already the stink was worse than the meat stalls at the market in the Dominican Republic. He had to keep the birds away. He was so goddamn tired. Jesus, he was tired. And the pain wouldn't stop. He touched fingertips to his face and felt the blisters, tight and dry across his cheekbones and on his forehead. The water in Bob's bottle was hot as a bath and burnt like acid on his cracked lips. He was used to the crowded streets of New York. The silence and the isolation unnerved him. He cursed again, cursed and whimpered.

'You're falling apart. Get a grip on yourself,' he said – and to the pilot: 'Dumb Spik.' But the pilot wasn't to blame. It was the nigger kid.

'I'm going to kill him,' Steve promised.

He had to keep the birds away. They were scared of the living and he lay down beside the pilot. With the shirt over his head, Steve couldn't see him but he was company and after a while the stink faded.

'Whatever they paid you, it wasn't enough,' Steve said.

The Colombians were probably already on a plane in to Nassau.

'The square mestizo, the boss?' Steve said to the dead pilot. 'He scares the shit out of me. You know? He's the kind that smiles and says it isn't personal and he's breaking your arm. Jesus! How the shit did I get into this? That goddamn kid . . .'

Steve awoke to find his right arm flung across the pilot's chest. Shame as much as the stink made him throw up as he scuttled away on all fours. His face and arms were afire but the breeze blowing cool off the ocean felt like ice. He shivered as he peered down through the dark towards the line of surf just visible beyond the black of the lagoon, then at his watch. Nine o'clock at night. He had slept six hours.

Bob would wait until one in the morning before risking the trip. Steve drank half the remaining water. One sandwich remained but the thought of eating turned his stomach. Picking up his stick he hobbled down to the beach and found the last of his traverse marks. Returning at the end of his third traverse he heard the scrape of a boat out on the coral.

Steve hid on his knees amongst the tufts of grass. Oars squeaked against their wooden pins and he saw phosphorescence drip from the blades. The boat was heading into the beach to his right and he scuttled sideways, watching the splash of the oars. His nerves were tight as the high string on an electric guitar. Everything was magnified. The stars shone like streetlights. The stench of rotting seaweed rose from the tidemark, the gummy scent of the thorn scrub, even the grass had a dry summery perfume that reminded Steve of the Hamptons.

The bows grated on the sand. Crouching low on his knees, Steve saw against the sky the kid vault into the sea and drag the boat up the shore.

Steve's muscles were stiff and the kid might be fast on his feet. He told himself to wait. The Ruger was light as a wand as he eased to his feet. Two steps. He smashed the butt of the handgun down like a club at the kid's shoulder but the kid moved and the butt struck him a glancing blow on the side of the head. The kid gasped and crumpled.

If he was dead, Steve was back to square one. In panic, he felt the kid's throat for his pulse, at the same time cursing him for having moved.

The boy was bigger than Steve had expected. Blood seeped from the side of his head and his shoulder looked broken but his pulse was strong. Ripping the pilot's shirt in strips, Steve bound his hands and feet. Then he drank the last of the water and filled the bottle from the sea, dribbling saltwater into the boy's eyes.

Steve had been partying at Aspen exactly one year back. A bunch of them had spent the day on Aspen Mountain. His salary was a hundred thirty-eight grand and he was due a five-figure end-of-year bonus. He had traded the Jaguar for a Porsche 911. A friend had given him a bottle of green gook that finally cured the leaf mould in his terrace garden. His blood test had shown negative. He had two steady live-out girlfriends plus the occasional weekend casual and had practised safe sex for over a year. Sure, a few people had been jealous but he didn't have a single real enemy. There were times when he worried that he was too easy-going to get right to the top. Then those goddamn de Fonterra brothers screwed his life and everyone treated him like shit. They were in for a lesson, every goddamn one of them, starting with this boy. Steve knew what he was going to do. He had spent hours thinking of nothing else.

The boy whimpered. The pain in his shoulder hit him as he tried to sit up and his face turned from black to flaky grey. Steve drew his pocket knife and opened the small blade.

Bob dropped anchor soon after one in the morning and paddled ashore. Steve met him on the beach. His face and forearms were blistered, his lips cracked, but he was rubbing his hands. Bob recognised Steve's excitement from men he'd worked for at the marina who'd just made a killing on the market or scored the woman they'd been after for months. At first Bob thought Steve was delirious.

Then he saw the kid up the beach.

Bob didn't want to believe what he was seeing. He tried to pretend to himself that it was a trick of the moonlight but that wouldn't wash and he collapsed on to his knees beside the boy. He felt the same way as he had at school one time when he had taken a bad beating from a bigger kid who'd stamped him in the gut.

Bob had hunted back on the farm. This boy's feet were too big for the tracks they'd found the previous night.

Bob looked up at Steve. Steve was still rubbing his hands.

'You're sick,' Bob said, 'sick . . .'

Bob made to get up but Steve had stopped rubbing his hands and had drawn the Ruger from his belt. The hole at the end of the barrel looked as big as the New York subway tunnel.

'Don't you ever call me sick,' Steve said. 'I'm the boss, that's something you'd better remember. You do what you're told. And there's another thing you'd better get into your dumb head . . .' He pointed to the boy. 'You're in this up to your goddamn eyeballs. I go down, you go down, so you'd better act smart.'

There was a part of Bob that didn't want to live any more. 'He's not even the right kid,' he said.

Steve grinned at him. 'Yeah, but he told me who is. Ma Bride's little boy, Jacket. This one we'd better dump out on the reef . . .'

8

The pathologist let Chief Superintendent Skelley and Trent out of the morgue and the two men walked back to Skelley's World War II jeep. The Bahamian police officer drove in silence to the beach where he had picked Trent up. The same old men were playing dominoes – perhaps it was the same game. The barbecue glowed outside the shack. Skelley paid cash for a couple of cold beers and told the owner, Skimp, to put two red snapper on the coals. 'Mind they're fresh,' he warned.

Trent broke off a wand from an oleander bush and walked down to a fallen palm tree on the edge of the beach from where he could watch his catamaran, the *Golden Girl*.

Skelley sat down beside him and passed him a beer. 'Skimp's putting fish on the grill.'

Trent didn't feel like eating. He said quietly, 'The boy's been worked over with a small blade. The cuts are all on the front so there's a difference, but it's not obvious. If it comes to court you'll need quality photographs back and front and a believable expert.'

He rolled the stick between his thumb and forefinger. A scrap of thin bark lifted and he peeled it back with great care – keeping his hands busy helped.

'There were two bodies,' Skelley said. He took the stick from Trent and drew a lozenge in the dust, a ring round it, and a line of dots to represent the coral heads in the lagoon. 'Bleak Cay. It's four miles off Green Creek on South Andros. A float plane flew in from Colombia on Monday night. The pilot hit the coral and broke his neck. The plane sank. Thursday morning a fisherman spotted a crowd of gulls on the reef and another flock on the cay. A boy was missing from the village so he rowed in and found the body on the coral. The pilot had been dragged up the

49

beach into the grass. Someone had taken his shirt. He was a spray pilot on contract to the DEA which complicates matters.'

Trent knew the DEA's resident senior agent: 'O'Brien?'

Skelley nodded. 'The pilot's project leader flew in from Bogotá this morning. He swears the pilot was straight. He's paying for the funeral out of his own pocket.'

Skelley passed the stick back to Trent. Trent didn't take it so Skelley set the point on the ground, leaning it against the Anglo-Irishman's thigh.

The soft roll of the surf drifted in to them from the reef. A car drove too fast along the main road. Skelley said, 'Damn fools, showing off.' He picked up a pebble and rolled it between his thumb and forefinger. Then came the sudden hissing shriek of an Hispaniola barn owl. 'They killed the boy.'

Trent fought to keep his mind blank. He didn't want to picture the boy's death. He was too expert at it. All the details would slip into place, then the return of the nightmares that had plagued him towards the end of his service with Military Intelligence. The plane crash was safer ground, less horrific. It was similar to sorting through his service record if it were stored on CD Rom, pictures and statistics flashing on the VDU: the times he had been picked up from jungle strips, strips in the desert, off the beach by submarine. He stuck with the pick-ups because they were the end of a mission and he didn't want to start at the beginning with the fear ahead of him and all the unpleasantness. He didn't want to start. 'You said all you wanted me to do was look, Skelley.'

'Life doesn't work that way,' Skelley said. 'You're the expert. I need you.'

'The *Golden Girl*'s my home. You could have come to the office.'

'You're never in your office,' Skelley said patiently. 'I'm asking for your help because I don't have a choice. Green Creek is an island community. You know what it's like. Closer mouthed than a Trappist monastery. The law's one policeman who spends most of the day fishing and keeps his eyes and ears shut in case the islanders won't play dominoes with him in the evenings. I send a detective in, he'll be spotted before he can get off the plane or the boat . . .

'Anyway it's drugs, Trent, so who can I trust?' Skelley didn't bother hiding his bitterness. 'I've had enough,' he said. 'There's an opening at the new resort down on St John's in the US Virgins. Head of security.

They want an outsider and they think the British accent adds class. The money's good, there's a decent house; schooling, medical insurance, car . . .'

St John's was less than sixteen square miles. 'Where would you drive?' Trent asked.

'I'm serious,' Skelley said. 'If they can get away with torturing and murdering children on my patch, I'm giving up. You can visit. I'll get you a special rate at the marina.'

Trent loathed marinas; for a committed police officer, resort security would be as despiriting as being neutered.

Picking the stick up, Trent poked at the line of coral heads. 'Which side was the plane?'

'South – fifty yards. There's a beacon at the south tip of the lagoon.'

Trent drew a line connecting the heads and the beacon.

'About four hundred yards,' Skelley said. 'The plane was a de Havilland Beaver.'

'Let's presume that whoever did it wanted information. The boy would have told him his life story in the first couple of minutes so you have a man who lost control or enjoyed what he was doing too much to call a halt. More probably the former,' Trent decided as he pictured the body – a lack of broken bones and the cuts were all on the boy's front.

'Scared and out of control with rage,' he said.

'The killer?'

Trent nodded. He had it now, clear as a movie. The killer facing the boy, the increasing tempo building to the final stab. 'I'd like Dr Jack to establish the exact cause of death.' Trent shuddered. But he couldn't escape the picture. 'If I'm right, he'll kill again so we need to hurry. It would help knowing more about the pilot. What's the DEA man's name? Anderson? I'll sail tonight, but I want to talk with him first.'

It was going to be a long night and Trent would need his strength. 'We'd better eat,' he said.

A little after eleven o'clock at night and the traffic was minimal as Skelley pulled the jeep into the staff car park round the back of the hotel on Paradise Island. The Chief Superintendent nodded to a security guard as he led Trent in through the service entrance. Anderson's room was on the third floor. A couple of minutes went by before he opened the door to them.

'Calling O'Brien,' Skelley guessed.

Anderson had dragged on a bathrobe over pink striped pyjamas that only a bachelor would have bought. He wore felt slippers with the backs worn flat so that he was forced to shuffle as he backed into the centre of the room.

There were a couple of armchairs, a straight-back at a desk, and a queen-size double bed. Anderson had pulled the blanket straight but the sheets were a mess underneath. The room was a mess. The American appeared to have unpacked in fits and starts, his possessions dumped on every available surface. A dark brown suit on a hanger and a white shirt and black tie hung on the open door to the bathroom ready for the pilot's funeral. Trent wondered if Anderson had mislaid a collar stud or a button. The TV was tuned to CNN with the sound turned down. An open bottle of Jack Daniels stood on the bedside table beside a tumbler that was half full. The ice cubes had melted – either Anderson had fallen asleep or was a slow drinker.

Skelley said, 'Mr Anderson, Trent's a friend who has helped your Agency on occasion. He's interested in your young pilot.'

Anderson said, 'Yeah, well why don't you sit down.' He was red in the face by nature so it was difficult to tell if he was blushing but he moved awkwardly, shuffling and scratching the back of his head like a boy told to stand up in class. 'I'm a visitor here,' he said. 'I mean, well, Mr O'Brien, he's the resident Agency man. He's who you should ask.'

'I've worked with O'Brien,' Trent said. His instincts were to like the American. He knew the type. One of the Good Ol' Boys. He had depended on such men in the days when his Control had seconded him to the CIA. If they said they'd get you out, that's what they did, or died trying. No committee or desk-bound superior back in Washington ever stopped them.

He said, 'You called O'Brien?'

Anderson shrugged. 'He'll be here in a quarter of an hour.' He didn't like it and he looked to Skelley. 'Listen, Vincente and I were friends and this boy's dead. Maybe there's a connection. I want to help but I'm under orders to button my mouth.'

Skelley crossed to the window. Resting his fingers on the sill, he looked down across the gardens to the sea front. Trent could see, beneath the police officer's thin T-shirt the muscles taut across his shoulders and up his neck.

'This is the Bahamas, Mr Anderson,' Skelley said.

'Perhaps they have room service,' Trent interrupted hurriedly. 'O'Brien will be here soon, Skelley. Have a beer.'

Anderson grabbed across the bed for the telephone and knocked it off the bedside table. The thump as it hit the carpet was like a bomb going off. Anderson cursed, shamefaced, and clambered across the bed. He ordered four beers, replaced the receiver and looked across at Skelley who hadn't moved from the window. Trent watched the American struggle with himself, then the words came in a rush.

'I'm in deep shit over this thing, Chief Superintendent, but for what it's worth, I'm on your side. Like Trent said, it's a few minutes till O'Brien gets here. That doesn't mean I don't have respect. I haven't lived in the States in years. Fact is, I don't fit.' Anderson looked across at Trent for understanding. 'Know what I mean?' He shrugged again, his face red, his body ugly as he sat slumped on the bed, disconsolate, but stubborn and honest. 'Listen, I advanced the cash for the goddamn plane the kid was flying. Vincente. I liked him, for Chrissake. Maybe this whole damn thing is my fault.'

Skelley turned to face the American. His head was close to the ceiling, the dome of his shaved skull reflecting the light. Tension made him appear even thinner than he was; framed against the black of the window, sinister – a snake about to strike – an avenging skeleton in a horror movie. Then his muscles went loose. He smiled down at the overweight American and said, quietly, 'You're a nice man, Mr Anderson. Thank you. I'll drink that beer when it comes.'

Instead of relief, Anderson looked as if he'd been kicked. 'It's worse,' he said. 'First Vincente has his plane torched. The same day a man with the Agency calls from Miami, says this de Havilland Beaver's coming up at auction.' He shrugged helplessly. 'You know how it is. The Agency's shitting bricks. They want a total clamp-down on information so the scandal doesn't get out.'

Skelley sighed. 'Politics . . .'

'I was never much good at it,' Anderson said.

O'Brien was short and thickset with a lot of muscle for a man in his mid-fifties. His face was tough but expressionless. His antique blue-stripe seersucker suit and faded blue cotton shirt must have outlived a dozen washing machines. His shoes were heavy and carefully polished, soles and heels protected by steel crescents. He wore a steel watch, a worn wedding band, and carried one of those obsolete leather satchels that failed bureaucrats in their last years of service use to disguise their lunch boxes. A low-grade commercial traveller on the Caribbean circuit in something unfashionable like heavy machinery or industrial chemicals would have been a reasonable guess – unless you looked in his eyes which were a cold pale blue, guarded and watchful. Very watchful.

He didn't betray surprise at Trent's presence. Nodding to Skelley, he dumped his open briefcase on the desk and dragged the straight-backed chair round so that he could sit with his back protected by the wall. Seating himself, he looked over at Anderson, waiting.

Anderson shifted uncomfortably. 'I told them I financed the plane.'

'Is that right?' Only O'Brien's eyes moved as he shifted his attention to Skelley: 'You should have called me.' He wasn't being rude. He was simply stating the position as he saw it.

Skelley kept control of himself – barely. He said, 'I'm investigating a boy's murder, Mr O'Brien.'

'Fact?'

'He was tortured first,' Trent said.

O'Brien nodded to himself. He spoke in the almost regionless accent of the expatriate who has spent his life fitting in, his words chosen carefully. 'Chief Superintendent, I've used Mr Trent in the past. We both know what he is. Before we get any deeper into this thing, we ought to straighten out whether he is here in any official capacity – that's with your government. With Washington he rates about the same as a loose magnetic mine. No offence intended,' he said to Trent. 'This is Agency business and no one is going to thank me for making you party to it.'

'A particularly vicious murder, Mr O'Brien,' Skelley corrected. 'You and I have shared aims most of the time. That's not so in this case. Your interest is in the drug angle as it affects the United States. I'm interested in the torture and killing of a young Bahamian boy. It's my case and this is my country and I won't have you interfering.'

Skelley searched the DEA resident's face for understanding but found no reassurance. He sighed and shrugged. 'I'm sorry, Mr O'Brien. Frankly I don't trust you. Not you personally, but your Agency. You've got rotten apples in the barrel, Mr O'Brien. Allowed to speak his mind, I'm sure Mr Anderson will agree. The aeroplane out on Bleak Cay proves it. If I went into the States the way you come in here, you'd

54

bounce me out on my backside. You can go over my head, Mr O'Brien, but we both know there are too many big houses and motorcars above me that weren't earned legitimately, so that wouldn't do you much good except on a short-term basis. You would also lose my friendship, Mr O'Brien, as well as my future co-operation.'

'Well, that's honest,' O'Brien said. A smile raised the corners of his lips an eighth of an inch. 'Nice if things were that simple. We'll give you all the help we can but there's ground we can't have you stepping on.'

'I don't require your help,' Skelley said. He looked across to Trent for confirmation.

Deliberate provocation and response – it was like a piece of theatre, Trent thought. He and Anderson were too small an audience so there was almost certainly a tape recorder in O'Brien's open briefcase.

Skelley had turned back to O'Brien. 'Only the four of us are aware that we know the boy was murdered rather than drowned. We are also the only people who know that I've asked our friend, Mr Trent, to take an interest. I should be extremely upset to learn that either of these bits of information travel outside this room and particularly upset to learn that they were on a report you or Mr Anderson wrote for your Agency. I wish that to be very clear, Mr O'Brien. Very clear indeed.'

'The murderers will be subject to the laws of this land. They will hang by their necks until they are dead. If they are American citizens and your President makes an appeal for clemency, my government will have my resignation.'

O'Brien looked almost sad. 'It won't work, Skelley. Whoever is behind this thing was in a conspiracy to smuggle narcotics into the US. That makes it our case. My instructions are to deliver the bodies to the US federal court in Miami. It may end up a little expensive, but that's what I'm going to do.'

Trent was reminded of the theatrical preliminaries to a dog fight, dangerous dogs, the stiff-legged parade round each other, the sniffing, the search for psychological weakness and for territorial advantage. Skelley black and immensely tall, O'Brien short, compact, white – greyhound and bull terrier. Trent smiled to himself.

The hotel was American. The furniture was American. Even the air they breathed had been cooled by American machinery. Stifled, Skelley turned to the window and tried to open it. The American latches defeated him. He spun suddenly like an uncoiling whiplash. Trent thought that he

55

would explode but he had himself under control. He leaned against the window with his hand behind him on the sill and spoke quietly.

'You people like to pretend that drugs are a mess created by the Latin Americans and by us out in the islands. You and I know this is a convenient fiction of US policy, Mr O'Brien. Your nation preaches the moral imperative of the market economy and it is the vast size of your market that controls the economy of your neighbours. Your wealth creates the mess. I could talk about lack of personal discipline in your society, Mr O'Brien, and you would agree, but that's another question. Right now we're dealing with what is almost certainly a drug-related murder.'

Skelley hesitated a moment, in all probability aware of O'Brien's tape recorder, perhaps simply drawing fresh fuel from his anger. He seemed to set himself much as a triple jumper does in preparation for his sprint.

'Mr O'Brien, I have a great deal of respect for you as an individual,' he began easily. 'I have respect for many Americans. But I have no respect at all for the powers that run your country. None, Mr O'Brien. I've never said this to you before, but I've never yet had the filth your nation creates kill a small boy who was under my protection.

'I won't have it Mr O'Brien.

'We're a small country with little means of support and our people are subject to normal human frailties. Your government uses aid and trade agreements to control our policies. Your banks control our financial institutions. Your criminal fraternities buy and sell our laws. The stick and the carrot, Mr O'Brien. In this case I refuse to be a donkey.

'You and I have used Mr Trent in the past. We are aware of his very special qualifications. I intend him to have a free hand. He will act in his own time and in his own way, Mr O'Brien.

'I wish to impress on you that I would consider you most remiss in visiting Andros or Bleak Cay until such time as he has completed his investigation.'

Trent had been watching O'Brien. The DEA resident looked suddenly tired, and said, quietly, 'You're making a mistake, Skelley.'

'Not Skelley, Mr O'Brien,' Skelley said, 'not until this case is closed. I am a chief superintendent of the Royal Bahamian Constabulary. I intend questioning Mr Anderson. I wish you to leave. You can do so peacefully or I will have you removed – but through the main lobby. That means scandal, Mr O'Brien, which you don't want.'

O'Brien looked across at Anderson, miserable on the bed. 'The Miami connection?'

Anderson nodded.

O'Brien sighed. He replaced the upright chair at the desk before picking up his briefcase. He turned back at the door, a small chunky figure, powerful in himself as well as through the powers of his Agency. 'You should have said yes to that job down in the Virgins while it was open, Chief Superintendent. As it is, you've picked dangerous ground for a fight. Nothing personal,' he said.

'That's my career down the chute,' Anderson said as O'Brien's footsteps faded down the corridor. He sat on his bed with his hands clamped between his knees while Skelley led him through the torching of Vincente's first plane and the financing of the de Havilland Beaver.

'How good a pilot was he?' Trent asked.

Anderson had recounted the first part in a flat, almost dead voice. He came alive as he described the Colombian: 'A lot of Americans serving overseas like to think we're superior beings. Fact is Vincente was about the best I've seen. A real artist, but careful, which is an unusual combination. Watch him take off and he'd be allowing for a squall before anyone had even seen it and he'd spray a pattern that used to scare the shit out of me it was so damn accurate. He had a lot of pride in everything he did. Not conceited or that macho bullshit but like he was showing us . . .' Anderson hunted for the right words: 'Not proving exactly. More that he did everything so you had to respect him.'

He looked up at Skelley. 'Yeah, respect, Chief Superintendent. He had a fiancée in Bogotá who gave him a tough time over working for us. The Gringo thing . . .'

He opened his hands, examining them. Blunt fingers of a manual worker, scars, a couple of nails permanently ridged. He shrugged sadly. 'I don't read much, Chief Superintendent. My Spanish is a little rough – you know? I mean I've been out in the sticks for fifteen years which is where I picked it up. And she'd been at school down in Cartagena. All that theta shit so the Indians can't understand a goddamn word. She thought I was a real slob.' He looked away at the black square of window as if it were a movie screen, staring at it with the fixed intensity of a child waiting for the film to begin. 'Maybe that's why I put up the cash. Proving to her that I cared.'

He wriggled uncomfortably. 'Jesus! You'd think I was gay with hots for the kid but it wasn't that. It's just that I've been down in Latin America a lot of years. They don't like us much. No reason why they should. So I wanted to do something.'

He'd gone by Vincente's parents' house on the way to the airport: 'I said I'd pay their fare over for the funeral. She was there, the fiancée. She told me to go screw myself. '*Dinero*,' she said, like it was a dirty word. 'That's all you gringos think of.'

Anderson wasn't complaining. But he wanted Skelley and Trent to understand how it had been. 'I don't have any family,' he said. 'Fifteen years in the jungle and it was Afghanistan before that. You don't spend much, so, yeah, I've saved and this man in the Cayman Islands does things with it that have turned out well so far, but I'm not J. P. Morgan for Chrissake.'

He was lost inside himself, watching the screen, the film of Vincente's life played out. How he had let the young pilot down by not thinking things through. 'They've got so much power,' he said of the drug cartels. 'They want a man's bank account closed, his mortgage pulled, his insurance cancelled, that's what happens. That's what I should have thought. That burning his plane was the beginning. And that he wouldn't want to owe me.

'If he'd wanted to fly drugs, he could have done it any time. He wasn't the type. That's what they don't understand in the States. They read newspapers or watch TV and think every Colombian's running coke into Florida. They don't think there's doctors and people like that, the same as there are back home. People with ordinary jobs. We're ignorant that way. We don't travel that much outside of the States. Except the backpackers, and they're mostly into dope so that's what they see and that's the message they take home. Most Colombians wouldn't let them in the house. Yeah . . .'

He turned from the window with a slight shrug. 'It's where I'd intended retiring. A small *finca*. I get on real well with the Indians.'

He straightened the black tie draped over the suit hanging on the bathroom door. 'Seems I'll be staying over the weekend while the Agency works out what happens next.' He picked a pair of black socks off the floor. He put them on the desk, picked them up again and dropped them on top of his open suitcase. 'You want anything, call me . . .'

Trent wanted to examine the crashed de Havilland.

There'd be no wind before sun-up, Trent knew as he studied the sky through the palm fronds above Skelley's jeep. The fronds hardly stirred and a thin haze of humidity ringed the moon. The *Golden Girl* carried an eighteen-foot Zodiac inflatable tender and a 50hp Yamaha outboard. Bleak Cay lay a hundred and twenty miles south-south-west of New Providence, a long distance in an open boat but the Zodiac was the only possibility if Trent wanted to see the crashed plane at first light and without drawing attention to himself. Skelley had sailed with him often and could handle the big catamaran.

9

The sea sucked lazily at the reef. The sun would lift over the horizon in half an hour. Now the light was cool and clear, the water within the lagoon a silky green jade.

Trent lay spread-eagled on the surface. He carried six pounds of lead on his dive belt and wore mask and snorkle, big pro-fins, dive gloves. Below him a shoal of tiny copper-coloured fish hung in the shadow of the wrecked plane. Beneath the fish lay sand patterned with minute ridges. A thin pale pointed stick waved from under the edge of the plane, a puff in the sand betrayed a flat fish.

Trent drew his feet in, almost touching his toes, then shot his legs straight up out of the water so that their weight, added to the lead, forced him smoothly down the upright wing. He equalised the pressure in his ears during the descent to the small cabin. Both doors and windows were open. The pilot's safety harness hung from the seat. Trent counted the short white tendrils of cord with frayed ends which floated from the cabin sides.

Trent eased back, each of his movements smooth and leisured. The big fins drove him down the extra few feet until he hung head down along the side of the plane, one hand holding to the doorway. He could see the prickles on the stick that waved from under the plane. He inched his free hand to the very edge of the plane's roof, then grabbed. The lobster kicked at his wrist but he had it tight.

Surfacing, he swam over to the Zodiac and dropped the lobster on to the floorboards. Then he turned and swam along a line back from the beacon through the coral heads. A pair of parrot fish butted at the wound torn in the coral by the plane's floats. Trent had hoped to find anchor marks the far side of the coral but the sand had been smoothed by five tides since the crash. Returning to the Zodiac, he undid his belt, drove up out of the water and rolled over the round hull.

He sat for a while gazing at the low ridge of scrub and sand. Bleak Cay. The lobster scratched at the varnished wooden floorboards. The sun swelled over the horizon and gold licked across the silken surface of the lagoon. Trent's thoughts went back to the dead boy. The beauty of the scene made the child's death even more appalling. Now the killer would have a second target – most probably another boy. He had to stop the killer. They had wasted a day. He must stay calm and he had to think.

He breathed carefully, his eyes closed as he counted slowly to one hundred. Then he touched the start button on the Yamaha and turned the Zodiac towards the reef. He had to tilt the propeller almost free of water as he crept over the coral. Once clear, he opened the throttle, bringing the inflatable up on to the plane. Then he eased off the power, listening for the change in engine note as the high-speed jet cut out.

Andros is one hundred and forty miles from north to south and forty miles wide. The second longest barrier reef in the northern hemisphere runs up the east coast – Yucatan to Belize is the longest. On the outside of the reef and seldom more than two or three hundred yards off-shore lies the trench known as Tongue of the Ocean. The cliff face is sheer and the trench is six thousand feet deep.

To the east of Trent the sun spilled fire across the horizon and drew lines of midnight shadow along the faces of the swells steepening against the coral. Ahead of him the shallows were mirrored gold. To the west the coast turned from shimmering sand to mangrove, then beach again with palm trees, more mangrove, mud glistening as the tide slipped over it. In the background lay the long low spine of the island cloaked in feathery pines.

The gentle hum of the Yamaha belied its power. Even at cruising revs, it drove the lightweight Zodiac skittering over the smooth water at thirty knots. Fishermen were out in their skiffs and Trent swung wide to avoid their nets. Out in the deep, a big CrisCraft, its white hull black against the dawn, seemed to float and swoop above the water like a seabird fishing.

He spotted the first tourist casting for bonefish from a Boston Whaler close inshore. A dive boat headed out from Kemps Bay; there were two more already on the reef off Congo Town.

As he rounded Driggs Hill a Hatteras eased clear of Southern Bight, Bahamian skipper on the fly bridge in spotless whites. Beer cans gleamed in the holders on the fighting chairs in the cockpit. Two Americans in Power Squadron caps looked up from checking rods and tackle to wave as Trent sped across their wake.

Next came Middle Bight, dividing South Andros from North Andros. A whaler lay tucked into the shadow of the mangrove, a portly Bahamian showing a skinny white man how to cast his lure. Then came ghosting towards him the great white spread of the *Golden Girl*'s spinnaker. To keep the lightweight balloon of Tyrelene filled in, the whisper of breeze required the touch of a master and Trent raised a thumb in appreciation of Skelley's expertise as he shot past and turned the Zodiac to come up under the catamaran's stern.

Skelley threw him a line and he made the tender fast. Swinging into the cockpit, he went forward and dropped the spinnaker, furling the sail directly into the big locker in the after section of the port hull. Back in the Zodiac, he shackled the line from the port davit to the Yamaha's holding handle, loosened the bolts and raised the engine while Skelley steadied it. With the engine lowered on to the tilting aluminium engine bracket aft of the cockpit, Trent connected the hoses from the catamaran's gas tanks and the battery terminals and swung the propeller down into the water. Under power the *Golden Girl* made fifteen knots over the smooth shallows. Her bow waves rustled back along the lean hulls, the propeller leaving a long white trail between the dark lines of the twin wakes.

Skelley hadn't been able to leave the helm since setting the spinnaker. Dropping down into the galley in the starboard hull, Trent filled a pot with seawater and set it on the stove with the lobster. Then he spread coffee beans to roast in the oven and peeled a clove of garlic. The lobster cooked, he shelled it and sliced the meat, put butter into a wok, crushed in the garlic, and added the lobster slices and four lightly beaten eggs. Plates in hand, he braced himself in the cockpit companionway as a thirty-foot day boat raced up from the south.

Bob eased back on the throttle to lessen his wake as he passed the big white-hulled catamaran heading south under power. A bearded man in the companionway raised a plate in gratitude and Bob waved.

Before leaving the house, Bob had given Steve a sleeping pill and told Mrs Bride not to disturb him.

Steve's Colombians were careful people. Steve had been instructed to wait forty-eight hours after the pick-up on Bleak Cay, then take the boat up past the settlement at Congo Town. If the pick-up had gone according to plan they were to fly a white swimsuit from the bow rails, black if the pick-up had gone wrong.

He was to tie up at the Chickcharnie Hotel, drink a beer on the outdoor terrace, then continue on beyond Moxey Town to Behring Point, then cut through to the west coast of Andros via Northern Bight, anchor off Yellow Cay for a half hour, then circle back to the east coast through Middle Bight and on home to Green Creek.

The midday heat was a poor hour for bonefishing and there were few skiffs or dories in the mangrove shallows. Any of them could have been crewed by one of the Colombians' messenger boys checking whether Bob was followed as he cut through the narrow winding channels that divided North from South Andros. The boat startled marsh hen off the mud and colonies of tern and oystercatcher.

Lying at anchor close in to Yellow Cay, Bob stretched out on the sun mattresses behind the cockpit and focused his binoculars on the shore. He had bought a hardcover edition of *Birds of the West Indies* at a secondhand bookstore in New York before flying south to Fort Lauderdale. He wasn't a twitcher with a checklist of the local birds. He liked to watch and occasionally he would leaf through the illustrations or check a bird call.

Watch wildlife, go fishing, fix motors. That was Bob's ideal life. Now he was an accessory to the murder of a boy. He didn't know what to do.

His criminal past was restricted to a few parking tickets, each offence the result of his taking longer over a job than he had expected.

Of course there was the smoke but Bob didn't consider marijuana a crime and did without it in any state where the penalties were severe. Now murder.

The horror was familiar from his childhood. There had been a pigeon with a broken wing that a cat got before he could release it back into the wild. A pet pig his dad butchered. A dog that got caught in a trap. A spaniel bitch that died of cancer. And his mother. Early lessons in the dangers of becoming emotionally involved.

Bob avoided thoughts of his mother. Her death had taken so long. There had been times that he had wanted to grab a pillow and hold it over her face to stop her agony. Cancer, like the bitch. Of the lung. She hadn't smoked. Perhaps it was the insecticides they used on the farm. More probably it was simple bad luck.

63

Luck was the closest Bob had got to a philosophy. There certainly wasn't any reason that he could see to what happened in people's lives. Good luck and bad luck. There was nothing you could do other than do your best at whatever you were doing. It went wrong, it went wrong, but it wasn't your fault, not if you'd done your best. Now he was coasting downhill with the power off, no brakes, no steering. The hill got steeper every minute. The crash would come with the arrival of the Colombians. Steve scared the shit out of him.

Steve had eaten one sandwich on Bleak Cay and nothing since except for a cup of light chicken broth prepared for him by Jacket's mother, Mrs Bride. Even the thought of food would have made him vomit. He flinched at the sunlight blazing in like a searchlight through a crack in the wooden shutters protecting Mr Winterton's master bedroom.

Mr Winterton's house on Fire Island had been raided by the police back in those days when homosexuality was considered a vice rather than the natural expression of man's sexuality. The shock to Mr Winterton's tender emotions had left him paranoid. He had ensured the privacy of future holidays by purchasing land on South Andros with no road access and with a small beach on which his guests could disport themselves without being spied upon. This was in the days before drug-traffic disturbed the economy of the islands, days when a labourer earned thirty dollars a week and was both grateful and polite to his employer.

The house had been designed by an attractive young disciple of the Bauhaus movement. As with most architects, his priority was to build a monument to his own talents rather than a home for his patron. From a distance the house resembled a giant staircase. The first step comprised a boathouse from which rails ran into the sea, a workshop and a sound-proof engine-room for the 11 kW diesel generator. The second step contained four bedrooms, each with its own bathroom. Then came the vast open-plan living area from which an impressive stairway rose to Mr Winterton's own quarters. These consisted of his bedroom, his dressing room, his library, and his bathroom – the latter furnished with more brass and marble than the entire presidential suite in a late-nineteenth century Chicago bordello catering for the new rich.

The house photographed well and had been illustrated in *House & Garden* and the *Architectural Revue*. These articles were compelling bait when tempting a young guest for the winter vacation and Mr

64

Winterton remained delighted with the result. He was a collector of kitsch which he exhibited to shock against a background of art magazine abstract paintings and formalist furniture. His greatest pride was in the bed he had discovered in Nassau – a true horror of gleaming brass with a red velvet heart centred on the mirrored headboard.

Steve lay propped up on the pillows. Despite the advice in travel magazines and the warnings of guides and dive instructors, sunburn remains the most prevalent affliction suffered by holidaymakers in the Bahamas and every doctor and nurse is expert in its treatment. Steve's face and forearms were wrapped in thin gauze saturated with burn pomade. Bob had taken the boat the previous morning to fetch the dressings from the hospital at Oakley Town.

Dosed with syndol, Steve had slept well. However, he was frightened that any movement would bring back the pain. He lay there in the big bed listening to Jacket's mother, Mrs Bride, down in the living-room. To avoid confronting Mr Winterton's private life, she had developed a walk that slapped her hard-heeled slippers on the tiles and her progress was easily followed. Steve had been delirious much of the previous day and Bob had kept her away from the master bedroom. Now Steve wanted a drink.

A half full jug of lime juice stood on the bedside table beside a tumbler with a hinged straw. Steve would have to roll on to his side to reach it. He looked at his arms. The blisters showed as lumps beneath the dressings. Fear flooded in as he remembered the boy on Bleak Cay. Tears pushed at the corners of his eyes. He wasn't sorry for the dead boy – he was sorry for himself.

It wasn't fair. He wanted someone to undo it all so that he could start again from before the de Fonterra brothers had re-entered his life. He wanted to wake up in his apartment, drink a glass of fresh orange juice, saunter out to the terrace in his bathrobe, water his plants, pick any dead leaves, then shower and dress in a clean suit and shirt crisp from Chin's Champion Laundry, read the leaders in the *Wall Street Journal* in the back of a cab on the way to the bank, check the market switch on his VDU, read his mail, get on the telephone, lunch at Denny's . . .

He closed his eyes, savouring it all: the sense of solidity, of safety, of success, of belonging to a privileged society. Platinum American Express card, American Airways Admiral's Club. The deprivation was unbearable. Suddenly the rage came, hot and total. He had nothing else and he opened himself to its flood, the heat comforting as it flowed through his limbs and up until his thoughts glowed and pulsed with its energy. Screw them, he thought. Screw them! He wasn't done yet. Not even close.

He pressed the bell push that hung from the headboard and followed Mrs Bride's footsteps as she mounted the stairs. She knocked and he croaked through dry lips for her to enter.

Jacket's mother was a short strong woman in her mid-thirties, very black. She hid firm pointed breasts, slim waist and rounded buttocks beneath a shapeless cotton dress. Worry, poverty, and hard work had prematurely aged her face. In emotions she was very similar to Steve – frightened, bitter, angry, vengeful. She hid these emotions from her employer and his guests and tenants behind a wooden exterior so that they thought her placid and stupid – a mule of all work was Mr Winterton's giggling description to his friends: 'And loyal! My dear, you have no idea. She walks seven days a week over that ridge to water the plants. Even when the house is empty. She actually prays for me every night . . .'

All this was true.

Mrs Bride believed in the word of the Bible. That the word had been translated first from Hebrew to Greek, from Greek to Latin into eighteenth-century English, then finally into a simplified modern English, the words in each successive translation chosen to conform to the prejudices of the translators, so that it now bore little resemblance to the original (which was anyway lost) made no difference to her. Her judgment of Mr Winterton and his friends was simple. They were alive. They were damned. They would burn in hellfire everlasting.

However, Mrs Bride valued her job. Each night she prayed to God to spare Mr Winterton His anger for just a little longer.

Initially she had approved of Steve. He had an easy charm and for the first month had kept to Mr Winterton's library, tapping into a laptop computer his treatise on the vagaries of currency speculation. With the arrival of Mr Bob with the boat, he had let his work slip. The two men had been out fishing day after day or simply raced the boat around the island or across to Nassau and back like any other rich foreigners. Life should be lived seriously, and not even the fish Steve gave her earned forgiveness.

What sympathy she possessed, she kept for herself and now she thought Steve a fool. Why else had he burned himself? Of course none of this was apparent as she poured lime juice and offered him the tumbler. If he was a fool then she would make from him what she could. Mr Winterton and the villagers, even Jacket, saw only the pittance of her salary – it was all she spent. But there was the other money that she earned in gifts and tips that she hoarded in a tin buried on the hardest stretch of the track home.

The contents of the tin gave her strength as did her steadily increasing knowledge of values. As ever indirect, here Jacket was her source. She would take him over to Mr Winterton's at weekends or in the school holidays and have him ask the foreigners the cost of their possessions.

Where, coming from an adult, these questions would have been suspect or rude, from Jacket they had charm and gave the foreigners an opportunity to boast of their affluence, thus committing themselves to generosity. And he was a boy, which helped. But she watched over him. Once she had found him bouncing on the big bed upstairs, Mr Winterton watching. She remained silent at the time but she had beaten him on the way home.

Given a further five years she would have saved and learned sufficient to set up in Congo Town as a pawnbroker. It was the power she wanted. The power to make those who had mocked her beg for help.

Steve grunted his thanks as he took the tumbler of lime juice from Mrs Bride. He pointed to the packet of penabol and swallowed two. Then he eased himself out of bed and shuffled through to Mr Winterton's bathroom. Squatting awkwardly in the shell-shaped bath, he sponged those parts not covered by dressings, patted himself dry and creamed his lips with the pomade in front of the huge mirror above the marble hand basin.

Bob had taken the boat up through Middle Bight to signal failure of the pick-up, then over to Nassau to check for messages at the fax agency. The mestizo had insisted on this forty-eight-hour wait before making contact. Steve wondered whether they were already in the Bahamas or were on their way. There came suddenly into Steve's imagination a picture of what they might do to his burnt face and arms. He shivered as he confronted himself in the glass, his eyes sunk, split lips, dressings oozing yellow grease. He had been good at acting sick at school and the huge bed tempted him. There was a chance that they would feel sorry for him. However, the Colombians weren't his mother. He had lost a day and he had to get moving. First he had to get his hands on Jacket. To be thwarted by that black little son of a bitch was more than he could stand. The size of the boy suddenly infuriated him. And that the kid's mother was downstairs – that close. He needed to get to work on her. He pulled on cotton slacks and took a loose, long-sleeved shirt with him down to the living-room.

'You're a truly wonderful woman,' he said as Mrs Bride changed his dressings.

He had hoped for a smile but she was an uncommunicative bitch. At least she had a light touch, he thought as she laid the fresh gauze squares from the refrigerator on his forearms. 'Jacket's a lucky boy to have such a mother,' he said. The cream had made his lips supple and he managed a smile of his own. 'He hasn't been over in a while.'

Mrs Bride had been so careful with the bandages, her gentleness paving the way, yet not seeing an opening that would appear natural. Now here was her chance. She took it carefully: 'Jacket over in Nassau, Mr Steve.'

Steve's surprise was obvious.

'Dat right,' she said. 'Jacket a good boy, Mr Steve. He savin' crawfish money to buy me a birt'day presen'. Shush,' she said as Steve tried to interrupt. 'Yo keep still, Mr Steve, while I get dis dressin' fix.'

She tilted Steve's head back and dropped a square of gauze on to his cheek. 'Dere, dat right. Yes, Mr Steve, Nassau. Nuttin' good 'nough on Andros for Jacket.' She nodded to herself. 'Monday, dat my birt'day, dat when Jacket guh be home.'

Four days! Steve would have gladly killed her. Instead he went up to Mr Winterton's library and put a hundred dollars in an envelope. He had reached the stairs when he heard the boat speed round the headland. No one had ever called Steve mean and he turned back to the library. He only had hundreds in his bill-fold. As the boss, he had to be more generous or lose face – two from him and one from Bob. Steve wrote Mrs Bride's name on the two envelopes and left them on the dining table, then went down to meet the boat.

Bob came ashore as if he wanted to be somewhere else. Anywhere else. He looked at Steve wearily. 'So you're up.'

'Right,' Steve said. He didn't want any shit from Bob. 'So what's new?' he asked, grabbing the newspapers Bob had fetched: the *Nassau Guardian*, the *Tribune*.

Both newspapers led with the Bleak Cay story. Neither of them named the dead pilot but the *Nassau Guardian* carried a photograph of the boy. The drowning was only linked by police suggestions that he might have heard the plane crash and was out hunting salvage when his skiff capsized on the reef. The *Tribune* reported the boy's victories in the ring and referred to trouble he'd been in at school. Steve let out a sigh of relief.

'Your Uncle Pete's flying in,' Bob said, handing him a fax. 'Says you're to meet him over at his sister's place.'

Pete was the Colombian. His sister's place was the rendezvous.

'Shit,' Steve said. 'That goddamn kid's over in Nassau – shopping! for Chrissake. Mrs B's birthday.'

His mind slipped into gear as he accepted the impossibility of finding the kid before meeting with the Spiks. Bob was at fault – all those hours to fix the goddamn motor – and he was no longer trustworthy. Nor did Steve need him. Already Steve could picture the new scenario. The mestizo was the greatest danger. Steve winced as he recalled their meeting at the Texaco station, the mestizo gouging his fingernail into the back of his hand. Son of a bitch. He had promised himself revenge on the goddamn hick.

The mestizo had arrived at Nassau international airport that morning as leader of a three-man trade delegation. They travelled on Colombian passports, the mestizo leader under the name of Frederico Perez. He was dressed in a reasonably cut gabardine suit and solid shoes that reeked of agricultural respectability. A black tie and a black button in his lapel added to the image. This was a serious man, a man with responsibilities. He carried, in a worn Samsonite briefcase, documents and price lists from the San Cristobal Vegetable Growers' Co-operative. The second man was equally square and tough, mid-fifties. The third was younger, perhaps still in his late twenties, of Spanish blood and consumptively slim. A prematurely receding hairline, metal-rimmed spectacles and a well-pressed but worn suit and shirt suggested the clerk.

The three Colombians were met at Immigration by a representative of the Bahamian Hotel Owners' Association and it was was the younger man who introduced Señor Perez and his colleague, Señor Roig. His own name was Jesus Antonio Valverde. He was a hoverer, a meek man, and rubbed his hands together. He spoke North American English with a slight lisp. He translated rapidly and accurately as they discussed hotel occupancy percentages on the twelve-mile drive into Nassau. There were two meetings arranged for that day – the first with a major supplier of provisions to the resorts, the second with four hotel managers.

10

Trent had attached rubber bungees to the tiller-bar and left the *Golden Girl* to sail herself while they ate. Skelley sat black and tall in one corner of the cockpit. Trent sat opposite him, an eye on the waters ahead. They ate in silence, Skelley sensing Trent's anger, Trent containing himself. He had played the scenario of the crash again and again since inspecting the wreck, slipping the facts into place as he had done so often in the past when dealing with terrorist attacks, keeping the details abstract, the blood and the torn limbs, so that his mind remained clear.

Back in the galley, he ground the coffee beans and washed the plates while the steam rose through the grounds in the moka pot.

Opening up the Yamaha, he squatted on the after bench in the cockpit, back against the tiller-bar. His thoughts were in order and he glanced across at Skelley once in a while as he marshalled his arguments.

'First this was a major operation,' he began. 'By the size of the cut lashings, cocaine rather than marijuana – twenty cartons roughly three feet in circumference. The receivers would have had a light on the coral heads in the lagoon. The pilot was an expert and knew his plane. If the light wasn't there, he would have landed from the beacon end. So we have a light but it's in the wrong place – say fifty to a hundred yards north. I checked the sand for anchor marks but the tide's washed them away.

'You can argue for a deliberate wrecking by the receivers or by a third party hijacking the cargo. That's common enough but it doesn't explain the dead boy. My guess is the receivers were late and the light was a fisherman. It's a coincidence but it's happened before and it fits.'

Skelley nodded. There were a dozen cases he could recall – mostly car lights that had turned out to be parked lovers rather than a reception committee.

'The men this end must have had a shallow draft boat to get in over the reef – probably an inflatable,' Trent continued. 'The fisherman hears them coming and hides on the cay. We're looking at two to three trips ferrying the cargo out to a mother boat. Coke out, gas in. Perhaps they ran out of time and hid all or part of the shipment on the cay. The fisherman watches and shifts it once they've gone. They come back the following night, the coke's gone, the boy turns up. That's one scenario.

'The second scenario has the fisherman trying to save the pilot, finds him dead and takes the coke. If he was a local he would have been in a skiff so he must be very light in weight to have got into the lagoon . . .'

'The boy,' Skelley said.

Trent shrugged. 'Almost certainly a boy. Whoever it was wouldn't have been able to get out again with the skiff loaded so we're back to the coke being on the island. The receivers find the crashed plane and the coke gone. They calculate the same way we do. They look for the coke, can't find it, so they wait for the fisherman to return.'

It had been easy so far – a matter of two plus two making four. Now Trent had to picture the boy's death again. He sat there looking ahead for the dark coral splodges of brown showing beneath the surface. The breeze of their passage came cool off the sea. A sloop a mile out beyond the reef had found enough wind to fill its sails. The *Golden Girl* ran steady as a train on rails. Fifteen knots . . . They would be there in less than four hours. Then what? His anger nearly surfaced and he swallowed, counting slowly. But the scene in Anderson's room at the hotel came back, O'Brien and Skelley playing their theatre of attack and response for the tape recorder in O'Brien's satchel. He had to forget it. Only the boy mattered – not the dead boy, but the killer's next target.

'The killer was late at the rendezvous,' he said quietly. 'He was responsible for the pilot's death plus the loss of at least part of the cargo. His bosses are going to be extremely cross so he's in panic. The boy turns up. One look at the blade and the boy would have told the killer where the coke was. The killer might still have killed him but he would have done it quickly and raced off to find the coke. That's not how it happened so he must have had the wrong boy. Probably a friend.'

The murdered boy had been tough, quick on his feet. So the killer had tied him first. The boy had known something, why else was he there? But not enough. The killer's panic had become ungovernable rage. Trent could feel the killer, his fury at being trapped, his frustration at being thwarted by the boy's ignorance. But he would have learned the one thing that mattered: the source of the boy's limited knowledge. He would have learned that much in the first few seconds. Why didn't he kill the boy and leave? Because he didn't have a boat? He was waiting. Perhaps he had been waiting all day.

'There were at least two of them at this end of the operation,' he said. 'One of them took the boat back so it wouldn't be noticed. The second man stayed on the cay. He was in trouble and the heat and loneliness got to him. He freaked. Right now he's looking for the other boy. Perhaps he's found him.'

He looked up. 'Don't play games, Skelley. Get on the radio. You need a hundred men on Bleak Cay. Once they've found the coke, the boy's safe. You should have done it yesterday instead of fetching me and going through that charade at the morgue and the hotel.'

'I wasn't sure,' Skelley said. He sat hugging his knees, all bone and bald head, his dark eyes slitted against the sun. 'We're not the same, Trent. You look at a dead boy. You look at the terrain. You see exactly what happened. That's what you did in your anti-terrorist job and you'd be dead if you weren't good at it. All I had was a possible murder, a crashed plane and a drug run.'

Trent looked at him across the cockpit. Losing his temper wouldn't help. He respected Skelley and liked him – liked him very much. Trent didn't have that many friends and he didn't want to lose Skelley's friendship. But there was the boy . . . The boy's danger ate at Trent like a cancer.

'Tell me the rest,' he said.

'The rest?' Skelley tried to look innocent but he was too nice a man to be good at deception.

'Come on,' Trent said. 'O'Brien?'

'Way above O'Brien.' Skelley unfurled his legs and leaned back as if easing his shoulders of a weight. It didn't work and he rocked forward, hands clasped, examining his nails. 'As Anderson said, the DEA's wetting its pants. There's a movement in the States to rethink the drug problem. The argument goes that the sums involved are too great for control to work. That leaves removing the reward motive through a form of legalisation.'

73

Skelley shrugged, not looking at Trent. 'You can see how it is. A scandal in the DEA supplies fresh ammunition to the argument. There's a lot of careers at stake and a big investment – surveillance aircraft, ships, radar. With the cold war over, manufacturers don't want to lose another market so there's pressure from all sides to keep this case quiet.'

'Despite the boy . . .'

'A black Bahamian boy . . .' The bitterness broke through with sudden ferocity. 'Not someone who rates very highly in Washington.' He looked across at Trent. 'I want the killer.'

Get him for me, Trent's Control had ordered time and again, no pretence as to what he wanted done. This was Skelley – Skelley who had said the second time they met, 'I should have had you off the islands the moment I saw your file.'

Trent had been working for O'Brien on the entrapment of a Cuban admiral deep in the heroin trade. He could remember with absolute clarity Skelley's expression as the police officer said, 'I should never have allowed O'Brien to mount an operation from the Bahamas that required a man like you.'

'You mean a killer,' Trent had said. The reputation was hard to shed – perhaps because of the demand put upon an understaffed profession with a high mortality rate.

He moved the tiller-bar a point to bring the catamaran on to a heading for Mars Bay. Then he looked across at Skelley. It wasn't something they could hide from.

'Chief Superintendent,' he said, 'if you wish me to do something for you, be precise. No euphemisms. I've heard them all. They don't wash.'

'That's not what I meant,' Skelley said.

It was the old plea, used down the ages by those in authority to exculpate themselves of the sins committed by their servants. Trent wouldn't have it.

'What about your hopes, Chief Superintendent? What do you hope I'll do for you?'

Skelley's shoulders were stiff with anger. 'Why should they get away with it?' he demanded of the sea ahead. 'They' were Washington more than the killers. A white president, white bankers, white officials. Trent could smell the Bahamian's racial revulsion.

'Christ, Skelley, how could you let them get to you this badly?' he

74

demanded. 'We're friends then suddenly we're white and black and all the never-the-twain-shall-meet crap.'

Skelley said, 'You don't know what it's like.'

No worse than being treated as a tame killer, Trent thought.

'I want them caught. I want them to hang,' Skelley said. He rounded on Trent. 'You know that isn't going to happen.'

'You've been catching people for too long,' Trent said. Keeping the peace was a constable's job. Proper policemen had a vested interest in crime. They needed axe murders to solve so they could earn promotion.

'How do we save the boy? That's what you should ask,' Skelley said, his own anger out now. 'If he's alive, that's what I'll do. I don't have a career and I don't give a damn for Washington. If that worries you, you'd better get out of the way. Maybe you'll be able to live with yourself. I hope not . . .'

Skelley swung his long legs out of the cockpit and crabbed forward, seating himself on the nylon webbing that served as a deck between the two hulls forward of the central cabin.

A dive boat surged towards them from the reef, fifteen holiday-makers on board, faces painted with sunblock. The dive had left them excited and happy and they waved beer cans and Cokes at the two men on the catamaran. The Bahamian crew recognised Skelley and were more circumspect. As the dive boat's wake lifted the *Golden Girl*, the Yamaha's propeller rose clear of the water and the engine raced for a moment.

'I'm sorry,' Skelley said. He repeated himself, louder this time. Then he made his way back and collected the empty coffee mugs, refilling them from the moka in the galley.

'Thanks,' Trent said.

Skelley sat beside him on the flat teak coaming at the after end of the cockpit. 'You're right. They get to you, they've won,' the Bahamian said after a while, quietly, and as much to himself as to Trent. 'I'm old enough to know better. Experienced enough . . .'

He looked ahead to the point protecting Green Creek. 'Where do we start?'

The dead boy first. They needed to learn his habits, who his friends were. School would be out by the time they dropped anchor at Green Creek. 'The boy's teacher,' Trent suggested.

*

75

She was known in the village as Miss Charity. Some of the villagers thought her superior. Certainly she was different. She was a childless spinster with no known sexual attachments. She had been to university in Jamaica, studying marine zoology, becoming politically militant.

The few openings in the Bahamas went to those with influence. Given her politics, it was ironical that she came from the wrong family, her father having stayed loyal to the white Bahamians whom he had served as a clerk in a lawyer's office. She tried the dive schools for a couple of years. She enjoyed the diving but hated being eyed by the customers, alienated by their repetitive attempts to bed her. The dive instructors were as bad but at least they were black. However, the books and fish charts they used were from the States.

She had been compiling her own book for three years. When completed it would include only the Latin and the island names of the fish and crustaceans. It would also list the fish by habitat rather than family so that an amateur out on the reef would know where to look in the book. As well as the book, there was her study of the coral head which she intended writing up as her Master's thesis. Teaching school in Green Creek wasn't a job anyone else wanted but it financed the hours she spent in the water and her photography.

Dummy sailed her out to the reef or a blue hole most weekends. He knew what she wanted and didn't bother her with idle chatter. Sometimes Jacket accompanied them. The boy was a keen student and she had been surprised at his absence from class for the past two days. Dummy was also missing.

Vic, an excellent swimmer, had drowned out on the reef by Bleak Cay and a plane had crashed there, killing the pilot. Though the constable hadn't said, the village presumed it was drugs. Vic must have heard the plane and gone out the following night. He had been a tough youth, a bully, and often in trouble.

There were no connections that Miss Charity knew of between the happenings on Bleak Cay and Jacket's absence from school or Dummy's absence from the beach. Vic's death made her anxious, that was all. Rather than stay anxious, she decided to seek out Jacket's mother, Mrs Bride.

Mrs Bride walked over the point to clean the homosexual American's house seven days a week and didn't return until mid-afternoon. Mrs Bride was another loner, and didn't take kindly to visitors. Miss Charity

76

decided to intercept her by accident on the path back from Mr Winterton's house.

A breeze had come up from the north and Trent set the catamaran's mainsail and ghoster, a headsail of light cloth cut flatter than the balloon-shaped spinnaker but almost as big. A thirty-foot day boat powered by an outdrive raced out from a small beach as Trent brought the *Golden Girl* round the point towards Green Creek. They had crossed paths with the same boat that morning and it had passed them again heading south a half hour ago. Two men were in the cockpit now, one of them in a long-sleeved shirt and a wide-brimmed sunhat, the other in a black T-shirt. The man in the T-shirt waved and Trent raised a hand in reply.

'Nice place,' Skelley said with a nod at the big white house rising in steps from the beach. 'Mr Winterton. He's what they call a corporate lawyer. Built it years ago and used to come four or five times a year but now it's two weeks at Christmas and a week at Easter. Lets it the rest of the time or lends it to friends. Says he has too much work.' Skelley shrugged. 'Seems a waste. He doesn't even have kids . . .'

The house was too grand for Trent's taste. 'What's it like inside?'

'Designed to entertain in. Big paintings that don't mean anything.' Skelley pointed ahead to a dark brown ragged line of coral a quarter of a mile off the beach at Green Creek. 'The best way in is round the south end.'

Fifteen or twenty skiffs were moored in the shelter of the coral, their hulls painted grey or black. The beach was standard gold. The village lay hidden behind a double line of coconut palms. Trent could see the tin spire of a chapel. Pines grew on the ridge behind the village, a few crows flapped, a pair of birds waited for a free meal; close to the sea, a big black sow roped to an iron stake rooted amongst the usual Third World litter of First World packaging.

Half the population congregated on the water's edge to watch the *Golden Girl* round the coral. Those of them who hoped to see a foreigner run aground were in for a disappointment. With her lee boards raised the big cat drew only twenty-six inches. Skelley went forward and bagged the ghoster. Trent signalled him to drop the anchor when they were a hundred yards inshore from the bar of coral. He sailed the Danforth anchor deep into the sand on two hundred feet of scope before coming up into the wind and dropping the main.

They mounted the Yamaha on the Zodiac and Skelley ran ashore. Putting on fins and mask, Trent swam over to the anchor with a small white buoy on a light line. The blades were all buried in ten feet of water. He dived and threaded the line through the hoop on the head of the anchor so that he could pull the anchor clear if it dragged and got caught under coral. Back in the cockpit he took a thirty-pound lead weight from the stern locker and ran it on a loop midway down the anchor rope. If the wind picked up, the lead would act as a spring, the catamaran having to lift it free of the water before the full drag of a surge came on the anchor.

Next he dealt with the sails. He laid the ghoster out forward of the central cabin and rolled it carefully into a long sausage. He lashed the sausage with loops of cotton, then folded the sail back on itself in a long zigzag and stowed it in its bag. Then he dragged the spinnaker out of the sail locker and treated it the same way. The sail bags were marked in big black numbers edged in luminous paint. Apart from the ghoster and spinnaker, there were three more headsails ranging in size from the number one jib that filled the complete triangle forward of the mast, down to a small storm jib. All the sails were lashed with cotton. Shackling the sheets to the foot of the number two jib, he ran the sail up the forestay ready to break out if he needed to get under way in a hurry. Lastly he shook all the lines, the sheets and halyards out and re-coiled them neatly, each in its proper place, so that there was no chance of confusion or of anything jamming if he had to slip anchor in the dark.

A couple of villagers paddled out in a skiff to inspect the catamaran. Trent tossed them a cold beer each and they discussed the wind the way boat people do, the villagers proud of their local knowledge and happy to share it. The headland curled any southerly squalls round to come back off the shore. They jabbed fingers at the beach where the direction the palm trees leant bore this out. The wind flattened any sea coming in over the coral so squalls were the only danger. Trent lowered a kedge anchor on thirty feet of chain into the skiff and paid out nylon anchor warp as the fishermen rowed the anchor a hundred and fifty feet towards the beach at a sixty-degree angle to the main anchor. If the wind got up he could let out more scope until the *Golden Girl* lay to both hooks.

The two villagers drank a second beer each in the cockpit. They were strong men, the sweat shiny on their bare chests, their faces suddenly lighting with the broad smile typical of Bahamian islanders. They spoke softly, the Andros accent less broad than that of New Providence, some

78

of the words different. Trent opened up the port-side locker to show them his dive bottles lashed upright in rubber cups and the small but powerful compressor.

They suggested dive holes and warned of currents along the edge of the Tongue of the Ocean. De Drop-off, they called it. One of them pointed to Bleak Cay.

'Plane guh down dere Wenesday night. You see it in de paper, mistuh? One of de boy drown on de reef. Cut all over de body. Writer mon from de papers come nosin' roun' but dey is guh now.'

'I'm not very good with those sort of people,' Trent said. 'Those people' were city people. The two fishermen nodded their agreement.

'I like to fish, go diving, sail,' Trent said. He didn't ask them to join him; it was too early in their relationship and he would have frightened them off.

The men got back into their skiff and rowed ashore.

11

For the first mile the path from Green Creek to Mr Winterton's house ran parallel to a sandy shore and was cool beneath the palm trees. Closer to the point mud had collected over the years and the palm trees gave way to thick mangrove swamp which forced the track back to the side of a steep ridge scantily covered with scrub. The day's heat lay on the ridge, the track was dusty, the scrub infested with small black flies. Miss Charity met Mrs Bride midway along the side of the ridge.

Mrs Bride had buried her three hundred dollars in the tin. She was having a good day. She wasn't worried by Jacket's absence. He was always off by himself and he was a sensible child, not fooled by strangers. She was naturally curious as to what gift he would bring her back from Nassau and, more, how much money he had. She had searched the hut a few times, hoping to find his hiding place. Jacket was an expert fisherman and crawfish were three dollars a pound up in Congo Town. She knew from gossip that Dummy had been up there selling at the resort more than once and she was certain that at least part of the catch was her son's. Twenty crawfish at a pound and a half each was ninety dollars. Thirty crawfish, a hundred and thirty-five dollars. Doing sums in her head made the walk pass quickly. She was halfway along the ridge when she saw Miss Charity.

Mrs Bride was suspicious – particularly of outsiders. Their tales of how easy life was in North America had led her husband to run off.

Miss Charity was an outsider.

Mrs Bride walked this track twice every day of the year and knew exactly how unpleasant it was in the late afternoon heat. She wasn't fooled by the teacher's casual greeting. The meeting was deliberate and she decided to make Miss Charity pay for her deceit by keeping her there in the sun with the flies biting for as long as she could. She was expert at relating unconnected details of a day's happenings, befuddling the listener with endless tangents, none of which approached a conclusion. She started with an account of Mr Steven's sunburn but without referring to him by name.

'Terrible,' she said with a shake of her head. 'Blister all up de arm. I tell de mon, camomile tea. Mrs Richie, she have de store use to keep it. Now dat new man. But dat how it is. Change. Everytin' change. Dat what I tell de udder one. Camomile. An' dat dere no poin' in goin' to de store since Mrs Richie give it up. Dat before you come, Miss Charity? Course it is. Seven year, or is eight? No, dat de year dat man catch de big marlin so it ten. An' de mon's face. De udder mon say he guh to de chemis' at de hospital. De drug store, de mon call it. De blister dat big,' she said, ringing her thumb and forefinger. 'Is liftin' like soap bubble.'

Miss Charity slapped at a fly that had settled hungrily on the back of her neck. If Mrs Bride had smiled more often, Miss Charity might have stayed there on the track till sundown. But the smile was a surprise and Miss Charity detected the underlying malice. She wasn't surprised. Only the naïve believe in the sweet simplicity of island communities. Nor did she care whether Mrs Bride liked her or hated her except as it affected Jacket.

She said, 'Mrs Bride, your son is one of the few children I teach who wants to learn. When he missed school yesterday and today, I decided to walk up here and ask you if something has happened to him. That's not being nosy. It's my job.'

'Not affer school hour,' Mrs Bride said, exultant in victory. 'Dere no school dis time o'day, Miss Charity. Yo ask me in de mornin', den it yo job. Mind, I leave de house 'fore school is in, so yo fine me at Mr Winterton or wait till I's home. I's home den de school done finish like now so you is back waitin' till de next mornin' fuh it yo job. Den de weeken' comin' and dere no school.

'I know 'bout job, Miss Charity. Proper work. An' bein' muddah. No fuh few minute in de day when de fancy take yo but feedin' de boy tree hundre' sixty-fie day in de year. Dat every year, Miss Charity, and I's walkin' dis path two time every day.'

Miss Charity almost fell as Mrs Bride shouldered her aside. God, what an awful woman, Miss Charity thought, as Mrs Bride strode off down the path. One hundred per cent bitch . . .

The meetings went equally badly for the three representatives of the San Cristobal Vegetable Growers' Co-operative.

With agricultural labour costs at a quarter the rate in the United States, Colombia could undercut North American prices by a third. The square-built leader of the delegation, Señor Perez, guaranteed regular supply. He argued that the smaller countries of Latin America and the Caribbean had similar interests in freeing themselves of North American economic domination. He argued quietly and patiently, nodding repeatedly as his thin Spanish-looking compatriot, Jesus Antonio, translated.

The Bahamians were sympathetic and even agreed in principle. However, ninety per cent of the investment they represented was North American. North Americans had a poor opinion of Latin American reliability. They liked to know who they were dealing with, preferably a single man. They were suspicious of co-operatives as un-American. There was a Cuban ring to the word.

In a break for a cold beer, one of the Bahamians led Jesus Antonio aside. The Bahamian was a warm man, portly and avuncular.

'We're talking reality here, power,' he said quietly. 'You people have to understand. We have a plane of your produce come in, the American suppliers over in Florida tell their DEA that there's drugs on board. The Americans have their own men here at the airport. By the time they've searched the cargo, half the stuff's rotten and our guests are eating canned beans.' He shrugged his heavy shoulders, his smile sympathetic. 'Yes, sir, I know. You people are farmers. We'd like to help, but it's not going to happen. That's something you have to accept and no amount of figures and argument are going to change it. You have to explain this to Señor Perez. He's a good man – that's obvious – but there's nothing any of us here can do.'

Jesus Antonio translated to Señor Perez. The mestizo crossed the room to the Bahamian and shook his hand, man to man. That's how it was. They both knew it, but Perez had tried.

The three Colombians hired a Hertz Ford. Fifteen minutes of careful driving assured them that no one was following. They pulled into the marina a mile beyond the Paradise Island bridge at exactly twenty minutes after eleven. A grey-haired boatman held the hose to the port tank on a thirty-six-foot fly-bridge Bertram alongside the fuelling dock. Perez ducked into the cabin. Jesus Antonio and the third Colombian drank a beer at the bar while watching the Bertram head out of the marina. Down in the cabin the mestizo sat with his legs spread against the movement of the boat, hands folded in his lap. A farmer, he was used to disappointment, to the vagaries of the weather and damaged crops. In the history of their family there had been many times when they had been saved from ruin by the de Fonterras. For no other reason would he have done business with the Gringo. He hadn't liked him. He was a young man to whom too much affluence had come too easily, a señorito.

Bob held the boat down to a steady twenty-five knots as he rode the sides of a slow swell that came rolling in from the north-east. At midday the sun had bleached the colours out of the sea and sky. Now, in late afternoon, the sky spread blue above the darker blue of the deep water. Ahead lay their rendezvous with the Colombian, two islets connected by a low strip of sand. Twin lines of surf curled round the islets a hundred yards offshore. The gap in the centre was some fifty yards across. The water was a pale green inside the reef, the sand connecting the two islets a solid bar of white gold.

Bob cut power as he turned in through the gap. He kicked a stern anchor overboard some sixty yards out, then raised the propeller and brought the bow gently on to the beach with a soft crunch. Running forward, he jumped ashore with a line and steel peg which he dug deep into the sand.

Bob longed to be about five thousand miles away – on one of these Greek islands he'd read about in the travel magazines, or the Philippines, or Indonesia.

He had never seen a corpse before except on TV where they didn't seem real. He didn't have the money to hide and he was sure that Steve would set the Colombians after him unless he made his case. He wasn't scared of them but he was scared at being involved in something this vile.

He had wanted sufficient cash to buy a small boat that he could fit out as a travelling workshop so that he could cruise and earn. This had been his dream for ten years and Steve's proposition had seemed safe enough. All he had to do was keep the boat running and get it to the right spot at the right hour. Steve had explained to Bob that he wouldn't even be breaking the law – or not the US law, which was the only law that counted.

Steve was the kind of successful citizen who made Bob uncomfortable because they didn't mess up and didn't understand why he did. He had known him as a banker who shared, with a bunch of equally successful friends, a nice house each summer out on East Hampton beach. He drove a Jaguar for a while, then a Porsche. He carried an entire concertina of credit cards in his bill-fold but had always paid cash up front for any job Bob had done for him, and there was a little extra in the envelope each time. That's why Bob didn't understand how a generous successful man like Steve could do such a wicked and terrible thing to a boy. Steve had to be sick.

He heard a thump in the cockpit and looked up as Steve appeared on deck. He wore a baggy blue long-sleeved shirt with the cuffs unbuttoned, loose Calvin Klein cotton chinos, Dunlop dockmasters. A floppy cotton sunhat perched on the bandages covering his forehead and he held his Ruger. He looked crazy – all that yellow gunk on his face – like a victim of a lab experiment that went wrong in an SF movie.

Bob said, 'Steve, the gun's a bad idea.'

'Don't worry about it,' Steve said.

Steve had been swallowing syndol all day. He felt a little light headed but he wasn't in pain as he checked the terrain from the foredeck. The sand bar was a hundred yards long. The two islands were round and four hundred yards in diameter. Neither island was higher than thirty feet and the vegetation was minimal. Like a flattened dumbbell, Steve thought.

A bunch of birds a foot and a half in height watched him from the curve where the bar met the eastern of the two islands. The birds had black heads and necks, broad crimson beaks, greyish brown bodies, white patches on the tail and on the wings, pink feet.

Every now and again one of them let out a loud wheeeep.

Steve drew a bead on them with the Ruger and said, 'Powee.'

Reassured, the birds went back to picking at the sand.

'Oystercatchers,' Bob said.

Steve had eaten a great many oysters back in his banking days. Doyle's Bar on 6th had been one of his favourite haunts. A half bottle of Moët Brut and a dozen Chesapeake Bay Blues before the theatre. A warm trickle of anger stirred as he thought for a moment of what he'd lost. 'You're meant to leave,' he told Bob. 'Pull the boat back a half mile and pretend you're fishing.' He knew Bob wouldn't go.

Sure enough, 'I don't like to do that,' Bob said.

Steve looked at him in acted surprise. 'Who gives a shit what you like?' He was a little frightened of the jump down to the sand – that the shock might bring the pain back. He took the packet of syndol from his shirt pocket and swallowed a couple.

'You want to go easy on those,' Bob said. He looked stupid standing there on the sand, black Carling Black Label T-shirt which someone who travelled must have given him, hick shorts, a cheap digital watch on a plastic strap.

The man was really dumb, Steve thought, really dumb to believe that Steve didn't know what he planned. Steve beckoned him over with the Ruger, leaned over so that he could get one hand on his shoulder, and vaulted to the beach.

'Thanks,' he said. Because of the burns on his wrists, he had put his Rolex Oyster in his shirt pocket. He took it out. Fifteen minutes remained before the Colombian was due.

'Weird but this must be about the first time you've been early for an appointment, Bob,' he said.

He fumbled getting the watch back into his pocket and dropped it. The watch strap was a darker gold than the sand. Steve made as if to pick up, then groaned and said, 'Shit, do me a favour, huh . . .'

Bob bent down and Steve struck the Ruger against the base of his spine.

Bob said, 'Why, Steve?'

Bob's apparent lack of fear annoyed Steve. However, there had been a time when Steve had liked the big man and he thought that he owed him an explanation.

'You're going to tell them about the kid and that it was all my fault,' he said. 'Bob, that's something I really can't allow.'

The oystercatchers screeched and took to the air when Steve pulled the trigger. It was the first time that he had fired the Ruger and he wasn't prepared. The massive recoil smashed back into the palm of his hand with the force of a club, his wrist felt broken, pain shot through his burns. His trousers and his shirt were a mess.

He sucked at his palm and kicked Bob in the ribs. 'Son of a bitch . . .'

Undressing, he scrubbed his clothes against the sand in the shallow

85

water. Having got the worst of the mess off, he hung the clothes up on the bow rail to dry and sat down on the Ruger in the slanting shadow thrown by the Tomahawk. The handgun was uncomfortable but he didn't mind. The deal was sorting itself out. That was the advantage he had – brains and education. The people he was dealing with were real peasants.

The evening breeze came cool off the water, its scent fresh and invigorating. The oystercatchers had resettled and were busy along the tide edge, their broad vermilion bills slashing at small crab and at the shells uncovered by the retreating tide. The birds were company and Steve found himself enjoying the tranquillity. That Winterton house was too remote but there were other houses on the beach. Once you were used to it, living on the shore was kind of nice. He had never played much golf – tennis had been his sport – but the long sweeps of freshly watered emerald green along the shore on Paradise Island were enticing with their plantings of palm trees and sea grape offering patches of shade. A decent clubhouse so you could eat out without needing the car and where you could meet new people without getting too committed. Security at the gates to keep the ordinary tourists out.

He could finish his book, then maybe in a couple of years join one of the banks on Shirley Street, not fulltime but as a consultant to privileged clients. Boesky was back in business, so was Milken. His own problems were a little more serious but he hadn't been to gaol. That's what some people didn't understand – that it was who you were that mattered more than what you did.

That lord over in England was the one that always made Steve chuckle. Chairman, as they called the president of a corporation over there, chairman of Guinness. He had lunch with his managing director and spent the rest of the afternoon buying 240,000 shares in his own company. An hour later his managing director launched the biggest takeover in British history and the lord said he didn't know it was going to happen. Four of them got charged but not the lord. All four were Jews, which Steve had pointed out to rile a few of his Brit associates. Coincidence, they said, nothing to do with the authorities being anti-Semitic. What a crock of shit.

12

Skelley returned from shore to the *Golden Girl* with a woman in her thirties. 'Charity Johnston,' he said, handing her on board. She stood in the cockpit as far away from Trent as she could reasonably get.

Trent could smell her anger.

Her eyes were black on brilliant white. They were set wide apart in a broad face marked by high cheekbones. The fierce narrow-bridged hook of her nose flared at the nostrils above a strong wide mouth, firm chin. Square shoulders and a deep ribcage told of hours out on the reef; leg and thigh muscles would have done a kick boxer proud. Her hair was puffed up in a steep-sided Afro that made her look taller than her five foot six or seven. She wore a black bandana around her forehead ninja style, a black Bob Marley T-shirt, black stretch jogging pants cut off an inch below her knees.

'Trent's a friend of mine and a fine diver,' Skelley said by way of introduction. And to Trent: 'Miss Johnston is a marine zoologist. She also teaches school.'

Trent hadn't time to navigate the undercurrents between Skelley and the teacher. He said, 'Why don't you sit down, Miss Johnston? What can I offer you? There's beer in the fridge, white wine, fresh juice. Or I can make coffee or tea.'

'Nothing,' she said, one word to define their relationship – nothing from him, nothing for him.

Skelley gave Trent a tired smile. 'I would have tried the constable but he's in Andros Town.'

For a moment the woman looked satisfied, as if in disappointing Skelley, she had scored a point – scored by being second. Then her face went flat again.

Trent wanted her to leave. She was too much a familiar from the past. One of those people who, at a very young age, had found emotional comfort in anger – and had fed on it, on and on, until it took them down the ultimate path to vengeance, the training camp halfway up a mountainside in Bolivia, Iran, or out in the Libyan desert, or in the Beka Valley, the terrorist cell.

Many of them were fine people apart from the rage – knowledge that had made his work so difficult and finally impossible. He had understood them too well and understood their anger – not always its initial source back in their childhoods but the latter fuel of being dispossessed of their heritage, of seeing their country sold by dictators and corrupt politicians; poverty, refugee camps, death squads; hospitals without drugs, schools without books; butter and meat mountains while people starved; lies concerning the safety of nuclear power stations, asbestos factories, mines, chemical plants. It was all fuel once the road was chosen. The terrorist cell offered the warm all-enveloping comfort of a child's nursery and bombs were the easy panacea.

He needed to break through her barriers and he said, 'Miss Johnston, Victor was your student. He was tortured and murdered.'

He saw the shock and he followed fast: 'Viciously tortured, Miss Johnston.' He sat opposite her, opening his hands on his knees, showing them empty – body language he had practised again and again until he had doubted who he was or even whether he existed.

'I need your help,' he said quietly, his voice flat, no pleading here, no weakness to which she could respond with her own emotions, but a statement of fact.

'The murderer is going to kill again. I need to know everything. First is there another child missing? Then who Victor's friends were, what he did in his free time, whose boat did he take? Did you notice anything in school? Anything different in any of the children?'

She looked at Skelley. She wasn't ready.

The Bob Marley T-shirt said it all. 'Kill Whitey' went the words of the song played in a million houses for twenty years, day in and day out. Most listeners might not consider the words literally, but the message entered the subconscious and hid there like a worm, eating away, eating and breeding and waiting to explode.

Trent had spent six years undercover in Ireland, six years of listening to the old men sing their songs late at night in small country pubs with the young registering the message of hate that to the singers was more romantic myth than a present reality. However, the young fed on it in the same way that the young Northern Irish Protestants fed on the word Loyalist each time it was used in the British newspapers and on the radio and TV to describe the killers from their community. The Loyalist community – so obvious a legitimising of murder yet the English, in their stubborn ignorance, refused to recognise it as such.

Loyalist para-military, the Irish Republican Army, Jihad, the Holy War, Shining Path, Jewish Conspiracy. Words and titles carefully chosen to legitimise murder.

He had to get her out of it. He had to have her help, not for himself but for the boy, the next boy.

'The Chief Superintendent asked for my assistance because I'm an expert, Miss Johnston. The Chief Superintendent says you're a marine zoologist. That makes you an expert observer. We don't have much time. I'd like you to think.'

He was out of practice. He had lost her. He could see it in her eyes even before she turned to Skelley: 'Bahamians aren't good enough for you?'

Skelley closed his eyes a moment. Then he said, 'Did you see the boy when they brought him off the reef? What I don't have is anyone who would have recognised that he'd been tortured with a knife blade. It doesn't happen here. Or it didn't happen till now. Trent knew the moment he saw the body.'

She turned on Trent, suspicious, but not knowing of what she was suspicious. 'Why are you special?'

'I know a lot about death,' he said, waiting.

She could feel it. She glanced at Skelley, then back at Trent, hooked by her own aggression. 'Yeah? How come?'

'I used to be a professional killer,' Trent said quietly. That was all. He swung down into the galley and filled the moka. He had set the fuse but he didn't listen to the harsh words, rapid and half-stifled that drifted down from the cockpit. He set the pot with two mugs on the saloon table and waited. The Yamaha started, the Zodiac speeding away to the beach.

Fear sat inside Charity like a stone. She had been enraged by her confrontation with Jacket's mother. Then came Skelley with his subservience to the Englishman's authority. At first she had refused to believe the two men. The Englishman's confession of his trade had jolted her – that the danger was too pressing for him to give a damn what she thought or felt. So she had told Skelley about Jacket's absence from school and recounted her meeting with Mrs Bride. Frightened for the boy, she had demanded to accompany the police officer but he wouldn't have her.

'You'd be more of a hindrance,' Skelley said.

She retorted angrily only for him to come back at her: 'You've got a bad mouth, Charity Johnson. Some day someone's going to kick your butt.'

'You're not man enough.'

Skelley had ignored her. Firing the Yamaha, he had raced for the beach and shot the Zodiac up the sand.

She watched him disappear into the trees, a scarecrow, all legs and arms. Her thoughts went back to the skiff she had spotted the night of the plane crash. She wished now that she had walked down the beach to check whether it was the *Jezebel*. Alone in the cockpit, she couldn't stand the anxiety.

Another minute passed before she ducked in through the cockpit companionway that led off the port side of the cockpit into the saloon. Though familiar with yachts and boats, she had never been on a catamaran the size of the *Golden Girl*. The spaciousness impressed her and the lightness of the accommodation.

At the forward end of the saloon the mast foot supported a table cupped by a horseshoe settee spread with handwoven Guatemalan covers. The Englishman sat at the table.

Big windows opened forward on to the bridge with domed hatches port and starboard in the cabin roof. The chart table lay to port of the companionway with Brooks and Gatehouse electronic equipment above: speed through the water, wind speed, depth indicator, barometer, satellite navigation. A Sailor radio was to port of the navigation equipment.

Hip-high cupboards lined the after bulkhead. A pair of wide-based ship's decanters for white rum and dark and a row of cut-glass tumblers were held in place by a fiddle rail. Afghan rugs lay on the blue carpeting. The bookshelves were full. A pair of nineteenth-century oil paintings of shipping on the Thames hung opposite each other beside the steps leading to the hulls. The tranquillity was too much for her. She wanted to scream at the Englishman. Her anger fought with her fear for Jacket, finally submerging it as she catalogued the Englishman's wealth.

She stood in the companionway, a dark shadow against the bright sunlight, not looking at Trent but sifting through his possessions in her mind, judging.

He could feel her contempt.

She said, 'Who did you kill to earn this?'

'It was given to me as cover on my last job. It was still in my name when I resigned.'

'You mean you stole it.'

He smiled. 'Some people thought so.'

'A thief as well as a killer.'

'I've been called worse, Miss Johnston.'

He sat at the table, coffee mug cupped in his hands, waiting while she stalked his territory. It was an old tactic from his past – this hope that she would find something familiar, a bridge into her own world.

The fear returned, suddenly thick in her throat. Having something to do helped while she waited for Skelley's return and she crossed the saloon to inspect the accommodation. The galley lay amidships in the port hull with double-bunked cabins fore and aft. The cabins had their own showers, hand basins and a head. Mexican bedspreads covered the bunks and there were matching curtains and bright rugs on white carpeting. The lone cabin in the starboard hull lay aft and was longer than those to port, plainer in its furnishings, and separated from the sail locker that opened to the foredeck by a head and shower. The cabins were very neat and well kept – like her own two rooms behind the school. She noticed the familiar bottles of photographic chemicals on a shelf in the master cabin head, the zinc sink and worktop. She opened the locker below the worktop. Rubber straps held an enlarger safe in a nest of bubble packing. The lens on the enlarger was a 1.4 mm Leinz. There were packets of printing paper wrapped in plastic and protected against the humidity by perforated envelopes of absorbent granules. She wondered what cameras he used.

He hadn't moved. Cup cradled in his hands, he sat waiting like a scruffy dog. But his indifference was a disguise. Everything was a disguise: the fisherman's smock and loose pants that hid his figure, the beard, the mop of dark shaggy curls that tumbled down the nape of his neck over the string of coral beads, the bushy eyebrows that shadowed his eyes so that she wasn't sure what colour they were. She remembered suddenly the way he sat in the cockpit, his hands open, backs resting on his knees so that she hadn't been able to see his fingertips. Even now they were hidden, left hand cupped over the right that curled away from her, thumbs tucked in against the cup. Though relaxed, the lump of muscle showed between thumb and forefinger. She wanted the hands unmasked – killer's hands. They obsessed her.

Her lips felt stiff and there was a dryness to her mouth as she pointed to the coffee pot. He gripped the handle in his left hand, fingers away from her. The right lay on the table curled in on itself like a crab.

He let her take the mug.

Then he looked up.

She had found something. He didn't know what but he could feel it in her – an increased concentration dragging at him.

He said, 'I could beg you but I was up all night, Miss Johnston, and I'm too tired to play games. The murderer wants information. Right now he is hunting for a friend of Vic's. When he finds him, he'll work him over with his knife and then kill him. This is one of your students, Miss Johnston. You can help me or you can accept responsibility for the boy's death. That is your choice in exactly the same way that it was my choice to help the Chief Superintendent or sail off to the Virgin Islands for a week's diving. The difference between me and you seems to be that you believe you have a choice.'

'You and I . . .' she said, falling into the trap.

'I'm sorry,' he said.

'That you get your grammar wrong?'

'That you won't help.'

'That's not what I said.'

'It's what you're doing.' The Yamaha roared off the beach and he gripped the table edge, about to rise.

The cobwebs of tiny white lines surrounding his nails were almost invisible. The scientist in Charity recognised them instantly as the mark of a scalpel. She saw the operating table. The nails ripped away from the torn fingertips. The surgeon frowning behind his mask as he repaired the

92

damage. She shook her head angrily, freeing herself. He had almost ensnared her and she cursed herself. They were Bahamian. They didn't need a foreigner's interference.

As Skelley ran the Zodiac alongside the *Golden Girl*, he called up, 'False alarm. One of Charity's kids over in Nassau buying his mother a birthday present . . .'

Charity Johnston closed her eyes for a moment, her relief showing both her acceptance of the threat and her emotional ties to the boy in question. Trent wanted to touch her as he would have a nervous horse, but she would have struck away his hand. He took pad, pencil and sharpener from the drawer beneath the charts. He dropped the pad on the saloon table and sat, sharpener in hand, giving the pencil a point. Skelley crouched in the companionway. The sun cast his shadow across the table, a dividing line between Trent and the schoolteacher.

'Let's start with Victor's friends, Miss Johnston,' Trent said. 'We're looking for a boy who would go out fishing at night, probably by himself.'

He built the picture carefully, his voice deliberately flat, his concentration on the pencil point so that there was no risk of confrontation. 'A boy who knew Bleak Cay well enough to take a skiff in at night through the reef. He was inside the lagoon so he was probably after lobster. He got the pilot out of the plane and towed him to the shore. Then he went back and brought up twenty boxes and hid them, so he's determined as well as courageous. He didn't tell Victor where, so he's close mouthed, perhaps a bit of a loner, which fits with being out on the reef by himself.'

'Jacket,' she said quietly. 'The boy who's gone to Nassau . . .'

She was certain and Trent didn't question her. He wrote the name on the pad.

'He's not a friend,' she said. 'He's small for his age. Victor bullied him – the village hero. He won cups every year and his father's big so no one did anything. Jacket doesn't have a father.'

It was in her character to have fought against the bullying whether she cared for the boy or not. But she did care for him – deeply. The control with which she spoke betrayed how close she was to panic.

'I'm sorry,' Trent said. He wanted to say more but the words stuck. His inadequacy gave her a point on which to concentrate her fear.

93

'Don't just sit there. Do something. That's why you're here.'

Trent looked across at Skelley.

'Anger isn't going to help,' Skelley said. 'The boy is the key to a million dollars of coke hidden on Bleak Cay. A police constable earns two hundred dollars a month. A detective gets three hundred, a sergeant four hundred. Tell me who to trust and how I keep the situation secret from the ones I don't trust. Already one set of people are searching for him. I call Nassau and I can name you a further dozen men in the drug business who'll know in minutes. There'll also be free spirits out hunting the boy. A miracle might keep him alive till nightfall.'

Charity watched through the saloon windows a skiff powered by an outboard run out past them towards the reef. The bow wave slapped against the *Golden Girl*'s port hull.

'Tell the villagers,' she said. 'They'll find the cocaine. Burn it.'

'I've been through that with Trent,' Skelley said. 'These people don't take risks, Charity. There's a possibility the boy knows something. They'll kill him. His one hope is that we get to him first. He's been missing a day and a half. We know he's in Nassau which gives us an edge. All they can do is have someone wait for the boy to turn up.'

Trent drew a circle on the pad and joined it to Jacket's name. 'Why haven't they talked to the mother?'

'She's at the Winterton house all day,' Skelley said.

'They don't work nights?'

'They messed up on Bleak Cay. Perhaps they're waiting for the big boys to fly in.'

'Possible . . .' But Trent didn't like it. 'Do we know what day the mother's birthday is?'

'Monday,' Skelley said.

'Did you ask what he's buying her?'

'She didn't know.'

Both men turned to Charity but she shook her head.

'How would he get back to Green Creek?' Trent asked.

Charity said, 'Saturday's mail-boat. If Jacket can't find a lift and he's got the money, he'll take the *Captain Moxey* to Kemps Bay – twelve o'clock from Potter's Cay dock.'

Trend said, 'It would help knowing how much money he has.'

'The Dane would know at Congo Town. That's where Jacket and Dummy sold their catch, Emerald Palms.'

'Dummy?'

'Jacket's friend. He's a deaf mute,' Charity explained, 'sixty years old. Sort of father figure. My friend too.' She gave a little shrug to deny the importance of the relationship but her hands trapped each other on the varnished tabletop, fingers twisted to stop them trembling. 'He takes me out to the reef. Jacket uses his skiff. He's not here,' she said. 'He must have sailed Jacket's catch up to Congo Town.'

'The morning after the plane crash?'

She nodded. 'He's the best bonefisherman on Andros. Sometimes he stays up there as a guide for regulars.'

Slides, Trent thought, layered slides building a portrait of the boy and his background. Charity was the photographer. She sat opposite him, square in her determination. Her eyelashes were long and, shuttering her eyes, gave an impression of sulky arrogance. Yet she was being torn to bits. He pictured the dead boy, saw his pain and the killer crouched over him.

The killer's boat must have broken down on Monday night. It was the only logical reason for the reception team failing to reach Bleak Cay on time. Trent wrote the days down in a column and added information:

Monday night	plane crash. Jacket finds pilot, buries coke.
Tuesday	a.m. Jacket tells Victor, then sails with Dummy to Green Creek.
	p.m. Victor murdered on Bleak Cay.
Wednesday	
Thursday	
Friday	
Saturday	mail-boat?
Sunday	
Monday	mother's birthday.

Wednesday, most of Thursday – two days in which nothing had happened. Unless they had already captured the boy. And perhaps his friend, Dummy. Probable . . .

He glanced up at Charity. He didn't want her to lose hope.

He said, 'Miss Johnston, my only aim is to save Jacket's life. I don't know what he looks like so I need your help. The villains know he's in Nassau – otherwise they would have questioned the mother. They'll have one team trying to pick him up, another team back here watching for him and watching the mother to see if anyone else questions her.

Green Creek's too small to risk putting in a stranger so it's probably a resident. If they pick him up in Nassau, they'll bring him back to Bleak Cay. If they learn that we know Victor was murdered they will presume we've got a watch on the cay. If so, they'll probably kill the boy and cut their losses.

'We have to keep away from the cay. Same goes for the mother. There's nothing for her to tell them that they don't already know so she's probably safe.'

He crossed to the chart table and studied the Andros chart. He needed to leave the *Golden Girl* off the beaten track. The west coast was mostly mangrove swamp with few settlements. The waters were sheltered, seldom more than twenty feet deep across the Great Bahama Bank that stretched for a hundred miles from the Tongue of the Ocean to the Florida channel, the diving as good as any in the world.

He said, 'I'd like you to go ashore, Miss Johnston. Put a notice on the school door that tomorrow's a holiday. Pick up your dive gear and your cameras. You'll need a change of clothes for Nassau. Act casual with anyone you meet; maybe a little irritated with Skelley for not having warned you ahead of time that he was bringing a friend over to explore blue holes on the west coast. Say something about the *Golden Girl* only drawing two feet with her boards up so we can cut through Middle Bight. You wanted Dummy to act as pilot but you can't find him. That explains why Skelley was up at the mother's house.'

Skelley ran Charity ashore. A skiff came alongside the *Golden Girl* and Trent chatted to the fisherman; a garrulous ancient with a bottle of Bacardi rum wrapped in a paper bag gripped between his feet.

Trent questioned him about the west coast, the blue holes. 'That schoolteacher woman, Skelley says she's a good guide?'

The fisherman grunted his dislike. 'She from outside. Know it all. Tink she better dan us. Out wid dat Dummy fella takin' picture and ask de name afterward. Dive dough,' he admitted, the fact irritating and he scratched behind his left ear, then spat over the side. 'Yes, sir, dive good. I's admittin' dat sure 'nough. But not so good she get where she want,' he added with a grin that showed three top front teeth missing. 'Universy, dat what she want but dey won' have her. Dat why she de Green Creek teacher woman. All dat learnin' in Jamaica and de pay four hundre' dollar de munt. Fishermen make dat wid no schoolbook an's she come down de bar tellin' us we isn' allow anchor out on de coral. Hundre' fifty mile long, de reef, sir. Bahamian anchor dere since Christopher Columbus wid no damage yo can see. Woman . . .' He spat again. 'Dey alliss interferin'.'

He reached down for his bottle, drank deeply and flashed Trent a sly grin. 'De teacher woman don' come down de bar now. Don' like de men talk at her de way men talk.' He squinted towards the shore where Charity was putting her gear into the Zodiac. 'All dat education, she don' like de men. Dat what dey say. Mine, I's too old for tryin'. Was a time dough,' he cackled and took another pull at the bottle before tucking it back between his feet.

Rubbing his hands in gleeful memory, he gave a little bob of his head as he watched Skelley push off from the beach in the Zodiac. 'Yo be careful, mon. De teacher woman, she don' like spear fish but touch and she spear yo ball.'

13

To Señor Perez his bodyguards were as indispensable as a Londoner's umbrella. The mestizo understood his own country well. He recognised his enemies more easily than his friends. He was slow to trust, swift to spot the unusual. He was a man of the land, by nature a producer rather than a businessman. He had flown to the Bahamas with Jesus Antonio because the Gringo, Steve, was his responsibility.

Jesus Antonio and his banker here in the Bahamas had arranged their papers. Jesus Antonio and the banker had assured Perez that he was safe in the islands and that to surround himself with his men would draw dangerous attention. Thus he permitted himself to be delivered by the banker's Bahamian boatman unescorted to his rendezvous and unarmed – for what danger could young Xavier de Fonterra's schoolfriend offer?

Steve listened to the thrum of a fast revving diesel approach the far side of the sand bar. He heard the anchor splash and the rev of the engine as the skipper set the flukes into the sand. He was tempted to walk up to the crest to see how many men were on the boat but it wouldn't have looked right.

Heavy shoes crunched over the sand. Steve was ready. He knew what picture he presented as he turned to face up the slope, naked, bandages oozing gunk, dazed expression like he'd been hit or was doped.

The boss mestizo stood looking down at Bob's corpse. Then at Steve.

Steve said, 'He broke the boat down the night the plane landed and had a kid set up the light in the wrong place. We got there and he jumped me, tied me up and left me out in the sun while he and the kid hid the cargo.' He raised his arms in case the mestizo hadn't understood that the bandages covered sunburn.

The Colombian turned the corpse over. Then he lifted one of Bob's hands and examined the heavy fingers, oil permanently embedded under and around the nails. Steve recalled watching Bob eat a sandwich once out at the Hamptons and how those crescents of black against the white bread had made him want to throw up. The Colombian was the same, heavy hands, heavy shoulders, heavy face. Weird how manual work did that to people – like dogs and their owners.

'You knew him well?' the Colombian asked.

'Yeah, on and off for a few years. He fixed my cars when they went wrong.'

The Colombian nodded. He said, 'Like myself, a peon. I agreed to work with you, señor, because of your past friendship with Señor Xavier. My family is much in the debt of Señor Xavier's family. Not financial debt, señor, but debts of loyalty that go back many generations.'

He seemed unconcerned by the Ruger that Steve slid from under his buttocks. 'I have a great contempt for you, señor. Yes, a very great contempt.'

Steve shot him, shot Bob in the first exit wound and curled the mestizo's finger round the butt of the handgun. The oystercatchers had taken off at the first shot and circled, screaming their wheeeps.

'Take it easy,' Steve told them. 'We're friends.'

Pulling his shirt down off the rail, he tore it into strips and wrapped one of the strips round his left wrist. Then he sat down and waited.

Only one man came over the dune, a Bahamian. A fringe of grey hair showed beneath one of those peaked caps with a white top the Brit yacht-people wore. There were epaulettes on his short-sleeved white shirt and he wore white shorts that were wide in the leg. What made him different from any other Bahamian boat handler was the machine pistol and the care with which he approached. Ex-military, Steve guessed, pleased. An expert was less likely to get panicked into a mistake.

Steve raised his hands high.

The Bahamian wasn't trusting like the Colombian. He said, 'On yo feet an' move couple of step back. Slow . . .

'Now yo tell me what happen.'

Steve nodded at Bob. 'He hijacked the cargo we had coming in. Staked me out in the sun.'

'Unhunh . . .'

'Then he brought me here. He had me tied up. He let me loose before

99

the Spik came over the hill so the set-up would look right. Said he'd kill me if I moved.'

'An' yo don' move . . .'

'And get shot. Who was that going to help?'

'De genleman,' the Bahamian suggested with a nod at the Colombian.

The Bahamian pulled Steve's pants down from the rail and dropped them in his lap. 'Yo better get dress.'

He emptied the Colombian's pockets into a white handkerchief, did the same to Bob. 'Who own de boat?'

Steve pointed to Bob.

'You sail it?'

'I know how to start the motor and how to steer,' Steve said. 'Navigation's something else.'

'We bes' get dem on board.'

They dragged the bodies over, the Bahamian doing most of the work. Then they heaved them into the cockpit of Steve's boat and down into the day cabin. The Bahamian inspected the cabin and nodded to himself. 'Dey real hard to sink, dese new boat.'

He tossed the pillowcase on to the beach, stripped the covers off the mattresses and laid them out at the foot of the cabin companionway.

Half-filling the pillowcases with sand, he heaved them on board and Steve emptied them into the covers. The Bahamian was finally satisfied when both covers and the pillowcases were full.

'I guh come roun' dis side de island an' yo follow me out,' he said. 'Don' yo get too close. We out thru de gap, yo keep off to de side so it don' look yo an' me is frien'.'

A golden sheen spread over the sea as the sun melted into the horizon. Steve settled his Raybans on the bridge of his nose as he followed the Bahamian's sports fisherman through the gap. Taking his hat off, he let the breeze ruffle his hair. He felt good – the same sense of completeness he had enjoyed back in the Dominican Republic cruising the girls at night in the German's car; the sense of being in control as he glanced down at the two bodies sprawled at the foot of the companionway.

The two motorboats drew away from the shallows out into deep water. With nightfall, the Bahamian hove-to and set out a sea anchor to control their drift as the two boats lay alongside each other. The squeak of the plastic fenders sandwiched between the hulls reminded Steve of chalk dragged across a blackboard as he drew quick diagrams of currency fluctuation for his juniors at the bank.

The Bahamian was busy preparing to scupper the day boat. Petrol floating to the surface would have attracted a fisherman or a passing yachtsman so he emptied the tanks first to allow the fuel the hours of darkness to drift clear. He chopped through the deck in a dozen places, smashed the ports, then went to work all the way along the hull, piercing the inner skin so that the water could seep into the flotation sandwich. Every little helped, even the ice box. He stopped every few minutes so that Steve up in the cockpit could listen for other boats. Finally he transferred the Bertram's two anchors and short lengths of chain over to Steve's boat for the added weight and the mattresses, fenders and wooden floorboards to the Bertram.

'That should about do it,' he said.

Steve boarded the Bertram while the Bahamian chopped holes in the day boat's bottom. The water was halfway up to the Bahamian's knees as he gained the cockpit. He swung over on to the Bertram and let the lines go. Then they sat in the cockpit watching the day boat slowly lower itself into the sea. With the deck awash, there were a few bubbles, then she was gone.

The Bahamian started the engine. 'Dat sunburn, yo better stay down in de cabin,' he told Steve. Like everything he said, it was courteous but it was a command. They docked an hour later alongside a short white pontoon with a gate leading to a path of coral slabs with thyme planted between them. The Bahamian whistled and two Rottweilers appeared at the gate.

'Keep close,' the Bahamian warned and led Steve along the path between clumps of flowering cactus and oleander. A New Yorker, Steve wasn't used to dogs. Their panting and the soft pad of their paws at his heels made him nervous.

Halogen lamps lit the property. Sea grape trees and big fan palms stood in the acre or so of clipped lawn that spread either side of the path. A dozen sprinklers swushed, the air cooled and cleaned of salt by the fresh water and perfumed by white blossoms of frangipani and jasmine.

There were no plantings close to the house which stood on an artificial rise with a big swimming pool at its foot. Trent would have recognised this openness as offering a wide field of fire and the swimming pool as defensive.

The house was low and white. There were wings left and right with a big covered terrace in the centre opening off an open-plan living area. Big white couches and armchairs faced out over the pool and lawns to the sea, the terracotta tiles polished and studded with huge green-glazed Thai pots planted with miniature citrus trees in blossom.

A Bahamian houseman came round the pool to conduct Steve to the terrace – black tie on a white shirt, black trousers and shoes, white jacket, the same grey hair as the boatman, the same respect disguising the same watchfulness.

Two men waited on the terrace. The senior of the two sipped a club soda. He was in his fifties, dark haired and Latin, tennis court fit, cool cottons, gold net watch strap, Italian house-shoes that must have cost three hundred dollars.

The younger one was tubercular and balding and wore a cheap suit and frayed shirt. He introduced himself as Jesus Antonio and beckoned Steve to one of the armchairs. He did the talking, speaking American-English with a slight lisp and addressing Steve as Steve as he took him through the happenings on Bleak Cay and on the sand bar. At first Steve thought he was simply the interpreter but he never once referred to his companion. He let Steve tell the story in his own time and without pressing for more detail than Steve offered. With the bodies gone to the ocean, Steve was confident as he finished with a description of the struggle between Bob and the mestizo.

'Your man got rid of the boat and brought me here.'

Jesus Antonio nodded and called softly for the houseman. 'A drink, Steve? What would you like?'

'Rum and Coke,' Steve said.

'Slice of fresh lime?'

'That would be great.' Steve wasn't nervous. He had made many presentations to the bank's clients and knew that his account had impressed the two men.

The hypnotic swush of sprinklers and the soft slap of the waves on the beach beyond the lawns all added to Steve's sense of well-being. Ice tinkled as the houseman returned with a heavy square glass on a silver tray. Steve thanked him. A sprig of fresh mint floated on the surface, the lime cut wafer thin. There was more rum in the drink than Steve would have liked and he sipped abstemiously. The older man picked up a book.

Jesus Antonio coughed into a clean handkerchief, then wiped his lips before folding the handkerchief back into his jacket pocket.

The silence began to prey on Steve and he sipped again, the ice cold against his tongue. Out on the lawn a Rottweiler barked once deep in its chest. Steve looked across the pool. The water shivered at the edges then seemed to swell outward into the clipped grass. The extraordinary brilliance of the stars drew his attention, then one particular star low to the south. Flames licked out from the edges of the star – tiny tongues of gold and vermilion that reminded him of the oystercatchers' beaks. He felt very tired and the glass seemed very heavy as he raised it to his lips.

Jesus Antonio spoke softly and the houseman crossed the terrace to take the glass. Steve felt lost without it. His hands lay big and empty on his knees. He was alone, all alone. No one understood. As he looked up through his tears at the star, it dropped suddenly. Dropped. Then all the others stars fell after it. At first one by one, then in great shooting sweeps of light until there were none left. The sky was absolute blackness, not black but blackness. The blackness shuddered, then turned inside out and swelled towards him, trembling at the edges.

He shrunk away from it, deep into the chair, but still it hunted him. He whimpered.

A soft voice said, 'Don't be frightened, Steve. Look at me. Look at me and you will be safe.'

He looked and saw the young man in the cheap suit – Jesus Antonio. He had brought a straight-backed chair out from the dining-room and sat close to Steve facing him, his knees spread either side of Steve's legs. He took Steve's hands in his. His dark eyes were soft with understanding.

'Tell me,' he said, 'tell me how it happened, Steve. Start with the bank . . .'

There were two of Steve in the chair, his real self that could only watch in silence as this other self wept and clutched Jesus Antonio's hands and told him everything: about the money laundering and the meeting with Xavier in Bogotá, the meet with the mestizo at the Texaco station, how he had found and rented the Winterton house and bought the boat for Bob to bring over from Port Lauderdale. Why they had picked Bleak Cay. The boat breaking down. Finding the aeroplane crashed. The boy's footsteps in the sand. Bob leaving him on the cay.

The fear came sweeping in on him as he told of the sun blazing down and the dead pilot and the gulls. How he had been all alone. How they had taken everything from him, all that he had worked for so that he was left there on the barren island with nothing. Nothing with which to protect himself.

Sobs shook him and Jesus Antonio held him in his arms, soothing his fears. 'Tell me,' he murmured gently, his lips close to Steve's ear as he rocked him gently, 'tell me, Steve. Tell me how it was when the boy came . . .'

There were only the two of them balanced in the pool of light. Beyond lay the blackness.

'Tell me,' Jesus Antonio urged, his voice so soft and kind and understanding. 'Be brave, Steve. Trust me . . .'

The blackness quivered. It would take him if he spoke. It would suck him out of himself, suck and suck until there was nothing left in the chair except a dry envelope of skin. He fought back out of Jesus Antonio's clutches, pushing at him, pushing at his chest. Jesus Antonio coughed into his handkerchief, a white handkerchief. Suddenly great rivers of scarlet flooded from the white down on to Steve's knees and spilled on down his legs, then rose as the water had risen in the sinking day boat. Rose up his legs and across his lap and over his hands and up his arms. He thrashed at it and fought to rise but hands on his shoulders forced him down into the chair.

'Look, Steve.'

The boy floated on the red tide. At first he was small but he grew huge and red like the tide on which he floated. He lay naked on a tray of shimmering steel. Crude arrows pointed into his flesh. Huge letters hung over the arrows.

A roaring came in Steve's ears and he fell like a stone, down into a black pit. There was no bottom to it. The young man held him by the hand. Their arms stretched and he could feel the flesh peeling off Jesus Antonio's hand as he clawed at it, knowing that if he let go he would be lost for ever. The roaring sucked at him and the blackness.

Jesus Antonio called to him. 'Tell me, Steve. Tell me about the boy.'

'I killed him,' Steve screamed and light seeped into the pit. He screamed again and there was more light. The rage came and he clung to it, its warm beat drawing him up until finally he was back in the chair. His voice was hard as he spat the words out, all of it now: the boy first and that Jacket had stolen the cocaine, then Bob ready to betray him and how he had shot him and the mestizo.

Finished, he sprawled exhausted in the chair. He felt a prick in his arm and looked down to see the shine of a hypodermic. Then he slept.

14

'Smile,' Trent suggested. He shoved a frosted can of Heineken into Charity's hand as she clambered into the cockpit from the Zodiac. 'You should even laugh a little. You're meant to be having fun.'

He grabbed her bags from Skelley and swung them on board. The dive gear weighed and he set it carefully on the laid-teak cockpit deck. Most of Green Creek had come down to the beach. Only a half hour of daylight remained and he wanted the villagers to see the *Golden Girl* set course for Middle Bight. He had sailed with Skelley as crew often in the past.

'Let's do it right,' he said to the Chief Superintendent once they had the Zodiac in the davits. 'No point in making the senior ranks of the Constabulary a laughing stock.'

The two men stood in the bows a minute gauging the wind and current before changing the number two jib for the bigger number one. Bound in cotton, the sail clung like a white sausage against the taut stainless steel forestay.

They raised the main anchor first, coiling the line into the anchor locker then carefully lifting the chain and anchor over the spotless white paintwork.

'We'll sail the second anchor out,' Trent told Charity, 'if you could handle the jib sheets.'

'He likes it to look casual,' Skelley mocked from the mast foot. 'It's called impressing the natives.'

Skelley raised the mainsail while Trent stood in the cockpit, one hand on the tiller-bar, the other ready with the mainsheet. Dropping to the side-deck, Skelley sauntered forward to take the anchor warp.

'Ready,' Skelley said and gave a sharp heave on the warp, swinging the bows of the catamaran on to the starboard tack.

Trent drew in on the sheet, cupping the breeze lightly in the mainsail so that the yacht ran down on the anchor.

Skelley coiled the warp quickly. 'Anchor up,' he called as the hook dragged clear of the sand.

Trent gave him ten seconds in which to stow the chain and hook. The beach was less than seventy yards away as Skelley strolled back along the port side-deck to the tackle that lowered and raised the lee-board.

Trent signalled him to drop the board and asked Charity quietly, 'Jib sheet ready?' She nodded and he said, 'Ready about,' thrusting the tiller-bar over. 'Now, please,' he told her as the *Golden Girl*'s bows swung through the wind.

The cotton lashings holding the jib snapped as Charity spun the winch. The wind caught the sail and it slammed open, taut as a warm drum. The catamaran seemed to lift under the added power. Water rustled fiercely down the long lean hulls which left only two darker lines behind them in the dark green of the sea. The sky was already sombre out beyond the line of tumbling surf that marked the Tongue of the Ocean. Aft of the yacht, the last of the sunset hung a streak of pale crimson behind the feathered ridge of South Andros.

Charity had been disgusted at school by the other girls' willingness to lose their dignity in pursuit of romance. Subservience to boys was implicit in much of their coyly giggling conversation. Subservience to the concept of white as good was equally implicit in the hours they spent struggling to drag and starch their hair into imitations of the waves and curls which they saw on the screen and in the fashion magazines. Their role models were white actresses, white fashion models. Charity had determined to be her own person and had avoided emotional commitments. The intensity of her fear for Jacket surprised her and she shied away, concentrating her thoughts on the Englishman.

She had prepared herself for the usual masculine skipper pantomime common to men she'd sailed with, shouted orders with either rage or panic edging the commands as they got under way. She found herself irritated at being deprived of her stereotype and further irritated when Trent asked her to take the helm and left her in command without giving instructions or checking her competence.

She eased the tiller-bar over to port and starboard to get the feel of the helm but also in hope of criticism for not keeping course. She had a retort ready. However, he had already ducked through the companionway to the saloon and down into the galley.

She knew suddenly that she hated him – not a generic hate but a personal hate. The reasons came to her: his arrogant self-possession. The armour he wore. The pretence that there were feelings behind the armour while the truth was that he was kin to a machine – a killing machine, self-confessed – further proof of his arrogance. There was his dismissal of her or, at least, his refusal to react to her antipathy. His refusal to react. Which brought her back to the machine. The all male machine, white, superior, arrogant.

Arrogant.

So arrogant that he didn't give a shit for what she thought or felt.

She wondered how much the Constabulary had agreed to pay for his assistance. He was expensive. That much was obvious from the upkeep of his yacht. Everything was of the best and in pristine condition, running and standing tackle, sails, paint- and varnish-work.

What was the going rate for a hit?

She considered asking Skelley.

The Chief Superintendent stood thin and tall on the aluminium cross beam connecting the catamaran's twin bows. Gripping the forestay with one hand, he held the other cupped above his eyes as he scanned the sea ahead for fishermen in unlit skiffs.

Charity despised the police. Rather than serve the law and the people, they were the corrupt tools of a corrupt government. Most of them were stupid and incompetent, fit for standing on street corners directing traffic. Proof was present in Skelley's need for the Englishman. Despite the colour of his skin, Skelley was half English himself; English by education and training. Even the uniform was a remainder of colonialism, as was the Royal.

The title stuck in her craw. Royal Bahamian Constabulary. Buffoons dressed in white sun helmets to evoke nostalgia in the tourists and make them feel secure as they shopped on Bay Street. Slavery of a people under whatever disguise, Trent was the slave master. That was the seat of Trent's arrogance. His contempt for black people, a contempt reinforced by his present employment. She saw it all. Exactly who he was and whence he came.

*

Trent had sliced a loaf of black bread kept fresh in the refrigerator since his last baking day. He worked with the lights in the galley turned low so as not to damage the deck crew's night vision. Having made sandwiches, he filled the moka, then carried the light supper up to the cockpit.

Charity sat with her arms spread along the tiller-bar, shoulders square, legs apart, bare feet planted flat on the deck. A sculptor would have been hard pressed to discover a more perfect model of female force and competence. However, the aura of antagonism she emanated reminded him of a thick fog through which he had to fumble his way without maps or torch.

Whatever direction he took would be wrong. Smile at her, keep his face straight, admire or ignore her breasts raised by the way she sat, their points thrusting against the thin cotton of her black sweatshirt; the broad strength of her thighs that gleamed in the dimmed light spilling up from the galley through the saloon.

He was unwilling to reharness his old skills into one more deception, even were it to allow him access to her. There had been enough play-acting in the eighteen years of his employment as an infiltrator of terrorist cells; eighteen years lived on a razor edge, danger never ceasing; the slightest slip of tone or expression; the continual hazard of being recognised from some other theatre of operation; never sharing his true thoughts; only displaying acted emotions; living as an integral part of the most tightly knit group, yet isolated from it inside himself.

To survive, he had kept himself under such strict control that his true emotions became embedded beneath the scar tissue of his fear. Now, even had he so wished, the battle to disinter them would have taken too long. He knew all this about himself, accepted it without liking. It was a curtain that hung between them, a curtain added to the fog of her aggression.

Trent moved behind the curtain efficiently but without pleasure, much of his thoughts on the boy, Jacket. A boy without a father.

Trent's own father had committed suicide. Trent had been eight years old at the time and had glanced into his father's office at the Gulf state racing stables he managed for the Sheikh. His father sat slumped at his desk, the old British army Webley revolver in his hand. Trent had met his father's look of entreaty. He had known that he could save his father, save him by throwing himself into his arms, by filling him with love. Ten feet of polished concrete floor to cross.

The intensity of his father's pain and despair had been too frightening. Trent had fled. He had crouched in the corner of an empty loose box hugging himself for fear of disintegrating beneath the desolation and guilt. A groom discovered him there an hour after the shot had echoed across the stable yard.

A further six months passed before his mother drove her old Jaguar convertible into a concrete wall on a curve that ended a fifty-mile straight of desert road. Years later Trent had learnt that his mother had been a compulsive spender, his father covering her excesses by borrowing without permission from the accounts he controlled. First there had been the British Cavalry regiment from which he had been allowed to resign his commission to avoid scandal. Then a procession of Jockey Clubs, Polo Clubs and racing stables. Finally the bullet at his desk . . .

Trent had absorbed languages on his parents' downward spiral, languages and a knowledge of horses and boats. His adoptive uncle and legal guardian, Colonel Smith, who later recruited him into the Intelligence service and became his Control, had sent him to the most prestigious of English public schools. As a result Trent had inhabited a social limbo.

He was marked by his accent as belonging to the British upper class yet was treated by this same class with wellbred embarrassment for his father's errors. Not part of them, he had more easily seen their faults: their class prejudice, their belief in their innate superiority, their anti-Semitism, racism, their ignorance and mistrust of any world outside their own narrow parameters.

There were times when he thought now that he could easily have turned traitor. The causes for which the terrorist killed had often seemed more valid to him than the interests of this society he defended. Colonel Smith had suspected him and had plotted his death at the hands of the SAS in an ambush in South Armagh.

However, it was always the terrorists' methods which Trent had loathed, the calculated use of violence against the innocent. As years went by, his loathing expanded to include violence against any target. He had witnessed too many errors both in target and of judgment. Violence was irrevocable.

This growing hatred of violence made him suspect in the Colonel's eyes, himself no less wedded to force than were the terrorists.

There was a growing certainty that Trent would be called to give evidence before a Senate Investigative Committee on the missions he had carried out for Langley during the cold war. There were too many careers at stake, careers of the old guard within the Intelligence community, the cold war warriors. Trend had to be silenced.

It had been a shoot to kill operation. Though wounded, Trent had survived through a combination of instinct and luck only for his Control to try again on Trent's final mission in Central America.

The Armagh bullet had left a crater in his thigh, its edges raised and resilient to his fingertips as he touched the scar.

Looking across the cockpit at Charity Johnston, he could hear Colonel Smith say the familiar words: 'Get her for me, Pat.' She was so much the type. Luck had protected her. That she hadn't met the right recruiter. Luck was all that kept most people from disaster – excepting the rich whose wealth protected them both from normal pressure and temptations and whose lawyers were ever present in case of need.

'In about half an hour?' he said to her quietly, leaving her the illusion of having made the decision.

She wasn't so easily fooled.

He made his way forward to relieve Skelley at look-out. There was a moment of temptation as he stood poised over the water on the aluminium cross bar, the temptation to dive into the darkness, to escape. A slight hum came from the forestay and he could hear, through the tearing hiss of the sea beneath the bows, the wind suck across the after edge of the jib. He gripped the stay to steady himself and his hand touched Skelley's.

The police officer said, 'Do we have a timetable?'

'For you?'

Skelley nodded. 'O'Brien's had a full day to get me pulled off the case.'

'They'll have to find you.'

'They do, there's no arresting officer. Then what?'

Trent didn't answer.

Only Skelley's head showed as he leant forward to peer down round the leading edge of the jib. Anger dragged the skin taut across his face so that there were no lines. His eyes were black pools hidden deep in the darkness of their sockets. The illusion of a disembodied skull was unnerving and Trent shuddered as he thought suddenly of the boy tortured and murdered on Bleak Cay.

Fear had unbalanced the murderer, making him unpredictable. He would be sealed within his own logic. Killing would come easily to him. He would be dangerous as a hunted cat brought to bay. Dangerous and vicious.

'O'Brien will get them,' Skelley said. Already there was a note of defeat. Big Brother, Trent thought. He felt Charity Johnston's presence behind them in the cockpit. Skelley's near impotence would be one more prod of the goad. How many prods before she slipped over the edge? Jacket's death might be the one.

What group would she join? He could list a score into which she would fit. Then the long trail from which there was no turning back and that had no end other than at the hands of the secret executioner. Perhaps in a jungle clearing, a camp out in the desert, a suburban safe house with refrigerators and a colour TV. It would happen in the hour before dawn. A shadow behind the spurt of flame was all she would see as the bullets beat through the sleeping-bag.

'At least get me the killer,' Skelley said, enforcing the image – Trent's Control flicking a photograph across his desk: 'Get him for me, Pat.'

The boy came first. Trent refused to think of him as already dead or in their hands. However, the smell of it was there. Two days without word of him. And there was Charity. She was personal, not something Trent expected Skelley to understand or share. The pieces slipped into place. How it would play. Jacket. A boy with no father. The boy had to be brave and they had to find him.

Trent sighed as he turned to the police officer. 'The boy's due Saturday evening at Kemps Bay. Sunday he's home. That's if we don't find him and the others don't get to him first.'

'Sunday night?' Skelley said.

'That's my guess. I'll aim to bring them to the school at Green Creek.'

Trent had tied pillows into rough shapes that rested against the saloon bulkhead in opposite corners of the cockpit. They looked like people in the soft light leaking from the saloon. Any passing fisherman would confirm a crew of three on the catamaran – the gossip spreading rapidly from settlement to settlement.

Charity and Trent sat across from each other in the Zodiac, the darkness thickening as the *Golden Girl* slipped away into the night. Beyond the catamaran lay the background of Andros, a few lights low on the coast, the tops of the pine trees black froth floating against the horizon.

To the east of them the surf warned of the Atlantic swells they would face when they crossed the Tongue of the Ocean to New Providence. Here, inside the reef, the sea was smooth, the breeze gentle. The skitter of a flying fish ended with a sharp plop, and a woman's voice, pitched high by anger, drifted to them from the shore.

Trent started the Yamaha and swung the bows of the Zodiac north towards Congo Town. The cool night air had lowered the pressure in the hulls and Trent had pumped in more air before launching the inflatable. Now, with her hulls drum hard, she sped over the sea at thirty knots. Darkness exaggerated her speed. They seemed to be poised on the brink of flight. The deep purr of the outboard formed a cocoon through which came only the sharp slap of the Zodiac's bottom against the water.

The Emerald Palms was Jacket's source of money and might be watched, so Trent beached the inflatable a mile out of town.

'I'm not a cripple,' Charity said as she pushed away his hand. They changed their clothes amongst trees, straightened their hair, then walked in uncompanionable silence along the shore. Ironic that the guests at the hotel would take them for lovers. The white and the black of it, Trent thought.

'Let's try looking as if we like each other,' he said as they entered the hotel lobby. He took her arm, smiling as he shepherded her across to the reception desk.

'Henrik in?' he asked the clerk as if he and the manager were old friends – acting the Englishman, self-conscious and embarrassed. 'Could we wait in his office?'

Alone in the office, she glared at him. 'You really get off on playing games.'

He was tempted to retort that he was trying to save a boy's life but adding fresh fuel to her anger wouldn't help the boy.

He needed to reach her, placate her. His own incompetence rather than her hostility froze the words before he could get them out. She turned away to the window, her square shoulders a solid bar across the glow of the pool area, the upright thrust of her hair a deliberate statement of their difference, of her blackness, an exclamation mark drawn to emphasise their natural hostility.

Dogs stalking the parameters of their territory, he had thought, watching O'Brien and Skelley in Anderson's room at the hotel. Here, with Charity, he was in danger of casting himself more as the coy bitch wagging its tail low to the ground as it obsequiously coiled itself round the legs of the big dog on the block.

The door opened. The manager's face registered surprise at being faced by a stranger.

'I'm sorry to break in on you like this,' Trent said before the manager's surprise could turn to irritation. 'We're looking for Jacket Bride. Miss Johnston teaches school at Green Creek. We have news of his father. It's quite urgent,' he pressed gently. He took a card from the old-fashioned pigskin wallet with the gold corners that had belonged first to his father and then to his Control. The card was redolent of success, or fraud, his name engraved above that of the agency he directed with the prestigious address on Shirley Street: Abbey Road Investigative Unit, offices in Kyoto, Tokyo, Singapore, Hong Kong, Nassau.

The manager had clearly read or heard something of Trent's business, perhaps guests gossiping. 'You're the insurance investigator. Marine fraud . . .'

'It's a favour we're doing a small agency in Florida,' Trent lied smoothly. 'The father's in hospital. We have an air-ticket for the boy.'

'Oh dear . . .' The manager's distress was genuine. 'But it's a relief that he's not in trouble. The constable from Green Creek was here earlier – not a man of great intelligence. Said the boy's playing truant. I told him not to be stupid. Jacket's a fine boy, responsible. One of my customers ran him over to Nassau. He's buying a bed for his mother.'

It came then, the manager's instructions to Jacket that he should go to the Royal Bank, the suggestion that he should start his search for the bed on East Bay Street.

15

Smooth crested, the great Atlantic swells marched out of the north. Trent drove the Zodiac up along the slopes at an angle of forty degrees. He cut power close to each crest for fear that a sudden squall would catch them and flip the light-hulled inflatable. The Zodiac seemed to hang for a moment, balanced on the summit, then came the skidding plunge down into the blackness of the valley, the vast wall of the next swell rearing over them.

From the crests of the swells the lighthouses of New Providence beckoned, north on Great Point and at Vincent Harbour to the south. Beyond the lights a low line of cloud grew along the eastern horizon, blanketing the stars. Below them plunged the ocean trench, six thousand feet of water, black and dead in its depth.

He had insisted that Charity lie forward on the floorboards as much for stability as for her safety. Climb, hesitate, plunge – so it went on, fifteen knots at best, thirty miles, two hours. There wasn't a moment in which he could relax until they gained the lee of the island. He opened the throttle as the swells diminished. Finally the sea flattened and he sped towards a secluded stretch of beach where a friend of his, a fisherman, had built a cottage.

The familiar anger had grown in Charity as she lay on the floorboards of the Zodiac. He had taken control of her as they always took control. Ashore, she watched him stretch the stiffness out of his joints, pivoting at the waist as he swung his arms left and right, then touched his toes a half dozen times. For a moment she was confused by what was strange in the scene. Then she realised, as he slipped away through the trees, that it was his absolute silence.

She heard a small animal scratch on wood, perhaps a cat. But it was the Englishman at the cottage door. A homeboy appeared with him out of the night-shadows and they dragged the Zodiac up, draping it with fishing nets. When the two men spoke, they did so with their arms round each other's shoulders, heads tilted to catch a whisper.

Excluded, she was tempted to scream. The threat to Jacket held her back. The boy's safety was dependent on Trent's expertise. Despite her antipathy for all Trent represented, she admitted his competence. His manner of handling the boat out in the swells had been admirable. Familiar with outboards and inflatables, she knew the concentration and strength required, yet he hadn't rested on the crossing. Nor had he given any sign of the fatigue that ate into his muscles. However, these signs of strength were an irritant. Her desire was for something immediate to criticise.

A trail bike leaned against the back wall of the cottage. Forced by circumstance into the subservient role, she followed as Trent wheeled the bike up the path to the highway.

Trent waited fifteen minutes for lights to appear in the distance. He readied himself as they approached, beckoning her on to the pillion.

The lights belonged to a pick-up truck. He kicked the engine alive as it passed and they rode without lights in the truck's wake to the turn past the lake.

He stopped a mile out of town, riding off the road on to a stretch of open verge. Dismounting, he said quietly, 'We need to talk.'

He had to have her co-operation and his instinct was to tell her everything but she was explosive and he couldn't read her well enough to be sure of her reactions. Expert in manipulation, he could have lied to her. There had been other times very similar to this when he had sat in the dark with a prospective informant or recruit and had nudged them ever so carefully down the road the demands of his mission required. Turned them, was the trade expression. His own needs of the moment had forced him to consider these recruits dispensable. His aim had been short term. That route he wished them to take was lethal had been unimportant when weighed against the alternative carnage wreaked by a terrorist bomb.

Trent's Control had worked on him over the years, programming his memory with film clips that remained as fresh now in their horror as they were when he had first inspected them: a pregnant woman spilled over the curb; the ribboned flesh of a child's face; a torn Paddington bear amongst the wreckage of a passenger plane, scraps of a child's dress spattered with red.

So innocent were the minute fragments of black plastic that had been the shell of the cassette player concealing explosives; blackened edges of Christmas wrapping, takeaway pizza box; a taxi cab splayed open outside a department store; strewn bodies dripping green and red beside the skeleton of a truck that had been loaded in the Beka valley with lettuce and tomatoes for the Beirut market; small charred faces at the shattered windows of a school bus.

He could smell it in her now as he had when she had first confronted him in the *Golden Girl*'s cockpit. The road so close and enticing. The temptation to do something. To show them. To teach them a lesson.

He considered sharing with her his interpretation of the doctrine of original sin taught him all those years ago by the monks at Ampleforth College: that each man and woman was born on the narrow platform at the top of a slide. Take a first step on the slope, however small and hesitant, and how far you slid into depravity was a matter of luck. No true difference but opportunity lay between Eichmann and the respectable English squire who refers at the dinner table to a Jewish politician as a fat Jewboy – nor was there any real difference between the mass of Germans who pretended ignorance of the death camps and the dinner guests who remain at the squire's table.

Vic's killer had slid to the very bottom. Now he was out there hunting the boy.

She had to be warned and he said, 'Most murders take place within the family. There are politicals, a few contract killings . . .'

'You,' she interrupted harshly.

He shrugged. 'If you like.' How she judged him was unimportant. 'This man's different. He's lost any feeling for anyone but himself so you can't reach him. Get in his way and he'll kill you with the same casual satisfaction he'd give to swatting a mosquito in his bedroom. The Americans want him. A man called O'Brien, resident head of their Drug Enforcement Administration. He'll be working to have Skelley pulled off the case and he knows I'm involved. He has sufficient influence to have the Immigration Department issue an expulsion order. Hence the secrecy.'

He turned to her, wanting her to look at him. She wouldn't. She sat with her knees drawn up, her profile fierce against the city loom, the squareness of the shoulders firmly set to withstand any entreaty he could make.

He tried: 'Miss Johnston, that happens, there's nothing you can do on your own. Tell O'Brien what you know, then leave it to the police.'

'We could do that now – are you that special?'

'There's a difference in priorities.' He shrugged again, uncomfortable in his disloyalty to Skelley. 'The Chief Superintendent and O'Brien want the killer. I'm trying to save the boy.' That much she had to believe; why else would he have crossed the sea?

'I need to get into my office on Shirley Street. It may be watched – that's something I need to know. I'd like you to enter at the front door to the office building. The police stop you, say I sent you to fetch my cameras. Tell them I'm with Skelley on South Andros. You're going to sleep on the office couch and catch Bahamasair back to Kemps Bay first thing in the morning.'

She said, 'Not everyone lies as easily as you do.'

'They haven't had the practice.'

Removing the spare office key and the key to the head of the stairs, he gave her the rest of the bunch. He dropped her two blocks down from Shirley Street. His own route was simple, across the car park of the adjoining building, up the fire-escape. The flat concrete roof was four feet higher than that of his own building. He watched for a while before swinging down and crossing to the parapet.

He had been right about the police. He had kept his own plans from Charity so there was no trace of panic as she argued on the sidewalk. Her natural indignation was an advantage as she demanded from a constable his warrant to forbid her entry. A second set of boots barked on the concrete, more argument, then the stinging slap of her hand on a man's face and an oath caught back.

Trent thought she had gone too far. However, she had learnt well the exact parameters of safe confrontation. In opening the doors, she rattled the bunch of keys against the plate glass.

Trent retreated across the roof to the service tower and down the single flight of stairs to his top-floor suite. Charity was silent in her trainers but Trent followed her progress by her police escort, his boots snapping like slingshot on the polished marble.

Once inside his suite, Trent quickly relocked the door. The floor of the reception area was carpeted in restful grey. An arrangement of dwarf palms in self-watering white plastic pots filled one corner, the upmarket end of marine and insurance quarterlies shared the bevelled glass tabletop, the table legs chrome to match two Barcelona chairs and a three-seater sofa. A John Lennon lithograph had centre place between two stills from the Beatles' film, *HELP* on the soft-grey wall opposite the windows.

A flush door opened to a corridor leading to a small bathroom. A glass door led through to Lois's office. Her desktop was clean, tweed upholstered chairs, more Beatles stills, IBM computer, two fax machines, telex, laser printer, bank of steel fireproof filing cabinets.

The door through to the executive office was panelled to be impressive. The office occupied the corner facing out over Shirley and Bay Streets to the channel separating New Providence from Paradise Island. From the conference table with its six chairs there was a view of the toll bridge and marinas. Two long sofas were upholstered in raw silk, Bohkara rugs. A slab of rose marble formed Trent's desktop. Two telephones and an intercom stood on the desk. That was all. His chair was covered in a tweed that matched the sofas. The executive tools were arrayed separately on a castor-footed side table: IBM Thinkpad 720c in a docking station equipped with CD Rom and a 17″ monitor, yet another fax machine, a Grundig satellite radio.

Trent's employer, Tanaka Kazuko, had bought the Paul McCartney watercolour at a charity auction, pen drawings by Yoko and Lennon from Sotherby's. Their matching frames were eighteenth century.

A side door to the corridor enabled Trent to escape without passing through Lois's sanctum. He eased the door open and smiled as he listened to Charity threaten her police escort with the Japanese Embassy if he dared step foot inside the suite without a warrant: 'No-manners nigger, yo jam me up 'nough, hear? Put dem dutty boot on dis carpet, Japanese goin' muggage yo up so yo tink yo fix de res' yo life.'

The door slammed on the constable's protest.

Charity marched through, a satisfied grin raising her lips as she pushed her fingers back through her hair. She saw Trent and stopped.

Finger to his lips, he turned the radio on and spun the tuner to a reggae station. 'I came over the roof,' he said and crossed to the executive icebox built in to a corner cupboard. 'Beer? Coke? I can make coffee . . .'

Looking round, he saw that he had lost her again. She turned away before he could explain that he had kept his movements secret to make her confrontation with the police easier.

Charity hadn't realised the status of Trent's employment till now. If anything, she had thought of him as a downmarket Jack Nicholson in Chinatown. She sniffed, wrinkling her nose at the scent of wealth. A vulgar display would have permitted her to feel superior but this was Business of the Month Club *House & Garden* – a sort of negative good taste designed to impress without offending anyone's sensibilities. The oldtime Bay Street Boys such as the lawyers her father had clerked for were more into fake antique British brass, leather and hunting prints. She supposed that there were Buddhist and Hindu shipowners who would have been uncomfortable if required to sit on the skins of dead animals.

She shivered in the air-conditioning.

'There's a shower,' he said, pointing to the corridor. 'The water should be hot.'

He kept a 9 mm Beretta automatic in the safe. Sometimes he carried it on the *Golden Girl*: however, he hadn't used it in months and the sea air was a killer. He laid a cloth on the marble desk, stripped the handgun and cleaned it meticulously, rubbing a fingertip delicately over each part in search of pitting.

She returned from the bathroom, her hair wet, and stood watching from the doorway as he reassembled the mechanism. He worked the action a half dozen times, then slit open a fresh box of shells with his thumbnail, loaded the magazine and slapped it home. He held the gun, reaccustoming himself to its weight as he sighted down the barrel at the late night traffic crossing the toll bridge.

Charity watched him stroke the steel as if he were in love with it, then play-act shooting cars off the bridge. The whole performance was obscene.

'Big deal,' she said. 'Bang Bang, you're dead. Do you get off on all guns or is this one special?'

He laid the Beretta down and folded the cloth over it. 'I'm going to get a couple of hours' sleep.'

Stretched out on a sofa, he looked across at her. She hadn't moved from the doorway. She had wrapped herself in a towel before leaving the bathroom. Her wet hair glistened and the light caught the droplets on her forehead and shoulders. Her look of sulkily regal arrogance was back in place. He supposed that she was waiting for a reply to her last attack.

'My father shot himself at his desk,' he said. She could make of that what she wished.

Trent lay in the dark, his thoughts going back over all the times that he had thought through childhood memories. His parents had not been true to their bloodlines. His father, Irish Catholic, dark, was always calm and thoughtful. His mother, tall, fair, English, was restless and impulsive – one moment sprawled lackadaisically in a deckchair, then leaping up, all energy as she demanded that they do something: Come on, darlings. Let's go to the beach – go sailing – riding – drive out into the desert – explore the souk. An only child, she had been an afterthought or accident of older parents who lived in a grace and favour apartment at Hampton Court. A distant relative of the Queen Mother, her father had been a diplomat with a reasonable pension but expensive tastes.

'They left nothing, not even the furniture was theirs,' Trent's Control had told Trent with a slight sniff of distaste for their improvidence.

Trent couldn't recall a single angry word between his parents. On the contrary, he had lived those early years in what he still thought of as an atmosphere of absolute love. His parents touched a lot. His father watched his mother whenever she entered or left or crossed a room. Even on horseback, his eyes were always seeking for her on the edge of the polo field or training gallop. Seeking for her, listening for the laughter that was her companion.

Trent had lain awake many nights trying to recall whether there had been a false note to her laughter, whether it had been artificial, too high pitched, nervous, verging on hysteria.

And he had wondered whether his father had watched, not from love, but for fear of what she would do.

There were times when the guilt was hardly bearable – guilt that he had been so obtuse and self-centred as not to sense his father's growing despair.

He hadn't been there when his mother killed herself. It had been part of the deal his mother had made with his Control – that Colonel Smith paid her debts, gave Trent a home, paid for his education. Trent had presumed for years that the Colonel had been in love with his mother – but it was Trent's father that the Colonel had loved. Taking her son was an act of vengeance for the father's death.

'He couldn't stand the shame,' Trent's Control had said, thus planting in Trent the conviction that he must do his duty at whatever personal cost.

Now there was this boy, Jacket, abandoned by his father. And the young woman asleep on the other couch.

He slipped to his feet and crossed to the window. The clouds were building. There would be rain before morning. If alive, the boy must be out there somewhere in the city. And the murderer?

Charity spoke out of the darkness. 'I'm sorry – about your father.'

The apology was difficult for her and he was grateful. 'I was wondering about the killer. What age, what nationality. What his status is. He's lost a million dollars in cocaine. If it's not his, he'll be under a lot of pressure.'

16

Steve woke to the snuffle of a Rottweiler down by the pool. At first he thought that he was dreaming. The big covered terrace, the soft light of lanterns outlined against the night sky, the white sofas and armchairs, the scent of orange blossom from the glazed pots. Then he saw the tape recorder on the coffee table. Underneath the recorder the shiny surface of a photographic print glistened. Memory came flooding back and terror.

They had spread a white bath sheet over the sofa to protect the cushions from the burn ointment. It was that detail that shook him out of any possible belief in escape. He knew, as he lay paralysed by fear of the recorder and of the photograph, that they had left nothing to chance. The table had been set far enough away so that he wouldn't knock it in a moment of restless sleep, yet close enough so that he could reach the controls without rising from the sofa. A beaded net covered a jug of lemon water on a silver tray beside the recorder. The tumbler had been left upside down as it would have been beside a hospital bed.

His head was clear, even his arms had been freshly dressed, but his mouth and throat were dry. Sitting up to fill the tumbler, he was confronted by the photograph of the boy laid out on the morgue table. Arrows pointed to individual wounds, each one lettered – but there were no references to a knife.

He looked up at the scuff of a soft-soled shoe on the tiles and saw the older of the two men step out on to the terrace. He had changed into cream pyjamas and a white dressing-gown. He carried a book, perhaps the same book, a finger marking his page. The book and his black hair and narrow triangular face reminded Steve of a priest, one of those at the Vatican, the ones with power. It seemed to Steve vitally important to know what this man read and he strained to see the title on the dust cover.

He had been too obvious and the man smiled. '*A Suitable Boy*, Vikram Seth.' He raised the book for Steve to see. 'Charming, erudite and wonderfully informative. In the city, people are too busy to read big books but out here on the islands we have time to develop our pleasures.'

It was the first time that he had spoken in Steve's presence. His voice was soft, his accent and precise pronunciation that of the erudite European for whom English was a second language. Steve had met his type at banking conferences: Scandinavians, Germans, Italians, Spanish, French. They appeared suave but there was always a veiled arrogance hidden behind their politeness, a belief in the inferiority of North Americans.

He sat facing Steve, one leg crossed over the other, a slipper dangling from his toes. He laid the book open on his lap, his hands on the arms of the chair. His fingers were long and delicate. Steve noticed that his nails were manicured.

'I am informed that you were a currency specialist, Mr Radford,' he said. 'Fascinating and useful. Now, sadly, you appear to have stumbled on an unsuitable business. Unsuitable to your talents,' he added with smile of pleasure at the linkage with the book title. One finger rose a half inch to indicate the tape recorder on the table, a bomb ready to blow Steve's life away.

'You seem to have got yourself into a very considerable mess,' the man said. 'There are many punishments for murder. In the Bahamas, they continue to hang people by the neck until they are dead – a barbaric custom inherited from the British.'

He smiled again, urbane, superior, in control – and powerful. Steve could smell it in him. And the sadism. He wanted to scream at him that they would never take him alive but he hadn't the courage. It had all been sucked out of him by the younger man, Jesus Antonio – sucked out and imprisoned on cassette.

'No doubt you are wondering of my own antecedents. Cuban,' the man said, 'but by way of Europe rather than Miami – a dreadful place. Only the more unfortunate or uncouth of my fellow countrymen chose to settle there – and of course the sweepings of our prisons.'

Insult on insult. Steve sipped again, but had difficulty in swallowing.

The Cuban smiled at him delicately. 'One must admire Castro for his sense of humour. Or perhaps you don't remember? Your president offered asylum to prisoners of the Revolution. The Commandante seized

124

the opportunity and shipped every petty thief and sexual delinquent to Florida – some hundred thousand of them. A great benefit to the exiled legal profession. But I disgress . . .'

And treat me like a goddamn peasant, Steve thought.

'I am a commodity broker, Mr Radford. My primary interest is in crude oil. Cocaine is an amusing and profitable sideline. Did you know, Mr Radford, that drugs constitute the largest import to the United States in dollar value, twice that of petroleum?'

Steve wanted to retort that it was a statistic he had used often when lecturing on currency movements. Every last Spik hated the States and every one of them longed for a Green Card. That was a statistic Steve wanted to shout in the Cuban's face but the Cuban was already continuing in that smooth, slightly mocking tone.

'I supply capital, organisation, and a financial cleansing service, Mr Radford. In both businesses I delight in contravening the laws of the United States. In oil through utilisation of Cuban refining capacity in contravention of the US embargo and in disguising both the source and the destination of sales and profit.

'Ah, how kind of you, John,' he said as the houseman appeared with two minute cups of coffee on a black lacquer tray. The Cuban pointed him to Steve. The tiny cup handle required a delicate touch and Steve blushed with anger as the cup rattled on the saucer.

The Cuban had taken his own cup and smiled his thanks. 'John, be kind enough inform Mr Valverde that our guest is awake.'

His eyes slid back to Steve. 'So what are we going to do with you, Mr Radford?' he asked with another of his little smiles. 'On the positive side you have shown ruthlessness and some imagination. The negatives include an unseemly lack of self-control and of loyalty to your associates. There are many who consider these the typical failings of North America where you have replaced responsibility and loyalty with insurance and the legal contract.'

Again he pointed. 'The tape will assure us of your loyalty, Mr Radford. Self-control might be achieved through a return to your former profession – a matter we can discuss once this unfortunate affair has been brought to a successful conclusion.'

He looked up to greet Jesus Antonio. 'Ah, there you are. I have been explaining my position to Mr Radford . . .'

And to Steve: 'Jesus Antonio is in the import business, Mr Radford.

He has assured his associates in your country that he will deliver Señor Perez's cargo this week. Now it is mislaid and he is in a delicate position. Your duty is to recover the cargo. Once this is done to Jesus Antonio's satisfaction, we can discuss your future employment. You have become indentured labour, Mr Radford. Fortunately for you I am a generous master. However, I punish carelessness with a degree of cruelty and I can assure you that the Bahamian hangman's knot would be preferable by far to your fate should you ever cross me.'

Steve watched him rise from his chair and cross the terrace, an arm round Jesus Antonio's shoulders. The two men talked quietly for a while, out of earshot, Jesus Antonio nodding agreement to whatever the Cuban said. Though the Cuban was issuing instructions, Jesus Antonio wasn't subservient to the older man. Their relationship seemed to Steve more one of family and there was an affection between them. He wondered if they were gay. It was difficult to tell with Spiks. They were always touching each other, kissing, all that shit.

The Cuban nodded to Steve from the doors into the living-room. 'Good night, Mr Radford.'

Steve checked his Rolex. It was four o'clock in the morning. The houseman came with a glass of warm milk on a tray for Jesus Antonio. Jesus Antonio crossed to the edge of the terrace and looked across the pool and lawns, searching the cloud bank in the eastern sky. He had changed from his threadbare suit into blue cotton trousers and cream safari jacket and he had combed his thinning hair straight back, more young executive than clerk.

He gave a slight shrug, shedding extraneous thoughts as he prepared himself for the day's work.

'This boy, Jacket,' he said turning to face Steve. 'You can recognise him?'

'I told you. His mother works for me,' Steve said.

'And he is in Nassau?'

'There or on his way back home to Green Creek.' Steve spoke pleasantly and he smiled the way he would have at a client of the bank.

'I'll arrange cover for Green Creek,' Jesus Antonio said.

Jesus Antonio had taken advantage of Steve while Steve was drugged, humiliated him. It wasn't something that Steve would forgive. He was frightened of him and hated him, not with the fire that had given him strength to kill Bob and the mestizo. He was too drained of emotional energy, so that this hate was on a low simmer. However, it was there, waiting. Even as he smiled obsequiously, he knew that his strength would return and that his opportunity would come. Not for months, perhaps, or even years. But he could see his way through the fear. He would be a banker again, the Cuban's banker. He would earn his trust. Little by little he would gain power through his expertise until finally he became indispensable.

He measured the terrace visually, maybe forty feet by twenty, the open-plan living area the same length but deeper. There had to be at least three rooms in each of the wings, one of them the Cuban's study – though he probably referred to it as the library.

Servants, pool, tennis court, boat.

All he needed was time, Steve thought as he slipped into the folds of the Cuban's power much as he would have into a suit he was trying on at Barney's. There was warmth in it, the familiar warmth of the executive elevator. It felt good.

Yeah, think long term, he warned himself. Think long term and be exceedingly careful.

The kid came first. They had to find him. And this time he wouldn't mess up. No rage. Get the information and dispose of him.

Jesus Antonio returned, a golf jacket slung over his narrow shoulders. 'The boat's ready. The constable at Green Creek will watch out for the boy that end. We'll search Nassau.'

17

Before leaving Green Creek, Jacket had left a note for his mother, telling her not to worry, that he was going over to Nassau to fetch her birthday present. The breeze had blown fresh off the ocean and Dummy held the skiff on course midway between the edge of the reef and the shore. To avoid discovery, Jacket lay on the floorboards by the mast foot. The rhythmic burst of the swell on the coral beat at him on and on until his eyes closed.

He awoke three hours later to his own scream as a monster reached with its talons into the steel cave where he hid with his father. Little breeze reached the bottom of the skiff and the sun beat off the tarred planks so that he was sweating as well as shaking with fear.

Green Creek was too small for secrets. Already Vic had the pilot's suitcase. Soon the plane crash would be public knowledge. The pilot would be found. They would question Jacket for days. They were the authority in a thirteen-year-old boy's life – Jacket's mother, the constable, Miss Charity.

A boy's intentions were unimportant to authority. It was the end result that counted. Whose fault was it? was the first question they asked. Jacket had learnt that much from life.

He felt ashamed to find himself thinking of the birthday present for his mother as something to save himself – like a bribe that the fishermen paid the constable when they caught crawfish in the off season.

A couple of Florida-registered sports fishing boats were moored at Emerald Beach Resort's private dock alongside the resort's dive boats and fibreglass dories.

The resort was modern and concrete. Each room in the main block opened to a private balcony facing out over a big pool to the sea. Palms and sea grape trees shaded the clipped lawn surrounding the pool area from which paths led to a dozen or so guest cottages. Hedges of pink hibiscus lined the paths, bougainvillea spilled over the walls, beds of red-leaved bromiads, stands of red and white oleander in the background, frangipani trees, flamboyants, a massive mango.

Dummy ran the skiff into the inner end of the dock and Jacket climbed the walkway round to the kitchen entrance in search of the head chef.

Once the chef had weighed Jacket's catch, Jacket and Dummy transferred the crawfish to the resort's holding tank. Dummy departed in search of an old client who employed him as a guide while Jacket followed the chef to the manager's office at the rear of the reception desk.

The manager was tall and pink skinned with pale blue eyes and pale straight hair. This was Jacket's third visit to his office. On his first visit the boy had been mesmerised by the manager's hands. It had seemed to Jacket that they had never been used. There wasn't a single cut or scrape or scar on the long thin fingers and his nails were very clean and neatly cut in perfect half moons. Everything about him was clean and he spoke a very precise English. He treated Jacket as an equal, a businessman.

'An excellent catch, Jacket. Excellent indeed.' The fingers tapped numbers on a desktop calculator. 'Forty-three pound seven ounces at five dollars and sixty-five cents the pound. Two hundred and forty-six dollars and thirty-four cents . . .'

He took a petty-cash book from his desk. Jacket's name was printed on the label centred on the stiff marbled cover: Mr Wilberforce 'Jacket' Bride.

The manager turned to a fresh page and wrote the date and the number of the catch and the amount in dollars. He signed the bottom of the page and passed the book and his pen and the calculator across the desk for Jacket to check and counter-sign.

Pressing the intercom, the manager ordered a gin and tonic. 'And a Coca-Cola for Mr Bride, please, Eddie.'

Turning back to Jacket, he said, 'Mrs Bride's birthday is on Monday. Have you decided on a suitable gift?'

Jacket shifted uneasily in his chair. 'A bed.'

He knew it was an unusual gift but the manager merely nodded and said, 'Very suitable.'

He punched in the total owed by the hotel: 'Fourteen hundred and eighty-eight dollars, thirty-seven cents – a considerable sum to carry on your person, Jacket. Do you have a particular store in mind at which to purchase the bed?'

Jacket had known the sum but hearing it from the manager made it real. The bed had to be exactly the same as the one up in Mr Winterton's bedroom. Mr Winterton had shown him the bed. He had invited Jacket to bounce on it one day of the school holidays when Jacket had walked with his mother across the point. The frame was brass. There were mirrors set in the headboard each side of a red velvet heart. Jacket had imagined his mother in it. She would be the queen of the village. Everyone would come to their hut to look and she wouldn't be ashamed any more of how they lived. Nor would he have to listen to her toss and turn through the night, nor fear her temper in the morning.

Mr Winterton had told Jacket that he had bought the bed in Nassau and had told him the price – thirteen hundred dollars. Jacket, who had never been to Nassau, hadn't asked the American where in the city. He had thought that Nassau was sufficient address. He had imagined a single store, like the one at Green Creek but infinitely bigger.

Uncomfortable, he picked at a tag of dry skin on the side of his left thumb. There were old scars on his hands and a coral scrape from the previous month streaked the milk-coffee paleness that lapped round the side of his left hand. He looked up to find the manager leafing through the telephone directory.

'Here we are. Furniture Dealers – Retail. Ace Cabinet Makers, no. Alina – that's in Miami. Atlantic Furniture – Miami again. Antique Warehouse, no. Central Furniture and Appliance, East Bay Street. That's a good address, convenient to the waterfront.'

The manager passed the directory open at the first of thirteen pages of retailer listings. Jacket tried to concentrate – the columns of store names and the advertisements were foreign to anything that he had imagined. The print shifted on the muddy yellow pages, amalgamating into a single blur. Ashamed, he rubbed his eyes on the back of his arm.

'You have decided on the type of bed?' the manager asked.

Jacket nodded. His nose needed wiping and he looked away through the office window to the sea so that the manager wouldn't notice. Then he thought that the light from the window would glisten on his upper lip and he turned back hurriedly but with his head tilted down and a little on one side. He sniffed quickly once.

'It's the pollen from the pine trees. I have the same problem at this time of year,' the manager said. He slit open a pocket pack of Kleenex with his thumbnail.

The delicate paper seemed to Jacket too insubstantial for use. He dabbed carefully at his nose. With nowhere else to put the tissue, he folded it and tucked it into his pocket.

'You need a point from which to start,' the manager was saying. 'Bay Street's easy to find and Central Furniture is a big store. Explain precisely what you want. If they don't stock it, there is a good probability that they will know who does.

'You may need to travel round town at some length. Fourteen hundred dollars is a great deal of money to carry in cash. I would suggest a cheque with a covering letter from myself to the manager of the Royal Bank. You can draw cash once you find what you want. Better still, the bank will issue you a banker's cheque for the amount of the bed and cash for your expenses. Yes, that would be best. Do you know what a cheque is, Jacket?'

The manager was already reaching into the top left-hand drawer of his desk. Jacket looked at the dark blue oblong book.

'It is an instruction to the bank to pay the specified amount of money, either in cash, or to a named individual or organisation. The store may be unfamiliar with banker's cheques so you should ask the manager for an accompanying letter. Let us arrange your transport over to New Providence.'

Jacket followed the manager out to the tiled pool terrace. A dozen guests sprawled on sunbeds beside the sparkling water; white tails, they were called in the Bahamas but to Jacket they were red and unnatural. Only two children leaping in and out of the water seemed at home.

The manager coughed behind his fist to attract the attention of a large grey-haired American reading *The Economist* in the shade of a sun umbrella, a glass of amber liquid and ice on the table beside him.

'One of our major suppliers of lobster, Mr Jacket Bride,' the manager said. 'If you would be so kind as to give Mr Bride a lift over to New Providence, Mr Green?'

The big man inspected Jacket over the top of his magazine. 'A pleasure, Mr Bride. Sleep on board. We'll be sailing at first light.'

Mr Green's yacht was a forty-five-foot Rybovitch with twin diesels. They trolled for marlin out in deep water, then ran back inside the reef to swim and picnic off a beach before making the crossing to New Providence and round to the American's berth at the Nassau Yacht Club. There were four fish to unload from the icebox, the biggest over eighty pounds. It was after nine o'clock in the evening by the time Jacket had finished helping the skipper wash the boat down.

The American had told Jacket to stay on board while he was in Nassau. The skipper told him, 'Yo righ' on Eas' Bay Street, boy. Gate guard let yo out in de mornin'.'

There was food on board, sandwiches that the owner left and which the skipper let Jacket keep, a couple of bottles of soda. Yachts and fishing boats passed up and down the narrow channel separating New Providence from Paradise Island. A half mile away Jacket could see headlights climb back and forth across the concrete arch that connected the two islands. He had never seen so many lights other than on TV.

The lights made him nervous as did the buildings that stretched as far as he could see along the New Providence coast. He had known Nassau was big, he had expected it to be strange. Reality was more oppressive and he was nervous of venturing out on to the streets at night. Mindful of the manager's warnings, he tucked the cheque and letter to the bank manager down inside his shorts next to his skin. Someone touched him there and he'd wake.

Unable to sleep, the boy lay tucked up in a blanket on the wheelhouse settee. He played the crash over and over again. Many planes had crashed on Andros or in the sea near by. Drug smuggling was familiar to every boy on the island. Grown-ups discussed the trade day in and day out at Green Creek's two bars and down on the beach while mending nets.

In the seventeenth century Morgan and Blackbeard were the Bahamian demi-gods, slavers in the eighteenth century, blockade runners in the time of the American Civil War, rum runners during Prohibition. Marijuana in the 'sixties and 'seventies. Now coke was king.

The boys of Green Creek recognised some of the people involved. Mr Corky, gold medallion and bracelets gleaming, as he raced round the island in his big jeep or his speedboat powered by twin Volvo engines;

Snape who lived in Congo Town, the police sergeant with the little finger missing on his left hand, the big government men who sailed over in their fast motor yachts from Nassau at the weekend; the American in the big house up the coast who had disappeared overnight; Fat Boy Lemming in his ragged shorts and silk shirts with the sleeves cut off at the armpit whose sixty-foot Cigarette was said to do eighty knots on a flat sea; Mrs Grindle who went to church each morning and handed out sweets and cards showing the Virgin Mary or Saint Joseph or the Lord Jesus with his bleeding heart exposed; the Drib brothers who, at school, had been the despair of the teacher, yet had got into the States illegally by boat and had made their fortunes in nine months of street dealing – true, of the three only the elder two survived: John had been shot dead on the corner of 5th and 7th by a Puerto Rican.

There were the foreigners in dark glasses who flew directly to their private islands where guards patrolled the beaches. Rare birds of passage these, spotting them required months of patient waiting and a great deal of luck. The boys recognised the watchers and teased them mercilessly. Florid Americans casting for bonefish in the shallows with the wrong action and the wrong trailer on their line. Black Americans pretending to be Bahamian and getting the accent right but making mistakes of vocabulary. The local narcotics agents were easiest to spot. They left deliberate trails so that the opposition would recognise them and know who to bribe.

And there were those others the adults referred to – the men in crisp linen suits with offices over in Nassau on Bay or Shirley Street and with private islands in the Berry group or Eluthera.

'Dat Mr So an' So, de liar man (or lawyer man), he a real king,' one would say.

'He a notin'. Is de banker man, de pink house wiv de tower an' de bright wife, dat mon makin' million dollar a mont . . .'

So it went on, hour after hour, story on story, myth and fact intermingled into a larger than life tapestry of Bahamian society. Every rich man was a reputed drug baron because drugs were easy to understand while the machinations of the Bay Street Boys, the bankers and the investment managers, were beyond the comprehension of the villagers – not because the villagers were stupid but because high finance was as much foreign territory to them as Greenland or Tibet.

Drugs were a few steps away across the street. Poor one day, rich the next. Or dead. Dead because you had seen something or somebody when you should have kept your eyes shut. As Jacket should have with the plane at Bleak Cay.

The plane had come straight down on top of Jacket the way a dung beetle flew at a light. Slowly the reality of his situation crept through Jacket's defences.

He had killed the pilot.

Not deliberately – and he managed to escape for a while into conversation with the smugglers. They were black because he was better at imagining black people and a homeboy would understand that he had been at Bleak Cay night-fishing crawfish.

For a while Mr Corky was central to Jacket's fantasy, his gold medallion and bracelets flashing in the sun, his hand at first heavy as he squeezed Jacket's shoulder, then relaxing as Jacket told him about his mother's birthday and Mr Winterton's bed. They were out on the track down from Congo Town, Mr Corky's big jeep parked in the shade of the lignum vitae that marked the halfway point to Green Creek.

Mr Corky fetched a Kalik for himself and a Coke for Jacket from the red cool-chest in the back of the jeep. He nodded over the lip of his beer, man to man: 'Don' worry yo head, Jacket, chile. We guh sort dis ting out.'

But it didn't last.

Fat Boy Lemming brought the police sergeant.

'Yo' a no manners boy, too fas',' the sergeant accused, grabbing Jacket by the arm and forcing it up behind his back. 'Why yo steal dem boxes, boy? Where yo put dem?'

Jacket rolled away from the image, his knees tucked up against his chest as he concentrated on the cars crossing the Paradise Island bridge. The structure of the bridge became invisible if he looked at it through slitted eyes. All that showed was a rainbow of moving lights. If only he had left the boxes in the plane, he could have pretended that he had seen nothing.

Or if he hadn't put the pilot's case in the skiff . . .

He bit into his knuckle, using pain to drive out the memory for a moment. Back it came, flooding in and he lay on the wheelhouse couch, trembling inside himself, the tuna sandwiches rolling in his belly and burning sour suddenly in his throat, the Coca-Cola burning.

'Dad,' he whispered. 'Dad, Dad . . .' But his father wasn't there and he

134

bit his lip, the tears coming as he thought of the case. He could have explained that he had found it floating. But they didn't take risks. Not the bad ones. The foreigners. They didn't care what you saw but only what you might have seen. There were articles written in the papers about them and clips on the TV news. Boats that they had commandeered, dumping the owners overboard, throats slit, adults, children. Full battles with machine-guns that left a dozen men dead for the sharks to eat so that the bodies were never found and the men had entered the Bahamas by private plane so that there was no record of their existence.

Foreigners. The pilot had been a foreigner. And Jacket scurried back for shelter amongst his own people but now the Drib brothers loomed out of his fantasy. Jook was the eldest, Jook because of his knife, and the stories told of how he wielded it over in New York to capture territory. There wasn't a sensible man on Andros who wasn't scared of him. Jacket imagined Jook grabbing hold of Vic: 'Nigger, where yo get dat case?'

'Jacket,' Vic would tell him quick as light.

Jacket moaned and beat on his thigh with a tight fist to drive out the picture of Jook Drib heading up to their hut hunting for him, but finding Jacket's mother.

He had to get back to Bleak Cay and dig the boxes up. He could dig them up and leave them for a fisherman to discover. That was the only way. The fisherman might make off with them or report to the police or to the coastguard – or to the Americans who would give him a reward. Whatever the fisherman did, the owner of the boxes would have lost them and be on his way out of the islands rather than trying to find out who was to blame for the plane crash.

That's what he had to do.

But he couldn't do it right away because Dummy had a job guiding and then would sail south to meet Jacket at Kemps Bay which was the nearest the mail-boat came to Green Creek. From there Jacket planned sailing his mother's bed home on two skiffs. He had to keep thinking about the bed. The bed . . .

18

Jacket had taken ten dollars cash from the manager at Emerald Palm, more than sufficient for supper and breakfast and the bus ride into the centre of town from the Nassau Yacht Club.

As always, he awoke with the rise of the sun. To keep fear from his thoughts he had to keep active. He washed in a bucket on the dockside, dressed in his clean khaki shorts, white shirt and old trainers, and packed his old clothes into a carrier bag.

The gate guard pointed him to the bus stop. Jacket, however, was shy of demonstrating his ignorance by asking directions as to where he should alight. The walk was at most a mile and half to the centre of town. The few drivers on the road this early drove faster than Jacket was accustomed to and he kept well clear of the roadway as he tracked his long shadow down the grass roadside then along the cement sidewalk towards Paradise Island bridge.

The apex of the single giant arch was higher than any God-made point on the Bahamas and the cars looked small as beetles up at the top. Jacket turned in beneath the bridge and walked up past the fish and conch stands and vegetable and fruit sellers to the mail-boat wharf on Potter's Cay.

A dozen of the inter-island boats lay bow to stern along the quay. The boats were eighty to a hundred feet in length and carried passengers and cargo. One of them had a forest of young palm trees from the nurseries loaded on the wheelhouse roof. The sailors were already stirring, some of them on deck.

Jacket found the Andros boat, *Captain Moxey*, halfway down the quay. He told a sailor that he had a bed to ship over to Kemps Bay. How much would it cost? The sailor asked what size and Jacket began to pace it out.

'In de box, mon,' the sailor said.

'Is not in a box,' Jacket said.

The sailor rolled his eyes to heaven. 'What you talkin' 'bout, not in de box? Every bed I see come in a box. How else dey bring dem from Miami?'

Jacket hadn't thought. However, a bed in a box wasn't part of his dream. In his dream he sailed the bed down to Green Creek. He arrived while his mother was at Mr Winterton's house. The bed would gleam in the sunlight and attract everyone else from the settlement.

The villagers would make admiring remarks as they carried the bed ashore and up through the trees to the Bride hut. It would be a victory parade. His mother would come home. Not knowing what he had done, she would climb the front steps and open the door and the bed would be there, sheets and pillows in their lace-bordered cases, everything just the same as in the house she cleaned every day.

Jacket had seen his mother, night after night, for months now in his imagination. He saw her standing looking down at the bed, not able to speak at first, slowly shaking her head in bewilderment . . . shaking her head because it couldn't be true, then finally turning to him and saying his name, that's all. Standing there saying his name in a way that would prove to everyone in the village how much she thought of him and how much she loved him. Then the teasing would end – the 'Hey, Jacket, yo able sit down dis day or yo muddah done all hackle yo up 'gain?'

Perhaps there would be an end even to her yelling at him: 'You jus' like yo pa,' so that everyone for a mile around heard, one hand twisting his hair while the other lashed.

Jacket had understood ever since his dad ran off that it wasn't what he had done or hadn't done that made his mother hit him. She was striking at life. Their hut. The daily walk over the ridge to Mr Winterton's. Not having a man to fix things that broke. Not having a man to bring in money or fish or coconuts. Not having a man. And having the village gossip behind her back.

Early in life he learned that she wasn't popular in the settlement. The villagers called her hard-head and stuck-up and accused her of eating wasp – and it was true that there was a sting to much of what she said. But Jacket understood, or thought that he did. He didn't want much out of life for himself. He wanted her to sleep easy and hold her head up and not yell at him or hit him, maybe even hug him now and then the way other mothers did their children.

He looked over at the boat with the coconut palms up on the wheelhouse roof. That was the way he wanted his mother's bed to travel, up high where everyone would see it all the way to Kemps Bay.

The sailor had lost interest in Jacket. Mooching back to the shade of the after deck, he had seated himself on a bale of cloth, resting his back against the bulkhead as he sucked on a big mango. Juice ran down his forearms and the front of his sweatshirt. Seeing Jacket approach, he wiped his mouth on the back of his arm before asking, 'Now what yo want?'

Jacket pointed to the roof of the wheelhouse. 'How much it coss up dere?'

The sailor laughed. 'Now yo is millionaire, boy.'

The captain appeared from the deck cabin. He was in his late middle age, medium black, squat and barrel-chested with a neck that resembled the stub of a palm trunk. He wore his captain's hat pushed far back on his head. He glanced from the sailor to Jacket. 'What goin' on?'

'Dis fool boy want to ship bed up dere,' the sailor said, pointing.

Studying Jacket, the captain scratched thoughtfully at his chest inside a drill shirt in need of an iron.

'What sort of bed, boy?'

'Brass and mirrors. Is fuh my muddah,' Jacket said.

'Is a whole bed, not broke down?'

Jacket nodded.

The captain shifted his scratching from his front to his back. Finally he spat over the side. 'Big bed?'

'Emperor size,' Jacket said proudly.

'Yo want de roove, dat guh cost fifty dollar, boy. Pay now and yo guh bring de bed down fuh Saturday nine clock.'

Jacket's ears turned hot. He could feel the sailor watching as he took the single ten-dollar bill out of the back pocket of his shorts. He held the bill out to the captain. 'Dat all I got 'fore I guh to de bank.'

The sailor viewed Jacket with amused contempt. 'Dis chile notin' but one big puppy show,' he said to the captain.

Jacket had the cheque and the letter in their envelope half out of his underpants.

The captain waved him to keep them hidden. 'Hannibal, you too fool-

fool. Why don' you shut yo mout'?' To Jacket he said, 'Don' pay no 'tention boy, Hannibal all confúddle up. You give me de ten an' come by any time wid de rest. Dat roove up dere yo reserve.'

Jacket thanked the Captain, handed over the ten dollars and walked back down the wharf. The traffic had thickened overhead on the bridge and trucks were unloading at the fruit and vegetable stands, men with muscles bulging to burst under the sacks and bales. Gulls and frigate birds squabbled above the fishermen's dock. There were two yacht clubs and four marinas within a mile of the bridge and boats were headed up and down the narrow channel, mostly dories, sports fishermen and dive boats, an occasional sailboat, a big catamaran under a red and white striped spinnaker. Only a few buildings rose above the dark hedge of palm trees lining the shore over on Paradise Island. Nassau, in comparison, was all brick and bustle.

West Bay Street is the main highway leading out beyond the resorts at Cable Palm – the so-called Bahamian Riviera. In the other direction Bay Street follows the coast out past the Nassau Yacht Club all the way to East End Point.

Downtown the street narrows and contains the western flow of the one-way traffic system. It is lined on each side with shops selling duty-free goods to the tourists who pour ashore from the cruise ships moored only a hundred yards away at Prince George Dock.

High-rise development is prohibited in Nassau and few of the shops occupy buildings more than one or two storeys in height. All the big names in a consumer society are either represented or are there in their own right, $100,000 necklaces, $50,000 watches, perfumes, heavy silks, exclusive luggage.

Interlaced with these purveyors of tax-free opulence are shops that cater to downmarket tourism: T-shirts, cheap drink, straw bags imported from Taiwan or China but sold at the old straw market.

A further block back from the shore comes Shirley Street, a shopping arcade for every form of legal thievery and tax evasion – lawyers and accountants, banks, brokerage and investment houses.

Jacket found the Central Furniture and Appliance Company on a corner site on the shore side of East Bay Street. It was a big store on two levels with its own parking lot on the side. The store hadn't opened yet.

Jacket cupped his hands against the window, peering in. A mirrored headboard gleamed darkly against the far wall but there was no brass.

He was pushed suddenly and a man shouted at him, 'What you dirty up dem window fuh, chile? You tink I guh notin' better do clean yo mess?'

The man had come round the side of the building. He carried a bucket and pole with a T of stiff rubber across the top. His sweatshirt and shorts were dripping. Three of his teeth were missing in the front. His hand left its wet dirty print on Jacket's shoulder.

Jacket ducked away from him and scurried on down the road. There were buildings on both sides now. The manager at Emerald Palm had told him to take a left up to the Royal Bank of Scotland. He found the bank. A notice on the door said it opened at nine a.m. With an hour to wait he walked on over the steep narrow ridge that ran parallel to and a quarter of a mile back from the shore.

The streets were shaded by big trees. Gardens spread left and right off the road at the summit of the ridge and he saw a huge house with a sloping roof part hidden in the trees. The Bahamian flag flew from a tall pole outside at the head of a sweep of gravel.

At the top of the ridge the road ran through a gorge spanned by a narrow bridge. The district beyond was more residential. Jacket plucked up courage and asked a lady in the front garden of a small house for permission to rinse the shoulder of his shirt out under the tap. Then he sat out in the sun waiting for the shirt to dry before heading back to Shirley Street.

The bank made him nervous. The façade of smoked glass set in concrete was foreign and it was bigger than the other buildings – bigger than any building Jacket had been in. Jacket watched from across the street the staff enter by the side door. The bells on St Andrew's church began to toll the hour as a tall elderly man in blue pants and a shirt with a badge on it and a peaked cap unlocked the main doors.

Two guards took up station inside, one on each side of the entrance. They carried pistols in their belts and short wooden truncheons. A half dozen customers had been waiting on the sidewalk. Jacket watched them cross to the counters. They were all adults in the bank, but that was to be expected, and the early customers were all men. The first of them was in the bank for only a few minutes. One of the guards swung the door open for him and they had a few words before the customer stepped back out on to the sidewalk and hurried up the road.

Now a young woman in a blue suit and long weave in her hair came up the street. The guards recognised her and smiled. It was all very friendly.

Jacket took his dirty T-shirt out of his carrier bag and used it to wipe the dust off his trainers. He felt the guards watching him as he stood up. He didn't look at them as he crossed the road and he didn't see the black Mazda that shot round the corner of Frederick Street. Tyres squealed on the macadam as the driver stamped on his brakes.

A second car sounded its klaxon. A police constable grabbed Jacket by the ear and yanked him back on to the curb. 'What you playin' at?' he demanded and cuffed Jacket across the back of the head.

The drivers glared and yelled at Jacket as he mumbled apologies.

'What islan' yo from dat yo never see traffic 'fore?' The constable forced Jacket's head round to the left. 'Dat de way de car come, boy. De car stop, dem has a red light up dere . . .' He yanked Jacket's head back to face the traffic signals suspended over the nearby intersection. 'De light red, de car come up Frederick Street. Clear, boy?'

The bank guards were watching Jacket, laughing to each other. He wanted to run and hide but the constable had him by the elbow. 'We is goin' cross now, nigger,' he said, shoving Jacket out into the roadway.

They reached the far sidewalk. 'Where you goin'? Insi' de bank?'

Jacket nodded.

'Dis chile belon' yo,' the constable told the guards, thrusting Jacket in through the swing doors.

With the two guards watching him, Jacket fumbled inside his shorts for the envelope containing the cheque and the letter to the bank manager.

They were all looking at him, the men and women in their clean shirts and ties.

The guard held up the envelope between thumb tip and forefinger and gave it a shake. 'Yo got a disease, boy, yo is givin' us?'

Laughter beat at Jacket as he mumbled that the letter was for the manager.

'Well de manager, he done go out.' The guard gave Jacket a shove towards an upright chair to the left of the door. 'Wait dere, chile. Maybe he back soon.'

The atmosphere of respect and the hushed voices were the same as in the big church at Andros Town that Jacket had attended twice for weddings in the family. A digital clock on the rear wall behind the desks ticked off the seconds and minutes and then the hours.

Jacket was thirsty and hungry. Worse, the enforced idleness brought back his fear of pursuit, not here in the capital – visiting Nassau for the first time, Jacket thought of the city as belonging to a different planet from Green Creek. No, the pursuit would be waiting for him when he got off the mail-boat at Kemps Bay.

He watched a big man in jeans and white T-shirt open a carrier bag and count money on to the counter. The man's shirt stretched tight over his shoulders and his biceps bulged below the short sleeves as he arranged the notes in piles, his actions casual and dismissive of the value. There was so much cash and Jacket shivered as he thought of the drug dealers. Nothing was important to them, or not on any scale that he could understand.

Jacket had heard his elders discuss with envy this attitude of the new ruling class. How Mr D or Mr G had driven a car into a tree and not even bothered having it towed away. Or an engine had seized on their boat and they had given the boat to a poor cousin. One hundred thousand dollars. There was always more where it came from. More cash, more cars, more boats, more people . . .

The bank manager arrived at half past eleven. Jacket recognised him at once by the deference shown by the guards and staff. The counter clerk took Jacket's letter through to the manager's office. The guard was summoned. The manager's raised voice pierced the hush as he came out of his office and crossed the lobby. 'Inexcusable . . .' It was almost a snarl.

He was a parrot of a man, short, round and red in the face, sharp beaky nose and thin mouth, his gestures abrupt and nervous. 'Mr Bride, my apologies. Yes, indeed,' he said as he grabbed Jacket's hand, leading him to his office. 'You've been here since nine. I'm ashamed. Coffee? tea? A soda?'

'Coke please,' Jacket mumbled.

'And a plate of biscuits,' the manager added into the intercom. 'Fourteen hundred and eight-eight dollars, thirty-seven cents,' he said, fingering the cheque from the Emerald Palm Resort as if it were a communion wafer. 'How old are you, Mr Bride?'

Jacket told him.

'Excellent, excellent . . . and in the habit of saving. That's the secret of a successful life. Yes, indeed, Mr Bride. Hard work, saving your money, sound investments. Rare qualities in the islands.'

He plucked a form from his desk. 'I am going to open a savings account for you, Mr Bride. You will be spending most of this money on your mother's bed. Quite right, that's what you saved it for. But that won't be the end of your fishing. The manager at Emerald Palm will transfer any money you don't require directly to your account here where it will grow, Mr Bride. Grow. Yes, indeed,' he said with a pleased bob of his head.

'You will acquire a history, Mr Bride. A history of credit that will permit the bank to lend you money when you are older, money for a new engine or a new boat so that you can expand your operation or make it more efficient. That's the future. Already rosy, Mr Bride. Yes, indeed. Yes, indeed.'

With each repetition of his favourite phrase, he bobbed his head sharply as if pecking seeds.

The cathedral clock tolled twelve as Jacket headed back downhill to the furniture shop on Bay Street. He had drawn fifty dollars in five-dollar bills and had hidden four bills in each of his trainers. Reaching the store, he found it closed until two o'clock.

19

Red and pink skins thronged Bay Street's sidewalks. The tourists seemed to Jacket enormous in their short pants and short-sleeved shirts. Their thighs bulged and shook, their chins quivered, their hair glowed blue and silver, the paint on the women's lips scarlet. Their voices were harsh, their language indecipherable. The population of North and South Andros is less than nine hundred, of whom sixty-two live in Green Creek. Jacket had never seen so many people in his entire life. The shops were packed. There were restaurants left and right, cloths on the tables and foreigners busy eating and drinking. Though hungry, Jacket never thought to enter. It wasn't his place. Nor was the sidewalk.

The cars and buses seemed a solid wall of glass and steel. Klaxon blared drivers' frustration. A haze of diesel and petrol fumes hung over the street. A fit of coughing bent Jacket double as he stumbled through the jostling crowd. A gap showed to the right and in sudden panic he ran blindly through the halted traffic. An open field of tarmac spread ahead. The sea sparkled to his left. A line of shiny coaches waited on the quayside where three cruise ships lay alongside Prince George wharf.

The furthest ship was longer than the settlement at Green Greek. Jacket counted the decks piled one on top of the next, ten in all. He imagined their interior. Pink ants teemed through the corridors, huge, hungry, carnivorous. The sun slammed down off the white paintwork and the heat beat up off the black tar. He could hardly breathe. He turned and bolted through the tourists queuing to board the coaches.

A constable took the boy for a fleeing pickpocket and grabbed at his shoulder. Jacket ducked and fled. He would be safe if he escaped over the ridge. He was panting as he raced up the steep road. The cliffs of the gorge threatened to imprison him. There was no sidewalk in the gorge and the driver of a long white limousine braked and shrieked at him.

Jacket charged on down the hill past the house where he had washed his shirt that morning. Homeboys thronged the sidewalk outside a wooden bungalow that would have been at home the better end of Congo Town. A hand restrained him as he cannoned off the thigh of a big man in dark trousers and a white shirt.

'Where de fire, boy, or is you leg short?'

Jacket couldn't answer. His chest heaved as he fought for breath and his legs trembled. The sun sat directly overhead, the light blinding and the heat, out from the shade, raised a stink of hot tar from the road that mixed with the cloud of diesel smoke billowing from a passing truck.

Jacket's stomach turned inside out but there was nothing to come up except for an acid dribble that burned in his throat. He swayed a moment and the man held him.

'You in trouble, boy? You play de trone?'

Jacket shook his head. 'I's from Green Creek.'

It seemed sufficient explanation. He looked up at the man for understanding. There were twenty or thirty in the group, men and women, all tidy as were the staff in the bank. One of the women recognised him.

'You de crawfish boy.'

He nodded dumbly.

'What gone wrong?' The woman squatted to face him. She was young, waved weave in her hair. A gentle perfume lifted from her white cotton blouse. Jacket longed for the comfort of arms around him, to rest his head against her bosom; sweat on his face, he didn't dare.

'I's hungry is all,' he managed.

'Den you come to de right place,' she told him kindly.

She pointed up the steps leading to the veranda. 'You go up dere in de cool, boy. Dey got de best food in town.'

A glass door opened to the front room. A big notice faced the door:

NO SMOKE
NO DRINK
NO LOCKS
NO HATS

145

NO MUSCLE SHIRTS
NO SOLICITING

A dozen square Formica tables were laid with cutlery, half of them occupied by the same type of smartly dressed people as waited on the sidewalk outside the side entrance to the takeaway counter.

A woman in a black dress viewed Jacket in surprise.

'What yo want den? Yo guh eat or is yo jus' lookin' how de big people is?'

Jacket shivered in the sudden cold of air-conditioning. He wanted to flee but the woman from the bank had entered behind him.

'Dis a good chile,' she told the waitress. 'You want crawfish, you speak to him nice 'cause he number one on South Andros. Dat for sure. He done open an account at de bank dis mornin'.' She ruffled a hand through Jacket's hair. 'Miss Lucy look after you, boy. You eat good and rest up a time.'

Jacket had drunk a jug of iced lime juice and Miss Lucy had served him a bowl of rice and beans with steamed conch, sitting awhile at the table with him.

'You eat up well. De food on de house.'

He told her about the bed for his mother and she kissed him at the door, her arms warm and filled with kitchen scent. Though he felt braver as he recrossed the ridge, he bypassed downtown Bay Street. The entrance to the furniture store was round the side. A big lady in spectacles sat at a desk to the right of the door. Jacket watched her for a while through the window. She smiled the second time she looked up. She seemed safe enough and finally he walked round and pushed open the door.

'What you wan', chile?' she asked, fumbling inside a big black handbag on a gold link handle. She took out a leather change purse. 'Ice-cream?'

It wasn't the response he had expected and he stood dumb a moment, studying his feet as he collected himself. Then he blurted out that he wanted a bed. The bank manager had given him a letter so that the store keepers would treat him seriously and he pulled it out of his breast pocket.

The woman was heavy, her joints stiff from sitting. A sigh escaped her as she forced herself up out of her chair and came round the desk.

'What your name, boy?'

'Jacket, mamma,' Jacked mumbled at the floor.

'Jack?'

He shook his head. 'Jacket.'

She cupped his chin, making him look up. 'How ol' you is?'

'Thirteen. I's a crawfisherman,' he told her. He tried to push the letter into her hands but she didn't want it.

'You payin' cash or you payin' time?'

'Cash,' he said.

'An' what type bed you wan'?' She had him by the shoulder, turning him towards the rear of the shop. The beds were arranged amongst matching furniture – side tables, chests of drawers, wardrobes. Lacquered plywood predominated, glistening black, deep reds, glossy creams. Three of the headboards were fans of mirror, both round and square cut, the glass leaves edged in black or gold. They gleamed at him in the sombre light of the store, splendid and enticing. But they weren't right. The frames weren't brass, nor did any of the headboards bear a red velvet heart.

The woman was kind and he was ashamed at disappointing her. He described the headboard and the gleaming brass at Mr Winterton's. 'Is bigger dan dese,' he finished, spreading his arms.

'Dat a bed you goin' to have make. Dese all comes in set,' she explained, pointing at a six-piece set in black lacquer edged with gold: 'Dat tree tousan' five hundre' dollar.'

For a moment the price weakened his confidence. However, Mr Winterton hadn't bought a set and the bed existed here in Nassau. 'Mr Winterton done buy it here,' he assured her.

She thought a moment, then drew him back to her desk and drew a street plan. 'You guh try Best Buy Furniture up on de mall,' she suggested, helpful, though without enthusiasm. 'Dat's a maybe. You take de bus.' She pointed him up Bay Street towards the terminal. 'Is a number twenty-four.'

The store on the mall was bigger than the first and inland in the safety beyond the ridge. The bus fare was seventy-five cents. Jacket thought it a lot to spend on a journey he could have walked.

Jacket was unable to judge which of the half dozen men and women were staff and which were customers. None of them paid attention to him so he crossed to where a grey woman counted money in at a window at

147

the back, her voice plaintive as she explained why she was late with her monthly instalment. Embarrassed for her, Jacket shuffled his feet, waiting till she was done.

The man at the window glared at him. 'What you want?'

'I's wanting a bed,' Jacket said.

'You don' see dis for payin' in?' Indignant at Jacket's stupidity, the man waved him away.

That part of the store was all stuffed chairs and sofas, low tables and dining sets. A bed end protruded beyond an opening in the wall to the left of the window. Shy, Jacket tiptoed to the opening and discovered the bedroom furniture in a rear hall. Again he found lacquer and mirrors but no brass.

Suddenly he was grabbed by the hair.

'What you tryin' tief, boy?' a young salesman growled, shaking him hard so the tears sprung to Jacket's eyes.

'I's wantin' a bed,' Jacket yelled.

'You don' have bed, dat yo muddah fault. You get on out 'fore I smack yo head.' The man gave him another shake, his hand up to strike. 'You hear what I say?'

Jacket had taken enough abuse that day. The bank letter gave him strength and he kicked the man hard on the shin. Ducking away, he darted to the street entrance, spun round and waved his letter as if it were a war pennant. 'Yo dead low-low peasy-head, why yo high-hat me?' he shouted. 'Yo tink yo Kin' George dat my dollar no good?'

And elderly man in a suit hurried out of an office behind the cash window. Looking from Jacket to his staff, he demanded an explanation for the fuss. Jacket thrust his letter at him. 'I's a crawfisherman. I's got fourteen hundre' dollar cash fuh buy a bed.' He pointed to the salesman: 'Dat man pull hair an' call tief.'

The elderly man rounded on the salesman. 'You apologise right now this minute, Wilfred. You hear?'

The salesman mumbled his apology while the elderly manager led Jacket back to his office. Once more Jacket described Mr Winterton's bed. The manager thought a while before picking up the phone. He dialled two numbers before giving Jacket a nod of encouragement. 'Happy House Furnishings. That's a block over and six blocks north. They've got brass. You take the bus on the corner of the mall.'

With a look of contempt for the salesman, Jacket left the store and turned north. He didn't take the bus. All those seventy-five-cent rides would mount up.

Forewarned, the staff at Happy House Furnishings had been kind and helpful to Jacket but the brass beds they stocked were small and without headboards. So his afternoon continued store to store, determination driving him back and forth across the capital. There were brass beds and there were mirrored headboards but never in combination and seldom of sufficient size. At some stores he was treated with politeness, at others with mockery or contempt. Time and again he was assured that he wasted his time – that the only way to acquire such a bed was to have it made in Miami. Politeness made him inspect catalogues. However, the same stubbornness and imagination that had driven him to hide the boxes now denied him the ease of surrender. A twin to Mr Winterton's bed existed somewhere in Nassau. Of this he was certain.

At home, other than for special occasions, he walked barefoot. His feet sweated in his trainers. The solid concrete and tarmac bruised his soles and raised blisters on the undersides of his toes. Street dust had dirtied his shirt and trousers.

In navigating the dunes and the waters of South Andros he was guided by familiar markers. A tall fir tree, the angles between two points, beacons, the white curl breaking on a reef. The bridge to Paradise Island gave him direction when to seaward of the ridge. Further inland he had only the sun. As the afternoon wore on and the sun fell behind the trees he had to hunt for fresh landmarks, a television aerial, a water tower.

His confidence increased as he grew more familiar with this new terrain and his imagination took control of his plodding feet. He was a spy for the Special Forces sent ashore to uncover support amongst the natives. The letter was his introduction to the resistance and he used it forcefully as he did the password the colonel had given him: 'I's a crawfisherman.'

The importance of his mission banished his anxieties concerning the aeroplane and the boxes hidden on Bleak Cay. The street he was on was wide and tree lined. The store to which he had been directed occupied a corner site. As he rounded the big windows he spotted the warm glow of polished brass on a mezzanine balcony. A young saleswoman with beaded weave and dressed in a short skirt and high heels reached the door as he shoved it open.

149

'I's a crawfisherman,' he announced for the umpteenth time, the letter ready.

'An' we's closing,' the woman said.

She tried to shut the door in his face but he jammed it with his foot, hunting beyond her for someone of greater importance. That much he had learned already – the higher up the ladder, the more helpful and attentive the service. He spotted a middle-aged woman wearing a flowered dress and spectacles on a chain. She was standing over by the office section.

'I's needing a bed,' he called, waving the letter at her. 'Cash dollar, mamma.'

Surprised, the manageress slipped the arms of her spectacles over her ears.

'Crawfisherman! Boy, you like to show sef, eh!' the young woman sneered as he slipped by.

She didn't worry him.

'Please, mamma, is a brass bed I's wantin'.'

The manageress led him upstairs. What he had taken for a large bed were labelled sections stacked against the windows, cellophane sacks of bolts and screws strapped to them. Expert now, Jacket saw at a glance that the beds were too small. There were no headboards.

Buoyed by his mission for the colonel, he had been strong when he entered the store, tall and thrustful. He felt himself shrink as he looked out over the city between the brass bars of the stacked beds. The sun sat low above the red and green roofs and trees, street upon street upon street filled with streams of cars, water tower in the distance. Already a dozen people waited at a bus stop with more trickling out of the building opposite. His shoulders sagged as he recalled the sixteen pages of furniture store listings in the telephone directory the manager of the Emerald Palm Resort had shown him. Checking each one would take a lifetime.

'You're looking for something special.' It was a statement. The manageress's voice was soft and she spoke in British English. She turned him, leading him by the hand, treating him as a child.

Shame made him keep his face hidden from her as they descended the stairs. At home they lived always with the background rhythm of surf breaking on the reef. Here it was the hum of air-conditioners.

He had been sweating out on the street and he shuddered within the chill clamminess of his shirt, his feet slippery inside his trainers as they crossed the shop.

Ushering Jacket into her office, the manageress turned to tell the sales staff they could leave. The office was neat and polished. The scent of floor and furniture wax reminded him of Mr Winterton's house. He needed to wipe his nose. The countless times that his mother had smacked him across the head stopped him from using the back of his hand and he looked quickly at the desk in search of a packet of the tissues the manager at Emerald Palms had given him. A folded newspaper lay beside an oblong of soft paper held in a leather frame. The office seemed to collapse in on Jacket as he saw the photograph of Vic centre page. It was a posed portrait of Vic in boxing trunks and gloves taken at the end of the previous year's championships.

GREEN CREEK BOXER BOY DROWNS ON BLEAK CAY REEF

Jacket was incapable of either reading the story or looking away. A knife pierced him deep below his wishbone. Vic had punched him there once and Jacket had vomited. Now he breathed very carefully round the pain, trying to isolate and contain it. Surf roared in his ears. The waves lifted the desktop almost into his face then sucked it back. The light ebbed and flowed with the wave pattern. The walls and ceiling of the office pressed down, their weight drowning him.

He dug his fingernails into the insides of his wrists, using the pain to force back the walls and steady the desk in the same manner as he controlled his misery when his mother hit him. It was fear now that he had to conquer. They had killed Vic. Jacket was certain. Vic would never have capsized a skiff in the surf off Bleak Cay. Nor would he have drowned so close to shore – he was far too strong and experienced a swimmer. They had been waiting for him on the cay. Jacket pictured the patrol boat, the landing party, their jungle boots shiny with seawater as they stalked the scrub, Vic fleeing from them, then trapped on the beach with nowhere to run. Vic raised his hands in surrender but they were cruel and merciless. One of them grabbed and shook him.

'What's wrong, child?'

The manageress had him by the shoulders. He read the anxiety in her eyes. She mustn't know. No one must know. But they knew. He could feel them sniffing for his trail the way the hounds did for wild pig in the pine woods. His legs gave and he snatched at the arm of the chair facing the desk.

I's all right,' he told her, his voice hardly above a whisper.

She didn't believe him. She had his letter from the bank and he saw in her eyes a spark jump as it did on the plug of an outboard, the connection made between him and Vic.

'He was a friend of yours?' she asked. 'Poor child.'

It wasn't clear which of them she was referring to. She took a tissue from her bag. Fetching a Coke from a tall icebox to the left of the office, she poured for him and, seated behind her desk, watched while he steadied himself. Then she questioned him about the bed and made him sketch it.

He had been taught by Miss Charity to be painstaking in drawing the reef fish after their field trips and he drew the bed with equal care, steadying his hand by holding his breath, his upper lip gripped between his teeth.

The manageress studied the drawing with seriousness. She explained that brass plate peeled in the salt humidity of the Bahamas. Mr Winterton's bed must be of solid brass to have lasted. Solid brass was expensive, a speciality item. There was an interior decorator way over on Graveney Road that used to stock such things. She wasn't sure that he remained in business. The only other suggestion she could make was the Antiques Warehouse on Rosetta Street. Both stores would be closed now.

Did he have a place to stay, she asked.

'On de boat,' he told her for something to say. He could be traced to the Rybovich at the Nassau Yacht Club. Nowhere was safe.

20

Jacket Wilberforce Bride was thirteen years old. He was wise for his age on his own territory, whether emotional or of terrain. Now he was lost.

His only knowledge of the world beyond South Andros had been learned from North American TV programmes. Ignorance made him incapable of differentiating reality from fantasy; episodes of *Miami Vice* were as real to him as his own life.

He understood the value of the hidden cargo. He knew to what terrifying lengths people would go to retain or steal it.

He was familiar with depravity and violence.

He had watched, evening after evening on the 16" screen down at Mr Jack's bar in Green Creek, the gangsters and drug traffickers torture informants. Seen them drill for the nerve in a victim's teeth. Watched them force slivers of bamboo under fingernails, tear out the nails with pliers, crush fingertips with a hammer, stub cigarettes on the flesh so that it smoked, brand with red-hot irons, hold a man's face to the kitchen grill, drip battery acid on it.

Vic would have told everything – everything he knew. Who he had taken the case from; that Jacket had told him that he had found it in a crashed plane out on Bleak Cay.

Now the hunt was on. First someone would have approached his mother. She would show the note he had left. Next they might search for Dummy out bonefishing with the American in Congo Town. Or Miss Charity . . .

Jacket's fear was as much for them as for himself, that the gangsters or the cops would grab them. Old-style Mafioso in snap-brimmed fedoras of the 1950s, the flash suits of 'nineties Hispanic-Americans – whatever

153

the period, lose sound on the TV and the cops were indistinguishable from the criminals.

He needed a role model. As he kept to the edge of the sidewalk in the deepening dusk he was Harrison Ford, *The Fugitive*. Then came memory of *Witness*, Harrison Ford as a good cop trying to protect a child who had seen a murder on a visit to New York. The murderers were polite. They had come hunting for the child and for Harrison Ford out on a farm where the Americans wore old-fashioned clothes and didn't own trucks or cars – Jacket hadn't understood why, nor had anyone else in Green Creek.

Jacket tried to escape into the war and his father but he couldn't free himself of the memory of the cops driving over the hill to kill the child. They had come early in the morning. Harrison Ford was unarmed when they came. They had shotguns and pistols.

Now they could be in any of the cars that passed. Jacket didn't know which way to look. He didn't know where to hide, where he could eat, where to sleep. He began to run. The cops had come for the child out in the country so he headed for the centre of town, the ridge. There were trees there and big gardens.

He found a gap in a fence. Headlights hit him as he squeezed through. Caught by the searchlights, he froze on the border fence. The Russian major was in the wooden watchtower. The lights slid on and Jacket broke through to the forest. He found a big old building gutted by fire. He gathered dead branches and curled beneath them in a shallow ditch below one of the crumbling walls. The building was the Royal Victoria Hotel, abandoned more than a decade before his birth. Jacket hid there in the ditch, flattening himself like a small animal, hungry, thirsty, desperately afraid.

They came searching for him later. He watched them from the ditch – first two men, then three more. They wore knitted wool berets over their dreadlocks. They were thin. They cursed and giggled as they stumbled amongst the brush close to the road, poking at the dead leaves. They lit matches. One of them crawled on all fours, nosing amongst the bushes. A sixth man came dodging through the shrubbery. He carried a woman's handbag and the others fell on it like squabbling seagulls, tearing at its contents, striking each other. One of them whimpered. Then the man on his knees yelped and they forgot the handbag as he backed out with a small plastic package. They sat in a circle, sniffing, scratching. Each flash of a match was followed by quick harsh intakes of breath.

154

The dust of the dead branches tickled in Jacket's sinuses and he gripped his nose, forcing back a sneeze. The men's conversation came in driblets between long silences, one man speaking at a time, the others nodding or not. A woman in a raggedy shirt shuffled out of the shadows and joined the circle. One of the men took off a shoe. He spat on the leather sole and flicked open a knife. The slow swish of the blade reached Jacket, on and on. Fresh spit added, more sniffing, more fierce inhalations.

The breeze stirred the dry leaves of Jacket's hiding place and he was late in controlling himself. He had been calm for a while. Terror embraced him as he sneezed. He flattened himself into the dirt as the men's footsteps approached, then drifted away. He thought that they had missed him. Carefully he raised his head to peek through the branches. A hand dug into his hair, yanking him out. It was the man with the knife. The point of the blade touched Jacket's throat. The man giggled. The corners of his mouth shone with spittle. He pushed Jacket out into their circle, thrust him to his knees.

'Dat one small dutty tramp,' one of them said.

Yet another held Jacket's head while the knife man pried a thin copper tube between his lips. The knife man blew in the other end, blasting the acrid smoke into Jacket's lungs.

Jacket's head exploded with coloured light as he doubled up, coughing and retching.

The men giggled as the woman reached for him. She dragged him into her lap, plucked at her skirt buttons. Sweat had left a paler streak down the inner side of her sagging breast. The nipple was dark and twisted. She pressed Jacket's face against it, rocking backwards and forwards as she crooned a baby's lullaby. The scent of her skin was sour, the bones of her chest sharp beneath brittle skin, her arms thin as sticks. Her strength gave out and Jacket slipped free. The trees swelled and circled him as he crept back to his nest.

He slept and the rain woke him. Light from the streetlamps leaked pale through the trees. The men and the woman lay higgledy-piggledy beneath a big lignum vitae. One of them stirred, then another. The heavy raindrops splattered off the leaves and they cursed, clambering to their knees, then to their feet, awkwardly, shoulders stooped and shuttered against the cold wind that snapped at them round the corner of the ruin. Their first steps were uncertain. One of them knelt coughing into the dirt.

They slunk away, not as a group, but one by one, their shadows melting and flowing amongst the dripping hibiscus and oleanders.

The rain coursed down the ruined wall into the ditch. Jacket lay shivering in a pool. The earth turned to mud beneath him, squelching and slippery as he pried his coverings apart. He squatted beneath the wall, drinking from a trickle that spilled from the broken corner of a projecting brick. He needed direction. He had been put ashore from the submarine. He had to get the weapons to the patrol stranded at Green Creek. The weapons were hidden in the bed. Only he could find them. The colonel had warned him how difficult and dangerous it would be: 'Your dad said you could do it. You're the patrol's last hope.'

Jacket's age was his disguise. They wouldn't be looking for a boy. The decorator's shop was out in the suburbs. The rain beat at him as he slipped through the fence to the road in the first hinted paleness of dawn.

The first signs of dawn were hidden behind clouds. Rain coursed down the window, warping the streetlights below. Trent thought of Skelley alone on the *Golden Girl*. The police officer would have set two anchors. In the lee of Andros, he was in no danger. However, responsible for Trent's home, he would be anxious as he crouched in the shelter of the saloon bulkhead in the cockpit and watched the shallow sea beaten into froth.

Trent wondered where the boy was – if alive.

He must remember to think of him by his name. Charity shifted on the couch and he asked quietly, 'Why Jacket?'

She told him.

A squall beat at the window.

'He's intelligent,' Charity said to reassure herself.

Trent showered and changed in to a loose safari, shirt, fawn linen trousers and a pair of viciously expensive Italian city sandals Tanaka Kazuko had bought him for Christmas. Back in his office he flicked on the desk light. Charity looked up at him from the sofa. He had thought that she had begun to accept him now that they had spent the night in the same room and had talked a little in the safety of darkness. Now he saw her suspicions flood back.

'I have to leave before it gets light,' he said. Guns in a civilian setting always tended to the melodramatic and he shrugged, embarrassed as she watched him settle the Beretta inside the front of his pants. He adjusted his shirt carefully. 'Does it show?'

It was the question teenage girls asked each other as they adjusted their straps in the rest room. She said, 'That's why I won't wear a bra.'

He smiled and she was surprised at wondering what he would look like without his camouflage, whether he had a chin. 'Do you always wear those beads?'

Again there was that slight look of embarrassment. 'They belonged to my mother.'

'Belonged?'

'She crashed her car.' He busied himself folding the cloth that had covered the handgun. Then he looked at her. 'Take a cab out as if you were going to the airport. Curse when you find you've forgotten your nephew's birthday present. Have the driver turn back and drop you by the bridge. There's a café the other side of the road.'

He took money from his wallet. He laid the bills on the desk without counting them.

Knowing she would refuse, he said, 'It's not real.' A slight movement of a hand indicated the office and the wealth implied. 'I have an expense account that I can't spend.'

He took a plastic rainproof from the coat rack in the corridor and buttoned it to his throat. 'Half eight? We can have breakfast before the furniture stores open.'

A watery dawn showed the marching whitecaps. The Bertram was less than a mile off the east coast of New Providence but the rain blanketed the shore and the entrance to the channel. Steve clung to the handrail inside the wheelhouse as the squall tore the cap off the wave and slammed it across the windscreen. Blind for a moment, the Bahamian skipper mistimed the rise of the boat and she slammed into the almost vertical wall of water. The sea smacked her back and she heeled fifty degrees, half her bottom rolling clear. The wave lifted her and the propellers broke free, racing the engines. The skipper cursed, spinning the wheel. The rudder dipped and bit. The bow came up into the wind.

Tucked in against the bulkhead, Jesus Antonio coughed carefully into his handkerchief, then folded it away into the pocket of his windcheater. He looked across at Steve and a slight smile lightened the normally sombre line of his thin lips. 'Breakfast's going to have to wait.'

The Bahamian skipper chuckled.

The clouds broke as Jacket walked up Graveney Road. His shirt and shorts were wet and filthy from the ditch. Water had seeped into his trainers and his feet squelched. He found the decorator's store set back from the sidewalk behind a white picket fence on the left side of the street. An iron grille protected the single shop window. All but a centre square of the plate glass was painted black as a frame for a velvet lined display box. A green vase stood in the box. The shop door was of solid wood so Jacket couldn't see in.

He crossed to the other side of the street and squatted facing east against the garden wall of a blue clapboard bungalow. The wet clothes chilled him and he was hungry. He thought of the men hiding in the jungle inland from Green Creek. The enemy were too close for them to risk a fire. More than twenty-four hours remained before the mail-boat sailed for Kemps Bay, then another night before he could smuggle the guns ashore.

The sun pried through the cloud. The warmth seeped though his shirt. He watched a red-leg thrush dig at the lawn of the house next to the decorator's shop. A first car drove up the road. A door opened to his left. A woman hurried to the bus stop on the next corner. Soon tiny god birds were humming their wings as they sipped at the hibiscus blossoms. A young man dismounted from a bicycle at the shop and unlocked the door. Jacket caught a glimpse of a stuffed chair as the youth wheeled the bicycle inside. The door closed.

A half hour later an older white man drove up in a small yellow convertible with the top raised. The youth met him at the door and they unpadlocked the iron grille from the window and carried it round to the rear. Then the older man moved his car into the shade of an acacia two houses down.

Jacket's trainers left a trail as he crossed the road. He knocked at the door gingerly and the youth opened it.

'I's a crawfisherman,' Jacket began as the youth grabbed for a broom resting against the wall.

He held it like a rifle and bayonet, stabbing at Jacket with the handle, his voice breaking as he screeched, 'Out! Out!'

Jacket backed up, his own voice high. 'I's not in.'

'You're not coming in,' the youth said. 'Will you look at the state of him. Oh my God, his shoes,' he cried, turning in protest to the older man hurrying from the rear of the showroom. 'Out,' he repeated, following Jacket down the short path, broom jabbing. 'Out, out.'

'I is out,' Jacket protested from the safety of the sidewalk. Desperate, he looked over the youth's shoulder to the white man. 'Mistuh, I's a crawfisherman. I's lookin' for a brass bed.'

The decorator said, 'Control yourself, Henry,' and stilled his arms. He inspected Jacket.

'I's slept out in de weader. I's not from here,' Jacket said. 'I's from Green Creek. Look . . .'

The youth squealed as Jacket fumbled inside his shorts for the bank manager's letter.

'Do shut up, and fetch the boy a towel.' The decorator pushed the youth towards the back of the shop. 'Hurry now.' And to Jacket: 'Take off those dreadful shoes.'

When the towel came, the decorator commanded Jacket to strip and leave his clothes on the doorstep. 'Henry will rinse them out under the tap in the back yard,' he promised.

He shoved the protesting youth out of the door before shepherding Jacket into the shop and seating him on a chair covered in creamy gold silk and painted gold on the delicately moulded brass corners. 'There, that's better. And you'll want something to eat and drink, I expect.'

He fetched orange juice and chocolate biscuits. Seated facing Jacket, he watched while Jacket ate. Moistening a finger, he dabbed a fallen crumb from the waxed tiles. 'Now tell me about your bed.'

Jacket had kept the drawing he had made for the manageress of the other store. The decorator recognised it at once. 'Good Lord, that's Charlie Winterton's!'

'Dat right,' Jacket said proudly. 'Mr Winterton done buy it in Nassau. Thirteen hundre' dollar. I's got fourteen hundre'. Is fuh my muddah birtday. I's a crawfisherman,' he added in explanation of his wealth.

'And a friend of Charlie's . . . it is a rather splendid bed.'

The decorator smiled gently as he leaned forward to brush a crumb off Jacket's lips. 'I've asked Charlie a hundred times, but he never will tell me where he found it.'

He indicated the contents of his shop. The chairs, tables and sofas were more delicate than those Jacket had seen in the other stores, the wood solid and polished rather than lacquered. Paintings hung on the walls – two of young white men in striped swimsuits that covered their chests and thighs, the colours in the paintings soft greys and blues.

'As you can see, not what I stock,' the decorator said. He took Jacket by the shoulder, steering him back to the office in the rear. 'I'll make a few calls and you can have a nice hot shower while your clothes dry.'

A door opened off the office to a bathroom that was all gleaming tiles. The decorator fiddled with brass taps above a deep shower tray, testing the temperature. Satisfied, he said, 'Now in you go. I'll fetch a clean towel.'

He flicked the used towel away from Jacket and gave him a gentle push. His look was familiar. There were those amongst Mr Winterton's guests who had followed Jacket with their eyes in the same way. Jacket crouched into the corner, sheltering himself with his hands.

'Don't be shy,' the decorator said. 'A friend of Charlie's . . .' He reached for Jacket. 'Turn round and I'll wash your back.'

The decorator's assistant screamed as he flung the door open. Jacket dived under the decorator's arms, sliding on his belly across the slippery tiles. The youth lost his footing as he charged the decorator and both men fell into the shower. Jacket scrambled into the office and grabbed his carrier bag with his papers in it and his old clothes. As he bolted for the door, he could hear the two men yell and slap at each other. He fled naked round the side of the shop to the back yard where his clothes and trainers hung dripping on the line. Dressing quickly, he bolted up the street.

Trent had brought Charity to Nassau only because she could recognise Jacket. He didn't want her connected with him more than was absolutely necessary and they had their first argument of the day at the furniture store as the doors opened. He wanted to enter by himself. She refused to be left on the sidewalk. He gave in to avoid a scene.

He related the same story he had given the manager at the Emerald Palm resort. The manageress was sympathetic. She recounted the boy's visit of the previous day; that, unable to satisfy him, she had directed him to Best Buy Furniture on the mall. So the trail began – but Jacket was alive.

Charity sensed Trent's relief. 'You thought he was dead . . .' She saw that it was true. 'That's what you deal in.'

In was an accusation, as if being who he was made him responsible for the danger the boy was in. Trent knew it of old, this attitude to his erstwhile profession. He was necessary to the safety of society as was the refuse collector or the driver of the night-soil truck.

He said, 'We need a phone booth. I'll call the bank.'

Steve made two calls from the public booth in the lobby of the Sheraton Hotel. To the Emerald Palm he was carrying out a financial survey for a French tour operator: what were their banking arrangements in Nassau? Given the Royal Bank, he called the manager. Steve had spent much of his working life on the telephone. He was fluent in its use and he and the manager spoke the same language. Steve gave Campbell as his name. He was employed as a bond broker with Merrill Lynch. He was sailing his boat over to Andros and had promised the manager at the Emerald Palm to give the Bride boy a lift home.

All the bank manager knew was that the boy planned on buying a bed for his mother. Jacket would be paying with a banker's cheque so must return to the bank. The manager would give him Mr Campbell's message.

Steve smiled as he replaced the receiver. It was easy now. Grab the kid as he left the Royal Bank. Take him to Bleak Cay. Once they had the coke, kill him and dump the body back on New Providence to concentrate the search well away from Steve's home ground. Over from Green Creek, the boy was unused to traffic. A hit and run would be simple and logical. Smash his lower spine with a club. Scrape a few flakes of chrome into his shirt.

Steve's old luncheon companions at Terry's would have recognised the evidence of a coup in the way he rubbed his hands together, his smile slightly sheepish, an almost adolescent spring to his step as he hurried across to the restaurant to join Jesus Antonio at a corner table.

Steve had expected congratulations, but Jesus Antonio's face remained expressionless. He looked very frail in the big room, dark eyes sheltered in bruised shadows. He had helped himself to a glass of milk. Separated by the glass, his hands never moved, their long narrow fingers pointing across the tablecloth.

'I'll have our men pick him up,' Jesus Antonio said in that soft voice imprinted on Steve by his interrogation. The Hispanic's lips were dry. He coughed once and for a moment his eyes were unhidden. Steve saw the pain, but also the contempt he had first encountered in the Treasury agent at the bank.

He watched Jesus Antonio fumble for his handkerchief. Yeah, cough your lungs up, Spik son of a bitch.

Trent called the Royal Bank, asked for the manager and announced himself as a detective searching for Jacket Bride on behalf of the hospitalised father.

The manager gave him the same information as he had given the earlier caller. He didn't mention the earlier caller – it didn't seem relevant.

Trent asked him to send young Jacket round to his office if he turned up in the morning or hold him at the bank if he came in the afternoon.

21

Jacket's clothes had dried on him on the long walk back from Graveney Road. The Antiques Warehouse was his last hope. Disappointment greeted him as he saw that a clapboard bungalow rather than a store occupied the corner plot on Rosetta Street. The boards and window-frames were freshly painted, even the tin roof. Scrubbed steps led up from a small front garden to the narrow veranda with its pillars separated by a painted rail and overhead fretwork. It was the right place – a wooden shop sign hung under the eaves.

There were similar houses on Andros – otherwise he might have turned away. Instead he opened the gate quietly and peeked in through the front door from the path. He recognised the interior from films he had watched on television: the highly polished table laid with lace mats and silver, the upright chairs, a corner cabinet displaying china, pictures on the walls, mirrors in gold or plain frames. It was a room for the respectable rich, European rather than North American.

He backed away quickly, stumbling as he hurried to close the gate. Safe out on the street, he looked back.

A white woman had come out on to the veranda, her face suntanned by custom rather than vacation. Her dress was at one with the furniture, mid-calf and expensive. She smiled at him, her tone matter-of-fact as she asked whether he had something to sell. 'Don't be shy,' she said, beckoning. 'I don't bite.'

Hesitant, he shuffled a foot. Her smile gave him courage. It was open, affectionate. Though she was white, she wasn't foreign; she talked with her eyes the way Bahamians do and the way she stood was Bahamian, her frame loose but upright, relaxed, confident.

He took a step back, a hand on the gate but not opening it. 'I's sorry, mamma, I's come to the wrong place.'

She leant a shoulder against a pillar, one foot crossed over the other, at peace with herself, not wanting anything from him, waiting.

He found himself drawn in through the gate. He halted at the foot of the steps.

'I's a crawfisherman, mamma. I's wantin' a bed fuh my muddah. Is a brass bed.'

She was accustomed to people searching for a specific piece of furniture. She called over her shoulder and a dark woman brought a glass of fresh lime juice. She made Jacket sit on the top step, not because she didn't want him in the house or on the veranda but because she sensed that he would feel more comfortable there.

'I like that,' she said when he explained why he wanted the twin to Mr Winterton's bed. She inspected the drawing while he told her of his search and she chuckled with delight at the picture of the decorator and his friend tumbling over each other in the shower.

She had never seen a bed like the one he had drawn. 'It must have been a special order,' she concluded. She recognised the bed as essential to his fantasy. Any other, however grand, would be a disappointment.

'Don't waste your money,' she advised. 'Find a smaller gift now and buy the bed for Christmas. Have it made in Miami.' She would order it. 'The factory will want a deposit.' The mail-boat didn't leave until noon of the next day. It was too big a decision to be taken quickly. 'Think it over,' she advised.

He was a hundred yards down the road when she called him back. She stood at the gate, a hand on her hip. He knew that if he ran to her, she would open her arms. He didn't know how he knew but he did know. He couldn't do it. His relationship with his mother had left him unfamiliar with affection and cautious of showing his emotions.

She told him of an Englishman who had intended opening a special kind of hotel for male clients. He had shipped the furniture in from Italy. 'Very rococo,' she said with a quick smile and a sketch of her hands. 'Chandeliers, big beds, lots of mirrors.'

The immigration department had expelled him. An old man, Lebanese, had bought the furniture. 'It's a long shot,' she warned. 'He may be dead.'

The Lebanese was something of a hermit and hated the telephone. She sought his address in a leather-bound directory.

'Let me know how you get on,' she said. Then she hugged him suddenly. He ran so that she wouldn't see his tears. The house was miles away. She had told him to take the bus. To do so would have lost her into the crowd. So he walked, hoarding her to himself, her scent and warmth fresh and unshared.

Trent and Charity had followed the trail, furniture shop to furniture shop. They travelled by taxi, Trent's story always the same. Finally they came to the manageress who had given Jacket the names of the decorator and the Antiques Warehouse.

The decorator seemed a more probable choice and they drove there first. The youth opened the door to them. A strip of sticking plaster bridged his nose and a streak of ointment glistened on the split on the right corner of his upper lip.

Panic filled the youth's eyes when Trent introduced Charity as Jacket's schoolteacher and himself as a private detective. He fled to the office. His voice, high pitched with fear, reached them through the door. The decorator appeared. Bruising had closed his left eye. He stood in the doorway, wringing his hands, stuttering his innocence.

'I didn't do anything. Really. I mean, well, Charlie Winterton. The boy said they were friends. It was a misunderstanding. His clothes were soaked. Poor child, I thought a shower . . .'

He turned to his friend cowering in the office. 'That's all that happened. Tell them, Henry?'

'I hope,' Charity said, her concern for the boy rather than for punishment. 'Where did he go?'

They had been too occupied with each other to remark the direction of Jacket's flight.

Steve sat with Jesus Antonio in the shade of a mango tree in the public garden below Princess Margaret Hospital. They were unremarkable, friends waiting for news of a medical examination, a birth, the outcome of an operation. The gardens overlooked Shirley Street and the entrance to the bank. Jesus Antonio held a cellular telephone on his lap.

Four of Torres's Bahamians were parked in a panel van in the car park the other side of the ridge. They could reach the bank in two minutes and thirty-eight seconds – or five minutes if delayed by the traffic signals at the junction of Frederick and Shirley. Delay didn't matter. They could pick the boy up entering or leaving. Traffic would dictate which of a dozen side roads they would take, either down to the sea front or inland beyond the ridge. They would wait for dark before transferring the boy to the Bertram. The constable was due back at Green Creek by dusk. An hour at the village bar and he would know whether there had been any movement out on Bleak Cay or whether the cay was under police observation.

Jacket had walked four miles out from the centre of Nassau. Shy of his ignorance, he hadn't asked what a Lebanese was, nor had he ever seen such a street except on the screen. Not a single patch marred the tarred surface and the line down the centre was white as surf. Evenly spaced acacias shaded wide verges of mown grass. Signboards threatened imprisonment or a fine of five hundred dollars for discarding litter. Iron gates closed off the private roadways while tall hedges and trees hid the houses beyond. The few cars that passed seemed quieter than normal cars. There were lawn sprinklers at Emerald Palm and the swish and pitter-pitter of rain falling was familiar. He found the house number on the gate post and a brass bell-push. Unsure of what to do, he backed away into the shade. A dog sensed his nervousness and barked on and on from behind the hedge until finally a man called it to heel.

Then a face peered at Jacket from between the bars of the gate. It was an old face, lined and bald, with a hook of a nose and a jutting chin sandwiching lips that had collapsed inwards over the guns. The man's body was hidden by the brick gate pillar and at first Jacket thought that he must be bent double or on his knees. Then the body appeared dressed in striped pyjamas. The man was no taller than Jacket. The dog came to his shoulder. It was the kind of dog that Jacket had seen guarding Mafia houses in gangster movies, black and lean with a pointed face. Its tongue hung out to the left and he could see its teeth sticking up like white rocks out of the dark gums.

He said, 'I's sorry, mistuh.'

A fierce wheezing chuckle burst from the little man. He said something that Jacket couldn't understand. His lips fell outwards when he spoke and he brushed a dribble away on the back of his hand before taking a double set of false teeth from his breast pocket. He wedged them into place before repeating himself: 'You haven't done anything yet.'

A second chuckle bent him double and he coughed into his fist. Finally he got his breath back.

'What were you going to do that you are already sorry for? Ring the bell? Throw a bomb? Or poison Hakim here?' he asked patting the dog's head.

'I's a crawfisherman,' Jacket began.

'I am a crawfisherman,' the little man corrected.

'Yes, mistuh,' Jacket said. 'Mistuh, is you a Lebanese?'

His head tilted to one side, the man looked like a bird. 'Why?'

'De lady at de Antik Warehouse say de Lebanese buy de bed I's wanting,' Jacket said. Then quickly, 'Mistuh, dat what de lady say but she never say what a Lebanese is. Dat's a good lady, mistuh, an' I's afraid to ask 'cause she tink I's fool.'

'You don't look a fool,' the little man said. 'You's a crawfisherman. I's a Lebanese. That's a lot to say through a gate.'

He gave another of his chuckles and looked at the dog. 'What do you think, Hakim? Shall we let the child in? He's our height.' He slapped the beast twice on the top of its head so that it seemed to nod. Then he took a bunch of keys from his pants and fitted one to the lock. 'In you come, crawfisherman.'

Gripping Jacket by the elbow, he steered him up the drive, the dog panting at their shoulders. The house was bigger even than Mr Winterton's but it was built all on one level. Lawns spread on each side and along the front, shrubs and trees with their lower branches pruned. A kidney-shaped pool surrounded a small island from which two palm trees grew at differing angles so that they formed a V against the bleached blue of the early afternoon sky.

The Lebanese urged Jacket on to the terrace and in through an arched side door to a big white-tiled kitchen. A huge icebox with four doors stood against one wall. The Lebanese took out a jug of fresh orange juice, put it on the table and found glasses.

'There we are,' he said as he poured. 'Sit yourself down, crawfisherman. I have a cook and a maid and two gardeners. They like to bother me with questions so I make them sleep in the afternoons. There's not much to do. One old man. Or one old Lebanese,' he corrected with another of his chuckles. 'Lebanon is a country,' he said. 'Drink up and we'll find it in the atlas.'

Though they faced each other across the scrubbed pine table, Jacket avoided looking at the little man. He was shy of him. He didn't understand who or what he was or why the Lebanese had brought him into the house.

He said, 'De lady say yo is a hermit, mistuh.'

'Nonsense,' the little man said. 'You're here. It's a matter of scale. I never did much like big people. Now that I'm old, I don't like them at all. But you're all right. You fit, crawfisherman. I don't have to peer up at you. That's something you ought to understand being small yourself. And I don't need people. I have my friends in here,' he said, tapping his temple. 'Lots of them. They come from books. Come along . . .'

He ushered Jacket through to the threshold of a vast low living-room. 'How about that,' he said, his delight bubbling over into laughter so that he coughed again.

It wasn't a real room, not one that Jacket had ever seen, even on the TV. The furniture was huge, the wood gold, the coverings red velvet. Outsize mirrors in gold frames flung scarlet images across the floor. Golden cords furled deep red curtains back from the windows that opened to a courtyard surrounded by pillars with bougainvillea trained over them. A small pond glistened in the centre of the courtyard. A statue of a naked young woman bent backwards over a smooth rock above the pond. Her legs were spread. One hand covered her eyes, the other trailed behind her in the water so that her breasts were thrust up.

The little man chuckled. 'Not what you ought to see, crawfisherman, but you see worse every time you watch the news on television. Starvation, murder, war. That's real vice. This is fun. A fun house. That's what I wanted. Not all that nonsense about good taste that I'd accepted all my life. Pretending that I was like everyone else while they whispered behind my back and were only polite to my face because I'm rich. No, no – I'd done all that for years. Then a silly Englishman ordered all this furniture from Italy and I thought, what fun. That's what I want. Look . . .' He trotted to a chair and bounced on the huge seat.

'Try, crawfisherman.'

Jacket was struggling to understand what the little man had said. About being small, he could understand. People sneering at the Lebanese. That was like Dummy. People throwing rocks at him, tripping

168

him up, mocking him while they pretended to say nice things. And being jealous and angry at him because he was the best bonefisherman on the island and was paid well as a guide. But all that about the furniture was a mystery. However, the Lebanese had the bed. That much was certain.

The Lebanese was saying, 'Come along. Come along.'

Jacket stepped gingerly on to the ripe-tomato carpet. The wool pile felt thicker, lusher, than the lawns surrounding the pool at the Emerald Palms hotel.

'Bounce,' the little man commanded. 'Try the sofa.'

Jacket couldn't. His mother would have smacked him had he dared even touch the furniture in Mr Winterton's house. 'Keep dem dutty han' off, Jacket, yo hear? fuh I hackle up yo backside 'gain.'

Stuck midway into the room, he said, 'Please, mistuh, I's looking for a bed.'

The Lebanese peered at him over the bulbous arm of the chair. 'What bed, crawfisherman?'

'Is with a heart,' Jacket said. He pulled out his drawing and the bank manager's letter and thrust them at the little man. 'Please, mistuh, I's serious. Is fuh my muddah. Mr Winterton done buy de one for thirteen hundre' dollar. I's got fourteen hundre'.'

'Fourteen hundred and eighty-eight dollars and thirty-seven cents to be exact,' the Lebanese said, reading the letter. 'How old are you?'

'Thirteen, mistuh.'

'And what do they call you?'

'Jacket, mistuh.'

'Why?'

'Is my dad,' Jacket said. 'He run off when I's four. He in de army now . . .'

The little man peered at Jacket over the arm of the chair, sniffing at him, searching through his defences, not questioning but seeking for the truth with instincts sensitised over eighty years of persecution, of being different – a freak. He recognised the territory of fantasy, knew it was as real to the boy as were his own ancient avenues of escape from pain.

He led the boy through his childhood, his mother's daily walk across the ridge to clean the American's house. The anger that was their constant companion. The bitterness that made her snap and slap. Jacket told of his hunt for the bed, of his vision of the bed on top of the mail-boat's wheelhouse, how the villagers would carry it in triumph up from the beach. How his mother would look when she saw it in their hut.

'I's huntin' dat bed fuh tree day. De bank close fuh four clock an' de boat guh in de mornin'.'

'And what makes you believe that I will sell you the bed?' the Lebanese asked.

Jacket had never considered for a moment that he wouldn't sell. The bed was Jacket's by right of the nights he had rowed out alone to Bleak Cay, the fourteen hundred dollars he had saved. The only necessity was that he should find it. He looked round the vast room and saw at once that he'd been wrong. The bed was part of all this, essential to the little man's fun as it was to Jacket's fantasy. He sat suddenly, not on a chair but on the step descending from the kitchen hall. He didn't want to cry, not in front of the Lebanese. He said, 'I's sorry, mistuh. De bed belong here right 'nough.'

'You'll give it up?' The little man frowned his surprise. 'Your dream, Jacket?'

'Dat yo dream furss,' Jacket said.

'Because I'm older? Does that give me absolute right? No opportunity for the young? No, no, that would never do. Come along.' The Lebanese took Jacket by the hand and led him down a corridor, throwing open doors left and right to a half dozen bedrooms, each one furnished with a vast bed surrounded by glistening furniture and mirrors. Each bed was different. Four-posters draped with lace curtains, one with angels at each corner, painted headboards of nymphs picnicking beside a river, Pan playing his flute. The bed with the heart was at the far end. It stood on white carpet, brass gleaming. Jacket saw his reflection in the headboard sliced into a dozen segments, the Lebanese beside him.

'We're going to need parcel tape and a role of plastic sheeting,' the little man said.

Jacket didn't understand.

'Well, you've got to have it. That's obvious,' the Lebanese said. 'My men won't be back for another hour. You'll have to take a taxi.' He chivvied Jacket down the corridor. 'Come along, come along. Off with you, boy. No time to waste . . .'

Trent's calm infuriated Charity. They were caught in traffic a half mile from Rosetta Street. Seated in the corner of the cab, his hands on his knees, he gave no sign of the tension she had suffered all morning and, worse, during the lunch hour when there was nothing they could do. A JCB had dug up a strip in the centre of the road short of the traffic signals at the crossroads ahead. There was no way past until the driver finished loading a dumper truck parked on the verge.

A cab pulled round the corner ahead and accelerated towards them the other side of the trench. Preoccupied with Trent she didn't register Jacket in the rear seat until the cab had already passed. Even then she wasn't certain and wasted time twisting round to look back through the rear window.

'That's him.' She was certain. She had spent too many hours in a skiff with the boy sitting up in the bows with his back to her for her to mistake the shape of his head.

22

Trent dropped a visiting card and a fifty-dollar bill over the driver's shoulder, jumped from the cab and leapt the newly dug ditch in the centre of the road. He didn't bother offering Charity a helping hand. All his concentration was on Jacket disappearing into the distance. He waved at a cab halted at the intersection. The driver spotted him and pulled across the traffic as the lights turned green.

'Shirley Street,' Trent requested and to Charity, as she slid in beside him, 'There's a chance the boy's heading for the bank.'

Steve knew Jacket from Andros. He associated the boy with Mrs Bride walking over the ridge and had expected him to come by foot. He had a clear view for a hundred yards either way and had been concentrating on the approach rather than the bank itself so that it was by chance and at the last moment that he spotted the kid already inside the bank talking to one of the guards.

'Shit! That's him.'

He glanced at his watch as Jesus Antonio dialled the van – half past three and the street was thick with impatient drivers anxious to get their business done before the banks closed for the weekend.

Klaxons sounded the other side of the ridge as the van driver forced his way out of the car park into the stream dammed by the light at the intersection with Frederick Street. The lights changed and the traffic eased forward. Steve cursed as a Lincoln town car braked in front of the bank, stemming the flow. The signals changed again bringing to a halt the cars crossing the ridge.

Steve couldn't see the kid. He said, 'Your men better know what the shit they're doing.'

Jesus Antonio coughed into his handkerchief. The light switched and they saw the van nose out into Shirley Street. The signals changed again before the van reached the intersection.

'They'll never make it,' Steve said. It was a repeat of his failure to reach Bleak Cay on time. The fear, the sweat, the sick feeling in the pit of his stomach.

The road ran straight as a ruler to the ridge. Trent and Charity could see the cars backed up from a mile away. They reached the bottom of the rise as the driver of a panel van forced his way out from the car park into the traffic. Trent counted the seconds and the distance the traffic moved at each change of the signals. The bank was a half mile away. Running would get him there faster than the cab. 'I'll go on ahead,' he told Charity.

The cab nearly caught him at the first change of the lights. From then on, he was ahead. Once over the ridge he put on speed down the slope. He had asked the bank manager to hold the boy if he came in the afternoon so he wasn't too concerned but he wanted to be sure, that was all. He turned into Shirley Street. There was no sign of the boy so presumably he was still in the building.

The van that had pulled out of the car park had halted at the curb opposite the bank below the hospital gardens. Drivers were hitting their klaxons in fury at the resulting bottleneck. Trent wondered why the van driver hadn't walked the three hundred yards from the car park.

The bank manager had greeted Jacket with relief. The second telephone call that morning had disturbed him. 'Your father's ill in the hospital in the United States,' he told the boy. 'You're to wait here until four o'clock. There's a detective coming with a ticket your father's sent.'

Jacket felt a surge of excitement, then disbelief. His father had never sent a single dollar. Now, after eight years, an air-ticket?

Suddenly Jacket accepted his mother's accusations: that his father was a coward; that he had run off because he was a weak man, incapable of facing responsibility.

Feckless, she always called him. Lazy and feckless.

Finally, here in the bank, Jacket understood. The money Jacket had saved proved her words. If he could do it, so could his father, a grown man – as could any of the men in Green Creek, yet few of them did. They preferred to sit and talk all day and half the night about what they would achieve if they were given a chance. Of what they could make of their lives if only they had a Green Card from the US Department of Immigration that allowed them to enter and seek employment in the United States.

Many men in the village had talked of the magic card for every day of Jacket's life; discussed its potency while they spent the little money they earned on beer or rum down at Mr Jack's bar. Some of them had two and three children by different women. Meanwhile his mother walked over the ridge each day. She was right. They were feckless and lazy.

And a detective? He could smell the danger as he could on the breeze blowing in off the deep water beyond the reef. They must have learnt of the boxes. They were setting a trap.

He said, 'My dad run off, mistuh. I's need de dollar for my muddah bed.'

With the bank in sight, Trent had slowed to a brisk walk. Charity was only a hundred yards behind in the cab. The traffic was moving at a crawl past the panel van. Trent hadn't seen anyone get out of the van. The driver must be waiting for someone – probably picking up wages for a factory or hotel.

Steve saw the Bride kid cross the bank lobby towards the entrance doors. There was no move yet from Jesus Antonio's men in the van. Steve wanted to scream at them.

The door to the bank opened. The boy stepped out on to the sidewalk. The sun was in his eyes. He hesitated a moment, not sure which way to turn.

The rear door of the van opened. Three men jumped down and headed across the road. Trent saw a puff of exhaust smoke as the driver started the engine. He was too familiar with kidnap to be mistaken. He shouted as he ran, not to warn the boy so much as to distract the men. He saw them grab the boy and the van pull out from the curb to block the street. Trent hadn't time to set himself for a shot or to use his knife.

Brakes screeched and there was the continual blare of klaxons as he dodged through the cars. They had the boy at the van now. One of them gripped a short club. A car barred Trent's approach. One of the men spotted Trent and swung to face him.

Trent dived high over the hood of the car and spun sideways in the air crashing into them at shoulder height as they thrust the boy in through the rear doors. Trent grabbed one of them by the neck and held on. The club slammed into his shoulder. He kicked violently, not caring where his feet landed so long as they were high enough to miss the child. The man he gripped by the neck punched him in the stomach. Trent held tight and got his teeth into the man's ear. The man yelled as Trent bit. The club struck the side of Trent's head. He fought to hold on as the blackness closed in. The club smashed again. Trent tried to kick one last time but his legs wouldn't work. He couldn't see. Then he fell down and down for ever.

Finally fingers pried his eyelids open and someone shone a bright light, first in his right eye, then in his left. They were talking. He couldn't make out what they were saying. Their voices mumbled on. Then he was moving in a cream tunnel. It didn't lead anywhere. Just on and on until there was a prick in his arm and the darkness swarmed back and grabbed him.

Frustrated by the traffic jam, Charity had jumped out of the cab. She saw the men grab Jacket. Three of them. She watched Trent run. There was nothing she could do. She saw him dive and turn sideways in the air, then a car cut off her view. She couldn't think against the screech of the klaxons. She beat on the roof of the taxi with her fists and screamed at a bank guard on the sidewalk. He was employed as decoration and didn't know what to do. She saw the roof of the van disappear down the street. She tried to get its number but there was too much movement. Jacket was gone. She reached Trent. He lay sprawled in the street, a sawdust dummy. A pool of blood surrounded his head. She wanted to kick him. She had never hated anyone so much. That he could fail Jacket. His gun, his big office, the *Golden Girl* – it was all front. Like advertising – fake to put up the price. Someone was shouting not to touch him – a policeman . . .

She leant against a car. A man in a white coat vaulted down from the hospital wall. A stethoscope hung round his neck, so he must have been on duty. Men slid Trent sideways on to a stretcher. Policemen ran from both directions, closing the road, stopping people from leaving until they had taken statements. She grabbed a sergeant by the arm, shouting at him that the boy had been taken. He wouldn't listen to her and she struck him. She couldn't help herself. She kicked back as a constable grabbed her by the elbows. At the same time, she was screaming silently at herself to get control. Getting arrested wouldn't help Jacket.

She shouted at the sergeant that she was with Trent. They immediately presumed that she was his girlfriend, his lover. They understood her panic. They would take her statement in the hospital.

She followed the procession up through the sloping garden into the hospital emergency ward. A dozen men crowded the stretcher. A nurse came running with a bottle of blood plasma.

Excluded, Charity stood in the doorway. She had been right all along. She should have done it herself, told them in the village what had happened out on Bleak Cay. Skelley and Trent had said that doing so would have put Jacket in greater danger. Now the drug smugglers had him. She hit the wall with her fist and watched the blood ooze out of her knuckles. She had to tell someone. Someone who would listen.

An inspector touched her shoulder. She grabbed him. 'The boy . . .'

Jacket had drawn twenty dollars cash. He hadn't asked the name of the Lebanese so the bank manager wrote a cheque for fourteen hundred dollars on Jacket's savings account and showed him where to sign and where to write the seller's name. The bank manager smiled as Jacket tucked the cheque inside his underpants. He said that the cheque wasn't cash; that it was worthless without Jacket's signature.

Jacket wasn't reassured and he was wary as he stepped out on to the sidewalk. The sun made him blink. Then he saw the men. Three of them. He had been hunted by Vic and his gang on innumerable occasions and recognised the men instantly for what they were – bully boys. He hadn't time to run. As they grabbed him, he let his muscles go slack so that he was dead weight, awkward to carry but noncombatant. He needed a distraction – one second of inattention. He was ready.

A bearded white man raced to intercept the men at the van. The white man dived over a car and twisted in the air, slamming into them at shoulder height. For a second shock loosened the men's grip. Jacket kicked and, wriggling free, rolled sideways under a car where they couldn't reach him. He slid out the far side and ran doubled up low on the ground, back through the traffic to the intersection and down the hill. Though he was safe, he didn't slacken pace until he was into the crowds of shoppers on Bay Street. A bus slowed and he ducked on board, sitting low in the seat so that his head wouldn't show. There were two stops to the terminal. He found a cab and told the driver that he'd been sent by his father's employer to buy a role of wrapping plastic.

In escaping he hadn't time to think. Now, safe in the cab, he tried to understand what had happened. He was certain the men weren't thieves. They were connected with the telephone call to the bank manager. To Bleak Cay. He wanted to hide in fantasies of his father but he had accepted reality at that moment in the bank. His father was gone, gone for good.

'People are watching,' Jesus Antonio warned. 'Walk slowly and don't look back.' He held Steve by the arm, steering him up towards the hospital buildings. Police had sealed off Shirley Street and were now running up through the hospital gardens in search of further witnesses to the attack.

'Separate and meet at the Sheraton,' Jesus Antonio said. 'Don't panic, Steve. A police officer stops you, ask what the fuss is about. Say you were inside the building. Show them your burns.'

They were wheeling Trent up the corridor to the X-ray department. 'Three men,' the inspector said. 'Brave of him . . .'

Charity was on the verge of screaming that he had let her down. But it was Jacket who had been kidnapped, Jacket who they would kill. Ashamed, she bit the words back.

The police officer was saying, 'The boy was a crawfisherman. He had fourteen hundred dollars in a savings account. Probably boasted to someone. At least he got away and he hadn't drawn the money in cash . . .'

'Got away . . .' He was mistaken. Or he was making some sort of sick joke.

'Like an eel. Down Frederick Street. Smart kid, never stopped to look back.' The inspector had his notebook out. 'It's the men we're interested in. Three of them and a driver. If you could describe them while the incident's fresh.'

Jacket had learnt street craft from TV spies and fugitives and hitmen. He knew exactly what to do. He switched taxis twice. Each time he walked a hundred yards, the roll of plastic over his shoulder. He stopped at shops, using the windows as mirrors to check the sidewalk. He changed pace, crossed the road suddenly, doubled back. He made sure that no one was on the street before ringing the Lebanese's gate bell.

The little man had changed and looked spruce and intimidating in slacks and a short-sleeved shirt.

'I's got a cheque,' Jacket told him proudly.

'An I's got de cook cookin' a feast,' the little man said, chuckling and rubbing his hands. He told his gardeners to wrap the bed while he showed Jacket into the library. A *Times* atlas was open on the desk. 'The Lebanon,' he said, pointing. 'And my name's Dribbi. Michael Dribbi. We're going to eat, then you're going to sleep in comfort, Jacket. My men will take you and the bed down to the boat in the morning.'

He made Jacket sit in the leather chair at the desk. Handing him a gold fountain pen, he spelled his name, watching while Jacket filled in the cheque and signed it.

'Splendid,' he said, folding the cheque carefully and slipping it into an envelope. He spun the dials on a small wall safe hidden behind a picture and put the envelope in a steel cash box.

'Must feel good,' he said, turning back to the boy. 'Knowing what you wanted for your mother. Earning the money and buying it.'

Jacket nearly told him then. He wanted to. He knew that he could trust Mr Dribbi. However, the Lebanese was so small and so old, so defenceless. He imagined intruders clambering over the gate. They would kill the dog first, cut its throat or poison it with a chunk of meat. Then they would torture Mr Dribbi the way Jacket had seen them do on TV. He was wrong to have come back to the little man's house. He had put him in danger.

Steve said, 'Your men messed up.'

He faced Jesus Antonio across the table in a booth in the American bar at the Sheraton Hotel. He was at home in the air-conditioned opulence that was so unmistakably American. The subdued lighting was familiar, the shape of the glass tumbler holding his vodka tonic, the feel of the carpet beneath his feet, the obedient smiling whispered servitude of the bar waiters.

As a vampire sucks blood, so he sucked confidence from the accustomed atmosphere. Though the thwarted kidnapping was a setback, he was exultant. Jesus Antonio's failure offered a start to Steve's undermining of the Hispanic's authority in the Cuban's hierarchy. Think long term, he warned himself. Long term. Five years, ten, and he would have constructed a base of greater power and independence than that of even a senior vice president at the bank.

For now it was essential that Jesus Antonio maintain control so that responsibility was his.

A newcomer to the business, Steve sought guidance with befitting humility: 'So what's our next move?'

Yet he could already hear himself reporting to the Cuban: Yeah, well, I warned him.

Silent, Jesus Antonio stroked the sides of his glass, studying the surface of the milk as if it were a gipsy's crystal.

'He was at the bank so he must have found his bed,' Steve prodded. 'He'll ship it on the mail-boat tomorrow – that's if your men haven't scared him off.' He felt a threat in Jesus Antonio's refusal to commit himself. 'He had a lot of bread on him for a kid. Maybe he'll think they were regular thieves.'

'He's a child,' Jesus Antonio said quietly. 'He made a mistake in hiding the boxes. He will try to undo the mistake.'

He looked up at Steve. His eyes were dark mirrors in which Steve saw his own reflection. He saw himself in bed at the Winterton house, his hopeless longing; the longing to be allowed to start again; start right back before the de Fonterra brothers had re-entered his life.

He shuddered in sudden fear of the Hispanic's perception. Rage came to him. Rage that Jesus Antonio should dare link him to the thirteen-year-old kid. Then he realised that the image was a product of his own fantasy. The Hispanic knew nothing of his feelings. Nothing that he hadn't been told. He recalled Jesus Antonio holding his hands as he drew from Steve the truth of what had happened on Bleak Cay. Their knees had touched, their faces so close that the Hispanic had seemed to inhale his substance.

'Goddamn but it's cold in here,' he said as he shuddered again. He looked at the tabletop, sheltering his eyes. Only the Hispanic's death would free him. And the kid. They had to go, both of them.

23

Charity sat in the waiting room down the corridor from the operating theatre. Police came and went, nurses, doctors. None of them paid her any heed. She was conscious of being without any rights – no relationship, except that Trent had been hit on the head in her company. If she had asked how he was they would have presumed that she was his mistress. Nigger and honkie staying on his boat or at his apartment or house.

A middle-forties Bahamian in expensive beige linen, club tie and a Panama talked in a corner with an older white American in wire-rimmed spectacles. The American's square build was disguised by an ancient seersucker suit, and an old battered leather briefcase hung open by his side. A second white American arrived, tall, blond and a lot younger. He wore heavy shoes and a belt with marks in the leather that told of a badge and pistol.

The Bahamian in the Panama looked to be important and the Bahamian police showed him respect. However, the zoologist in Charity took note of the small signs that betrayed the true hierarchical structure. Power lay with the cheap seersucker. A stillness in his poise showed lack of anxiety or concern for the Bahamian's opinions. He never raised his voice so that the Panama hat was forced to stoop slightly. It was all part and parcel of the man, his choice of clothes, the angle of his head, the square stance that avoided being pugnacious because no one in years had argued with him on his own territory – and, though this was the Bahamas, it was very much his territory.

A black Bahamian surgeon joined the threesome, mask hanging down below his chin. He stretched and wriggled his shoulders; an occasional gesture to the scalp accompanied his description of Trent's wounds.

Finally they wheeled Trent down the corridor. A bandage covered his head. The standard bottle dripped sugar water into his arm. A catheter dribbled urine into a plastic bag. The left front wheel of the trolley squeaked and she imagined the Americans thinking that it was typical of the Bahamas.

The American in the seersucker suit nodded to her on his way out of the waiting room. She didn't know whether to smile or not. Or ask him how Trent was. He wasn't a doctor. They were all gone. She sat alone with the smell of disinfectant and of floor polish. She was on what her brother called slow-boil level. She recognised the state.

She had expected to be given orders by the police that she could argue against. Instead, having taken her description of the attackers, they had ignored her; making her feel both unimportant and an interloper in some all male game which was too complicated and serious for a woman to understand. A young woman.

Young women who showed interest were pushy. Young men acting in the same way were said to show promise. Hold it, she warned herself. Slow boil was all right. Move up a level and she would do something that would get her thrown out of the hospital.

As she watched the procession thin behind the trolley, she was reminded of religious parades in the Bahamas, the manner in which the men sneaked off for a quick drink and forgot to rejoin. Bahamians did the same with their women.

She followed the procession down the corridor and took note of which room Trent was in. Then she returned to the waiting room. Nobody bothered her. She didn't bother anyone. She hardly existed.

She waited half an hour. The last ten minutes passed in a frustrating crawl despite the patience taught her by her profession. She walked down the corridor and round the corner. The squeaking wheel had left a dull tag on the polished linoleum every eight inches. A tall medium-tough plainclothes Bahamian policeman in his early thirties leant against the wall opposite Trent's door. The young blond American in the leather belt sat beside the door on one of those upright dirt-green fibreglass chairs that nest inside each other.

The American was cleaning his nails with the file on a stainless-steel nail-clipper. He looked up at Charity, then carefully folded the file back into place and dropped the clippers into his shirt pocket. Charity could read his mind better than she could a map. She thought of it as the little-woman syndrome – run along now and play, this is men's business, serious.

He smiled at her and said, 'How can I help, lady?'

Charity wanted to say: By getting out of my goddamn way. She settled for: 'I want to see the patient.'

The Bahamian police officer had swung off the wall. Tall, he looked down on her, his slight smile of sexual awareness infuriating – based on the presumption that she and Trent were sleeping together. A man who slept with a woman gained respect while the woman was a tart, particularly when the bedding crossed the colour line.

'Which patient?' the Bahamian asked, wanting Charity to commit herself.

'Mr Trent,' she said.

His smile widened a fraction. 'What's your relationship?'

She said, 'Get the fuck out of my way,' and grabbed the door handle.

The American's hand closed on her wrist, hard enough but not so hard as to leave a mark that might tempt an assault charge. Terror of lawyers had been bred into him. Added to which he was possessed by the standard WASP fear of blacks and women.

'I'm sorry, miss. No visitors.'

'You're his doctor?' she asked.

The Bahamian said, 'He being deported. Illegal immigrant . . .'

'Bullshit,' she told him. 'He's a Bahamian resident. He's managing director of the Bahamian subsidiary of a Japanese-owned multinational.' She sounded weird even to herself. She hated multinationals. But she was in her stride now. Skelley had accused her of having a bad mouth. Skelley didn't know shit.

She said, 'You try keeping me out of his room and I'll have the Japanese Ambassador come here personally and kick your dumb arse. Now get the fuck out of my way, you black son of a bitch.'

'Listen, sister . . .' That was as far as the Bahamian got.

'Sister?' she shrieked. 'Who gave you the right to call me sister? Slave shit. Get down on your goddamn knees and bark to your honkie masters. Do I get in now or do I call the embassy?'

'Steady down, lady,' the American implored. He had taken out a small cellular telephone. He punched buttons, listened, nothing happened at the other end.

'Japanese,' he said, his face straight. He turned to his Bahamian colleague. 'You want to try a phone in the lobby? See what they say?'

The Bahamian sneered and sauntered off, his stride deliberately heavy and masterful.

Once the Bahamian was round the corner, the American said, 'I have to search you.'

Charity didn't argue.

He opened the door enough for her to squeeze through, as if keeping it part closed diminished his offence. 'Do me a favour and be quick, lady.'

They must have drugged him. He lay on his back, his mouth part open, the sheet folded neatly back below his shoulders. His arms were underneath the sheet and she whipped the sheet back expecting to see his hands bound and his arms strapped to his sides. They were loose and she chided herself for being melodramatic. His body was made dramatic by the scars of his career.

She understood now why he wore those loose smocks and three-quarter-length trousers. Bullets had caused some of the scars and it struck her as extraordinary that none of them had been fatal; an inch left or right, up or down, would have been enough. The chunks of scar tissue must remind him of the closeness of death every time he looked in the mirror.

She tried to picture his attack on the three men exactly. She couldn't recall his having looked round for help. He hadn't time to think. He had acted automatically. She wondered at the training that could make him sublimate his sense of self-preservation time and again. Ivanov's rats in a maze. Reward and response. Brainwashing . . .

As she touched the lip of the bandage wrapping his head, she realised that fear of the answer had stopped her asking how badly he was hurt. His breathing seemed steady. She wanted to shake him. Make him open his eyes. Tell him Jacket had escaped. She had told Trent the boy was intelligent.

The young American peeked round the door, beckoning.

Out in the corridor, she heard the heavy tread of the Bahamian police officer approach.

The blond American had propped himself against the wall and looked half asleep. He grinned at her. 'The slave thing, lady – my folks were serfs back in Russia. Turf shacks and whips. Run away, they hanged you.

183

First generation in the States, indentured labour. That's slavery except there was a time limit – if you survived; a lot didn't. Same with the Chinese. History. Thought you'd be interested.' He jerked his head at Trent's door. 'Do me a favour, lady. Forget I let you in.'

The Bahamian returned looking pleased with himself. The surgeon would see her. 'Down de corridor an' on de right . . .'

She sat in the office, waiting. The surgeon arrived in company with the chunky white American in the seersucker suit.

The surgeon introduced the American as Mr O'Brien: 'Mr O'Brien has an official interest.'

So this was the man in whom Trent had told her to confide. As always, an American rather than a Bahamian. She felt the indignation thick in her throat as she did each time she passed the United States Customs and Immigration officials at Nassau international airport.

He settled himself into an upright chair, his old battered briefcase open between his feet. Presumably the brass catch was broken.

'Here, in the Bahamas?' she asked.

The American had taken off his wire-rimmed spectacles and was busy cleaning the glass on a worn but spotless white cotton handkerchief. His eyes seemed unfocused without the lenses. 'An observer,' he said with a small smile and a shrug of apology that barely moved his thick shoulders. 'I share a common interest with Chief Superintendent Skelley.'

The surgeon knew who Charity was. Miss Johnston, he called her, his smile a permanently fixed crescent, nervous and obsequious. He had been castrated by internship in the United States. Lawyers hovered like vultures in his imagination. Rather a dead patient than attempt a procedure too advanced to be supported by the statistics necessary to fight a malpractice suit. Trent's employment by a Japanese multinational was an added and unfamiliar danger. Having the American listening increased his discomfort – two witnesses to his diagnosis.

'I understand you're a friend of Mr Trent's, Miss Johnston. He has a medical history that gives cause for concern.'

'You mean he's been shot a lot,' Charity said.

'And other things.' The surgeon was unfamiliar with the language of violence. 'Accidents,' he tried, but the word didn't fit the patient's scars. 'Yes, well, anyway, concern . . .'

He opened his hands, the palms pale and scrubbed. 'Three blows to the head, Miss Johnston. Fortunately only one was direct. Concussion, of course, though, at this stage, one can't be certain. However, that's the fear. Optical damage. Yes . . .'

His hands fluttered and swooped to fiddle briefly with a gold Sheaffer fountain pen, a fake ivory paper knife, and a small silver button discovered in a plum pudding one Christmas dinner at Government House.

'The first X-rays don't show a fracture,' he said. 'We'll take more in the morning, of course, but for now, rest. Yes, definitely . . . We've administered a sedative, saline drip to obviate dehydration, a small transfusion in the theatre.' His hands paused in mid-flight above the desktop and he looked up for a moment, fixing Charity with a look of embarrassed entreaty for understanding and belief. 'The plasma is screened, Miss Johnston, so there's no worries as to HIV. We've taken samples, of course, of Mr Trent's blood.'

He looked round at the American. 'That's really all. For the moment, of course. As I've said, in the morning. Yes, in the morning. But till then, no strong light. A minimum of movement. And I'll be looking in, of course, as will Mr Reginald and Dr Franklyn . . .'

Safety in numbers, spread the possible blame, do every test imaginable. Charity longed to slap him. Fish didn't bring suits against marine biologists, not even in the United States. Nor did poor Bahamians who could afford and received only the most basic of treatment in this same hospital.

She said, 'What you're telling me is that you don't know shit.'

Her insult plucked him from his chair. His hands froze, fingers curled into talons of barely suppressed rage. 'Miss Johnston! How dare you? Here, in my office.'

'Your office, bullshit. This is a government hospital.'

He said, 'Your emotional commitment does you more credit than your manners, Miss Johnston.' His shoulders were stiff with indignation as he turned to the American: 'Love affects women in strange ways.'

'Love! I hate the son of a bitch,' Charity said but the surgeon was already at the door.

He bowed to her. 'Despite your deplorable behaviour, the patient will receive the best treatment possible. Good night, Miss Johnston.'

'Son of a bitch,' Charity said, and to O'Brien: 'Skelley says I've got a bad mouth.'

'What does Trent say – about the boy?'

She wasn't ready. She hadn't expected him to be direct. He sat very still, his hands folded in his lap. The round wire-rimmed spectacles gave him a superficial look of innocence but the eyes behind the lenses were a very pale grey and very careful. She recalled the attitude of the superior Bahamian in the Panama hat – the only partially hidden respect he had shown O'Brien. It was the man as much as his position, whatever that was.

She asked him and he said, 'I'm an employee of the US government, Miss Johnston. What people call a bureaucrat, a minor functionary.'

Like shit, she thought. She had to keep control. Shooting off her mouth wasn't going to help. 'What reason do they have for deporting him?'

'You'd have to ask your minister for immigration.'

'Your man's on guard outside his door,' she retorted.

O'Brien's smile was infinitesimal and never touched his eyes. 'A favour to an old friend, Miss Johnston. Mr Trent has enemies. Right now he's not in a state to defend himself.'

She saw him lying in the bed, the network of scars relating a history she couldn't read.

The American seemed to read her mind. 'I could give you a list of terrorist organisations worldwide that have him on their hit list. He tell you that's what he did? Infiltrate?' He looked at her, waiting – as Trent had waited for her to commit herself in the saloon of the *Golden Girl* the previous afternoon. Less than a day and a half.

'He doesn't always think,' O'Brien said.

She pictured the street outside the bank. Jacket blinking in the sunlight. The three men. The van. 'He didn't have time.'

She didn't know how much Trent wanted her to tell the American – or if he wanted her to tell him anything. Or what was best for Jacket. We have different priorities, Trent had warned her. Mine is to save the boy.

O'Brien was waiting. That's what they were good at – waiting. The professionals.

She said, 'I'll wait.'

'Till he comes round . . .' He searched his briefcase for a yellow pad of stick-on labels and a plain wooden pencil. He moistened the lead before writing a telephone number. 'Night or day, Miss Johnston, you need help, ask for me by name.'

24

Four golden angels stood guard over Jacket at Mr Dribbi's house, one at each corner of the huge bed where he lay curled up tight beneath the blankets. The boy had felt stifled by the softness of the duck-down pillows and had dropped them to the floor.

Out in the corridor Hakim, the Dobermann, pricked his clipped ears as the boy stirred and whimpered. Released from the kennels, six of Hakim's relatives patrolled the grounds. Old Mr Dribbi sat reading in his library. Sleep didn't come easily to him. Most nights he dozed a little in his chair before making for his bed at three or four in the morning.

Hakim eased the library door open with his nose, trotted over and thrust his head between the little man's legs. The dog went on pushing for attention while Mr Dribbi fondled his ear absentmindedly.

'*Qu'est-ce que tu veux?*' Mr Dribbi finally asked.

The dog trotted to the door, then looked back.

'*Bien, bien . . .*' Mr Dribbi pushed himself out from the chair and followed the dog across the big living-room and down the corridor. He hesitated, hearing whimpers come from the child's bedroom. Only when Hakim scratched impatiently at the door, did the old man open it.

Hakim ran to the bed and pawed at the sheet. The boy yelled and sat bolt upright. The child's terror reminded Mr Dribbi of his own tortured nights in those days before he accumulated the financial power to protect himself and distance himself from his business. Seated on the bed, he drew the boy into his frail arms and rocked him gently, crooning in a mixture of French and Arabic and English.

Jacket calmed and Mr Dribbi questioned him carefully, softly prying through the surface for the roots of the boy's fear.

The story came in dribs and drabs. First the attack outside the bank.

Then the night Jacket had spent in the ditch at the foot of the gutted hotel, that he had thought the drug addicts were hunting him.

Mr Dribbi's voice was tender, his touch light, his arm thin and harmless round the boy's shoulders. Hakim, the protector, lay on watch by the door, stubby tail twitching approval of the friendship.

Aided by the soft glow of the bedside lamp, the boy's confidence grew. He told of the long row out to his lobster ground and of the lamp he used for fishing. How the lobsters formed chains on the sand.

There was more but the boy wasn't ready yet. Mr Dribbi, a fisherman himself back when he was a child on the Mediterranean coast, fetched cups of hot chocolate from the Thermos the maid left at night in the kitchen.

They sat beside each other, sipping in companionable silence, one very old, one very young, white and black, hook and broad nosed, very much of a height.

Mr Dribbi didn't encourage the boy to continue, rather he left him to pick his own time and route and to progress down it only as far as he wished. The old man imagined the scene as Jacket told of the aeroplane crash and the dead pilot, that the boy believed he was at fault because the lamp was his. How he had hidden the boxes. His fantasies of his father. His recognition in the bank manager's office of the truth: 'Is like my muddah say, he no good, Mistuh Dribbi.'

Mr Dribbi took a silk handkerchief from his pocket and wiped the child's eyes. 'Shush, little one. What matters is that you were brave, very brave. Blow,' he commanded and held the handkerchief to the boy's nose. 'We must decide what to do.'

He carried their cups out to the kitchen, washing them in the sink while the child composed himself. He fetched a box of handmade truffles from the refrigerator, then decided that they would be bad for the boy, too much sugar late at night. He peeled an orange instead and arranged the segments on a saucer.

Back in the bedroom, he watched the boy suck the juice before asking him, 'Who have you told?'

'You de fuhst, Mistuh Dribbi,' Jacket said. 'I's fright fuh de police. Dat sergeant wid de short finger, he in dat business. I hear de big people talk at Mistuh Jack bar 'bout it all. Dere no one I can trus' till I meet wid you.'

The old man searched back through his own distant childhood for comparisons. He had never known his father, never known who he was. He had learnt early to keep his own council, to duck and weave and pretend innocence and ignorance. As for the police, they were the natural enemy. But he had been a child of the street and of purchased love, wise at Jacket's age in the ways of a corrupt city as the boy was wise in the ways of the sea and the closed island society.

'I's goin' to dig de box up,' Jacket was saying. 'A fisherman goin' to find dem. He de one tell de police.'

The old man nodded. The decision was logical given the boy's limited knowledge of the world. Logical. Sensible. Safe. The boy had the courage and strength of character to carry it through.

'I's home Sunday. De man all in de church or in de bar. Dey talk all day 'bout dat bed,' Jacket said. Meanwhile he would dig up the boxes, then hide until they were discovered.

Mr Dribbi gave the plan his blessing and settled the boy under the bedclothes, sitting with him until he slept. A good child, Mr Dribbi admired courage. The coincidence was unfortunate. However, such coincidences were common in a country of only a quarter of a million inhabitants. Mr Dribbi returned to his library.

There were those of his contemporaries and younger who had refused awareness of the electronic revolution. Many of them were dead or in prison. Mr Dribbi hadn't spoken on the telephone in thirty years, wire taps were too effective. For many years he had done business by coded cable and by telex received and sent from agencies. Now he used an IBM laptop. He connected a LAN link to the computer, switched on and punched in his security codes. Less than three minutes from start to finish and his coded message, untraceable and secure, awaited collection from an electronic bulletin board.

Art dealers are adrenalin addicts. Lend them a hundred thousand dollars and they will use it as a deposit on a million-dollar painting. Lend them a million, they will make a deposit on a ten-million-dollar painting. The Cuban, Torres, was of similar character. His dealings in cocaine were easily financed from his own resources but not the tankers of crude and refined petroleum products that plied the oceans at his command. Add a refined lifestyle and he would never be free of Mr Dribbi's very private bank.

Politics make the oil market volatile: war, threat of a coup, embargo, a strike of oil workers, fire in an oil field, fresh discoveries, even an election in an oil-producing country. The Cuban's aim was to own sufficient crude to manipulate the price. The global commodity market never sleeps, only the local branches. One of his secretaries picked up Mr Dribbi's coded invitation to early breakfast from the electronic bulletin board at five o'clock.

Jacket woke early. Mr Dribbi's maid had taken his clothes the previous evening. Shy with only a towel to cover himself, he sidled out into the garden where Mr Dribbi sat sipping coffee beside the pool in the early morning sunshine.

The little man beckoned him and slipped an arm round his waist. 'A great day for you, Jacket. The bed is yours. Now to ship it.'

The cook brought the boy freshly pressed orange juice and two crisp bread rolls warm from the oven. The maid beckoned him to dress in his laundered shorts and shirt.

A car arrived while Mr Dribbi's gardeners were loading the bed in its plastic wrapping on to a light truck. The newcomer was white, middle aged and smartly dressed, his dark hair shiny and swept back from a high forehead. Mr Dribbi introduced him to Jacket as Mr Torres.

'Jacket is a lobster fisherman,' the little man told his visitor. 'A fine young boy. He has bought a bed from me for his mother.'

As he introduced Jacket, the little man laid a hand on the boy's shoulder as if to emphasise the unusual closeness of their relationship. 'Jacket has been spending the night.'

The visitor appeared embarrassed as he shook Jacket's hand – uncertain perhaps of the boy's exact standing.

'I's from Green Creek,' Jacket said. 'Dat over in Sout' Andros, mistuh.'

One of his familiar little chuckles escaped Mr Dribbi. 'Mr Torres is from Cuba – by way of many countries. Come along, Jacket.' He led the boy aside.

'My men will go with you to the docks,' he said, taking an envelope from his pocket. There were ten new twenty-dollar bills: 'You tip each of the men twenty dollars, the same to the maid because she did your laundry and to the cook. The cook has a picnic packed for you.' He hugged the boy. 'Now off you go. Do exactly what we arranged last night. Come back soon. This house is your house. Understand?'

The boy sniffed as he nodded.

The little man said, 'Tut tut,' and gave him his handkerchief. 'That's to remember me by, Jacket.'

Mr Torres and President Castro came from similar backgrounds. Their fathers had emigrated from Spain and had amassed largely by theft and violence estates of some ten thousand acres each in the west of Cuba. Both these sons of the landed had enjoyed an elitist education at the hands of the Jesuits. President Castro progressed to socialism while Mr Torres thought of himself as an aristocrat. Mr Dribbi invited Mr Torres to take breakfast in the kitchen to irritate him. Also because he considered it the least likely room to be subject to electronic eavesdropping.

First he dispatched the cook to the market and the maid to her housework, then he busied himself at the stove: coffee, scrambled eggs, freshly crisped bread. He sat the radio on the table tuned to a reggae station and switched on the liquefier. Satisfied with the noise level, he joined Torres at the kitchen table.

'Men are so gullible, Pedro,' he began with a little chuckle. 'Did I ever tell you that my size enabled me to sell my virginity once a week for nearly four years? That's how I made my initial stake. I have been in my present business ever since. In all these years, Pedro, I have never once been questioned by the police. I tell you this to impress upon you that I am a professional. Sometimes I fear that you are something of a dilettante.'

He had been sitting, shoulders hunched, studying his cupped hands. Now he looked up. His dark eyes were totally expressionless and his words, though spoken softly, bit with icy anger. 'Your associates have made fools of themselves. The boy tells me they were late at the rendezvous, then made a mess of kidnapping him. Who was the rescuer?'

Torres, so smart in his summer suiting, coughed into his coffee and had to wipe his lips before answering. 'A British insurance investigator who works for a Japanese agency. Apparently he lives on a yacht. There's no connection with us. The boy's father . . .'

'Nonsense,' Dribbi interrupted. 'The father's a runaway. Someone's mounting an operation against you. Perhaps against me. I wish this matter cleared up.' He tapped once with a finger on the tabletop. 'The boy intends digging the boxes up and leaving them for a fisherman to find. Have your men follow him. Don't touch him till he's done, then clean house.'

A sigh escaped the Cuban. 'Jesus Antonio?'

'Everyone,' Mr Dribbi said. 'Fetch in a team from outside.'

Pedro Torres called Jesus Antonio on his cellular phone. 'The child's going to do what we want all on his own. Follow, that's all.'

Mr Dribbi was a careful man. He laid the clothes he required out on the bed and watched the maid pack his suitcase. Then he sent her up the road to find a taxi. American Airlines flight 5718 landed at Dallas Fort Worth at 12:12. He was shepherded through customs and immigration by a member of the airline's flagship staff and settled into the Admiral's Club. His onward flight to Frankfurt, Germany, boarded at 14:20.

Meanwhile Pedro Torres flew Eagle to Miami. He expected to be back in Nassau by late evening.

'The rats are on the move,' O'Brien reported.

25

A nurse had brought Charity a pillow and blanket. Exhausted, she slept for six hours on a couch in the waiting room and was only awakened by the clatter of buckets as the cleaners started work. The smell of disinfectant and cheap floor polish was a reminder of university. For a moment she was disorientated. A nurse offered her coffee and she sat in the cubicle watching the night staff scurry to and fro as they prepared to hand over to the day shift.

The young American guarding Trent's room found her. His relief was due in twenty minutes. The Bahamian policeman's replacement had called in to say he would be late. The American had offered to wait: 'If you want to see your boyfriend, I'll fix it with my relief. Give me half an hour.'

Charity smiled her thanks. She was used to her role as Trent's lover; correcting the American wasn't worth the effort; nor would he have believed her.

The second American was black, small and battered. He gave Charity a grin more suited to one of her students than to a plainclothes cop.

Trent was lying in the same position. Charity presumed that nurses and doctors had been in and out through the night. Someone had put his coral beads on the side locker. She had never noticed the small leather sheath attached to the clasp. She supposed that his hair hid it. She slid the knife free and found it surprisingly heavy, the point sharp as a needle. The handle was simply an extension of the blade.

She flicked water from the carafe over Trent's face. She sensed the moment he awoke. Watching him was like waiting for an old 8086 computer to boot with the monitor turned off. At least a minute went by before he opened his eyes.

'Oh, it's you,' were his first words.

He reached for her hand, saw the knife and took it, tucking it under his pillow.

'I'm a little woozy,' he said. It was his excuse for having touched her – an automatic denial of any relationship. He felt the turban of bandages: 'What's the damage?'

She was angry at him for not asking if Jacket had escaped. 'Maybe concussion. They're going to take more X-rays.' He would find out so she told him: 'I gave the surgeon a hard time.'

He'd had a lot of practice in hospitals and kept his head still as he fumbled for his watch.

'Saturday morning, ten after six,' she said. 'They've got a couple of guards on the door. You're due to be deported.'

He didn't seem surprised. 'O'Brien?'

She nodded. 'I didn't tell him anything. You said if something happened to you.'

'You thought I meant something more final than a bump on the head?'

'Three bumps. Jacket got away – in case you're interested.'

He was silent for what seemed a long time. She said, 'I can't stay for ever. One of O'Brien's men let me in because he thinks we're lovers.'

'The boy, he'll go to the mail-boat . . .'

Trent would have said more but the white American stuck his head round the door. 'Lady, hide, will you. The doctors are coming.'

She hesitated.

The guard was close to panic. 'Lady, for my sake, huh? They'll have my balls. I've got a wife an' kids.'

She thought of ducking under the bed then realised that she would be seen when they checked the drain sack from the catheter. The wardrobe was the only alternative. Cramped in the dark, she couldn't decide whether to laugh or scream. She heard them transfer Trent to a trolley, then wheel him away. She waited five minutes then slipped out. The corridor was empty. She ran down through the gardens and across Shirley Street towards the mail-boat wharf under the bridge on Potter's Cay.

For Trent it was familiar territory. They took X-rays, shone lights in his eyes, checked his reflexes, changed the dressings. Watching the three doctors huddle, he was reminded of American sports coaches, heads together, their opinions whispered to keep the opposition in ignorance.

He wanted to protest that the doctors were on his team, that he had a right to be included in their conversation. They wouldn't have paid attention. Finally they summoned nurses to wheel him back to his room. A small black American and a large Bahamian accompanied the trolley.

The medics' leader said, 'You've had a good deal of luck over the years, Mr Trent. That's something that you shouldn't push unnecessarily. We'll keep you for a few more days. A minimum of movement.'

The doctor slid the palms of his hands against each other, admiring their smoothness as if he were a salesperson at the stocking counter at Harrods. 'Yes, rest, Mr Trent. Your girlfriend might be a mistake. We have an expression here in the Bahamas with which you may be familiar: to eat wasp. It implies a rough tongue, Mr Trent. Your young lady would appear to exist on a diet of particularly ferocious forest hornets.' The doctor smiled at his simile, delighted with himself, his superiority established. 'We'll give you something to help you rest, Mr Trent.'

The nurse slipped the needle into Trent's arm.

Trent's limbs weighed a ton when he awoke. His mouth felt and tasted as if it were stuffed with old socks. The catheter burned. A dull ache ran from the nape of his neck over the top of his skull into his right eye. He smelt someone in the room. He stirred, raising his right hand to his forehead, then slipped it under the pillow, feeling for the smooth steel his knife handle. He opened his eyes a crack so as not to destroy his vision with too much light.

O'Brien's stocky figure stood outlined against the window facing out over Paradise Island channel. Trent sighed and reached for the bell.

A nurse came and he told her to remove the catheter. When she protested that he must ask the doctor, he said, 'Do it, or I'll do it myself.'

O'Brien waited in the corridor while she complied.

'What was done to the boy out at Bleak Cay was a lot worse,' Trent said when the American returned. 'Put a guard on Jacket until you have the killer.'

O'Brien had taken up station again at the window. Perhaps he felt more at ease with something to look at or pretend to look at. He nodded at the bedside locker. 'I brought you a bunch of grapes.'

Trent closed his eyes. He needed to argue. The energy wasn't there.

195

He wondered if that was the drugs or whether he was getting old. The pain gave a little leap over the top of his scalp and stabbed him a quarter of an inch above the right pupil. He fumbled for the glass of lemon water on the locker.

'What did the boy do?' O'Brien asked.

'Hide the coke. That's a guess,' Trent said. 'He was out at the cay fishing for lobster when the plane crashed.'

The American nodded. 'The reception committee were late or broke down.'

There was no inflection the American's voice. Trent tried to understand. He rubbed a hand over his scalp to iron away the pain. It didn't do any good. He was tired and he wasn't sure that he wanted to understand.

O'Brien said, 'Did you ever think that a double might be a double double? Or be a double double without knowing that he was. Your man, Philby, for instance?'

'Because MI6 and the CIA were too dumb to catch him?'

'I believe in the dumbness,' O'Brien said with a slight smile. 'It's the man I can't believe in – being a traitor all those years.'

O'Brien drummed a little tattoo with his fingertips on the window: 'The problem we're into is all the layers. All the need-to-know shit. You end up not knowing enough to make a judgement except in office terms. It's not much of a proposition to sell to someone you respect.'

'Is this code for saying your man in Miami who arranged the sale of the plane was part of an operation?

'I don't know,' O'Brien said. 'These things come from different places. This one's out of New York. It's the receiver. We need him to have the coke in his hands. He's an amateur, used to the good life. Bright, capable of calculating the odds. We offer him a deal, we think he'll break.'

'He's a murderer,' Trent said.

'He wasn't when they set this thing up.'

It was always they. Trent wanted to warn O'Brien that he was taking the first step on to the slide. O'Brien had removed his spectacles and was polishing the lenses. He didn't have his briefcase with him. Perhaps the room was wired. It was the name of the game – covering with a record of what was said.

'Skelley knows?'

O'Brien didn't answer.

Trent said, 'You and Skelley are friends – or doesn't that mean anything?'

'I'm under orders.'

There had been a time when O'Brien had been choosy in what orders he obeyed. Also he had kept his spectacles in a metal case rather than on his nose. Three or four years and he'd be retired.

O'Brien threaded the wire frames back over his ears. 'We get the amateur, he'll give us a real pro. Man we've been after for a good many years,' he said. 'Not just drugs. Oil – an embargo breaker. There's strong Treasury and State Department interest.'

Trent was sure there was more to O'Brien's agenda. He had worked with the American in the past and knew how devious he could be. O'Brien would have his own target. Someone bigger than the embargo breaker. Trent could smell it in O'Brien now: the desire for a last few years in Washington behind a big desk – the desire to hear kids whisper behind his back that he had been a legend in the field. There had been a time when O'Brien had despised Washington. Trent remembered Anderson back in his hotel room struggling with his conscience. He said, 'And you drop Anderson down the tube.'

'Anderson has sticks in his hair,' O'Brien said. He removed his spectacles again. He didn't know what to do with them. He had already cleaned the lenses.

Trent wondered how well he could see without them.

'You've got a few sticks yourself,' O'Brien said. 'You rescue the boy. What does that tell the opposition? That they're under surveillance. Maybe even that they've been targeted. Your girlfriend's here. She wanted to get on the mail-boat with the boy!' His disgust was obvious. 'These are serious people, Trent, and you use a schoolteacher. You used to be a professional, for Chrissake.'

He turned away from the window. The light struck one side of his face, the other side was in shade. He stood very still as he looked down at Trent, the set of his shoulders square. 'I want you out of the way till this thing's over. Understood? And don't threaten me with the goddamn Japanese. Screw the Japanese. Buying real estate gives them the right to pay taxes, not control the US government or any part of it.'

'It's possible they haven't heard,' Trent said. The pain came again gouging deep into his right eye. It was a little better with his eyes closed. 'Go away,' he said.

He slept and was wakened by a nurse changing the drip bottle. Charity had replaced O'Brien at his bedside. Her fists were clenched and impatience gave an anguished twist to her shoulders. Trent thought that she might physically eject the nurse but she restrained herself until the door closed. Then she said, 'The police wouldn't let me on Potter's Cay.'

She had backtracked and crossed the bridge to a point directly above the mail-boat wharf.

'Jacket turned up with his bed. They loaded it on top of the wheelhouse. I yelled at him. He couldn't hear, there was too much wind.'

The police had fetched her off the bridge.

'They said they needed to check my evidence but that was crap. They were holding me till the mail-boat left.'

'They don't want you to get hurt,' Trent said.

She didn't believe him. 'They said you were sleeping. I had to wait two hours. What did the doctors say? Are you sick or have you given up?' She kicked her toes against the wall, scowling at him. 'Tell me so I know what to do. Or what attitude to take. There's no point waiting for you if you've given up.'

He didn't know.

'Everyone is important here except Jacket. All he is, is a black kid. No one gives a shit. They're going to use him as bait, right? Answer me, you son of a bitch.'

'White son of a bitch,' Trent said.

'And a comedian. Jesus!' She stuck her fingers into her hair and lifted it.

Trent watched the tight small curls open then spring back into place as she let go. He wanted her to go away, leave him in peace. There wasn't anything he could do. One person. This was a big operation. Anyone who got in the way would get crushed.

She said, 'There's a plane to Congo Town first thing in the morning but I'm out of cash.' She hated the admission. It was asking for help. Becoming a kept woman. 'In case you've forgotten, banks are closed Saturday and Sunday. I don't have credit cards.'

26

Steve and Jesus Antonio stood in the shadows of the quayside bar at Kemps Bay as the *Captain Moxey* docked.

The plastic wrapping failed to disguise the magnificence of Jacket's bed. The story of the small boy buying the bed for his mother spread to the quay and a crowd gathered to see it swung up on the derrick.

Dummy had co-opted his friend, Glasgow, an elderly fisherman with a skiff of the same size as the *Jezebel*. The two men had lashed poles across the thwarts of their boats to form a catamaran that would support the bed.

Unloading was too important a task for the boatswain. The captain assumed command as the deckhands, one at each corner, lifted the bed into the cargo net.

The chief engineer took charge of the donkey engine at the foot of the derrick. The engine coughed a couple of smoke rings then fired true, the single cylinder thumping powerfully.

The captain positioned himself at the foot of the bed, right arm raised, forefinger pointing aloft. A hush fell on the crowd as the finger slowly circled.

The engineer slipped the clutch on the winch and the line to the cargo net eased taut.

The captain checked the positioning of the hook in the net then again raised his arm.

Jacket bit on his knuckle as the bed slowly rose from the wheelhouse roof. The captain shoved his peaked cap back so that he could watch the bed swing up against the sky. The brass frame gleamed and there was a gasp from the crowd as the evening sun flashed off the mirrored headboard.

The engineer swung the derrick slowly to port carrying the bed out over the ship's gunwale. Ropes trailed from the bed legs. Two of the deckhands dived overboard and clambered on to the twin skiffs.

The clutch whined as the engineer eased the brake. Dummy, Glasgow and the deckhands grabbed at the ropes, leading the bed foursquare on to the floating platform aft of the mast steps. The crowd cheered as it settled. The men lifted the corners of the bed one by one, prying the cargo net free.

The engineer swung the derrick back and the captain beckoned Jacket to stand in the cargo hook. 'Keep tight hold of the rope, boy,' he warned as the engineer winched Jacket up.

Jacket looked down over the crowd. Sunlight flashed on spectacle lenses as a white man leaned clear of the shadows at the dockside bar; the angle of his jaw was frighteningly familiar, the receding hairline, the handkerchief. The same man had been in the gardens at the Princess Margaret Hospital when the kidnappers had tried to grab him. Jacket froze, shock loosening his grip on the rope. The crowd gasped as he grabbed with his other hand, hauling himself upright.

The gasp turned to renewed cheering as the engineer swung him out and down on to his bed. He grinned shyly, his wave hesitant. Already Dummy and the fisherman were lashing the bed down and stepping the masts. They cast loose and set the sails. The thin cotton sacking fluttered in the soft evening breeze, then filled and billowed out port and starboard. They had rigged a steering oar between the two hulls and Dummy squeaked at Jacket, gesturing him to take the helm as they ghosted away from the quay.

Jacket looked aft, straining to see into the shadow. His fear eased as they glided out into open water. He was at home on the sea. The spatter of water under the twin bows was comfortingly familiar as was the soft pressure on the scull. Nassau had been an aberration. The man with the handkerchief came from one of his fantasies.

A dozen skiffs with outboards followed, speedboats, a pair of Hobbie cats, three tourists on sailboards. A Bertram sports fisherman brought up the rear of the procession. A man on shore blasted on a conch. The skipper of a sixty-foot American motor yacht sounded his klaxon. The captain of the mail-boat accepted the challenge with three dots and a dash, V for victory.

Dummy and Glasgow waved and clapped Jacket on the back. He was safe now. They would be back at Green Creek by dawn. Then all he need do was sail out to Bleak Cay and uncover the boxes.

The strange craft made three knots as it crept down the coast with the night closing in. The sunset painted the western sky in layers of pinks and reds beyond the island; to the east the slow thrash of the surf beat on the outer reef.

Jacket lay asleep on the bed. He was in a dream of Bleak Cay, digging the boxes up only for the sand to crumble beneath them so that the more he dug the deeper they sank. Above the hole stood his mother, hands on her hips; beside her, the man in glasses with the handkerchief. Their faces were blank but laughter spilled from their open mouths. His father appeared opposite them and Jacket screamed a warning but he was too late. The side of the hole collapsed and his father disappeared into the sand. The man with the handkerchief stretched down a long thin arm and grabbed Jacket by the shoulder, shaking him. He came awake with a scream, slapping at Dummy's hand. His scream woke Glasgow.

The old fisherman saw the sweat streaming from the boy. He smiled kindly, touching Jacket on the shoulder. 'You all right, chile?'

Jacket nodded.

Glasgow wheezed as he chuckled at a thought he'd had while on watch. 'They goin' call you Bed Jacket now on.'

Jacket smiled weakly and looked away to the east. Dawn dyed the underside of a roll of clouds above the Tongue of the Ocean a pale rose.

'Goin' blow a storm 'fore de day finish,' Glasgow said. He signed to Dummy the clouds bursting and Dummy nodded and swung a finger from east to west, pointing above Andros at an angle of forty degrees, the sun time he expected the cloud to break.

As they headed in towards the point separating Green Creek from the Winterton house the sun lifted over the horizon and spilled a stream of molten gold, shimmering across the sea to lap against the white concrete blocks and warp the windows with flame.

A small flock of snowy plover rose from the mudflat beyond the point. The beat of their wings and their triple whistle pierced the background suck and spill of the sea. The yellow flash of a loggerhead shot between the trees and a pair of scissor-tail frigates took up station off Green Creek beach, waiting for the fishermen to clean their catch.

Dummy made his way to Jacket at the helm. The two elderly men stood by the sheets as the boy brought the bows round, jibing the sails. The rising sun struck the bed's headboard and lit the boy's face.

Fat Charlie was first of the fishermen to spot the makeshift catamaran. Soon skiffs were heading out and a small crowd grew on the beach. Looking north, Jacket recognised the blue of his mother's cotton work-dress on the path traversing the ridge to Mr Winterton's house.

The two men dropped the sails as Jacket brought the twin skiffs into the beach. Hands grabbed the bows, dragging the boats up the sand. Teeth flashed and questions spattered him: where had he bought the bed? how much had it cost? how had he fetched it over from Nassau? He found himself unable to speak and Glasgow answered for him.

Jacket flinched as he saw the constable shoulder his way through the throng. Already one of the men was slapping him on the back, calling him Bed Jacket. They wanted to see the bed, see it in all its glory. They wanted to be part of Jacket's legend.

The bed was lifted clear of the skiffs by a dozen men while a further dozen shouted conflicting instructions and warnings. The bed was no longer Jacket's. It had become public property. The men of the settlement carried it up through the palms, across the main street, and up through the first pines to the hut. Jacket's schoolmates pranced beside it. His new name had caught and become a chant.

'Bed Jacket, Bed Jacket,' the kids sang.

Silence fell as the men set the bed down in the sand yard at the foot of the front steps.

'Bigger dan de damn hut,' a man said.

Quaker Pete, the village carpenter, pushed his way to the front and mounted the steps. 'Jacket boy, you has de key dere?'

Jacket went round the back and entered through the rear door. He squatted on the floor. Seeping through the crack in the walls, the rays of sunlight showed him the poverty of their home. He didn't want people seeing inside. Already waves of laughter beat at him through the thin planks. He thought of Mr Dribbi's house.

The slap of bare feet mounted the rear steps and crossed the floor, big feet with splayed toes. 'You have yo'sel' a cry, boy. Notin' be shame of,' Quaker Pete said.

He was tall and broad, his voice soft as he lifted Jacket on to the plank bed. 'De Lord Jesus born in a stable, boy. You do a fine act. Dey goin' talk 'bout notin' else fuh year but how yo sail dat bed down from Nassau

202

Town. Yo dad goin' hear over in de Unite' State an' he goin' come home prou' of you, boy. Yo ma too when she back fro' de Winton house goin' kiss yo good. She goin' sleep fuhst time in year. Yes, sir,' he said with a slow nod. 'We goin' take dat door off. Me and Christian. We goin' take de ol' bed out an' we goin' put de new bed in. Don' worry yo head. We get it all fix 'fore yo ma get back. Yo jus' sit dere an' take yo'sel' a rest.'

Jacket couldn't rest. There were the boxes on Bleak Cay. He heard Quaker Pete chide the villagers outside and call to Christian over their heads to fetch tools from his workshop.

Peeping through a crack in the door, he saw the constable leaning against a tree. The constable wasn't part of the crowd so he was there for a purpose. Victor must have told someone that Jacket had seen the plane crash.

Jacket slipped out the back door and up the dune through the pines, then circled back to the beach. Dummy and Glasgow had unlashed the two skiffs. Jacket shoved the *Jezebel* off the sand and pushed the bows round. Raising the sail, he pointed the skiff out to the south of the sheltering coral.

The fear was back and he fought it with thoughts of his father and Quaker Pete saying that news of the bed would reach him over in the United States. Jacket knew that it wasn't true. He didn't care. He needed his father. He needed him this one more time.

Jacket's father was in Washington. He had sent the message by radio – the radio Jacket kept hidden up in the dunes behind the hut. The German raiders were coming that night. They would land by submarine first on Bleak Cay to pick up the explosives.

The fantasy grew layer on layer, shifting only to re-form. The man with the handkerchief was the Germans' guide. Jacket had to get there first, uncover the explosives, then set the fuse. When the Germans landed he would blow them up.

The breeze dropped. In the humid heat of the morning, the cloud bank thickened out over the Tongue of the Ocean. There was a threat in the clouds now, the grey centres loosening their spume into the rolling crests that hung over the deep waters.

Jacket could smell the storm ready itself to plunder the coast. He saw the submarine, dark and low, lying off the beach. Wind and rain tore at the palm trees as the soldiers spread along the shore line. They carried

203

their guns angled across their chests. Rain streamed down their faces, white in the lightning; their knuckles white and shiny; boots dripping as they crouched their way through the trees towards the scientists' camp. The perimeter lights flickered as the generator lost power to the storm. The new torpedo the Allied scientists had tested all that month on the range gleamed blue in its cradle as the lightning pried under the tarpaulin.

Jacket had warned the scientists that morning but they hadn't believed that the man with the handkerchief was a spy. He was one of their team. He had worked with them for months.

Jacket had brought the land mines in from the store on Bleak Cay and laid them along the tree line a hundred yards in from the beach. He had been a fool to go back for one last load from the store. Now it was too late to change direction. The submarine lay between him and Green Creek.

The cleaning team employed by Torres flew in by private plane from Miami, landing at a small strip on the Elutheras. There were four of them. They were exiles from Cuba, tidy men, middle aged, nondescript. One of them had been a pilot with the Cuban air force. Two served with the marines in Angola. The fourth had been a weapons instructor in the Cuban Special Forces. They had been employed to dispose of a Bahamian boy, a British insurance investigator, a retired Gringo banker from New York, a consumptive accountant from Colombia with US residency, the five-man crew of a Bertram 36. Their targets would be on Bleak Cay. A sixty-foot Cigarette day boat waited for them.

Skelley's sister, Lois, shook Trent awake. She was almost as tall and thin as her brother. She said, 'What's going on? You've been in the hospital two days and no one tells me. Now I find out someone's been sleeping in the office. A woman, according to the janitor.'

Trent tried to concentrate. His head throbbed and there was a sluggish feel both to his mind and to his body. Narrowing his eyes, he squinted at the corner of the window, forcing it into focus.

He said, 'How come the police let you in to see me?'

'The janitor called me at home.' Lois had used the radio and finally raised the *Golden Girl* only to reach her brother. 'He said I should check with cousin Ralph at immigration.' She shrugged. 'We're too small a country for secrets. Wilfred at police HQ said you saved a boy and were in the hospital. Janet at the US liaison office said the Americans want you on ice for a few days.'

She had called Trent's employer, Tanaka Kazuko, at Abbey Road's head office in Kyoto. Tanaka Kazuko had called a friend at the Japanese Foreign Ministry. Thirty-eight major Japanese corporations had opened financial services offices in the Bahamas. Were the climate to be thought unsympathetic, they could enjoy equally useful tax and trust regulations in Bermuda, the Dutch Antilles or the Cayman Islands.

Lois grinned. 'It didn't take long.'

A thought nagged at Trent. Something he had noticed without noticing. Twice he was nearly there only to have his concentration slip.

'So what do the doctors say?' Lois was asking.

They had replaced the catheter. The doctor had said, 'I know it's uncomfortable, Mr Trent, but we want you immobile a little longer.'

Lois was at the wardrobe, bundling up Trent's dirty clothes and hanging up a clean shirt and slacks. She took his wallet out. There were a few small bills. She said, 'Your Amex card's missing.'

He said, 'Charity must have taken it.'

Charity had caught the early morning flight to Congo Town and the bus on to Green Creek. The village seemed deserted with everyone up at Jacket's hut. Quaker Pete and Christian had lifted the front door off and were taking out the door frame. Jacket was missing. She turned and ran down to the beach. The *Jezebel* was missing. She looked out to sea. Clouds were building out beyond the reef. A 10hp outboard hung on the transom of Fat Charley's skiff. She waded out and checked the fuel tank.

Trent watched the nurse change the bottle. She was young and attractive and he smiled at her as she smoothed his hair back with a damp cloth. Then he remembered. It was the night nurse. Sweet dreams, she had murmured as she changed the bottle.

He could feel the world slipping away. He had to hold on and he had to be very careful. He closed his eyes. At the same time he dug his nails into his thigh. He heard the door close on the nurse. He pushed the sheet back and pulled the needle out. Then he slipped it back again under the bandage so that it looked as if it were still in his vein.

*

205

The American Airlines staff cosseted Mr Dribbi on the flight from Dallas Fort Worth to Frankfurt. He was escorted from the aeroplane by the airline's flagship staff and shepherded through to the waiting limousine. However, no amount of extra attention could entirely protect him from the weight of his years and he settled back into the rear seat of the Mercedes, a rug over his knees, and slept as the chauffeur cut round the city on to Autobahn 46 and the route to Zurich.

One of his eighteen grandsons accompanied Mr Dribbi on the road journey. Forty-six years old, he was a graduate of the French École de Mathématique and employed as a senior credit controller at the Dribbi Agriculture Fund and Produce Bank.

They were still two hundred and fifty kilometres short of the Swiss frontier when the grandson tapped at the glass partition and instructed the chaffeur to pull into an autobahnhof. Mr Dribbi was feeling poorly. He was helped up to a bedroom. A doctor was summoned from the nearby town.

'Exhaustion,' was the doctor's opinion. Ridiculous for a man of eighty-five to fly halfway round the world, then undertake a six-hundred-kilometre road journey. The doctor made plain his opinion of the grandson, his selfishness and lack of caring for the tiny old man.

A gentle heart stimulant and a large bill were administered by the doctor. A half hour later an English travelling salesman slipped out of his room on the second floor. A man in his early sixties, he was marked as a patent failure by his blue serge suit which was shiny at the knees and elbows and along the edges of the collar and front. His tie was equally worn, as was his shirt. He was clean, however, and tidy, his hair and moustache clipped short, black shoes properly polished, his clothes carefully pressed despite their age.

The grandson spotted him on the stairs, signalled, and let him into Mr Dribbi's room. 'Mr Brown, Grandfather.'

Mr Dribbi beckoned him to the bed.

Mr Brown said, 'You're very kind, Mr Dribbi, not to pick a younger man.'

'I rather hope you'll last me out.' Mr Dribbi gave one of his little chuckles and pressed a photograph and a slim brown file cover into Mr Brown's hands. The Englishman stared at the photograph for perhaps half a minute before turning to the file. There were two sheets of paper: one showed the plans of a house and its grounds, the other listed general information as to security, the staff and the possible contents of the rooms.

'Quickly, and a very thorough job, if you please, Mr Brown,' Mr Dribbi said.

'Indeed, sir, very thorough.' Having returned the photograph and file to Mr Dribbi, Mr Brown fetched a small brown cardboard suitcase from his room, paid his bill and drove back along the autobahn towards Frankfurt in his ancient black Volkswagen Golf.

27

The needle had leaked half the drip bottle. The wet sheet woke Trent. He lay very still, sampling the pain that remained in his head. He squinted at the door frame, following the sharp edge up and over and down the other side. His vision was good and the pain was little more than a normal headache. Charity had accused him of giving up. It wasn't that simple. To begin with there were two men on guard outside his door. It was only a detail, of course, a detail that Charity had overlooked. She would be on South Andros by now. So would Jacket. Firing off half-cocked wouldn't help either of them. He had to backtrack.

He began with the attempted kidnapping. He put himself in the thoughts of the organiser. The receiver had failed to pick up the cargo. The aeroplane had crashed. Murder. The failed kidnapping.

He reviewed the power structure. The soldiers who had fluffed the kidnapping, the amateur from New York, the embargo breaker, O'Brien's quarry. Add the exporters and the importers, perhaps a boatman or two, a private detective. It was all very messy.

He understood the DEA. They wanted to hide any scandal behind a good arrest. He wondered why they had left him his knife. He fumbled for it under the pillow, feeling the familiar cool of the clean steel.

Perhaps no one who had seen the knife had recognised it as a weapon. Perhaps leaving it was an oversight.

On O'Brien's part? Never.

Who had O'Brien picked as his ticket to Washington? Some big establishment figure, an untouchable? Too risky for this new O'Brien. No, the target would be someone they had been trying to entrap for years, someone they had almost given up on. Someone so careful, he'd become a myth. Anyone that careful would be very upset by the mess. He would be cleaning house.

For a moment Trent wondered whether conscience had made O'Brien leave him his knife for self-defence. It didn't matter. He reached for his watch – 14:10. He was surprised. The sombre light had made him think it much later. He swung his feet to the floor and looked out of the window into the cloud face. Not a breath of air stirred the treetops in the gardens below – it was that hour before the breaking of a Caribbean storm. He needed clothes, money, transport out to the airfield – say half an hour minimum, a further half hour to find a plane and pilot willing to cross to South Andros, and an hour's flying time. The way the weather looked, there wasn't a hope.

He pulled on the shirt and slacks Lois had left and slipped his feet into his boat shoes. There was just the one chair. Picking it up in both hands, he stood with his back to the wall on the left side of the doorway so that he would be hidden. Then he hurled the chair through the window.

Two plainclothes cops, one black, one white, burst into the room, saw the broken window, cursed and charged over to look down into the gardens.

Trent was out of the door and down the corridor before they realised they had been tricked. Though he needed to conserve energy, he jogged up the back through the hospital car park and over the ridge before hitting the road. A cab dropped him at the mall and he called Lois from a phone booth. He hummed the Beatles melody 'Yellow Submarine' while he waited and went on humming a few bars when she answered, then switched to the theme from *Bridge Over the River Kwai*. She hung up after the first bar.

He found a cab outside the mall and had the driver drop him a mile further inland. Then he walked a block and caught a bus back to the foot of the Paradise Island toll bridge and walked to the top where he stood leaning against the parapet, watching the yachts and fishing skiffs scurry back to their berths in the marinas. The rain would come in another three quarters of an hour. He wanted to ride the front.

Lois picked him up in her Ford Fiesta. She had borrowed her neighbour's dog to explain the bedspread on the rear seat. Trent lay flat on the floor with the bedspread covering him.

Lois pulled into the marina, drove round the dock and parked. Tanaka Kazuko's powerboat, the *Yellow Submarine*, lay at the outer end of the last pontoon. Painted bright yellow, she was a Sunseeker 45 Apache day boat powered by triple Mercruiser 500 gasoline engines. On a flat sea she was capable of seventy knots. Trent's employer used her three or four times a year to impress clients. Trent acted as skipper.

Lois had picked up the keys from the office safe. She looked very unhappy. 'The Beretta's missing.'

'I had it,' Trent said.

'You're sure you know what you're doing?'

Trent was anything but sure. He said, 'I think there's going to be a mess. See if you can reach O'Brien. Tell him to get a heavy squad down to Bleak Cay right away.'

The elderly marina attendant jogged round from the club house. 'She all fill up, Mistuh Trent.' He squinted at the cloud bank. 'De Japanes genleman guh be good an' mad if you hackle up de *Submarine*.'

Trent vaulted on to the bathing platform and made his way forward through the cockpit to the controls. There were three racing seats mounted on hydraulic shock absorbers. He switched on the exhaust fan first to clear the bilges of any fumes. Then he fitted the keys and fired the triple engines. The boatman had cast off the stern lines and followed him on board, squeezing along the narrow side-deck to the bows.

Trent gave the engines a couple of minutes to warm before giving him a nod. The boatman unsnapped the bow line shackle and stepped over on to the next yacht.

'Have a nice day, Mistuh Trent,' were his parting words as Trent eased the big day boat out of its berth.

Clearing the marina entrance, Trent settled himself into the helmsman's seat and buckled the safety-harness before thrusting the triple throttles open. The exhausts roared and the huge power rammed the Sunseeker's bows out of the water. She gave a little shimmy of her stern as the propellers drove the transom down and lifted her bows. Then her bows levelled out, slapping the ripples, rose again, quivered, then, as Trent adjusted the trim tabs, steadied and drove straight down channel like the point of a dagger.

The hull of the *Yellow Submarine* weighed over five tons. The engines weighed a further one and three quarter tons. She carried three tons of gasoline and a quarter of a ton of water. With her engines turning at three thousand rpm, the speedometer indicated fifty-five mph. She was forty-five feet long on the deck. Only the after seven feet of her hull touched the water. The channel was clear ahead and Trent eased the revs up to four thousand, the speed to sixty.

Glancing for a moment at the cloud he calculated that he had half an hour. It wasn't enough. He opened the throttles a further half inch and the speedometers crept to seventy. At that speed a floating log, even a lobster pot awash ahead, could hurtle the yacht out of control.

The purple black of the cloud bank split the sky into dark and light. He could feel the weight of the approaching storm. It seemed to tilt the *Yellow Submarine* to starboard. He yanked the safety-harness tighter over his shoulders as the boat shot out of the channel. There was a slight oily roll to the sea now and the *Yellow Submarine* leapt and slammed from low crest to low crest. The weight, as she slammed, shook the hull. Thick padding and the shock-absorbers that supported the seat cushioned Trent, nevertheless the smash of the hull against the water punched up through his feet into his spinal column. The shock knifed the pain over the top of his skull and down into his right eye. He counted out loud to blank out the pain. He counted to one hundred then started again. He had no time to think now of anything but the boat and the sea ahead. The careful procession of numbers built a barrier behind which he crouched, one hand on the wheel, the other playing the throttles as he fought to marry the speed of the boat to the wave pattern. He felt the boat as his father had taught him all those years ago to feel a horse between his thighs. He had to be one with the machine. Any separation, however minuscule and even for the smallest fraction of a second, could bring disaster. Each different tremble of the hull or change in vibration of the engines carried a message to which he had to respond instantly and without thought. An hour and a half to Bleak Cay if he could outrun the storm.

There was no definition to the sun above Bleak Cay. Rather the haze had split it into ring upon ring of ever paler light that spread across ten degrees of the afternoon sky. In the distance the first rain squalls showed as ragged scraps of black net against the deep grey of the curling cloud bank. There was no wind yet to bring the scent of the rain and the sullen stillness of the humid air lay heavy across the Great Bahama Bank. A slow swell lifting from the north-east seemed separate to the slack and oily surface of the sea. Even the surf out on the edge of the Tongue of the Ocean seemed muffled by the weight of the approaching storm.

The gulls, the oystercatchers and plovers had long since fled to the protection of the pine woods and mangrove swamp on Andros. Now nothing moved except for the black skiff, Jacket at the oars.

High tide and Jacket rode a slow swell in towards Bleak Cay. A grey peak of rock on the shore in line with a thick clump of grass was his first mark, then hard to port for two strokes on the oars, swing straight, ten degrees port, then hard to starboard, straighten and run through the last of the coral into the lagoon.

The surface of the lagoon shimmered black and pathless beneath the spread sun. The stillness isolated the skiff and magnified the squeak of the oiled wood against the pintals, the drip of the blades and the sound of his own rapid breathing.

Jacket beached the skiff and stood for a moment on the shore, hunting his bearings. He had hidden the boxes at night. Now, in this strange light, the heat twisted the crest of the cay and there was almost no shadow. He felt Vic's presence and he shivered as he climbed the low spine. A purr drew his attention north, heat warped the sea so that for a while all he could see was a white arrowhead slipping and sliding through the layers of mirage. The arrow was on a heading to leave Bleak Cay well to its east.

The first flash of lightning cut across the face of the cloud. He counted, a mile for each second – four, five, six. Then the thunder broke deep and rolling. He turned back to watch the arrow melt and swell in the heat. The shape of it was clear for a few seconds – a sports fisherman with a tender in stern davits. He saw a flutter of white as two matchstick men stowed the awning on the fly-bridge.

A trickle of breeze stirred through the clumps of coarse grass; he felt it cool on his spine and in his armpits as it dried his sweat. The breeze brought the scent of rain, fresh and rich. He glanced up at the sun, faint now in the deepening haze but still pulsing in the centre. Another flash tore across the deep grey of the cloud, then another. The twin blasts of thunder chased and intertwined so that the explosion gained intensity as it broke over the cay.

Jacket shivered as the wind lifted the back of his shirt and pried into his trouser legs. The surface of the sand shifted, rivulets formed and built tiny drifts against the roots of the grass clumps.

Foolish tourists, he thought as he watched the sports fisherman. The boat was making twenty knots over the glossy water. He could see the dark lines of the spray chines veering back from the bows. The chines flung two wings of glistening spray arcing out over the darkness of the sea and he could hear the deep purr of the big gas engines. She was too small a boat to be out in the coming storm and he wanted to stand and wave and shout at the skipper to head back for shelter into the lee of Andros's west coast. Instead the boat swung in a slow curve in towards the south-east side of Bleak Cay.

There was no entrance to the lagoon and the cay was too low to protect the boat from the wind. However, she would be sheltered from the worst of the seas as long as her anchor held. Jacket lay flat on the crest of the cay watching.

Though only thirteen years old, he was expert in the ways of the sea and watched with a critical eye. The skipper needed to drop his hook at the midway point along the south-east edge of the reef to avoid the waves that would soon curl round the ends of the lagoon. There was good sand outside the reef, deep against the coral. The shelter of the cay would give a circle of safety perhaps eight hundred feet in diameter. He could see the skipper now up on the fly-bridge. He had expected him to be white rather than the black blob that showed below the white cap. The boat was a Bertram 36.

Far in the distance another boat raced south, a sixty-foot Cigarette – the imported cleaning team. One of the ex-marines sat at the wheel. The other three Cuban exiles squatted in the cabin checking their weapons.

A further hour behind, the *Yellow Submarine* leapt and slammed over the smooth swell. Trent didn't dare look round for even a moment but he could feel the front of the storm press on his shoulders, the cold and the scent of the rain.

The storm sped out of the north-east. Charity had seen the Bertram 36 slip into the lee of Bleak Cay. She had no time left to make for shelter. She tilted Fat Charlie's outboard, lifting the propeller clear of the water and grabbed the sculls, thrusting the bows of the skiff into the twisting channel that opened to the lagoon. The *Jezebel* lay on the beach. She shouted for Jacket.

The first heavy drops of rain hit the backs of Jacket's legs and left dark circles on the sand. He looked over his shoulders into the black wall of cloud as lightning ripped its face. There was only a second's pause before the thunder slammed down on him. The sand seemed to shiver and throb under the explosion.

The crest of the wall broke over the sun and the rain came blasting in across the lagoon. He drew the legs of his shorts tight to stop the wind driving the rain up his thighs as the curtain swept over him and hid the Bertram.

In the moment of the boat's disappearance, Jacket recalled the man with the spectacles and the handkerchief peering at him from the shadows at Kemps Bay as the engineer swung him aloft on the cargo hook – and the Bertram 36 that had followed up at the rear of the flotilla that had accompanied him the previous evening.

He lay shivering in the dark of the storm, hands cupped over his nose and mouth so that he could breathe in the downpour. Visibility had shrunk to a few yards. Lightning whipped through the darkness. Thunder was almost continuous. As the rain collected, torrents carved gashes in the sand.

Jacket crawled down towards the dune where he had buried the boxes. When he had first landed, the heat and strange light had confused him. Now he was half blinded by the rain which pounded the vegetation flat so that none of the marks remained. Lost, he fought his way to the beach against the full force of the wind. He found the rock where he had hidden the skiff the night of the crash and retraced his course to where he had left the pilot, then turned inland at an angle and marched steadily in short steps, as he had that first night with the boxes, along the slope, counting as he marched – a hundred and twenty-two steps.

He tripped on a root and the wind tossed him tumbling down the face of a dune. Desperate now, he dug like a dog into the underlip only to discover the sand empty. Thunder drowned the footsteps of his pursuers. The wind whipped away their cries as they sought him along the shore. Lightning knifed at him out of the twilight. There was only one man who could help and Jacket turned to him, no more than a vague dark shape in his parachutist's uniform, the colonel's stars on his shoulders and the three rows of medal ribbons hidden in the gloom.

'Start again,' his father urged quietly. 'Keep low. Hunt for the remains of the picnickers' fire.'

Jacket obeyed orders, again marching the 122 steps. Then he stopped and searched the sand for the stains of charcoal. A black leak across the grey lead him to the dune and he dug hurriedly. The mines were there.

Solder sealed the tops of the canisters – hours of work to open them and pour out the poison gas the Russians planned to use in the attack. His last hope was to lay a chain of mines across the island, a chain that would lead the attackers to the store. Then Jacket could detonate the stockpile, killing them all.

He carried the first mine to the top of the cay and rolled it down towards the beach, the wind driving it. He fetched a dozen mines in all. Then he set a further seven down from the peak to the dune where the rest were buried. Five more and the line crossed the cay from east to west. The landing party must detonate the mines no matter the direction of their attack. Jacket's duty was to escape and warn headquarters.

He slipped down the beach towards the skiff. He kept low as his father had ordered. He listened, through the thunder, to the surf crash on the edge of the lagoon and the waves break up the beach. The waves would be eight foot high on the reef. The wind was gusting at eighty knots. He had as much hope of escaping out through the channel as he had of flying.

He crept along the sand, feeling for a familiar landmark that would tell him the depth of water. An hour to high tide and the gale was driving the sea into the lagoon. Already the water had risen two feet above the morning's high water mark. The water would pour westward out over the reef as the tide turned and the wind dropped. That was his one chance to escape – to ride the tide out over the coral directly under the guns of the enemy fleet. Turning, he scrambled back and lay, his hands cupped round his eyes, watching for the landing party to appear out of the rain.

28

They were seven on board the Bertram: Steve and Jesus Antonio, the boatman and the four failed kidnappers. They had waited for the constable at Green Creek to call. Then, sure that the kid was on his way out to Bleak Cay, they had cut west through Middle Bight before heading south.

The boatman had taken his time threading the sports fisherman through the shallows to the west of Andros. Rounding the point, they had spotted through binoculars the skiff against the almost black background of the approaching storm. The kid had borrowed a small outboard.

Steve had wanted to grab him at sea but the boatman had refused. The storm was coming fast and he wanted to get the Bertram safe into the lee of Bleak Cay with both anchors out. The rain swept in like a wall across the cay then slammed into the anchored yacht. A splash of surf on the edge of the lagoon showed through the murk and gave the boatman a mark. He stood huddled in the wheelhouse watching to see if the anchors dragged as the sports fisherman bucked and veered under the thrashing of the storm.

The stink of hot engine oil permeated the cabin. The four Bahamians read in Steve's face that he wanted to retch. They winked and grinned at each other. Black apes, he thought. Every damn thing had gone wrong. Now they were close to success and Steve was determined to stop the kid escaping.

He said, 'One of us has to get ashore and make sure of the skiff.'

'Den dat man goin' be you,' one of the Bahamians said. His companions chuckled.

They had no respect for Steve. He thought of appealing to Jesus Antonio. The Hispanic hid behind his handkerchief, his face pale as typing paper in the gloom of the cabin. Steve wondered if he was dying. There were drugs for TB. Antibiotics. It had to be more serious. AIDS, Steve conjectured as he recalled wondering if Jesus Antonio and the Cuban were lovers. The diagnosis fitted the Hispanic's look of exhaustion, his skeletal shape undisguised by what clothes he wore.

Steve wondered if Torres was infected. If so, Steve had less time to infiltrate the financial structure than he had expected. He thought of the two men dead. It was going to happen. He was sure suddenly and felt a familiar surge of power. He would allow nothing to stand in his way. Looking across the cabin at the biggest of the Bahamians, he said, 'You can swim. Come on. The two of us can make it into the lagoon.'

Challenged, the big man shrugged and pushed himself up off the seat. The others watched as Steve wrapped his Ruger and a box of shells in a plastic bag.

'Dat a chile we affer,' the big man said and again the others chuckled. However, they were less contemptuous now as they watched Steve push his way out into the storm.

'Yo out yo mine?' the boatman demanded as Steve shouted at him above the wind to lower the small whaler from the transom davits. Only the boundary of coral surrounding the lagoon frightened Steve. Once into the lagoon, they could make the shore.

He ordered the big man into the bows of the whaler to keep her from being flipped by the wind. Starting the 20hp outboard, he signalled the boatman to cast them off. The gale grabbed them as they eased out from the lee of the Bertram. Blinded by the driving rain, Steve almost lost control. As he opened the throttle, luck more than skill forced the bows into the wind.

Steve steered straight at the low surf driven out of the lagoon against the reef. He didn't care where he hit. He needed speed, that was all, enough speed to slide them over into clear water. The weight of the Bahamian forward held the bows down as they plunged into the line of waves. Coral ripped at the whaler's bottom. The outboard kicked up. Steve ran forward and dived flat. His right foot struck as he kicked, then he was through into the lagoon. He didn't look for the Bahamian. The big man could take care of himself.

Less than a hundred yards to the shore – three lengths of the Olympic pool: Steve swam with the style taught him at private school, six beats of his legs to each stroke. He reached the beach and knelt, staring up through the rain at the flattened tufts of grass on the dune ahead.

Charity had to fight to hold the skiff on course as the wind drove her into the lagoon. She shouted Jacket's name as she plunged the oars into the water, thrusting the heavy skiff towards the beach. She ran ashore beside the *Jezebel*.

The rain half blinded her as she faced into the gale to drag the skiff's bows up the sand. She turned inland, forearm sheltering her eyes, and shouted again. Thunder drowned her voice. She considered searching for the boy but the rain had washed away any hint as to the direction he had taken. Fear might drive him out to sea if he returned to the *Jezebel* and found a second boat. Better to wait and she lay low in the lee of Fat Charlie's skiff, the rain driving over her. She thought of Trent safe in the hospital.

Driven by the wind, the swells chased the shaped transom of the forty-five-foot Sunseeker south down the Tongue of the Ocean. The *Yellow Submarine* was equipped for fair-weather picnics on sheltered beaches. Her hull and engines were massively constructed but there were no spinning discs mounted in the windscreen to toss aside the sea and rain that burst against the steeply angled glass. Trent stood at the wheel, his feet planted on the deck so that he could absorb the motion of the boat and see over the foredeck. Half blinded, he navigated by feel, running the day boat at maximum speed for the conditions, playing the throttles and the wheel so that she surfed down the face of the seas at an angle of thirty degrees, then surged fast to the top of the wave ahead. A moment of inattention and he would bury the bows in the swell ahead. The next swell would catch the stern and throw the powerboat broadside on for the following sea to swamp and bury.

To the west he saw through gaps in the rain the white wall of surf thundering on to the barrier reef. He had to cross the surf to reach Bleak Cay. The few gaps were hidden in the storm. However, the tide was already high and the wind was driving the sea on to the Great Bahama Bank, the water abnormally deep. If he could pick the gap off Congo Town he could run south inside. The faster he drove the Sunseeker, the less water she would draw. At full speed only the out-drives would project below the surface. Eighteen inches.

*

Something struck the skiff lightly. Charity peered over the hull. A shadow crouched looking down at her from a low dune above the beach. 'Jacket . . .?' she called tentatively.

The shadow was too big.

Rising out of the sand, a white man fought his way down against the wind. She recognised him as he reached the foot of the dune. He was the smaller of the two Americans staying at the Winterton house. Not even the dark of the storm could hide his surprise: 'Miss Johnston . . . from the school.'

She didn't understand what he was doing on Bleak Cay. Then she saw the revolver. It was the biggest handgun she had ever seen. She had the advantage of the rain behind her. As she ducked and turned to run, a thick black arm slammed round her throat and yanked her off her feet. She gasped in terror, then lashed out with her bare feet. Her assailant chuckled and shook her as if she were a dog. 'Yo behave, lady 'fore I kick yo head in.'

'Get her off the beach before the boy comes,' the American snapped. He searched the skiffs and found a length of cord and a torch. He put the torch in his pocket, then followed the big Bahamian up the dune into a hollow. The Bahamian held Charity while the American tied her hands behind her back. Then he looped the cord round her neck and pulled it so that she had to hold her hands high or throttle herself.

The American was enjoying himself. Steve – that was his name. She knew he was going to kill her. Not right away. Later, after he'd had his fun. The way he had killed Vic. Fear sucked the last of the warmth out of her body. She tried not to shake. She had to think. There was nothing she could do for herself. Jacket – she had to warn him.

Jacket lay on the spine of the cay, peering westward through the murk to where he knew the Bertram heaved and tugged at its anchor. The scene shifted in Jacket's imagination: sometimes the Bertram was a patrol boat, sometimes a submarine, German, Russian, Japanese, Vietnamese. He recalled a dinghy hanging in the stern davits. They would need to launch it to ferry the boxes out. Heading into shore against the wind was impossible – the gale would flip the tender bow over stern. So the crew were still on board.

Jacket crouched low as he reached the beach and scurried south to where he had left the *Jezebel* behind the dune. He kept to the water to hide his footmarks, following the line of burst foam along the sand. The sea warmed his bare feet while the rest of his body shivered in the wind.

He was a scout for the main party. If they caught him, they could shoot him as a spy. Jacket's father was senior officer of the forty rangers imprisoned in the island camp. Jacket had found them. Now he had to get the news back to base. To do so he had to sail the skiff below the guns of the fort and slip the blockade. His only hope was to do so now under cover of the storm.

The sea had risen well above normal high water and he was certain that he could float out over the reef. If he lay in the bottom of the skiff and let the storm drive him clear . . . then ship a scull aft and angle the skiff at thirty degrees to the wind until he gained the lee of Andros.

Easy, he thought.

Tell everyone in the village that he had seen boxes on Bleak Cay. He would start in the store, then Quaker Pete's workshop, Mr Jack's bar. Tell the constable and the schoolteacher last of all.

He thought of his mother. With the storm battering the ridge, she would stay at Mr Winterton's house overnight. Jacket would be safe home before she returned. Once again he tried to imagine her first reaction to seeing the bed but the video stuck, blurring the frame, and he switched back to his father as he had last seen him squatting close to the prison compound perimeter. He had lost weight but otherwise seemed in good health. He wore a camouflage cap, the peak pulled low. His teeth, as he whistled softly at a parrot in a tree on the outside of the fence, were very white in the shadowed black of his face. He had played with a short piece of stick, flicking it up and down as he whistled. One of the guards up in the tower watched him. Twenty yards of swept dirt separated the fence from the undergrowth where Jacket lay. Mines were buried in the dirt, there were trip wires and the fence was electrified.

Stealing the patrol boat was the only hope. If he could bring the boat close inshore, sling the anchor over the wire and rip the fence down.

He reached the dune behind which he had hidden the *Jezebel* and, rounding it, saw a second skiff and a shadow poised above it. For a moment he thought that the shadow was part of his fantasy. Then came the crash of a rock smashed through the bottom of the boat.

Jacket screamed. He turned and ran up the slope, ducking and weaving through the scrub. They would search for him now and he threw himself down, trying to think. First how many of them? The Bertram sports

220

fisherman was too small to carry enough men for two lines spanning the width of the cay. The hunters would sweep from one end or the other, searching the scrub and the hollows.

He had fled south from the *Jezebel*. Now he doubled back to the line of boxes. Though the rain washed most of his tracks away, he remained careful as he searched for a vantage point, where possible keeping to the grass clumps. He found a hump close to the western shore. Searching he found two flat rocks. He part buried them as stepping stones on the beach, a yard apart. Now all he could do was wait and hope that finding the boxes would distract the search party.

The Cigarette slid out of the dusk. The helmsman was expert. He slammed the boat alongside the Bertram tumbling the crew to their knees. The other three Cubans leapt on board. One of them shot the boatman in the wheelhouse, the other two hosed the interior of the cabin. Only Jesus Antonio survived. He had been in the head.

He had expected the cleaning team. It made sense. He would like to have known if Torres had given the order or whether it came from higher up. The dying didn't matter to him – now, quickly, or in the hospital in six months with tubes trailing in every direction. His money was well hidden and amply sufficient to keep his mother in the condo he had bought her in Naples, Florida, and to finance his brother and two sisters through college, give them a better start than he had enjoyed – the good life, he thought.

Racial loyalty delayed the bullet. The Cuban even gave a small nod of acknowledgement and Jesus Antonio answered with one of his narrow smiles, a sort of mutual introduction, one professional to another.

'There's no need to kill the boy. He doesn't know anything,' Jesus Antonio said. This late, it was the best he could do for his immortal soul. He saw the Cuban's finger tighten. He needed to cough and he would like to have crossed himself. He hadn't time.

Steve had wanted to search for Jacket. The big Bahamian had insisted they wait for the rest of the men to disembark.

'De skiff smash. Where de boy go?'

Steve hadn't sufficient authority to argue. He threw Charity on her belly in a hollow above the Bertram's anchorage. Rain cloaked the boat. Bahamians hated rain. Dumb idiots, they would have to swim to shore so

221

what difference did the rain make? They were so goddamn lazy. He hated them. He hated their colour, their fat-lipped flat-nosed features, their belief in their physical superiority, their arrogance. Jesus! How he hated them. Goddamn niggers with delusions of grandeur because they'd inherited a bunch of islands from their masters that weren't worth shit without the white Americans who built and owned anything that mattered, houses, hotels, golf courses, banks, the whole goddamn lot.

She could feel the rage build in the American. Every few minutes he kicked her in the ribs. She kept picturing Trent dodging the cars as he raced up Shirley Street. She had seen people run in just that way to catch a bus. She wanted Trent right now. She wanted him and she hated him because thinking of him gave her moments of false hope. There was no hope.

She didn't want to die. There was a dreadful fear in her, fear of the pain that would come first. Somehow she had to make it quick. She thought of doing something that would make Steve kill her. However, there was Jacket. She was his teacher. Despite her fear, there remained in her a stubbornness and pride and anger that together fuelled her determination to save the boy. She had sailed out to Bleak Cay to save him. It was all that she could ever achieve. She wouldn't allow the American to deprive her of that one victory. She thought of the book of fishes that had been her constant companion in much the same way as the bed must have filled Jacket's imagination. She thought of the neatly catalogued photographs in her room behind the schoolhouse. She wondered whether anyone would use them. She pictured Trent picking through them, studying her files. She imagined his guilt.

The storm front had run well to the south and what had been a solid blanket of rain had begun to shred, giving Trent glimpses of South Andros. A few lights sparkled along the shore. Dark cloud sped low across the sea, streamers whipping at the crest of the island that showed as a long low lump against the slightly paler sky to the west.

He visualised the gap in the reef leading into Congo Town. It wouldn't look the same with the surf high and driven from the north. He would be broadside on to the waves pounding across the channel entrance, immensely vulnerable.

He would have greater control heading into the sea than surfing the

222

waves. To do so he would have to turn the Sunseeker through one hundred and eighty degrees. He had never taken the *Yellow Submarine* out in such conditions and was incapable of judging how she would behave. He required a smooth swell to spin on. The waves were hard to judge in the deepening dusk. If he judged badly a steep wave would fall on the powerboat.

He tried to absorb the rhythm of the swell as he ran on past the settlement. He had banished Charity and the boy from his thoughts. His concentration was on the helm and the lift of the *Yellow Submarine*'s stern as he slowed to allow the seas to run on under the hull. Twice a wave passed that would have served. He thought that he had the feel of their approach. Another came, the same slightly more sluggish rise. As the wave lifted the hull he dragged the wheel hard over and nudged the throttle so the propellers kicked the stern round.

The sea dropped away and the next came at him. It was a solid wall fifteen feet high capped by a white crest already curling to pounce on the deck. There was no way over the top. He slammed the throttles open and held to the wheel, his backside braced against the edge of the seat. Fifteen hundred horsepower punched the Sunseeker into the wall. The yacht shuddered as the massive weight smashed down into the open cockpit. He was in the wave, ten feet of water above his head, a mile and a half of sea below his keel. He had to hold the wheel steady or he was lost and he was done for if the engines faltered. He felt the bows leap free. Then the cockpit rose and he burst into the air.

The *Yellow Submarine* shook herself loose of the tons of water cascading off the deck and out of the cockpit. He heard the whine of the automatic bilge pumps. The next wave was ahead. Less steep. No breaking cap. He had no time to think, no time to assess the damage. The motors were running. That was all that mattered. Already his hand was on the triple throttles, cutting power as the bow rose. Still the water sluiced off the deck and out over the transom. For a second the powerboat hung poised on the rounded crest of the huge swell. He saw the lights on the coast. He drew the bow over to starboard ten degrees, then straightened her again to meet the next wave.

The turbulence increased as he edged slowly towards the reef, the seas were more broken, the waves more threatening. Twice more he was caught by a breaking crest but he was in control now and knew how the Sunseeker would react to the controls. On this course the wind whipped the water off the windscreen and he was able to strap himself back into the helmsman's seat.

He looked again at the surf. He couldn't do it on his own. He had one chance. He slid back the waterproof panel protecting the VHF switch and microphone and called the coastguard station on Nassau Point. He needed both hands on the controls a dozen times and had to drop the mike. Finally he got his message through: Call the police station at Congo Town and get someone down to the beach with a spotlight or a car.

'I'll come in on a bearing of two twenty degrees,' he told the coastguard.

'Man, dis wedder, dat a bad-bad entrance, dere no way you make it,' the wireless operator protested.

'Thanks for the encouragement,' Trent said. He dropped the mike as the *Yellow Submarine* slid down into the next valley. A wave charged at him, steep as the first. He met it straight as the crest slammed down on his head. He surfaced coughing water and half blind. The yacht rose and he grabbed for the mike. The wave had ripped it off. He swore and looked to the shore then down at the compass. He had allowed ten degrees to give the police time.

A squall slammed the top off the next wave. He rubbed the back of his arm across his eyes. Tension tore at the muscles across his shoulders.

Two degrees more and the police would be too late. Bahamians were infamous for their lack of speed. However, they were the best sailors of small boats in the world. The duty constable would understand what was at stake. If the coastguard had got through on the telephone; if the constable was in the police station rather than playing dominoes. Trent cursed again. He had forgotten it was Sunday night. There wasn't a chance in hell of finding a policeman on duty.

He hadn't a doubt that the boy had gone to Bleak Cay. He was equally certain that Charity had chased after him. And the killer would be on their tails. So there wasn't an option. His only chance was to take it fast. It wasn't a proper chance but it was the right thing to do – get the *Yellow Submarine* up out of the water. He knew what would happen if he missed the entrance but he didn't think about it.

He shoved the throttles forward and took her in along the top of the first swell. The swell left him. He was already travelling at thirty miles an hour. He was broadside on to the next wave. The swell lifted him sideways as he tried to claw up its face. For a moment he thought he was going over, then she righted and he had made another hundred yards.

The seas steepened. Their thunder against the reef melded with the roar of the huge engines. Trent yelled at the top of his voice. He yelled and went on yelling, anything to keep his mind free. He knew it would happen. He had always known that he hadn't a chance. A twenty-foot wall slammed the *Yellow Submarine* sideways, then lifted her and flung her over as if her ten tons were no more than a cork. Trent couldn't see. It didn't matter. It was finished. For a second he thought of undoing his harness, of letting the sea take him. Then with a massive corkscrew the *Yellow Submarine* tore herself clear. She was heeled at an angle of sixty degrees when the next wave hit. Trent slammed off the power and she dropped dead into the trough. He thrust the throttle forward again to catch the power before the engines died. The next wave was round topped. The *Yellow Submarine* rose as if on a hydraulic lift and he saw car lights blaze from the shore. He was too far north. He spun the wheel to bring her back with the seas on her counter.

One minute, two, then it was time and he spun her again with plenty of power and charged straight into the surf. White water enveloped him, mountains of it falling. He thought that the policeman had got it wrong. Then he felt the *Yellow Submarine* steady. There were no heavy seas, it was all froth. And he was through.

He brought the bows round and opened the throttles the last inch to lift her clear of the coral heads. Fifty mph, sixty, sixty-five. He had nothing with which to signal the police but the roar of the engines would be enough to tell the constable that he was safe.

The cleaning team had searched the Bertram for guns and dropped them overboard. They considered cutting her loose from her anchors but there were other targets on the cay. Once they were all dead, the Cubans could dump them on the Bertram and let her drift away over the Great Bahama Bank. She might end up washed ashore on the Florida coast or be swept by the current down towards Cuba. Either way, there was little expectation of her being found until they were safely home in Miami.

Having disabled the Bertram's engines, they launched their small Zodiac inflatable from the Cigarette. They put their weapons in the tender, pulled on dive fins and swam, pushing the Zodiac towards the lagoon. They swam at an angle to enter the lagoon well away from the direct path in from the Bertram. On reaching the surf, they heaved themselves up on to the inflated hulls to keep their bodies clear of the coral. With the tide high and the storm driving the water into the lagoon there was plenty of depth. They landed on the south tip of the cay, dragged the Zodiac up the beach and spread out.

More than an hour had passed since the man had smashed the rock through the two skiffs. Though the rain still fell, the darkness was the dark of approaching night rather than of the storm. A mile away the white caps rode the huge waves out of the Tongue of the Ocean, steepening across the seventy to a hundred yards of shelving rock before hurling themselves against the final barrier. The wind had begun to drop but still it carried the crash of battle across the Great Bahama Bank and with it came patrols breaking free of the outer reef to race forward and probe the defences of the lagoon and on across to burst on the sand.

The searchers came at Jacket from the north. First Jacket heard a man cough and spit. Then came a cry as one of the hunters found the first box. Jacket ran to the beach. Two steps on the flat rocks took him into the water. Immediately lowering himself into the sea, he paddled on his hands round the edge of the hunters' line.

The tide had turned and he could feel its pull as the water poured out of the lagoon. He kept to the sea for a hundred yards then eased into the shore, searching for somewhere he could land without leaving marks. Finally he found the worn trunk of a dead palm tree that must have been bowled in over the reef by a previous storm.

Crouching low as he balanced on the tree, he leapt for a tuft of grass and landed on one foot. A second step took him on to more grass, then a flat piece of coral. Someone called his name, low and urgent. He dropped flat, listening, trying to understand the trap. Again he heard his name. A woman's voice. He was sure. Then an American, a man, whispering fiercely, 'Jacket, where the shit are you?'

A torch shone for a moment behind a cupped hand. Two faces showed in the soft glow. Miss Charity and Mr Steve.

The relief was so total and sudden and unexpected. Jacket almost fell. It was as if his cords had been cut. For a moment he couldn't move. Then he managed, 'Here . . .'

He had forgotten that they couldn't see him in the dark. He giggled and Miss Charity heard him.

'Run!' she screamed.

He thought that someone was behind him.

He ran hard, feet stumbling on the uneven ground. Only twenty steps and he was safe. Twenty steps. He didn't dare look round but he could hear them coming behind him. He yelled, 'Mr Steve, help,' and threw himself into the American's arms.

29

'Run,' Charity shouted.

She had expected Jacket to flee and had planned to hurl herself against the American's gun. It would be over then, no further fear.

Surprise froze her as the boy ran into Steve's arms. Steve flung Charity aside and she fell choking against the cord around her neck.

'Welcome,' Steve said to Jacket. His smile was a little crazy as he grabbed the boy by the hair, forcing him to his knees.

'Eat steel,' he said and giggled as he pried the pistol into the boy's mouth.

He looked up for a moment as the big Bahamian said, 'Yo sick, mistuh.'

The Bahamian strode away to distance himself from what was happening. A man appeared over the edge of the dune, his shape indistinct in the last of the drizzle. The Bahamian waved and called. A soft phut followed a flash. The Bahamian's face split and he staggered.

Charity lashed out with her feet and caught Steve on the back of his legs. He stumbled and whipped his pistol free. As Jacket fled down the dune, a second man appeared, closer, crouched. Steve dived flat, rolling. Sand spat at him, the soft phut of silenced automatics. A third man loomed out of the rain. Steve tried to steady the big revolver. He fired once. The big Magnum bullet lifted the assailant off his feet. The man who had shot the big Bahamian cursed and dropped behind the dune. Steve fired again, not aiming, but keeping the attackers down as he scrabbled to the beach.

Charity thought that they must be police – white, so O'Brien's men. She called and two of them rose out of the sand. They were neat bodied, middle aged, black hair slicked back by the sea and the rain. They approached carefully, swivelling packages of transparent plastic.

The leader said, 'Shit, a woman.' And, to Charity, 'So who are you when you're at home?'

'A zoologist. I was caught by the storm.'

'Yeah?' He wasn't convinced, or didn't care.

A third man had stopped to inspect the one Steve had shot. 'Goddamn Magnum,' he said.

They carried satchels and the plastic-covered machine pistols. They weren't police. Not even American police. They were too quiet and they spoke with an Hispanic accent. The leader took a roll of tape out of his satchel and strapped Charity's feet. Suddenly the thunder of a boat's engines split the quiet.

Trent cut power well out from Bleak Cay and nosed the *Yellow Submarine* in towards the anchorage in the lee of the east coast of the little island. The big engines were almost silent as he crept out of the dusk. Two boats lay alongside each other. He slipped the engines into reverse, easing the *Yellow Submarine* back into the cover of the rain.

He presumed that the boats would belong, one to the killer and his team, the other to those sent to tidy up the mess. The second team was the more dangerous, professional killers. He was caught between the demand for speed and the need for caution.

If they remained alive, Charity and the boy's only hope lay in his ability to grab the attention of their pursuers. He turned the wheel and slammed open the throttles. The engines thundered. He thought for a moment of Tanaka Kazuko and had time to smile as the *Yellow Submarine* lifted.

The speedometer showed fifty mph as he hurtled out of the rain directly at the two yachts. He expected shots, though he wouldn't hear them above the thunder of the triple Mercruisers. No men were visible on either boat. At the last moment he brought the helm hard over and cut power.

As the *Yellow Submarine* dropped, her weight, aided by the swing of her counter, built a wave that caught the Bertram broadside on. In the sudden silence Trent heard the splintering of the Bertram's wheelhouse as she smashed into the Cigarette. He ran forward, dropped the anchor and let two hundred feet of chain and warp whip out of the hawsepipe.

229

Easing the throttles, he slipped alongside the Bertram, jumped on board and dropped flat on the deck.

One man sprawled dead in the wheelhouse, four more in the cabin. Chips of fibreglass spattered over his head as a gunman hosed the wheelhouse from the shore. The engine covers were open, the fuel pipes fractured. He rolled across the deck and dropped on to the Cigarette. He hoped to find a gun but they were too professional. He hadn't time for a thorough search. He found a tool box and grabbed the hammer.

The windscreen disintegrated and he heard the screech of bullets as he lay flat to smash open the dashboard and gain access to the ignition wires. The warm engines roared to life. He backed the Cigarette, hoping to drag the anchor. The flukes had caught in coral. He had to get out on to the foredeck. Muzzle flashes sparkled across the lagoon. Two automatic rifles with silencers. Pure luck if they hit – bad luck, he corrected with another slight smile as he sliced the anchor warp with his throwing knife.

He rolled back across the deck to the cockpit, turned the wheel and opened the throttle. The engines kicked the Cigarette round and he straightened, running the day boat out of range. Ducking into the low cabin again, he opened the butane taps on the gas stove mounted in the galley counter. He settled himself in the helmsman's racing chair and fastened the safety harness.

The Cigarette pitched and slammed as he drove her out of the lee and round the beacon marking the south tip of the reef. He imagined the gunmen following his progress. They must be running now across the cay. The surf smashed over the low racing boat as he turned back towards the shore. He was a hundred yards off the reef when he opened the engines full and drove in at the heaving line of white that showed the edge of the lagoon. He tucked his feet up on to the dashboard, legs flexed to absorb the shock. The Cigarette hit twice as she crossed the coral. One of the propellors tore loose and the engine screamed. The other engine drove on. He clapped open the safety harness and dived clear with the Cigarette only fifty yards from the beach. Twisting in the water, he looked back out to sea to protect his night vision. As the boat hit the shore a spark leapt to the butane gas in the bilges. First the butane exploded, then the fuel tanks. Huge sheets of flame leapt into the sky and lit the beach.

Trent didn't look. Two to three minutes for the men on the cay to get their sight back: he swam fast and sprinted up the shore, throwing himself flat and rolling into the protection of a dune. He needed a gun. Any kind of gun. Then he heard Charity scream.

He had her pinpointed midway down the cay from where he lay. He crawled, belly flat to the sand. She screamed again. He shouted then. He shouted that he was coming in: 'Shoot me and you don't get off the cay.'

Flames danced behind him. Standing with hands above his head, he made a great target.

'Get your arse over here,' a man yelled.

He walked towards the voice. Though he kept his hands high, he watched the ground – tripping could get him shot. He saw the shadow, black and small, crouched in the sand shaking. Trent whispered, 'There's a knife on my beads. You're going to have to come in and cut me loose.'

He didn't know whether the boy had heard. Even if he had heard, terror might stop him from understanding. Trent couldn't risk repeating himself.

One man knelt with Charity pulled back against his chest, a knife to her throat. There were two others, one each side of her, forty yards apart so they couldn't be taken by surprise. Professionals, as he had expected – Hispanics.

He said, 'Hi, who's the girl?'

'Get down on your goddamn knees,' the one holding her ordered. 'There's some clown out there with a cannon.'

They had brought a roll of tape. They strapped his hands behind him and his feet. 'You're the detective?'

'That's right,' Trent said. 'Your boat's gone, so has the Bertram. That leaves mine and the keys are hidden. The DEA's due once the wind drops and they can get the helicopters off the ground. You think I'm bluffing, fine, because it doesn't matter. Have a look at the torch burning on the beach. That'll bring them in. You want off, let's deal.'

They had to recognise their situation.

'Earning good money isn't worth much when you're dead,' Trent pushed.

The man on the right switched to Spanish, his accent Cuban. 'He came in because the woman screamed.'

The one to the left nodded agreement. 'Cut her a little.'

'Yeah, take them out to the man's boat,' the first one said. He was the most anxious of the three.

231

The leader was cool as an insurance underwriter. He said, 'We don't get the American before he reaches the boat we'll be climbing on board into the mouth of his cannon.'

'And the boy,' the man over to the left said. 'We need the boy.'

The first man, the anxious one, was about to argue but the leader was on his feet. 'Let's do it,' he said. He picked up a Stirling machine pistol wrapped in loose transparent plastic so that he could shoot without getting sand in the mechanism.

The other two were similarly armed. Extremely professional, Trent thought.

They fanned out, three men on patrol, each with more combat experience than most hoodlums get to watch on TV.

They had taped Charity's feet. The cord binding her hands behind her back was looped round her throat. She lay curled up on her side facing him. Her muscles twitched and trembled. Rain and the sweat of her fear formed rivulets that ran down her face into the sand.

'I'm sorry. I'm a little late,' Trent said. The boy was out there close by. To give the child courage, he had to sound very calm. He said, 'I brought my boss's boat in through the reef at Congo Town. Some trip. She rolled right over, three hundred and sixty degrees.'

He saw Jacket then. He was twenty yards away. He was naked and looked very small.

Trent said, 'Don't give up, Charity. It's not over yet, not by a long chalk.' He smiled at her. 'I never did understand the chalk bit. Must be something to do with school? That's your department.'

The boy took a step forward.

Trent wanted to scream at him to hurry.

Then the boy froze and Trent heard steps padding quickly across the sand.

Jacket couldn't move. His terror was too great. He watched the man walk out of the darkness. It wasn't Mr Steve. It was one of the others. One of the ones with the guns wrapped in the same sort of sheeting that he had bought to protect his mother's bed. It was so long ago. He wanted to get it over with now. All he had to do was cry out and it would stop. Everything would stop. He waited for the man to see him but the man seemed blind. Then Jacket remembered again his father saying, 'We've got natural camouflage.'

Only it hadn't been his father. His father had run off to the United States and was never coming back. Jacket felt the tears on his cheeks. He couldn't stop them but they didn't matter.

He had said it to himself, 'We've got natural camouflage.' It was true. He was invisible.

He recognised the man with the beard. He was the man who had hurdled over the car outside the bank to save him from the men with the van.

The other one had taken out a knife. He squatted down with his back to Jacket. He said to the man with the beard, 'You've got five seconds to tell where you hid the keys or the woman gets it.'

He touched the point of the knife to Miss Charity's breast.

'Well?' the man demanded. He kept his voice low so his companions wouldn't hear him.

The man with the beard said, 'I don't give a donkey's arse for the woman.'

It wasn't true. If he hadn't cared, he wouldn't have walked in to try to stop them hurting Miss Charity. Jacket eased one foot forward. He had escaped from Vic and his friends a hundred times. What was difficult now was having to do it on his own. Not having his dad to help. Absolute silence. He mustn't even swallow.

The man with the beard seemed very calm and was watching him, though not directly. Jacket felt the man's confidence in his ability. It beat into him warm and strong and he eased another step forward. It was the same as stalking fish. The movement had to be very slow, but continuous – a sort of controlled drifting.

It was the anxious one of the trio who had returned. Trent could smell in the Cuban the standard contempt felt by the Latin American Hispanic for the Gringo's softness. The boy had to be given strength. Trent kept watching him, willing him on.

He said to the Cuban, 'I worked eighteen years for the British government infiltrating terrorist groups that made you boys seem like nursery maids. I know where it's at. You'll kill us once you know where the keys are.'

The boy was close now. Ten yards. Trent smiled at the Cuban and spat casually at the man's feet. 'I'll see you dead first, *gauchito*.'

The Cuban lashed out with the butt of his gun.

Trent laughed at him. 'Try the woman, *maricon*. She's more your size.'

The Cuban cursed and rounded on Charity. He wanted Trent to see what he was doing. She shuddered as he slit her shirt but she didn't whimper.

The boy saw his chance. Five steps and he knelt at Trent's head. He found the knife. The blade sliced through the tape. Trent grabbed the hilt. The Cuban had to face him.

'Hey, little whore,' Trent said in Spanish. 'One day I'll have your mother and your wife and your sister all in the same bed.'

As the Cuban spun round, his throat was unprotected. At that same moment Trent felt the cramp grip his right thumb. The tape had been too tight. The blood wasn't circulating. He rolled at the Cuban, lashing out with his bound feet as he dragged his thumb back. The knife had dropped.

The Cuban clubbed him across the knees. Then the Cuban saw the boy and laughed softly. He had forgotten Charity. She was only a woman. She had been at his mercy. She punched her feet out, catching him in the base of the spine. He lost his balance for a moment. Trent got his legs in and dived at him, clawing for his throat. Surprise was on Trent's side and he was heavier than the Hispanic but he was unarmed and his legs were bound. The Cuban rammed his fists up betwen Trent's forearms, bursting his hold. They rolled, the Cuban on top, punching at Trent's eyes while driving his knees at Trent's groin. He was fast. Victory was his once he could break away. Trent clung desperately to his waist, trying to hold him close and heave him over so that he could use his weight. There was nothing scientific in their fight. It was brute force against brute force. Their wet clothing hindered them. Finally the Cuban managed to throw himself back. Breaking free, he grabbed the pistol from his belt.

Trent heard himself say, 'I'm sorry, Charity.'

Then the Cuban fell. Both men had forgotten Jacket.

The boy had found a rock. He struck again at the back of the Cuban's skull. Trent heard the bone give. He rolled away from the dead man. Automatically he searched for his knife. He severed the tape binding his feet before cutting Charity loose. He knelt holding her by the elbow. 'Can you walk?'

The horror of Steve's hands and the Cubans' were imprinted on her body. She struck Trent away.

Trent turned to Jacket. He had to be very casual or the child would go into shock.

He didn't touch the boy. Simply smiled at him. 'We'll take you home soon. My boat's out beyond the reef. I'll just clean up here, then we can swim out together. The three of us. The storm's about over.'

The boy nodded and Trent asked easily, 'How many more are there?'

'Dere only Mr Steve an' de udder two,' the boy said.

'Good,' Trent said with another smile. 'Now get in the sea. Both of you. Don't move till I whistle.'

He picked up the Cuban's Stirling, checked the magazine and took a spare from the Cuban's satchel. The other two had headed north. He followed. They weren't expecting him. He didn't think that they were the sort to surrender. He had to offer them the chance. Otherwise it would have been easy. It was what he had been trained for.

A gun thundered. A .45 Magnum. One shot, then a second, five seconds separating them. That would be the one the boy had called Mr Steve, O'Brien's amateur whom the DEA expected to break, the killer Skelley would give his career to see hang. Trent thought of leaving him to the cleaning team. They had been paid to do the job. Or he could wait for the police. Then O'Brien would get him. Skelley was correct, they would do a deal that Charity would recognise as one more betrayal – a betrayal taking her a further step towards the edge.

One of the Cubans shouted to his companion. Then both called to the man Jacket had killed and cursed when he didn't reply. They hadn't time to search for him. They were about a hundred yards apart close to the beach on the north coast of the cay. The killer must be out in the water, hiding, frightened, desperate, potentially very dangerous.

Steve had seen a movement and fired twice to hold the pursuit off while he scuttled back into the lagoon. He stood with only his head above the water. They couldn't find him there – not unless they came into the sea. He'd get them then outlined against the shine on the sand. He had five shells left in the Ruger and a box in his pocket. The water wouldn't harm the shells. He didn't know who the men were. He didn't care. He intended killing them.

He stood with the water lapping his mouth, thinking about the one he had killed earlier. How the big Magnum bullet had smashed him off his feet. Remembering kept the fear out. It was all round him, waiting. He had to keep very tight hold of the Ruger and keep his teeth clamped together. He didn't understand what was happening. Where the flames had come from. He didn't understand anything. He had thought that he had won. Jesus Antonio and Torres were on the way to the cemetery. He had even imagined himself at Torres's graveside. He had rehearsed what he would say and what expression he would wear.

They had never given him a chance to show what he could do. It wasn't fair. His thoughts went to his father, an accountant with the state government. Loyalty was his father's favourite topic. Loyalty and service and debt to the community when he could have been making triple in private practice. Steve would have gone to Yale after his prep school scholarship. Then maybe Oxford for a couple of years like that son of a bitch, Xavier de Fonterra. With that background, the bank wouldn't have dumped on him. He would have been too valuable. And now a goddamn nigger brat had screwed him up.

His rage and his fear were equally balanced as he searched the beach for movement. He was going to get them. Then he was going to get the kid and that black slut from the school. School, shit! It was a tin shack. What goddamn right did she have sticking her black nose into his affairs?

He had brains on his side and had kept his head under market pressure at the bank. What would they do? Eventually get off the cay. He needed to get between them and the boats, catch them on their way to the reef. He imagined them wading from the beach – Kapwumf, Kapwumf.

30

Trent watched the two Cubans from a shallow dip a little to their rear. They lay a hundred yards apart on the down slope of the last dune before the beach at the north tip of the cay. The wind had cleared most of the cloud and patches of the beach shone dimly where the tide had retreated. It wasn't a lot of fun getting ready to go out into the water after a man armed with a .45 Magnum, particularly when you couldn't hear him because of the surf. Trent hadn't any sympathy for them but he accepted a kinship. No doubt the Cubans got paid more than he had when he worked for military Intelligence. However, they got killed if they failed, while Trent would have lost his job. He hadn't wanted the job – not even when first recruited by his guardian.

Trent was less than twenty yards from the closest Cuban. He said quietly in Spanish, 'The Gringo's mine. Leave your Stirling where it is and back up on your belly.'

The Cuban lay very still, calculating.

'Do it,' Trent said. 'I used to kill for my government. I'm not an amateur.'

The Cuban said, 'I was in Angola. Three years.' Getting shot was a death he could accept. The alternative was being hanged by the neck. He swivelled fast, not really trying so much as wanting it finished with.

The *phut* of Trent's silenced Stirling alerted the last Cuban and gave him a general area. He hosed the dune.

Trent lay very still in the dip, watching the sea as the bullets whined away to the south. He expected Steve to fire at the muzzle flashes. Instead there was silence – he had underestimated the American in thinking of him as the quarry. There wasn't time to offer the Cuban a way out. Trent fired once then raced down the dune.

The storm had increased the current flowing from the north. As he waded out, Trent felt the surge tug at his legs. Walking in on the killing team had been a risk calculated on their desire to escape. Steve wasn't rational. Trent imagined him in the gun store. The huge size of the Magnum must have impressed him. However, it was a revolver that demanded a great deal of strength and expertise.

The Stirling weighed Trent down and he dropped it. Then he let the current take him.

The weather in the Caribbean was quicker to change than up north. A gale had blown an hour ago; now only small dying squalls spun across the lagoon. Steve had expected to wait but they were already there outlined against the sliver of moonlight that glinted palely to the east beyond the cay. They were forty yards offshore in line with the boats and watching the beach. Only their heads showed. The nigger kid was small so the bitch was squatting.

Steve's line of interception had taken him thirty yards further out. The suck and surge of the tide as it ran out of the lagoon covered his approach. He had been cold earlier on. Now warmth flooded his limbs. He felt joyous. He was smiling. He wanted to be right up close so that he could see their faces. He imagined their fear. Twenty yards would do it. He held the Ruger flat on the water and slid his feet forwards, feeling for rocks or coral. Brains always won – even at tennis, he thought as he recalled moving his opponents round the court back at school. Steve had plotted each point as he had plotted this ambush. He had tried to explain to his father, but his father had been indignant, accusing Steve of unfair play.

He sighted along the dripping barrel of the Magnum, drawing the bead on the teacher's head. He would take her first. He wanted the boy to see her head burst.

He held the Ruger two handed and used both thumbs to ease the hammer back. He was too close to miss. He said, 'Bang, you're dead.'

Charity thought, He wants to see me die. Cats were like that. Playing with their victims. She wouldn't give him the pleasure. Then she thought of Jacket. There was a chance he could escape while Steve shot her. She began to turn, slowly, very frightened, hating to give the white pig his satisfaction. Then she heard Trent.

*

238

'You're sick, Steve,' Trent called. 'If you're lucky they won't hang you.'

The current had swept him further out than the other three. They were separated by some forty yards. The five-second interval between the two shots Steve had fired at the Cubans gave Trent the American's rate of fire. He mustn't get too close yet he had to keep advancing. He needed to keep Steve's attention and keep him mad.

'I knew it the moment we saw the boy in the morgue,' he called.

The muzzle of the Magnum was big and black. He closed his eyes to protect his sight and kept on walking, only his head above the surface.

'Yeah, sick,' he said. 'They'll lock you away for life in the insane asylum.'

The explosion shook him. By the angle of the barrel the recoil must have thrown the bullet a yard over his head. He wondered if the American had reloaded since firing at the Cubans. Three more bullets if the American hadn't reloaded – five if he had.

He watched Steve fight the big gun down and aim. The second shot went the same way as the first. The gap was down to twenty yards. Trent cupped his left hand and jetted water at the American. 'You're a punk. I want you alive.'

The American fired. Three.

Charity understood what Trent was doing. She grabbed Jacket, holding him quiet. She didn't want to watch. She couldn't stop herself. She saw the barrel of the big revolver leap as Steve fired. Four shots and still Trent came at him. The gap was down to ten yards. Only Trent's head showed, beard dripping, John the Baptist on a tray. She wanted to shout at him to duck but he advanced on Steve without pause, not fast but steady, looking him straight in the eye.

Four shots, so he had probably reloaded. The distance between them was too short now for the American to miss. Trent saw him lick his lips as he took aim. Then he heard the click of the hammer on the empty breach.

The American collapsed physically, no fight left in him nor hope. Trent took the Ruger and told him to face the beach.

A stomach spasm doubled Trent over and he retched. Bile burnt in his throat. He spat and washed his mouth. The current floated the trail of vomit towards Charity and the boy. 'I'm sorry,' Trent said.

239

They found the Cubans' inflatable drawn up on the beach and paddled out to the *Yellow Submarine*. The after end of the yacht was a mess, the radar arch ripped off and the cockpit gutted.

Steve sat huddled in a corner of the helmsman's cockpit. Charity held Jacket against her side. Trent dropped anchor close to shore at Green Creek. Despite the rain, the flames out on the cay had brought a few of the villagers down to the beach. Deeply suspicious, they watched in silence as the small party came ashore, then followed at a distance up the road. The men at Mr Jack's bar looked up as they passed.

The lights were on in the schoolhouse and a police jeep stood parked outside. Trent held Steve by the elbow, steering him in through the tin porch. There was only the one classroom: four lines of desks, an open area where Charity stood, then a small stage used by visiting politicians for election meetings. Skelley sat on the edge of the dais. Someone had fetched his uniform over from Nassau. He looked very smart and official. The peak of his cap shaded his face from the light of the one electric bulb so Trent couldn't see his expression.

Trent gave Steve a little shove to keep him on the move up the centre aisle.

Skelley seemed to inspect the American for a while – or possibly he was recalling the correct wording: 'Stephen John Radford, I arrest you in the name of the law for the murder of Victor Horatio Nelson. You have the right to remain silent. However, anything you say may be taken down and used in evidence against you.'

Village hall theatricals, Trent thought. He wondered if O'Brien had given Skelley Steve's name or whether Skelley had been involved from the start in whatever was happening. He laid Stever's Ruger and the ammunition down on the stage beside Skelley. 'Bleak Cay's a mess. O'Brien should have sent men.'

Skelley gave a slight nod. 'They're on their way. The weather held them up.' He turned his attention to the boy. 'So you're Jacket Bride . . .'

'Leave the boy alone,' Charity said. She hadn't let go of Jacket for even a second since their final confrontation with Steve. She held him now round the shoulders, keeping him tightly protected by her body warmth against the slight chill of the schoolroom. She stood tight muscled, legs a little apart, bare feet planted firmly on the wooden floor. This was her school, her territory, the boy was her pupil.

'You make me sick. Whatever shitty little game you're playing, we're not part of it.' She included Trent in her attack.

The beating of the helicopters thudded in the distance. Two flew on to Bleak Cay. The third landed on the beach.

Skelley took out a handkerchief and flicked sand from his highly polished toe caps – clearing for action, Trent thought. Something was going to happen. Trent could smell it. He needed to see Skelley's face. He edged forward into the open space in front of the dais but Skelley looked away to the American.

'Stand right there where I can see you, Mr Radford.' Skelley pointed to a spot in front of him and Steve shuffled forward.

'Did you know that we hang murderers here, Mr Radford?' Skelley asked. He withdrew his automatic from its holster and laid it on the dais. It was all very deliberate, carefully rehearsed. 'Which one of us do you hate most, Mr Radford? Who are you going to blame in those few seconds before they drop the trap? Did you know that a voiding of the bowels is normal? That's quite a comedown from being a smart New York banker, Mr Radford.'

Trent made to interrupt.

'You don't like it, get out,' Skelley said. 'All those New York parties I hear about, expensive liquor, cocaine, beautiful women throwing themselves at you. Did you suffer a surfeit, Mr Radford? Need a new thrill? Torture? Killing children? Young Victor out on Bleak Cay? Is that what it takes to get a smart banker off, Mr Radford?'

Steve had been almost comatose since surrendering his gun to Trent. Now Trent saw life seeping into him. The hate.

As Steve moistened his lips, the tip of his tongue showed bright pink in the glow of the electric light. 'It wasn't like that. You don't understand . . .'

'The fun in torturing children? Correct, Mr Radford. Perhaps you'd enlighten us?' Skelley had crossed his legs. Hands clamped round his knees, he rocked back a little, waiting. 'Come along, Mr Radford.'

His aping of a sadistic schoolteacher suddenly infuriated Charity. 'Stop it, Skelley . . .'

The Chief Superintendent looked up. His face was a polished black skull, even the eyes were dead. Trent saw it suddenly. Skelley was going to kill the American. Throw away all his years of service, all his training, the last of his faith in justice.

The door opened on O'Brien and two Bahamian police officers. A gust of wind entered with them, disturbing the dust, gold flecks that swirled below the light. O'Brien carried a wad of papers in one hand, his ancient briefcase in the other. He blinked for a moment in the harsh light of the unshaded bulb.

He said, 'Good evening, Miss Johnston,' and gave the boy a brief nod. He ignored Trent. Holding up the papers, he said, 'I've come for the body, Chief Superintendent.'

He turned his attention to Steve. 'Mr Radford, the Bahamian authorities are handing you over into my care for conveyance to the United States of America. There you will face charges of conspiracy to import an illegal substance, cocaine to be exact. You have a right to appeal your extradition. If you wish to accompany me, you should say so. Nothing complicated, Mr Radford. A simple expression of your desire to be transferred to the jurisdiction of the American Federal Court and your acceptance that you will be charged on reaching American territory. I'm sure the Chief Superintendent has already mentioned the alternative.'

'Lots of black people in American jails,' Skelley said. 'We blacks like a piece of white tail, Mr Radford. But you'll have heard as much.' He grinned and turned to face O'Brien. As he did so his elbow struck his automatic. The pistol spun off the stage and across the wooden floor. It rested against Steve's feet.

'Don't pick it up, scumbag,' Skelley said.

Perhaps it was the insult that made Steve grab the gun. No one else had moved. Indecision held Steve for an instant. Then he rounded on Jacket. 'You first,' he said.

Trent had raised his arms in surrender. His hands rested on the back of his neck. His arm flashed over as Steve brought the pistol up. His knife took Steve midway up the side of his throat. The American dropped the pistol. He seemed surprised as he touched the knife handle. Then he crumpled.

Charity saw the pain in Trent's eyes, the self-disgust as he stooped and plucked the knife from Steve's throat. He wiped the blade deliberately on the American's shirt and slipped the knife back into its sheath.

He was accepting responsibility. He had done nothing else for four days. None of it had been automatic. None of the bravery.

He picked up Skelley's automatic and fired into the floor. The first two shots blew the dust around – blanks. The third smashed a hole in the wood. He gave a little shrug and tossed Skelley the automatic.

Skelley said, 'The *Golden Girl*'s at the yacht club at Coakley Town.'

'Thanks,' Trent said.

Charity wasn't sure what to do. The American didn't interest her. The role he had played was too complicated. Whether he was puppet master or puppet. She walked over to Skelley.

She said, 'I said you weren't man enough to kick my butt.' She hit him flat-handed across the face. 'That's for Trent. He's too dumb to do it himself.'

As she turned away, Mrs Bride charged in through the door. She saw Steve on the floor and hesitated. Then she grabbed her son, shoving him towards the door, screaming at the men at the same time, threatening them. She didn't need to know what had happened. She could make it up to fit whoever she decided to blame for whatever she decided to blame them for.

Trent wanted to protect the child. It wasn't the role he had been set, the role Skelley had cast him in from the beginning. He didn't blame Skelley for using him. It was all in the files, who he was, what he was. He existed to be used.

Charity was at his side. She said, 'Let's go.'

'Killers get you off?' he asked.

Charity wanted him to know how much that hurt: Skelley, O'Brien, the police watching, the gossip, the whole scene.

'I'm sorry,' he said. His shame was another weapon against her.

'Screw you,' she said. It wasn't enough. 'Jesus, someone must have screwed you up with a lot of guilt when you were a kid.'

She took his arm. Her fingers were broad nailed and tough, tattooed with the scars of the reef. He didn't resist as she pulled him round. 'Leaving with me isn't optional,' she said.

Mrs Bride led Jacket up the street. He was a hero and she was careful of him, hugging him against her side as she passed Mr Jack's bar.

He tried to speak but she shushed him. She didn't want words in public. She wanted him up at their hut, alone, so that she could find out what he had done. She couldn't trust what little the villagers had shouted to her as she charged the schoolhouse. The teacher woman was involved.

That much was certain and dangerous. The teacher woman might get credit.

She pushed the boy up the back steps into the house and lit the kerosene lamp. The bed glowed in the soft light, the lace-bordered sheet turned down below the fluffy pillows. The bed took up too much room and she had to squeeze through to the table.

'Sit dere,' she told the boy. Her boy. 'I's goin' make tea.'

Jacket sat waiting. The fear remained in him and he shivered every now and again. He tried to blank out what had happened out on the cay but it kept coming back – Mr Steve and the big gun. He touched the corner of the white top sheet. As the wind drove the sea spray and the rain at him, his fingers tightened, dragging the soft linen. Mr Steve called and he ran to him. He couldn't stop himself. Mr Steve grabbed him, holding him close. The blood from Mr Steve's throat jetted down over Jacket's head, warm and sticky. The boy moaned and tumbled sideways on to the bed. He lay there curled in on himself, clutching the sheet in both hands, stuffing it into his mouth so he wouldn't cry.

Small on the huge bed, the boy looked like a sick fledgeling in a nest, wet and crunched up. His misery blocked Mrs Bride in the doorway. She wanted to go to him, cradle him. She was too familiar with misery. Anger, bitterness and a vengeful God had been her constant defences in the nine years she had lain longing in her body for arms to hold her, the feel of warm breath on her face.

She forced herself into the hut and put the tin tray on the table. Steam rose from the teacups. She tried to sit beside the boy but her legs wouldn't bend. She touched him on the shoulder. He shivered. She wanted to say his name but it was suddenly too strong a reminder of the man she had lost.

The agony of those first years of her husband's desertion knifed into her belly – the boy so small in his father's jacket. The child's love for his father, so absolute, had reinforced her sense of failure; that she couldn't hold her man. She recalled her sense of shame in front of the village. The women had mocked her while the men, judging her easy prey, had fumbled at her in the shadows. She had resisted always. Love was too dangerous, too easy a trap. The discomfort of the hut had supported her resolve. There was no room in it for a man. Now the bed threatened her. So much comfort and splendour begged to be used.

She shook the boy and he rolled on to his back, his knees drawn up.

'Dat a goo' bed,' she said. 'Yo all wet an' ditty, mussin' up de sheet.'

Jacket looked up at his mother. Her face was in shadow and she was shapeless in her loose dress. He could feel her pain. It had been there always, binding her and too thick for him to penetrate. He had thought that the bed would help. He wept for her softly. There was nothing more he could do.

Boots dragged in the sand outside. Jacket had time to say, 'I's alrigh', Mama,' before the tall policeman peered into the hut.

The policeman said, 'Your boy may be in danger, Mrs Bride. We'd like him to come with us, somewhere where we can protect him. A few days.'

END PIECE

Mr Brown had built a network of contacts helpful to his profession. On Mr Brown's arrival in Florida, one of these supplied him with the necessary materials for his work neatly packed in a waterproof briefcase. Another arranged Mr Brown's flight from Fort Lauderdale into a small airstrip in the Bahamas. There he was met by a boatman over whom lay the very faintest shadow of suspicion that he had informed the police of a smuggling operation.

Though only twenty-five feet long, the motorboat had a small cabin equipped with a shower heated by butane gas. The shower was important to Mr Brown. He liked a good wash after work. The charter was for the rest of that day and all night with a drop-off at a beach on the coast of Paradise Island. Mr Brown didn't argue the charter fee and paid half in advance.

They spent the afternoon and evening at an uninhabited cay, the boatman fishing while Mr Brown dozed over a book. Now in his sixties, he found air travel quite tiring.

On the night voyage, he changed into a thin coverall of dark blue cotton, then joined the boatman in the cockpit, only now giving the Bahamian his exact destination. He wished to be let off a half mile from the coast. The boatman helped him into the small black inflatable tender.

He rehearsed the boatman one last time: 'Remember, I flash three times, then twice. You flash twice and then three times.'

Mr Brown eased the little grappling anchor overboard a hundred yards from the beach and slipped into the water. He used the waterproof briefcase as a swimming aid and carried in a child's small blue nylon backpack a compressed-air dart-gun, a water pistol and a wide-bladed surgeon's scalpel. He approached the shore a little to the left of the smart private dock. The gardens were lit by halogen lamps and Mr Brown paused a moment to admire the shrubbery and the perfectly kept lawns.

One of Mr Brown's closest friends had worked for many years as a chemist in the scent industry down in Grasse before transferring to a heroin laboratory on the outskirts of Marseille. At Mr Brown's request, he had perfected early in their relationship a chemical duplicate of the scent put out by bitches when in heat.

With only his head and hand above the surface, Mr Brown squirted the grass with his water pistol. Soon two Rottweilers came sniffing along the shore. Mr Brown silenced them with the dart-gun. The darts weren't lethal – Mr Brown liked animals. He also appreciated them in his work, they made the human guards inattentive.

He used the same darts on two housemen, cutting their throats with the scalpel before slipping into the house. He found Torres reading on the terrace and having killed him, noted the title of the book. He thought that it must be a good book to have so engrossed the Cuban. He enjoyed a good read, especially in winter when he couldn't work in his garden.

He discovered a secretary in the library and four servants in the quarters to the rear of the house. Having dealt with them, he set his briefcase open on the hall table. It contained a small magnetic detector, a thin slab of semtex and ten small canisters of phosphorus equipped with timers.

The magnetic detector led him to the floor safe in Torres's bedroom and he set a five-ounce charge of semtex across its top. The safe in the library was in the wall and required a larger charge. Lastly he distributed the canisters and set their timers for three a.m.

Slipping back into the water, he swam out to his boat. He swam slowly out of respect for his age and he towelled his face and hands carefully before paddling out to his rendezvous with the boatman. Looking back, he thought that it was quite a pretty house, in some ways a pity to destroy it. However, Mr Dribbi was an old and very good client, very regular.

He apologised to the boatman for tracking water down into the cabin. Having taken a warm shower, he changed back into cotton slacks and shirt, then rejoined the boatman in the cockpit.

The boatman looked at him sideways, his curiosity uncontrollable. 'Eweytin' go good, mistuh?'

'Splendidly, splendidly,' said Mr Brown, rubbing his hands together. Reaching Paradise Island, Mr Brown paid the boatman the second instalment of his fee. The darkness was deep beneath the trees dividing the beach from the street where, this far out of town, the lighting was dim and irregular. Mr Brown asked the boatman to accompany him: 'Only as far as the road. At my age, you know, muggers and such like. One has to be so careful.'

Mr Brown's garden was mostly clay and digging kept his muscles firm. He had no trouble cutting the boatman's throat. He left the body beneath a sea grape tree, crossed the main road and walked along the grass verge to the car park. It had been a good night's work. Mr Dribbi would be well pleased.

Trent had only agreed to inspect the house at O'Brien's insistence that Jacket's safety was involved. They picked their way through the smouldering ruins. Any papers, any documentation, had been destroyed by the intense heat. Phosphorus, Trent presumed. Two safes had been blasted open, their doors twisted steel, no attempt at robbery. It was a cleaning mission, very professional. The two men retreated to the lawn. Black scum covered the pool. Trent said, 'Fetch me a dog. Any sort of dog so long as it's male.'

A constable brought a young Alsatian.

The dog almost writhed itself into a knot as it sniffed along the water's edge.

Trent said, 'Torres was the DEA target?'

O'Brien nodded.

'You want to tell me who you were after?'

'Dribbi.'

Trent had served in Ireland for the latter part of his employment with Military Intelligence, then for the final months in Central America; nevertheless the name was familiar – the connection he had already made, the Middle East, Beirut. A Lebanese who had controlled much of the drug traffic out of the Beka valley; in return for protection from Islamic militants, he had financed some of their terrorist operations against external targets.

'Small man, a banker?'

O'Brien nodded again.

Trent said, 'Christ, he must be nearly ninety.'

'He's never even been questioned by the police,' O'Brien said. He seemed almost embarrassed. 'He was Torres's banker. When he built his

251

retirement house here, he bought up the furniture for an upmarket whorehouse that never opened. He sold the boy his bed. Coincidence.'

Tent said, 'He was born in a Beirut whorehouse.' Details were returning: 'The Dribbi Agriculture Fund and Development Bank, Zurich. We targeted him through a fellow banker.' Trent nodded at the burnt house: 'Same result. Same workmanship.'

A freelance, the Americans had the cleaner filed as a Russian defector from the KGB. He had been used back in the early 'sixties by one of the funny branches of the CIA that blossomed under Kennedy.

'We had a feeling he was one of ours,' Trent said. 'The bed's a coincidence that damn near got the boy killed.'

'It still might,' O'Brien said. 'The boy stayed overnight. Torres turned up for breakfast.'

Trent looked out to sea. He had left the *Golden Girl* at Green Creek and had told Charity he would be back by nightfall. The situation would be easier if Dribbi had retired – easier to ignore. 'Where is he now?'

'Zurich,' O'Brien said. 'Skelley has the boy under protection.'

Trent hadn't much faith in police protection nor did the Bahamians have the manpower to continue it indefinitely. He could feel O'Brien waiting. There was anger in him as he turned back to face the ruins. First Skelley had used him. Now the DEA agent. He said, 'The mother's a horror. Charity says the boy's bright. Get him a scholarship somewhere good.'

O'Brien said, 'No problem.'

Trent nearly hit him. He said, 'You're the problem.'

'Dribbi,' O'Brien corrected. He scooped up a handful of pebbles to play with. 'I've got funding to replace the old man's yawl. We're giving him an outboard.'

Trent watched a pair of hummingbirds dip their beaks into hibiscus blossoms over to the left of the pool. The breeze blew patterns in the oily black soot floating on the pool surface. He imagined Charity in the classroom. He had tried to enjoy a private life during his first years with Military Intelligence. It hadn't worked. There were too many compartments to protect, too many secrets. Now that he had a chance he was being pulled back. He wanted to walk away from it all, tell O'Brien to clean up his own mess. There was Jacket to consider. He recalled his own years at private school. The financial scandals attached to his father had been common knowledge amongst his fellow pupils. It hadn't been easy.

The click of O'Brien's stones irritated him. He said, 'Put one of your own men on the boy. Once he's safe, get him into a school where he'll fit.'

O'Brien nodded. 'California – everyone fits.'

Charity took Trent's arm as they walked to the beach from the schoolhouse. It wasn't so much a mark of affection as a raising of her battle flag in front of the villagers, a statement that she didn't give a damn for their gossip. They shared a beer in the *Golden Girl*'s cockpit while he told her everything he knew about Dribbi. When he had finished, she said, 'He has to be stopped.'

'People have been trying for seventy years,' Trent said. He took the barbecue from its locker, mounted it in brackets projecting outboard from the transom and lit the charcoal. Dropping down into the galley, he prepared the salad he had fetched back from Nassau.

He brought the salad and the cutlery up to the cockpit on a tray.

Charity watched as he laid a pair of red snapper on the coals. He was very neat and proficient in everything he did – very self-contained, she thought as he unfolded and laid the table. Even in bed there was a part of him he wouldn't let go – as if he was watching himself.

She said, 'That's what you used to do, stop people like Dribbi.'

'That sort of thing,' Trent said. He slid the snapper on to their plates and drew the cork on a half bottle of chilled Argentinian Chardonnay.

She said, 'You're a little weird, Trent. You won't let me help in the galley but you want me to tell you to go kill someone.'

'I want you to know who I am,' he said.

'Judge you,' she corrected. She had been judging people all her life. 'Trent, that's something you have to do yourself.'

He mixed the dressing into the salad and turned the wooden spoon and fork towards her so that she could help herself.

'Why haven't they stopped him?'

'Dribbi?' He shrugged. 'There's an unwritten convention that prohibits disposal of people above a certain rank. Otherwise people who give the orders would risk being in the firing line.'

'You can't protect Jacket?'

'Not indefinitely.' He took their plates down to the galley and brought coffee. They sat in silence for a while listening to the surf.

Finally she said, 'I think I'd like to go ashore.'

She dived overboard and he watched the trail her legs beat through the water. He waited until she had reached the beach before taking the cups below and washing up.

It was quite easy once Trent had taken the decision. He flew to London first for a meet with the man who would have been his new control had he stayed with Military Intelligence. Trent required a very small quantity of a viral poison developed by the Bulgarian Secret Service in the days of the cold war. The Bulgarians had favoured needles fitted to the tip of an umbrella.

Trent waited twenty-four hours before flying back to the Bahamas. He travelled on an Australian passport in the name of Richard O'Neil, an international lawyer with offices in Liechtenstein. He looked the part, clean shaven, short hair, blue contact lenses; a good lightweight blue suit bought off the peg at Vince Moloney's, Melbourne Cricket Club tie. O'Brien collected him at Nassau airport and dropped him fifty yards down the road from Mr Dribbi's house. Trent handed the gardener a card on the back of which he had written in small neat capitals, 'A Mr Patrick Mahoney has asked me to consult you.'

He was made to wait twenty minutes before being shown up the drive. A maid led him to Mr Dribbi's library. The little man sat behind a cherrywood desk. A tartan cashmere rug covered his kness. His Dobermann, Hakim, lay by his side. Dribbi looked very frail after the previous day's flight. He pointed Trent to a chair.

Trent said, 'It might be useful if we played a radio during our conversation, Mr Dribbi.'

A very small smile moved the banker's lips as he complied. Trent was reminded of Punch, a combination of fun and violence.

He said, 'I am instructed to inform you that you were the subject of discussion at a meeting chaired last week by my client. I understand that there was strong argument in favour of termination, Mr Dribbi. A more liberal view prevailed. This is your prison, Mr Dribbi. There are those who might consider it over comfortable; however, wealth is privileged under any penal system.

'Should you leave your house, you will be killed, Mr Dribbi. You will be killed should anything untoward happen to a Mr Jacket Bride. You will be killed should there be the slightest rumour that you or your bank continue to fund narcotic traffic.'

Trent took an expensive ballpoint pen from his breast pocket, unscrewed the top and rolled a gelatin capsule containing viral poison on to the polished cherrywood. 'An earnest of my client's commitment. This commitment extends to your children and grandchildren, Mr Dribbi. The contents should be examined with great caution.'

Back in O'Brien's car, he said, 'The boy should be safe.'

'We've got him a scholarship to a school in California, five hundred kids, strong sports programme,' O'Brien said. He tapped the wheel a couple of times, uncomfortable in his thoughts. 'The teacher said I should drop him over at your boat.'

'Charity?'

O'Brien nodded. He was careful to avoid Trent's eyes as he checked the traffic at a T-junction. 'Private school – it's what you asked for.'

Trent found a note pinned to the pillow in his bunk: 'Have taken my gear up to Woods Hole. Seems there's a good chance they'll give me a fellowship. Take good care of yourself.'

She hadn't signed it. Charity was a difficult name.

Lois found Trent in the cockpit. She had brought a gift-wrapped state-of-the-art satellite telephone sent by Tanaka Kazuko. Trent smiled as he read the note: 'Even a Brit can learn to keep in touch.'

Punching in Tanaka's private number connected him to an answering machine. He said, 'Trent. I'll be away a couple of weeks. I need to grow my beard back.'

He made coffee down below in the galley. A slight movement of the yacht alerted him.

The catamaran looked a lot bigger lying stern to the quay than it had at anchor off the beach at Green Creek. The cockpit was bigger than Jacket's mama's hut.

The man was there suddenly in the companionway and Jacket saw the knife he had thrown at Mr Steve. Jacket had expected the man to look the same. Beard and untidy hair, Trent had been familiar. Hundreds of boat bums cruised the Bahamas each year, living off the fish they speared, selling crawfish to the smart yachts, smoking, getting drunk on the beach. Now the man looked like the white men Jacket had seen in Nassau carrying cases smaller than the one he had taken off the aeroplane.

He said, 'Is me, Mistuh T. Dat what de man at de gate say I call you. Dat righ'?'

'Right,' Trent said. He hoped sight of the knife hadn't unnerved the boy. He considered peeling an orange with it to diminish the threat. The boy probably wouldn't eat the orange. Or he might eat the orange to be polite and the memory would make him sick.

The boy said, 'Is Miss Charity. She say yo goin' take me de new school in de State.' He held up a white plastic supermarket bag. 'Dis my stuff.'

'Right,' Trent said again. He didn't know what to do with the boy. Touch him. Leave him alone.

The boy said, 'I's sorry, Mistuh T.'

'No . . .' The moka burped and bubbled, releasing Trent into action. Memories of his own childhood held him as he squeezed fresh oranges for the boy. Trent's adoptive uncle had always taken him by taxi to the railway station to catch the train back to boarding school. They would stand on the platform, nothing to say to each other, their only communication the crisp five-pound note his uncle took from his pigskin wallet. Somehow he had to do better for the boy.

Giving the boy space and time was important and Trent sat across from him in the opposite corner of the cockpit, waiting while he drank his orange juice.

'I used to be a sort of spy,' he began. He didn't speak directly at the boy or look at him and he spoke in short sentences, giving Jacket ample time to absorb the information. 'Living undercover. That's pretending. Like being an actor. Except you do it all the time. Even at night, in bed by yourself. What you're doing, going away to school in the States. It's the same thing in a way. A sort of mission. The man who prepares you and sends you in is your Control.'

He risked a glance across at the boy and a quick smile. 'That's me, Jacket. Short missions, you may have a radio and report every hour. Longer ones every week. That's what we'll do. For this operation the telephone's safe. Anything you need, call. Anything. That's what Control is for. Support.'

Trent's adoptive uncle had been his Control and had betrayed him, trapping him in an ambush in South Armagh. The first bullet had torn through Trent's left thigh. Now, in the cockpit, he traced the ridge of scar tissue.

A sleek two-deck motor yacht, one of Camper & Nicholson's charter fleet, eased up channel. A cruise ship sounded its siren out in the roads as a tug butted alongside.

Trent looked across at the boy. 'I'm putting you in because I know you're brave and can do the job.'

Trent shopped with Jacket in Miami. He didn't want the boy looking different from other boys at the school and had the valet service at the hotel put the clothes through the washing machine ten times; same with the laces for the boy's two pairs of trainers – it was the type of detail that Trent had learnt early in his years with Military Intelligence. They found a used 35mm Canon with three lenses at a camera shop and Trent bought the boy a new Swiss army knife with all the gadgets. Trent spent an hour up in the hotel room familiarising Jacket with the camera. The knife was the sort of present boys would expect a boy to bring to a private school. So were new fins and a quality dive mask.

Trent paid for an upgrade to first class on the American Airlines night flight to San Francisco and booked a Buick with Hertz. A Cadillac would have been dangerously pretentious, a Chevy too downmarket.

Having something immediate to do helped at the start of a mission. Eating was the best occupation with boys and Trent telephoned the school from San Francisco airport to check what hour the students ate lunch. He kept his speed in the Buick down to forty-five mph, timing their arrival with a half hour to spare.

The boy sat beside him, numb.

Trent had been the same when they were putting him in.

He kept on trying to say something. It didn't matter what; anything that would break the silence, get the boy talking. He decided to say that there should be a sign to the school and gates that the boy should look for. He prepared the words time and again, chose the next tree or barn as a mark. The most that came out was a cough, mostly not even that.

The sign came and he turned in through the gates, driving between football fields, an Olympic swimming pool with concrete seats, tennis courts in the distance – O'Brien had said the school was strong on sports.

The buildings were 'fifties concrete with metal-frame windows set in a convex crescent at the foot of a low wooded hill. Wide steps led up from the driveway to a terrace outside the main block. A bunch of boys leant

257

over the railings watching the car approach. Most were white, a few were probably Latinos – no blacks.

Trent got out of the car and went round to the trunk for Jacket's two hold-alls. He felt safe with his head in the trunk. A teacher came down the steps.

'Mr Trent?'

Trent said, 'Yes,' and put the hold-alls on the ground so they could shake hands.

Jacket hadn't moved.

The teacher called up to the terrace at a white boy spinning a football. The boy was taller than Jacket but about the same age. The boy put on a show for his public, pantomiming reluctance as he dragged his feet down the steps – not a good beginning. Trent wanted to get back in the car with Jacket and drive off. Or just get back in with him and sit for a little while. Doing so would have blown the boy's cover. He walked round to the driver's door so there would be room between them and said, 'Well, this is it.'

Jacket was used to Dummy's silence. He could drift off into his own world. That hadn't happened in the aeroplane, nor in the car. The territory was too strange for him to find reference points on which to build his fantasies. And there was the fear of school.

He had been able to escape Vic and his gang back at Green Creek; there were only four of them and he was familiar with every tree and fold in the ground. Five hundred students was more than he could imagine – more, even, than the hounds the islanders hunted pig with through the woods. He had thought that keeping silent and not thinking of anything would make the journey go on and on so that they would never reach the school. Now that they had arrived his only defence was to fold in on himself. If he could keeping folding inwards, he would disappear. Hugging himself would have made it easier but it was too obvious and he had to be very careful or they would notice and grab him back.

He was about halfway inside himself when Mr T stuck his head into the car and said, 'Well, this is it.'

Jacket smelt the fear in him. It was the same fear for Jacket that the boy had smelt in Dummy the times they had been caught out in the *Jezebel* with the wind rising. Reassuring Dummy was difficult because he

258

couldn't hear. Mr T was easier. Jacket needed a little while to fold back out of himself. Then he said, 'I's goin' be OK, Mistuh T.'

He got out of the car and shook hands with the teacher and with the white boy carrying the football.

Mr T held him by the shoulder. Jacket had already told him that he would be OK. Saying it again with everyone listening would have made Mr T look foolish. He had to say something, so he said, 'Yo speak wit Miss Charity, tell her I's fine.'

The white boy had picked up one of Jacket's hold-alls. Jacket picked up the other and followed him up the steps. He knew that Mr T didn't want him to look back.

He followed the white boy across a hall, up stairs and along a corridor. The white boy opened the door to a room and dumped Jacket's hold-all on the floor. A blue blanket covered the single bed, small wardrobe, chest of drawers, a wooden desk.

The white boy leant slouching against the wall by the door, sneering and tossing his football. The slap of the leather against his hand was a deliberate threat. Jacket recalled a film about the US school for army officers where they did things to new cadets. He crossed to the window and watched Mr T get into the hire car. Jacket knew that Mr T wouldn't leave. He'd drive halfway to the main road before turning back. He'd come up the stairs to fetch Jacket.

Jacket sat down on the bed to wait. He couldn't hear Mr T out in the corridor. That was something he had noticed, how Mr T moved like an animal up in the woods, silent all the time. He remembered Mr Steve rising out of the sea with the big pistol. He had known that Mr Steve was going to kill him and kill Miss Charity. Jacket had wanted it to happen quickly so the fear would stop. Then Mr T came walking through the sea towards Mr Steve, Mr Steve shooting at him. The fear had dropped out of Jacket the way it did at night once he saw the crawfish below on the sand.

He said, 'I's a crawfisherman.'

The white boy wasn't interested but he said, 'Yeah? What's that?'

The picture Jacket built was real rather than the customary fantasy but he did it in the same way, layer on layer: first lighting the lamp and how the crawfish looked; the *Jezebel*, creeping out of the house, that he had to get into the lagoon; that the entrance was too shallow for anyone else in Green Creek. Looking at the white boy would have broken the spell so he looked at the wall.

The white boy stopped bouncing the ball. 'How far is it out to the cay?'
''Bout six mile.'

The white boy said, 'No shit. At night. You don't get scared?'

Jacket looked at him then. The boy's eyes were too pale a blue for Jacket to read, blond hair cut short as an old brush, bigger than Vic, heavily muscled. He was dressed the way Mr T had dressed Jacket, jeans, T-shirt, trainers. He leant very still against the wall, waiting for Jacket's answer.

The dry skin lifted as Jacket picked at a coral scar on the side of his right hand. 'Mos' de time. I's pretend I's in de war,' he said. 'De ranger or de one in de green berets. Dat help.'

He looked up again.

The white boy said, 'Yeah.' He turned the football over a couple of times. Then, not looking at Jacket, looking out of the window, he said, 'Me too.'

The ball spun as the white boy flicked it up. He caught the ball cleanly, passed it round behind his back, flicked it up again and let it drop low down into his right hand. Head at an angle, he grinned at Jacket.

'Coming back to school. It's training camp and I'm some big star with the Cowboys.'

'I's a spy,' Jacket said.

He recalled the chant that had followed him up the beach when he had landed at Green Creek with the bed.

'Bed Jacket, dat what dey call me.'

'Cliff,' the white boy said. He tossed Jacket the ball. 'Let's go eat.'

2/97

Gandolfi, Simon

White sands

E.R.

28
Day
Book

X